A NORTHANGER ABBEY
DOUBLE FEATURE

THE CASTLE OF WOLFENBACH & THE NECROMANCER

ELIZA PARSONS
LAWRENCE FLAMMENBERG

Edited by
ANN MARIE HORMEKU

WFP
WORDFIRE PRESS

The Castle of Wolfenbach, A German Tale by Eliza Parsons, first published in 1793, and *The Necromancer; or, The Tale of the Black Forest* by Lawrence Flammenberg, first published in 1792, are works in the public domain.

The Necromancer; or, The Tale of the Black Forest translated in 1794 by Peter Teuthold

This new edition edited by Ann Marie Hormeku
Foreword copyright © 2022 by Dr. Sandie Byrne

EBook ISBN: 978-1-68057-363-3
Trade Paperback ISBN: 978-1-68057-362-6
Hardcover ISBN: 978-1-68057-364-0

Cover design by Ann Marie Hormeku and Allyson Longueira
Cover artwork image by Zishan Liu | Adobe Stock

Published by WordFire Press, LLC
PO Box 1840
Monument CO 80132
Kevin J. Anderson & Rebecca Moesta, Publishers
WordFire Press Edition 2022

Printed in the USA

Join our WordFire Press Readers Group for new projects, and giveaways. Sign up at wordfirepress.com.

A NORTHANGER ABBEY DOUBLE FEATURE

CONTENTS

FOREWORD

DR. SANDIE BYRNE

In Jane Austen's *Northanger Abbey* the heroine, Catherine Morland, and Isabella Thorpe, a young woman older by four years and much experience, shut out rainy mornings in Bath by reading novels (Jane Austen, *Northanger Abbey* (1817/1818); reprint ed James Kinsley. Oxford, Oxford World's Classics, 2003, p.23. Subsequent parenthetical references will be to this edition). The first is Ann Radcliffe's *The Mysteries of Udolpho* (1794), which is to be followed by Radcliffe's *The Italian, or the Confessional of the Black Penitent* (1797) and other gothic romances recommended by a friend. Isabella promises a list of ten or twelve but, characteristically, delivers only seven. She is already a connoisseur of the genre, but Catherine is an instant devotee, and rapidly becomes steeped in its conventions and language. Gothic romance was still popular when Austen began *Northanger Abbey* (then titled *Susan*, subsequently *Catherine*), probably in 1794, and completed it in 1798-9, but though the manuscript was sold (for £10) in 1803, the publisher, Thomas Crosby, chose to shelve it. Retrieved in 1816, revised, and published posthumously in December 1817 (though dated 1818) *Northanger Abbey* was parodying a genre that had had its day.

It is the work of Ann Radcliffe that possesses Catherine and whose plots she superimposes on her experiences at Northanger, but the tropes (confinement, secrecy, deception, violence, abduction, mysterious manuscripts, hidden objects) and settings (ancient buildings, forbidden areas, locked rooms) are staples of the genre. Austen's satire is directed at the reader of gothic as much as, or more than, the novels themselves; not only the genre's recycled settings, characters, and incidents, but also the extent to which deeply immersed readers project the fantastic and improbable onto the quotidian, are disappointed to discover that they are not living amid theft, abduction, and murder, and miss the real suffering around them. The novels recommended by Isabella's friend Miss Andrews, of which two are printed in this volume, provide plentiful examples of those tropes. Like many gothic romances, they are set in an imagined past and abroad – an Other not subject to the rational and law-bound society of England, a place where superstition outweighs rationality, banditti roam the mountains, and the brooding anti-hero can abduct, cheat, immure, and murder to his heart's content. Ann Radcliffe's writing normalises the seemingly supernatural elements in her plots, perhaps making them more suitable for ladies' reading, but the novels on Isabella's list make no such concessions (p.25).

The novels handily noted in Isabella's pocket-book (some slightly mistitled) other than Radcliffe's are Eliza Parsons, *The Castle of Wolfenbach, A German Tale* (1793) and *Mysterious Warning* (1796), Regina Maria Roche, *Clermont* (1798), Lawrence Flammenberg, transl. Peter Teuthold, *Necromancer, or the Tale of the Black Forest* (1794), Francis Latham, *The Midnight Bell* (1798), Eleanor Sleath, *The Orphan of the Rhine* (1798) and Carl Grosse, transl. Peter Will, *Horrid Mysteries* (1796) Catherine's only concern about the quality of these is "but are they all horrid, are you sure they are all horrid?" (p.25) On the testimony of Miss Andrews, Isabella confirms that they are. The Oxford English Dictionary provides several definitions for "horrid," the most applicable here current in 1602-1854: "[c]ausing horror or aversion, revolting to sight, hearing, or contemplation; terrible, dreadful, frightful; abominable, detestable." Henry Tilney would no doubt take Catherine to task, as he does for her all-purpose "nice," for this use of a signifier of the unpleasant to identify something she clearly enjoys. The title of *Horrid Mysteries* shows, however, that the term was associated with the gothic, and Catherine is learning the teen argot of the day from Isabella, who lards her speech with "amazingly," "sweetest," "particular" and a great deal of exaggeration.

The titles of the "horrid" novels were thought to be fictions of fictions, until early in the twentieth century when contemporary reviews proved their existence, and in the 1920s the texts were gradually discovered and made available to readers. Had these novels not had the Austen connection, it is likely that their republication would have made little impact, but the connection is there, and it has encouraged readers to explore this once-popular genre and to reconsider its appeal to contemporary audiences.

When Catherine announces that she has "heard that something very shocking indeed will soon come out in London," Eleanor Tilney is startled: "Indeed!—and of what nature?" (pp.81-2) When Catherine informs her that "It is to be more horrible than anything we have met with yet [....] uncommonly dreadful. I shall expect murder and everything of that kind," Eleanor is astonished at her composure. After some teasing, Henry explains that they have been at cross-purposes, that Catherine refers to a forthcoming publication rather than a riot. That Eleanor had, her brother surmises, immediately "pictured to herself a mob of three thousand [...] the Bank attacked, the Tower threatened, the streets of London flowing with blood" (p.82), perhaps reminds us that the period when gothic romances and gothick architecture were fashionable was not a peaceful time. There was war, there were riots, and there were justified fears of invasion and revolution. The Gordon Riots of 1780 were in living memory even when *Northanger Abbey* was published, and Eliza de Feuillide, Austen's cousin, was caught in a riot in London reported by the Times in June 1792. It is perhaps not surprising that contemporary anxieties should take the "horrid" form, nor that some women as well as men should produce repeated episodes of confinement and escape. *The Orphan of the Rhine*'s Julie is kidnapped, the Countess of Wolfenbach and Countess Eugenia in *Mysterious Warning* are imprisoned. Castles such as Wolfenbach, Renaud (*The Mysterious Warning*), Elfinbach and Monferrat (*The Orphan of the Rhine*), and

Cohenburg (*The Midnight Bell*) may represent an exaggerated, gothic version of domestic containment and constraint. Though some gothic heroines are passive victims of male subjugation, however, others fight back, demand agency, and do not wait to be rescued by a male hero. There are also female gothic villains, including Fatima in *The Mysterious Warning*.

Genre fiction such as the gothic gave women as well as men the chance to earn money from writing, though rarely enough to live on, and it is notable that of the seven "horrid" novels, four were written by women. All but one were published by the Minerva Press, which paid its authors £10-£20 for a novel. The payment of £500 for *Udolpho* was unusual and, significantly, the contract was between the publisher and Ann Radcliffe's husband.

Gothic romances enacted fantasies of desire as well as of violence. *Horrid Mysteries* in particular is vividly sensual and represents physical as well as spiritual love, the plot of *The Castle of Wolfenbach* concerns a woman fleeing a would-be incestuous uncle, and the heroine of *The Orphan of the Rhine* has to escape the lustful attentions of the Marchese de Montferrat. Above all, they offered the strange pleasures of the encounter with the sublime, the feeling of awe close to terror that is evoked by the supernatural, terrifying landscapes and imposing, brooding architecture. *The Castle of Wolfenbach* and *The Necromancer* provide those in true gothic excess.

—Dr. Sandie Byrne
University of Oxford
Oxford, ENG, 2021

THE CASTLE
OF WOLFENBACH

ELIZA PARSONS

VOLUME ONE

The clock from the old castle had just gone eight when the peaceful inhabitants of a neighbouring cottage, on the skirts of the wood, were about to seek that repose which labour had rendered necessary, and minds blest with innocence and tranquillity assured them the enjoyment of. The evening was cold and tempestuous, the rain poured in torrents, and the distant thunders rolled with tremendous noise round the adjacent mountains, whilst the pale lightning added horrors to the scene.

Pierre was already in bed, and Jaqueline preparing to follow, when the trampling of horses was heard, and immediately a loud knocking at the door; they were both alarmed. Pierre listened, Jaqueline trembled; the knocking was repeated with more violence; the peasant threw on his humble garment, and, advancing to the door, demanded who was there? "Two travellers," answered a gentle voice, "overtaken by the storm; pray, friend, afford us shelter." "O!" cried Jaqueline, "perhaps they may be robbers, and we shall be murdered." "Pho! simpleton," said Pierre, "what can they expect to rob us of." He opened the door, and discovered a man supporting a lady who appeared almost fainting. "Pray, friend," said the man, permit this lady to enter your cottage, I fear she has suffered much from the storm." "Poor soul, I am sorry for her; enter and welcome," cried Pierre. Jaqueline placed her wooden armchair by the chimney, ran for some wood, and kindled a blaze in a moment, whilst Pierre put the horse into a little outhouse which held their firing and his working implements, and returned with a portmantua to the lady. They had only some bread and milk to her, but they made it warm, and prevailed on their guest to take some. The man, who appeared an attendant, did the same.

The lady soon got her cloaths dry, but she wanted rest, and they had no bed to offer. One single room answered all their purposes of life; their humble bed was on the floor, in a corner of it, but though mean it was whole and clean. Jaqueline entreated the lady to lie down; she refused for some time, but growing faint from exhausted spirits and fatigue, she was compelled to accept the offer; the others sat silently round the fire: but, alas! horror and affliction precluded sleep, and the fair traveller, after laying about two hours, returned again to the fireside, weary and unrefreshed. "Is there any house near this?" demanded she. "No, madam," replied Jaqueline, "there is no house, but there is a fine old castle just by, where there is room enough, for only one old man and his wife live in it, and, Lord help us, I would not be in their place for all the fine things there." "Why so?" said the lady. "O! dear madam, why it is haunted; there are bloody floors, prison rooms, and inscriptions, they say, on the windows to make a body's hair stand on end." "And how far from your cottage is this castle?" "A little step, madam, farther up the wood." "And do you think we could obtain entrance there?" "O, Lord! yes, madam and thank you too: why the poor old souls rejoice to see a body call there now and then; I go sometimes in the middle of the day, but I take good care to keep from the fine rooms and never to be out after dark." "I wish," said the lady, "it was possible to get there." Pierre instantly offered his service to conduct her as soon as it was light, and notwithstanding some very horrible stories recounted by Jaqueline she determined to visit this proscribed place.

When the morning came, the inhabitants of the cottage set out for the castle. The lady was so much enfeebled, from fatigue and want of rest, that she was obliged to be placed on the horse, and they found it very difficult to lead him through the thickets. They at length espied a fine old building, with two wings, and a turret on the top, where a large clock stood, a high wall surrounded the house, a pair of great gates gave entrance into a spacious court, surrounded with flowering shrubs, which lay broken and neglected on the ground intermixed with the weeds which were above a foot high in every part.

Whilst the lady's attendant lifted her from the horse, Pierre repaired to the kitchen door where the old couple lived, which stood in one of the wings, and knocking pretty loudly, the old woman opened it, and, with a look of astonishment, fixed her eyes on the lady and her servant. "Good neighbour," said Pierre, "here is a great gentlewoman cruel ill; she wants food and sleep, we have brought her here, she is not afeared of your ghosts, and so therefore you can give her a good bed, I suppose." "To be sure I can," answered Bertha, which was the woman's name: "to be sure I can make a bed fit for the emperor, when the linen is aired: walk in, madam; you look very weak." Indeed the want of rest the preceding night had so much added to her former feeble state, that it was with difficulty they conveyed her into the kitchen. Bertha warmed a little wine, toasted a bit of bread, and leaving Jaqueline to attend the lady, she made a fire in a handsome bedroom that was in that wing, took some fine linen out of a chest and brought it down to air. "Dear, my lady," cried she, "make yourself easy, I'll take care of you, and if you ar'nt afeared, you will have rooms for a princess." Pierre and Jaqueline being about to return to their daily labour, found their kindness amply rewarded by the generosity of the stranger, who gave them money enough, they said, to serve them for six months. With a thousand blessings they retired, promising however to call daily on the lady whilst she staid at the castle, though their hearts misgave them that they should never see her more, from their apprehensions of the ghosts that inhabited the rooms above stairs. When the apartment was arranged, the lady was assisted by Bertha and laid comfortably to rest; she gave her some money to procure food and necessaries, and desired her servant might have a bed also.

This the good woman promised, and, wishing her a good sleep, returned to the kitchen. "God bless the poor lady," said she, "why she is as weak as a child; sure you must have come a great way from home." "Yes," answered Albert, the servant's name, "we have indeed, and my poor lady is worn down by sorrow and fatigue; I fear she must rest some time before she can pursue her journey." "Well," said Bertha, "she may stay as long as she likes here, nobody will disturb her in the day time, I am sure." "And what will disturb her at night?" asked Albert. "O, my good friend," answered she, "nobody will sleep in the rooms upstairs; the gentlefolks who were in it last could not rest, such strange noises, and groans, and screams, and such like terrible things are heard; then at t'other end of the house the rooms are never opened; they say bloody work has been carried on there." "How comes it, then," said Albert, "that you and your husband have courage to live here?" "Dear me," replied she, "why the ghosts never come downstairs, and I take care never to go up o'nights; so that if madam stays here I fear she must sleep by day, or else have a ground room, for they never comes down; they were some of your high gentry, I warrant, who never went into kitchens." Albert smiled at the idea, but, resuming his discourse, asked the woman to whom the castle belonged? "To a great Baron," said she, "but I forget his name." "And how long have you lived here?" "Many a long year, friend; we have a small matter allowed us to live upon, a good garden that gives us plenty of vegetables, for my husband, you must know, is a bit of a gardener, and works in it when he is able." "And where is he now?" said Albert. "Gone to the village six leagues off to get a little meat, bread and wine." "What! does he walk?" "Lord help him, poor soul, he walk! no, bless your heart, he rides upon our faithful little ass, and takes care never to overload her, as we don't want much meat, thank God. But where will you like to sleep?" added she; "will you go upstairs, or shall I bring some bedding in the next room?" Albert hesitated, but, ashamed to have less courage than his mistress, asked if there was any room near the lady's? "Aye, sure," answered Bertha, "close to her there is one as good as hers." "Then I will sleep there," said he. His good hostess now nimbly as she could, bestirred herself to put his room in order, and was very careful not to disturb the lady. Albert was soon accommodated and retired to rest.

I n the evening the lady came down into the kitchen, much refreshed, and expressed her thanks to the good woman for her kindness. "Heavens bless your sweet face," cries Bertha. "I am glad to my heart you be so well. Ah! as I live, here's my Joseph and the ass." She ran out into the court to acquaint her good man with what had befallen her in his absence. "As sure as you be alive, Joseph, she is some great lady under trouble, poor soul, for she does sigh so piteously but she has given me plenty of money to get things for her, so you know it's nothing to us, if she likes to stay here, so much the better." "I hope," said the old man, "she is no bad body." No that she an't, I'll swear," cries Bertha; "she looks as mild as the flowers in May." They had now unloaded their faithful ass, and entered the kitchen with their provender. Joseph was confounded at the appearance of the lady; he made his humble bow, but was very silent. Bertha prepared some eggs and fruit for her supper; she ate but little, and that little was to oblige the old couple; she then asked for a candle, and said she would retire to her room. Joseph and Bertha looked at each other with terror, both were silent; at length Joseph, with much hesitation of voice and manner, said, "I fear, madam, you will not be quiet there, it will be better, to my thinking, if a fire was made in one of the parlours and the bedding brought down." "There is no occasion for fire," answered the lady, "but merely to air the room; however I am not in any apprehension of sleeping in the room above, at least I will try it this night." It was with great reluctance the honest couple permitted her to retire; Bertha had not even the courage to accompany her, but Albert and Joseph offering to go, she ventured up to make the bed, and her work finished, flew down like one escaped from great danger.

The men having withdrawn, the lady seated herself at the dressing table, and having opened her portmantua to take out some linen for the ensuing day, she burst into tears on viewing the small quantity of necessaries she possessed; she cast a retrospection on her past calamities, they made her shudder; she looked forward to the future, all was dark and gloomy; she wrung her hands. "What will become of me, unhappy as I am, where can I fly? Who will receive a poor unfortunate, without family or friends? The little money I have will be soon exhausted, and what is to be the fate of poor Albert, who has left all to follow me!" Overcome with sorrow, she wept aloud. When, turning her eyes to the window, she saw a light glide by from the opposite wing, which her room fronted, and which Bertha had informed her was particularly haunted. At first she thought it was imagination; she arose and placed her candle in the chimney; curiosity suspended sorrow—she returned and seated herself at the window, and very soon after she saw a faint glimmering light pass a second time; exceedingly surprised, but not terrified, she continued in her situation: she saw nothing further. She at length determined to go to rest, but with an intention to visit every part of the house the following day.

She got into bed, but could not sleep. About twelve o'clock she heard plainly a clanking of chains, which was followed by two or three heavy groans; she started up and listened, it was presently repeated, and seemed to die away by gentle degrees; soon after she heard a violent noise, like two or three doors clapping to with great force. Though unaccustomed to fear she could not help trembling. She felt some inclination to call Joseph, she then recollected Albert was in the next room; she knocked at the wainscot and called Albert! No answer was made. She got out of bed, and throwing on a loose gown, took her candle, and, opening the door of the next apartment, went up to the bed; she saw he was buried under the cloaths. "Albert," said she, "do not be afraid, 'tis your mistress with a light;" he then ventured to raise himself and though but little inclined to mirth, she could not refrain from smiling at the fright he was in; the drops of perspiration run down his face, his eyes were starting, and he was incapable of speaking for some time. "Pray, Albert," said his lady, "have you heard any particular noise?"

"Noise," repeated he. "O Lord! all the ghosts have been here together to frighten me." "Here—where," asked she, "in this room?" "I believe so," he replied; "in this or the next I am sure they were; there was a score or two in chains, then there was groans and cries: but pray, madam, leave the candle a minute at the door, I will throw on my cloaths and get down into kitchen and never come upstairs again." "Well, but, Albert," she, "I must stay in my room, have you more cause for fear than I have?" "No, madam, thank God, I never did harm to man, woman, child." "Then take courage, Albert, I will light your candle, and, I shall be in the next apartment, and will leave my door open, you may either call to me or go downstairs, if you are a second time alarmed." It was with reluctance he obeyed, and repeatedly desired doors might remain open.

The lady retired to her room, for some time hesitating whether should dress herself or go into bed, she at length threw herself down in her night gown, but could not sleep. Strange and various were her conjectures respecting the lights she had seen, and the accountable noises she had heard; she was not surprised that the weak minds of the old people should be terrified, or that Albert, who was likewise far advanced in years, above sixty, should shrink from alarms which had given her a momentary terror; but as she did not suffer her mind to dwell on the causes being supernatural, she conceived there must be some mystery which, on the following day, if her health permitted, she resolved, if possible, to explore. Towards morning she fell into a profound sleep, undisturbed by groans or noises of any sort.

A lbert, who, by his terror and apprehensions of seeing those ghosts that had so greatly frightened him, was prevented from sleeping, got up the moment day appeared and crept down stairs, here he was soon after joined by Joseph. "How have you slept, my good friend?" asked he. "Slept!" replied the other; "why, who could sleep d'ye think, when chains were rattling, ghosts roaring and groaning doors banging with violence enough to shake the foundation of the walls?

Lord help me, I would not live in such a place no, not to be master of the whole estate." "Aye, I knew how it would be," said Joseph; "it's always the same business when anybody comes here to sleep; we never hear any noise else." "Why, then your ghosts are very rude unsociable folks," answered Albert, "for strangers can do them no hurt, and there's room enough, me thinks, in this great house for them to have their merriments, without coming to frighten honest travellers, that never desire to interrupt them." "I don't know how it is," replied Joseph, "but as to merriment, sure there can be none in groans and cries, and they do say that cruel wicked deeds have been done in this castle, and I suppose the poor souls can't lay quiet." "Dear me," cries Albert, "I wish my mistress may be well enough to go farther, though poor soul, she doesn't know where to go to, that's true." "Poor lady, that's bad indeed; has she no parents, nor husband, nor uncles, nor aunts, nor—" "Yes, yes," said Albert, interrupting him, "she has some relations, but what of that, better she had none, I believe for her—O, here comes Bertha." On her entrance the good morrows and enquiries were repeated; Bertha expressed her sorrow for the lady and immediately ascended the stairs to see if she was not frightened out of her wits by such a cruel disturbance.

She soon returned with the lady, and breakfast being quickly set before her, she endeavoured to eat, but her appetite was so indifferent as to cause great pain to the friendly Bertha.

Joseph mounted his favourite beast and repaired to the town that he might procure necessaries for his family, superior to what he had bought the day before. After his departure, and that Albert was gone to look after his horse, the fair stranger demanded of Bertha if she could give her any account of the owners of the castle. "Why, madam," answered she, 'the present lord of this estate is—aye, his name is Count Wolfenbach; he married a very handsome lady at Vienna, and brought her here; it was then a beautiful place very unlike such as it be now; but howsomever they say he was very jealous, and behaved very ill to the poor lady, and locked her up, and there she was brought to bed, and the child was taken from her, and so she died, and 'twas said the child died, and so everybody believes "tis their ghosts that make such dismal noises in the castle, for soon after my Lord the Count went away, Joseph who worked under the gardener, was ordered to take care of the house; and I lived then under the cook, so we married: all the other servants were discharged, and so we have lived here ever since. My Lord came here once or twice, but the ghosts made such a noise he could not stay. Several gentry have slept here at times, but nobody would stay a second night, and so we have all to ourselves by day, and the ghosts, or what they be, have got all the rooms by night and then they be quiet enough." "Pray," interrogated the lady, "can I walk through the rooms and examine the opposite wing?" "To be sure, madam, you can, if you be so bold, but neither I nor Joseph ever goes there, because that's the part where the poor Countess died." "How many years ago was it?" "Near eighteen, my Lady for next Christmas we have been married so many years, and I was fifty-three and Joseph fifty-two when we came together; not very young to be sure, what of that, we live very comfortable, only a little lonely or so." "Well," said her guest, "I shall be glad to walk through all the apartments." "I will attend you, madam, except to the other side, there I never goes."

A fter breakfast was over, the lady and Bertha walked upstairs; they went through several fine apartments, the furniture rich though old fashioned; one hung with family portraits she was particularly pleased with; two attracted her attention greatly, which Bertha told her, she had heard say, were the present Count and his late lady.

After going through the body of the house they came to the doors that led to the other wing: "Now, for goodness sake, dear Madam, don't go no farther, for as sure as you are alive, here the ghosts live, for Joseph says he often sees lights and hears strange things." "My good friend," replied the lady, "you may return, but I certainly will look into those rooms." "O, pray good, your ladyship, don't go now." She persisted however in her determination, and on Bertha's leaving her she opened the door which led to a gallery, and a handsome staircase, on the right hand she saw a suite of four rooms, all well-furnished, two as bedrooms, one handsome sitting room, the other a library, well filled with books, in handsome cases; these two last rooms, she observed, exactly fronted the one on the opposite side, where she had slept. Having examined those apartments, she saw, on the other side of the gallery, two other doors; these, on trial, she found locked. She then returned and went down the staircase; after the first landing place the windows were shut, and when she came to the bottom she entered a hall, in which were three doors. One she attempted to open; immediately a murmuring noise was heard, and the instant she opened the door, another at the end of the room was shut to with great violence. The lady for a moment stood suspended; she trembled, and deliberated whether she should return or not; but recovering resolution, she entered; a candle was burning on a table, the windows were closed up, there were books and implements for drawing on the table; this convinced her the inhabitants were alive, however, and going to the door, she said aloud, "Whoever resides in this apartment need not be under any apprehensions from the intrusion of an unfortunate woman, whom distress has driven to this castle, and only a melancholy kind of curiosity has induced her to explore a part of it proscribed by everyone."

She had scarcely uttered these words when the door opened, and a lady, attended by an elderly woman, appeared. Both started; but the visitor, in a confused manner, apologised for her intrusion. The other taking her hand, placed her in a chair. "Perhaps, madam," said she, "this may prove the happiest day of my life, and I may rejoice that your curiosity and courage is superior to those terrors by which others have been intimidated." "At least, madam, you will do me the justice to believe," answered the lady, "that I would not have been guilty of this intrusion, had I known these apartments were really inhabited, but be assured, madam, your secret is perfectly safe with me." "I do not doubt it," replied the other, your countenance is a letter of recommendation to every heart." She then ordered her attendant to bring some refreshments, which consisted of biscuits and fruits.

The woman being withdrawn, the lady of the house said, "However, madam, I may rejoice in seeing a female of your appearance, I cannot help lamenting that one so young should know sorrow, or be driven to seek an asylum in such a melancholy place as this castle." "I am indeed, madam, an object of pity," replied the other, "without friends, a home, or one acquaintance to sooth my sorrows. I have fled from oppression and infamy, unknowing where to direct my steps, or what will become of me." "Surely," said the former lady, "heaven directed your steps here, that we might communicate comfort to each other: griefs, when divided become less poignant; I have known years of sorrow, yet I still support life in a feeble hope of one day being restored to happiness." "Alas!" replied the other, "not one shadow of hope can I derive from either past or future prospects; and as I have intruded thus upon you, madam, it is but fit you should know who and what I am. I was born, as I have been told, at Fribourg, and lost both my parents in my infancy. My birth was noble, but my fortune very trifling. The first thing I can remember was a gentleman who I was taught to call uncle, an elderly woman his housekeeper, and a young girl attendant on me; we lived in the country, about three miles from any town or village. As I grew up masters were hired to attend me, and by their skill and my own attention, having nothing to divert my mind from my studies, I became tolerably accomplished at twelve years of age, when my masters were discharged. We received no company; a few gentlemen called now and then, but those I never saw. My uncle was exceedingly fond of me; his name was Mr Weimar, mine Matilda Weimar. Our ancestors, he said, had been Counts, and persons of high rank and fortunes, but by war and prodigality, they had been reduced to comparative poverty; therefore it was fortunate for me he had never been married. I think I am naturally affectionate and grateful, yet I never felt any degree of either for my uncle; and, young as I was, have frequently taken myself to task when I found a repugnance to return his caresses.

"I devoted my whole time to my studies; my uncle, when I was about fifteen having some property in France, was compelled, by the failure of a house, to go there in person; at first he talked of taking me with him, but changed his mind, and gave me in charge to his housekeeper and an old servant called Albert, with strict orders I should never go beyond the walks belonging to his castle. Nothing could exceed the tenderness of his behaviour at parting, and for the first time in my life I was affected. I returned his embraces and shed my tears. 'Ah! Matilda,' said he, 'are you indeed sorry I should leave you?' 'I am, indeed,' I replied. 'Then you shall go with me,' cried he, eagerly; but striking his forehead, he exclaimed, 'No! that will not do; dear Matilda, my sweet niece, keep yourself retired, apply to your studies, I shall soon return, and, I hope, make you the happiest of women.' I felt at that moment real gratitude and affection; I promised strictly to obey his commands, and by my endeavours to improve my mind, deserve his love and esteem. He quitted me with extreme reluctance, and for several days I found the want of his company and conversation, but by degrees I grew reconciled, and as Agatha and Albert were respectable and intelligent persons, for their stations in life; I made them both my friends and companions. This was really the happiest period of my life I was capable of amusing myself with music and drawing, in the evenings I walked in the garden and adjoining wood with Agatha, returned with a good appetite, and slept quietly.

"My uncle remained in France near nine months, he constantly wrote to me, and I was punctual in my answers; at the end of that period he returned; I was overjoyed to see him, but the pleasure I felt and expressed fell very short of the rapture and transport with which he embraced and praised me; he dwelt on the improvement in my person with such delight, that I felt confused and uneasy; the attention which used to give me pleasure now was painful, and I repulsed his caresses involuntarily. He told me he had brought me a present of some books and drawings, both of which he knew would be acceptable to me; I acknowledged his kindness with an apparent gratitude, yet I was in reality but little thankful, though I could not account for the increasing coldness of my behaviour. After a hasty supper I retired to bed, notwithstanding his wishes to detain me, and after I was alone I began to reflect on my conduct so cold and thankless, towards so kind an uncle, whose affection for me seemed greatly increased. I was displeased with my own reflections, and resolved to behave better to him the following day.

"The next morning I rose early; my uncle was not up, Agatha met me going into the garden. 'My dear Miss,' said she, 'you were very shy and unkind to your uncle last night; the good man loves you dearly, and 'tis not your business to be shewing him such slights, I can tell you.' Though conscious I was wrong I was amazed at the freedom of her observations, as she was not much the room with us; I therefore made some trifling answer and pursued my walk.

"It was plain my uncle had taken notice of my coldness, and complained to her: I was mortified and vexed; after taking two or three turns I went into the house, and met my uncle in the breakfast room; I assumed the kindest manner possible in my salutations to him and I saw he was highly gratified by it. He produced his books and drawings, the latter were very beautiful, but the attitudes and want of decent drapery confused and hurt me, for although I had never received any particular lessons on delicacy or modesty, yet there is that innate virtuous principle within us, that shrinks involuntarily from anything tending to violate that sense of decency we are all, I believe, born with; I therefore could not examine them with the accuracy I wished, much less praise them, as I saw he expected. 'Are they not exquisite pieces?' demanded he. 'They are very fine drawings, I believe, Sir, but I think the subjects of them are exceptionable.' 'My dear girl,' he replied, laughing, 'you know nothing of the world; whoever excepts against the subjects of drawings, or the attitudes of statues? 'tis the execution and proportions that attract our notice, and I assure you, my little prude, there is nothing objectionable in any point of view, in those drawings before you, nor in the books, which are now most in repute among the fashionable circles in France.'

"Though my reason was not convinced I made no further scruples, but thanked him for his attention to my amusement, and, breakfast over, retired to my own apartment, having my presents carried there, that I might examine them at my leisure.

"From this time my uncle's behaviour was to me unaccountable he was forever seeking opportunities to caress me, his language was expressive of the utmost fondness, he praised my person in such glowing colours as sometimes filled me with confusion. In short, madam, not to tire you, within three months after his return I began to be extremely uneasy at freedoms I scarce knew how to repulse. One morning after dressing I went into the garden, a thing unusual with me at that hour, and going round a serpentine walk, which led to a summer house, I thought I heard voices there; I stopt at the back of it, which, as well as the front, had a door that opened into the garden, and plainly heard Agatha's voice, saying, 'I tell you, Sir, there is no other way, send Albert off for a few days, or turn him off at once, for he loves Miss Matilda as if she were his own child, and therefore we must get rid of him; but you are so long settling your mind—get into her room at night when she's asleep, I'll take care nobody comes there, or tell her roundly at once you are not an uncle to her—I would not longer stand upon ceremony.' 'Well, Agatha, I'll take your advice, and dispatch Albert tomorrow, and the next night I will be happy.' You may suppose, madam, I was scarcely able to support myself. Having heard thus far I tottered from the summer-house, and got into the shrubbery, where I threw myself on the ground, and preserved myself from fainting by a copious flood of tears.

"Overwhelmed by my own reflections, without a friend or habitation to fly to for protection, uncertain whether this man was really my uncle or not, yet convinced he had the most diabolical designs against me, and that in his house I could not be safe: it is impossible to describe my feelings and distress; at length I arose and recollected what the horrid woman had said of Albert, it was my only resource. I walked from the garden towards the stables; most fortunately I met him coming from them. 'Albert,' said I, hastily, 'I wish to speak with you, follow me into the park.' The man looked surprised—'Me, Miss—I follow you?'

'Yes, immediately,' I replied. I walked quickly to the park, he came after me; when out of sight of the house I turned to him— 'Albert, do you love me? Are you willing to serve me?' 'Aye, that I will, dear Miss, to the last drop of my blood.' I then, without losing time, told him the plot designed against me, and what was determined with respect to himself. The good creature was struck dumb with surprise, but recovering himself, 'By my soul,' cried he, 'I will save and serve you whilst I have breath, from such devils. My dear young lady be easy, I have a sister who lives at Lucerne, she will be proud to serve you; 'tis a long journey, but never fear, you can ride behind me, as you have often done in sport: I'll manage the business tonight, never fear—get up a little early in the morning and meet me here.' We then concerted our whole plan, and I returned to the house with a lighter heart, and got to my apartment unobserved.

"I was soon after summoned to dinner; when I saw my uncle I turned faint, he flew to me with tenderness—'My dear Matilda, are you ill?' 'Only a sick headache,' I replied, disengaging myself from him, and sitting down. 'I fear you have been reading too much.' 'Very likely, Sir; I shall be better by and bye,' was my answer. I could eat but little, yet I tried to do it, and also to rally my spirits to avoid suspicion. When Albert was removing the cloth, 'I have a great favour to ask your Honour.' 'What is it Albert?' said my uncle. 'Why, Sir, I have got a sister married at a village near Lausanne, and the poor soul does so long to see me, that if you could spare me for a week, I should be mightily obliged to you?' 'For a week!" replied his master, pleasure dancing in his eyes, 'you may set off tomorrow and stay a fortnight, it cannot be less time, to give you any comfort with your friends.' The poor fellow bowed his thanks and withdrew.

"I now exulted in our prospect of success in my deliverance: I grew more cheerful, my uncle was tender and affectionate; I bore his caresses without any repulses, but left the room soon as possible. I employed myself in packing up a few necessaries in a small portmantua, with what little valuables I had, and was tolerably supplied with money, as I thought, knowing little of the expences of a journey. I did not go to bed,

17

and about four in the morning, when the whole house was buried in sleep, I took my portmantua, and with some difficulty carried it downstairs, opened the doors with the greatest precaution, and, to my no small joy, found Albert walking upon the green; he took my load from me, and, without speaking, led the way to the stables, fastened on the portmantua, and getting me behind him, we rode off as fast as possible. Previous to my quitting the room the preceding evening, I desired my uncle not to wait breakfast for me, as I believed I should scarcely rise sooner than ten, as I had not slept well the night before; I therefore thought we should have some hours start of any pursuit, and we proceeded on to Lucerne the very opposite road from Lausanne, where Albert had asked permission to go to.

"After a tedious and painful journey we got safe to Lucerne. Alas! how great was our disappointment; this sister, on whose protection I relied, had been dead three weeks, and her little shop and stock given to a young woman who lived with her, and only a small legacy left to Albert. What now was to be done? The mistress of the house humanely offered me a bed for a night or two; vexation and fatigue compelled me to accept the offer: my poor fellow traveller was more affected than myself. We consulted what was next to be done; he then recollected he had a relation at Zurich, and proposed my going on there. He said it was a good city, and some way or other, doubtless, I might procure a living by my talents. Small as this hope was I had no alternative but to embrace it, and the next morning we pursued our journey; the day before yesterday was the second day of our travelling from Zurich. The storm came on just before our entrance into the wood, we took shelter for some time, but the trees getting thoroughly wet, and the night setting in, we rode through it, in the hope of meeting some friendly cottage; we were fortunate to our wishes, and by the inhabitants of that cottage we were conducted to this castle."

She then proceeded to relate the conversation she had heard, relative to its being haunted, with her terror of the preceding night, and determination to explore every apartment in the castle. "I hope, madam," added Matilda, "the relation I have given, though tedious and little interesting to you, will apologize for my abrupt intrusion here." "Dearest madam,' answered the Lady of the Castle, "can you think it possible I should be uninterested for a situation like yours? Young, new to the world, with uncommon attractions, without friends or protectors, surely misfortunes have taken an early hold in your destiny; but do not despair, my good young lady, Providence never forsakes the virtuous, but in its own good time will relieve us from every difficulty; an assurance of that truth has supported me under the bitterest calamities, and though I am at present dead to the world, I flatter myself I may be of some service to you, but do not think of quitting this castle yet; happy should I think myself if I could enjoy your society always, but 'tis a selfish wish and shall not be indulged; however, our confidence ought to be reciprocal, and you shall know, in part, the peculiar distresses which have driven me to this asylum, though my confidence must be limited from restrictions I dare not break through." "I fear, madam," answered Matilda, "however eager my curiosity and anxiety may be awakened by your uncommon situation, I must for the present postpone the gratification of it; my long absence will, I am sure, cause much trouble to my hospitable entertainers, and therefore 'tis time I should return." "Well then," said the lady, "when may I hope to see you again?" "After dinner madam, I will attend you." "I shall think every minute an hour till then," replied the lady. They parted with mutual regret. Matilda carefully shut the doors, and returned to Bertha's apartments, with a lighter heart and a dawn of hope.

O n her entrance into the kitchen the good creature clasped her hands and shouted for joy; "O good God be thanked," said she, "that I see you once again; my dear lady, where have you been and what have you seen?" "An excellent library of books," replied Matilda. "And did you see no ghosts, nor hear no noises?" "I saw no ghosts, but I certainly did hear noises." "Lord have mercy upon us! and so, had you courage to stay?" "Yes, I stayed to view the apartments, but I was a little frightened I must confess." "O, dear heart, but I hope you won't go again." "Indeed I shall," said Matilda, "I intend to sit there very often, and shall borrow some books to bring home with me." "O, madam, don't be so hardy, who knows what mischief may come of it one day," "I have no fears, good Bertha; if we perform our duties towards God and man, Providence will always preserve us from evil." Ah! Lord, madam, you talk so good; I am sure I never did hurt to anybody, nor Joseph neither, and when no company comes here we be as quiet as lambs, and yet methinks I do wish for folks sometimes, because you know 'tis very lonely—but will you have your bed made below stairs tonight?" "No," replied Matilda, "I will sleep in the same room, I have no apprehensions at all now." Bertha wondered at the lady's courage, but said nothing.

Albert had before this requested to sleep below, for as they were ghosts of quality, who never condescended to visit kitchens, he thought himself perfectly safe on the ground floor.

When dinner was over, Matilda said she should go to the library and fetch some books. Bertha looked quite woe begone, but was silent: not so Albert, who had been informed of the perilous adventure his young mistress had undergone in the morning; he besought her, with tears in his eyes, not to trust herself again in the haunted rooms. "If any harm betides you, madam, I shall be a poor miserable fellow for the short remnant of my days." "Be not uneasy, my friend Albert, no ghosts can hurt me; 'tis the living only I fear, not the dead; assure yourself I shall return in perfect safety."

Saying this she went upstairs, leaving Bertha and Albert under great consternation. "Well, the Lord love her," said the former, "she must be a pure good creature to have so much courage—I hope no harm will come on't." "I hope so too," cried Albert, wiping his eyes. "She is the best sweetest tempered young lady that ever lived;—ah! I little thought to have seen such a day as this for her."

Whilst these two worthy creatures were expatiating upon her praise, Matilda pursued her way to the Lady of the Castle, who was expecting her with impatience, and warmly embraced her upon her entrance. "How mortifying the reflection," said the lady, leading her visitant to a chair, "that the unexpected happiness I enjoy must be purchased so dearly as by your peace of mind; what delight should I feel in your society, if distress and misfortune had not driven you here!" "Believe me, madam," answered Matilda, "your presence and conversation has greatly alleviated those sorrows which oppress my heart; and if my company should be productive of pleasure to you, I shall feel much less regret for the causes which compelled me to seek this castle as an asylum for an unhappy orphan, though but a temporary one only." "Ah! my dear young lady," replied the other, "you are but young in the school of affliction; you can look forward with hope, you can feel only for yourself, and, God forbid, you should ever know the sorrows of a wife and mother, who knows not but that she is childless and cut off for ever from those endearing ties." "O, madam," cried Matilda, interrupting her, "forgive me that I have revived such terrible images to your mind; let not my curiosity occasion such painful ideas, at least we will enjoy the present hour with mutual satisfaction, and defer your painful recital 'till another day." "Charming girl," said the lady, "I accept the delay you offer me, and am happy that I can assure you of an asylum whenever you grow tired of this castle. I have a sister in France, married to the Marquis de Melfort, she is one of the best of women; she is no stranger to my situation and has repeatedly wished me to come into the world and reside with her, but I have powerful reasons for refusing, though she is the dearest friend I have on earth, and I am certain will rejoice to offer you an accommodation in her house, and a place in her heart, as she has no children to engage her attention." Matilda made the warmest acknowledgements for this kind offer, but said, unaccustomed as she was to the busy world, she was apprehensive Paris would be the last place she ought to reside in, particularly as her uncle might go there, having property and friends in that city, and she might run the hazard of being discovered.

Whilst she was speaking, the lady's attendant entered with a letter, "Joseph has just brought this, my lady." "Joseph!" repeated Matilda, involuntarily "Yes," said the lady, smiling, "your friend Joseph is my friend also; this letter is from my sister—but bid our old friend step in." Joseph entered but started back with surprise when he beheld Matilda seated quietly in the room,—"Good Lord!" cried he, "how came young madam here?" "This lady's courage, you see, has penetrated through our secret and now we have no occasion for any reserve before her, she will as carefully guard it from your wife as you do." "Lord! I am sure," answered Joseph, "it goes to my heart to keep anything from poor Bertha, she is such a good creature, but women's tongues will blab sometimes, to be sure, and as I have sworn to your ladyship, God forbid I should break my oath, though often and often I have longed to tell my wife." "However, Joseph," said the lady, gravely, "I depend upon your honesty and oath." "You have nothing to fear, my lady, eighteen years' practice has learnt me to hold my tongue; have you any further commands?" The lady replying in the negative, he made his bow and retired.

"That man is a faithful good creature, I owe my life to him; I know nothing of his wife, though I am told she is a worthy woman; but as a secret should never, if possible, be trusted to chance or accident, I made him swear not to reveal mine, without permission from me." Matilda exprest her satisfaction that the lady had such a faithful servant, and taking a book from the table, requested she would open her letter.

This being complied with, she presently exclaimed, "Alas! my brother and sister are going within a month to England, perhaps to stay some time; yet why should I grieve at that, they cannot come to me." Then reading on, she again cried out, "My dear Miss Weimar, if you will accept of my sister's protection, it is now at your service: hear what she says, after expressing her regret that I cannot be of her party, 'I wish I could meet with some amiable female companion, to take the tour of England with me; there are so few of one's acquaintance that are desirable as intimate friends, that nothing can be more difficult than to obtain such a one as I am anxious to have. Young ones we cannot meet with, and I cannot bear the idea of being plagued with the ridiculous fopperies of an old coquet; for I am not yet so much of a French woman as to think there is no difference in ages, and that a fine drest and high coloured lady, though near to her grand climacteric, shall be indulged in all the expectations of youth and beauty."

"Now, my dear Miss, you are exactly the lady that will suit my sister; it is not proper, at your age that you should be buried here, otherwise it would be the greatest felicity in the world for me to enjoy your conversation." "I certainly, madam," answered Matilda, "should think myself most fortunate in attending the Marchioness but indeed my finances are so slender, and the necessaries I have are so trifling that I am unable to take a journey of consequence. When I left my uncle's house I was so entirely ignorant of travelling expences, that I conceived I had plenty of money to last a considerable time, but I find myself much mistaken; my little stock is considerably diminished, and I must try, by my industry, soon to support poor Albert as well as myself." "I am happy," returned the lady, "that I can obviate some of your objections. I have a large store of linen I never can wear in this place; I have a good deal of money by me, for I do not spend half the income allowed me; you must—you shall do me the favour to accept my little assistance, as from a mother to her child, I will not be denied." "Your goodness, madam," said Matilda, "overpowers me, but, alas! poor Albert, I cannot forsake him." "Nor shall you, my dear young lady; a faithful servant like him is an acquisition to any family: my sister, I am persuaded, will rejoice to receive him; tell me, therefore, you accept of my proposal, and I will write instantly: we shall then know when it will be absolutely necessary you should join her, that I may not be too soon deprived of the pleasure I now enjoy. I shall leave it to yourself to acquaint her, or not, as you please, with your story, 'tis sufficient I recommend you as a friend of mine." Matilda could form no objection to this kind offer in her desperate circumstances and whilst she amused herself with a book, the lady wrote her letter, and having read it previous to its delivery to Joseph, her young friend expressed her warmest acknowledgements for the favourable manner in which she was mentioned in it.

This business settled, the lady took her into the next apartment, the windows of which were also closed. "This room," said she, "opens into the garden, where I walk occasionally of an evening, when not liable to observation. In these drawers, my dear Miss, there are plenty of necessaries all at your service; tomorrow we will examine them." "I cannot find language, madam, to express my gratitude." "Do not attempt it, be assured your acceptance of my little assistance is a sufficient return for what you consider as an obligation. But pray tell me how you came to venture visiting these apartments, which are generally believed to be haunted?" "As I never had my mind occupied by any ideas of ghosts," answered Matilda, "and could not conceive any actions of my life had subjected me to the terror of supernatural visitations, I believed there must be some other cause for the appearance of lights which I traced in the windows above, and for the noise I heard in the night, though I confess the latter did terrify me; I resolved therefore to visit these rooms, although I was told in one of them there was blood on the floor and horrid inscriptions on the windows." "Your information was true," answered the lady, with a sigh she could not suppress, "it is the room above which answers the description you have heard; another day, when I have related my melancholy story, you shall see it. I am much pleased with your courage, which proceeded from a right principle: when the mind is conscious of no evil actions, nor any deviations from rectitude, there is no cause for fear or apprehensions in a thinking sensible person, and I hope, my dear Miss Weimar, you will never want resolution on similar occasions; judge always for yourself, and never be guided by the opinions of weak minds." "You are very good, madam," replied Matilda, "in favouring me with your approbation; I shall think myself particularly fortunate if you will condescend to instruct me, for it is with shame I confess, more attention has been paid to external accomplishments than to the cultivation of my mind, or any information respecting those principles of virtue a young woman ought early to be acquainted with." "You are truly good and amiable," said the lady; "born with sentiments of virtue, and natural understanding pointed out the right path to happiness, pursue it through life, ever remember it is better to suffer from the follies or vices of others than to feel self-condemnation from a sense of your own: the one, time and patience may subdue, or at least blunt the sharp edge that wounds you; but, for the other there is no consolation, self-reproach admits no healing balm, that can enable us to stem the torrent of oppression, or the evils which arise from our own misconduct. You will pardon the freedom you have invited, my good young lady; when you know my story, you will find I am qualified to speak on the subject from very painful lessons, which I pray heaven you may ever be a stranger to."

She now took her hand and led her to the other room, where refreshments and pleasing conversation made the two hours Matilda passed there the most pleasing she had ever known. When she took leave they parted with regret, and proposed meeting at an early hour the following day; when the lady promised to relate the events that had compelled her to a seclusion from the world, and the motives which induced her to alarm every stranger that came to the castle.

Matilda stept into the library, and selecting two or three books, returned to her friendly hostess, whose surprise and pleasure seemed equally gratified by seeing her in safety. Joseph came in soon after; he looked with increased respect and kindness, but was entirely silent as to their meeting in the lady's apartment. When the hour of retiring came, Matilda repaired to her room with great cheerfulness, and when Albert, with tears, entreated her to sleep below, she replied, "You may, my good Albert, if you chuse; but I shall sleep perfectly quiet above stairs; be under no apprehensions for me," added she, smiling, "I am no longer a stranger, and have not the smallest apprehensions of being molested this night." She took up her candle and left them. "Well," cried Bertha, "the Lord be good unto her, for sure she is the best and most courageous lady I ever saw in my life; I believe it would kill me if any harm was to happen to such a sweet creature."

All now retired to rest, and Albert thought himself quite safe on the ground floor from the quality ghosts. In the morning they met with great satisfaction; every one eagerly demanded of Matilda if she had slept undisturbed; she assured them she had, and was greatly refreshed. This account pleased them all. Albert went out to assist

Joseph in the garden; and his mistress was preparing to visit her friend, when Jaqueline made her appearance from the kitchen with Bertha. Matilda was extremely glad to see the good woman, enquired after Pierre, and thanked her for the good accommodations she had procured for her in the castle. "Dear me," said Jaqueline, "you cannot think how glad I am to see you, my lady; I was a-coming yesterday, but I was busy washing, and, Lord help me, this morning before day I was afrightened out of my wits, for I heard some horses galloping by the door, and I thought I heard this lady screaming most piteously; so, says I, dear heart, Pierre, I am afraid some mischief has happened to young madam, so I'll be sure to go to the castle when I have hung out my cloaths; so Pierre he went to fell wood, and I made all haste here, and glad to my heart I am to see you all safe." Matilda thanked the friendly woman for her attention, and after a little chat left the two gossips together, and hastened to the lady, telling them she was going to sit in the library. She crossed the apartment and descended the stairs, saw the lady's room open, and walked in; no one was there, but a great appearance of disorder in the room, one of the stools thrown down, a candle on the floor, another burning on the table, and several things scattered about; she was surprised—she knocked, she called, she had no answer.

Terrified beyond expression, she ventured into the other room, where the bed was; it was empty, but had the appearance of being laid on; a little cabinet, which stood on the drawers, was open and emptied of its contents. She returned; she went through the several rooms that were open, all were desolate; she once more went back to the ground floor. The candle was nearly extinguished, she took up and lighted the other, and, on looking round, she saw the door that opened from the bedroom into the garden was ajar, and on trial it opened; she then readily conceived the lady must have been carried away through the garden, but by whom it was impossible to guess; robbers would never have incommoded themselves with females.

She came in and was about to shut the garden door, when she thought the sound of footsteps reached her ears—-she trembled and stopt, presently a door, the opposite side of the bed, opened, and Joseph appeared: she was overjoyed—he looked surprised; "O, Joseph," cried she, "what is become of your lady?" Astonished at the question, the poor fellow repeated her words, and added, "Good Lord, madam, has not your ladyship seen her?" "No," replied she; "I have searched every room in vain, and found this garden door open." "O, she is carried off then," cried he, "and we are all undone—O, my dear, dear lady, you are betrayed at last." Tears burst from his aged eyes; Matilda sunk into a chair, overcome with sorrow, "But," said she, when able to speak, "how could anyone enter, there is no door forced?" "Yes, madam, there is," answered Joseph, "I found the kitchen door burst off its hinges, and came in trembling for fear of what had happened." "From whence could anyone come into the kitchen?" "Why, madam, there is a private passage underground, from the garden to the under apartments, which is unknown to everybody, as I thought, but to the lady and myself; but it must be discovered by somebody, and we are all undone. Hasten, madam, out of this place, I will fasten up the doors and follow you." "Joseph." said Matilda, "can you meet me in the garden by and bye, I wish to speak with you." "Directly after dinner, madam, I will wait upon your ladyship; I will look about a little, I think no one will come here in the open day." Matilda retired, with trembling limbs and a beating heart, to her own apartment; here she ruminated on what had happened to her friend so recently gained, and so irrecoverably lost— "Alas! poor lady," said she, "who knows what evils she may have to encounter with; a stranger as I am to her story, I have no clue to guide me who may have carried her off, or by whom the cruel action was committed; doubtless it must have been her cries that alarmed Jaqueline—What will become of me? How are all my flattering prospects vanished?"

With these bitter reflections she passed the hours 'till dinner time came; she then went down, but with a countenance so altered, that Bertha started back and cried out, "O, for a certain young madam has seen something and been frightened!" Albert looked with anxious curiosity, "Be not uneasy, my good friends," said she: I assure you neither ghosts nor noises have terrified me, but I am not very well; after dinner perhaps I may be better," "Heaven send it," cried Bertha. Albert joined in the wish and Matilda, affected by their kindness, went into the parlour, where her dinner was served up, not in state or profusion indeed, but good wild fowls, eggs, salads, and fruit. She waited impatiently until she thought Joseph had nearly dined, and then walked towards the garden; in a little time Joseph joined her, and walking before, conducted her to a distant part of it, where a small arbour in a shrubbery appeared almost choaked with weeds; he led her into it, she sat down— "Now, Joseph, for heaven's sake, tell me everything about the dear lady." "That I cannot do," replied Joseph shaking his head: "my oath will not permit me; but underneath this stone," said he, stamping his foot, "is an underground passage, one end of which goes to that part of the castle, and opens into a private place behind the kitchen; the other end goes through to the end of the wood, I believe, for I never had courage to go so far on, but this morning, when I went down the passage, and came round, I found both doors forced off their hinges below, and was much afraid to come up, where I found you, madam: who it is that has been so wicked, I can only guess, and Lord have mercy on the poor lady, I fear no good will come to her." "But how come the garden door open; could they convey her through that into the road?" "Yes," replied Joseph, "that was the way, for after you went upstairs I went into the garden, and the great gate, at the end, was unbolted just at the end of the wood, and I do suppose they had horses waiting there, or a carriage. The few jewels my poor lady had is taken from her little chest, but there are no locks broke on the drawers, and her pockets are left behind, on a stool, with everything in them; 'twas no robbers, my lady, I fear." "I fear so too," answered Matilda, with a deep sigh; "I dread that she is fallen into worse hands—" "Into worse than I fear has got her," said Joseph, "she cannot be fallen—Lord how I rejoiced she had got your ladyship with her." "Aye, Joseph," resumed Matilda, "I grieve for her and feel my own loss;—Do you know her sister the Marchioness?" "I saw her once after my lady was married; they say she is very happy—God help us, 'twasn't so here." "Your lady has wrote to the Marchioness relative to me; did not you take a letter yesterday?" "Yes, my lady, and if there be any answer to it I shall be sure to have it, and you may open it, you know, because the good lady never wrote to anyone else." Poor Matilda knew not what to do; she was desirous of staying 'till this answer arrived. She was anxious to explore those apartments that were locked, and after some hesitation asked Joseph if he would meet her there, tomorrow morning. "Aye, sure, that I will," returned he, "and as I left the lamps burning in the passage, if you like, I will go down this way with you now." "No," said she, "not now; I will meet you tomorrow in the library, and we may return this way, for I own I should like to see it, though 'tis plain the passage must be known."

They now separated, and Matilda found no possibility of gratifying her curiosity, Joseph's oath being against her, and she too much respected her friend to urge a violation of it on any grounds.

She returned to her apartment and amused herself for a short time with a book; but the agitation of her mind would not admit of entertainment; she threw it aside and called for Albert; he instantly attended her. "My good friend," said she, "I propose remaining here a week or ten days, perhaps not so long, to refresh myself; how far are we from Zurich?" "About a day and a half's journey, not much more." "Well then, Albert, we will wait a few days until I am more in health unless you are very anxious to get there.' "Me, my dear young lady, Lord bless you, I want to go only on your account, it's all one to me where I am, if you are safe." Matilda was pleased at his answer and exprest her gratitude for his kindness in such terms as brought tears into his eyes. "God bless you, madam, I'll go with you all the world over." He bowed and retired. "Good creature!" exclaimed Matilda, "heaven has blest you with an honest feeling heart; how much superior are thy sentiments to those of better understanding and cultivated talents, when their minds are depraved by the indulgence of irregular passions!"

She sought to compose her spirits, and wait with patience for the expected letter, which she thought must determine her future destiny. She had recommended to Albert not to stir from the house, lest he might be seen by any one that knew him in passing the road, which caution she observed herself.

The following morning after breakfast she repaired to the library; ah! thought she, what transport, if I should find the dear lady returned! but no such happiness awaited her; she entered the apartments with a beating heart, and remained near ten minutes in the library before Joseph made his appearance. "Well, Joseph," said she, hastily, on his entering the room, "how are things below stairs?" "All the same as they were yesterday, madam; the doors were fast, and everything as I left them." "I have a very great desire," said she, "to see that room where the inscriptions are, and which I find is locked up, can you open it?" "Yes, I can; the key is below, but if I may speak my mind, I think you had better not go." "Why so," demanded she. "Why, because, to my thinking, it's a dismal place, and will put me in mind of sad doings." "You make me more curious—pray indulge me, Joseph?" "Well, madam, I'll go with you, but 'tis sore against my mind." He went down, and soon returned with two keys, but with evident reluctance in his countenance; "I believe one of these is the key," said he; "there used to hang three upon the peg; the other is gone, or left in the closet door perhaps yet: I don't think my lady ever came up to open these rooms." Whilst he was talking he was trying the keys; neither of them would open the first door, the second he unlocked presently; they entered. It was a dressing-room, handsomely furnished; they tried the door which opened into the other room, it was fastened on the inside. "This is very strange," said Joseph; "I will go down again and see if I can find the other key, if you are not afraid to stay alone." "Not in the least," said Matilda, who was examining the room very carefully. The windows were very high and grated with bars of iron, the hangings were dark green damask, everything was handsome, yet the grated windows made it appear gloomy.

Joseph now returned with a countenance of horror and dismay "O, my lady, I can find no key, but looking about the kitchen, behind the door I found a large knife, all over blood." "Gracious heaven!" cried Matilda, "what is it you tell me; I tremble with apprehension; let us force that door, at all events." "I intend it," answered Joseph, "and have brought a bar with me for the purpose." The door in the dressing-room being the slightest, after a good deal of labour, the old man burst it open. What a scene presented itself! a woman on the bed weltring in blood! Both uttered a cry of horror, and ran to the bed; it was the elderly attendant of the lady dead, by a wound in her throat.

The sight was too much for poor Matilda, she sunk fainting into a chair; Joseph was frightened out of his wits; he flew down as fast as possible, and returned with water, he bathed her face and hands and she revived.

"O, Joseph!" cried she, "the lady—the dear lady! what is become of her in such bloody hands?" "The Lord only knows," answered he, looking with terror towards the closet. Directed by his eye Matilda arose and walked to the door; the key was in it; she unlocked it, and was about to enter, when casting her eyes on the floor, she saw it was all over stained with blood, dried into the floor—she started, and involuntarily retreated, but Joseph, who had looked round said, "You may enter, madam, nothing is here." With trembling steps, she entered the closet, her heart beating with terror; it was a large light closet, with a very high window, grated like the other, hung with dark green stuff; two stools covered with the same, and a large wardrobe in it. On the floor was plainly mark'd the shape of a hand and fingers traced in blood, which seemed to have flowed in great quantities. "Good heavens!" cried she, "some person was doubtless murdered here too." "Intended to have been murdered," answered Joseph, wiping his eyes, "but thank God she escaped then." He said no more. Matilda, extremely terrified, hastened out of the closet, when the poor creature on the bed met her eyes. "O, Joseph!" exclaimed she, turning with horror from the scene, "what is to be done with this unfortunate woman?" "Dear, my lady, I can't tell; I have neither strength to dig a grave, nor can I carry her down." "It is plain," said Matilda, "the wretches who have carried of the lady, murdered the servant to prevent discovery." "I fear," cried Joseph, "my turn will be next—my mouth will be stopt from the same fear." "God forbid," said Matilda; "but as I have now no hopes of finding the lady, and it will be dangerous to entrust another person with the secret, I think, Joseph, if we can find a small trunk or chest, to fill it with the linen and necessaries your lady offered me, and convey it to one of the rooms in the other wing; I will write a line and leave it on the table: yet, on second thought, it will be useless, should she escape, she can never think of coming here again: we will therefore lock and bolt up every door; you can take the keys of the places below to your own kitchen, and now and then come through the passage to see if all is safe." Poor Joseph, with a heavy heart, agreed to this.

They had now stayed some time, and thought it best to separate and meet again after dinner: they gladly left these horrid rooms, and returned by different ways to their own habitation.

When Matilda came to her apartment, the terror of her mind was unspeakable; all she had seen, all she had heard crouded upon her remembrance, and gave her the most horrible ideas. She could not think Joseph's fears unreasonable; if he was supposed to be in the secret, his life was not safe, and in his fate the whole family might be involved. "What can I—what ought I to do?" cried she, shedding a torrent of tears, "no friend to advise me, no certainty of a place to receive me, if I go from hence, and a probability, that, if I stay, I may be murdered;—what a dreadful alternative is mine!" After giving free vent to her tears, she endeavoured to compose her mind, by addressing the Almighty Power to protect her.

Sweet are the consolations which religion affords! In all our difficulties and distresses, when supplicating the Supreme Being with fervor and a perfect reliance on his goodness, we feel a resignation and confidence, that enable us to support present evils, and look forward with hope to happier days. Such were the feelings of Matilda: she rose from her knees with serenity; she recovered resolution and firmness; "I will not despair," said she, "the Almighty will preserve a friendless orphan, unconscious of guilt, that relies on his protection." She dried up her tears, and met the family as usual.

When dinner was over, she returned to the library; Joseph soon joined her, they went down to the deserted parlour. Matilda could not help shuddering. Joseph found a trunk, the drawers were opened, and she took out such necessaries of every kind as she thought she must want, yet left plenty behind. In one drawer she found a purse, with a good deal of money in it; here she hesitated; the lady had told her she would supply her, yet she knew not to what amount: Joseph persuaded her to take the whole. "Be assured, madam, my dear lady will never return," cried he. After much hesitation and reluctance, she at length divided it, and then taking a pen and ink, she took an inventory of the cloaths and money, with an acknowledgement to repay it when able, and locked it in the drawer with the purse.

Having packed up those few things she had selected, and requested Joseph would take it, by and bye, to a room near hers, she said, "I cannot be easy under the idea that the poor woman above should lie there to decay; is there no way to place her in a decent manner?" After some pause Joseph said, "There is a large chest in the back-kitchen, with old trumpery in it; if I take them out, perhaps we might get the body there, but I fear I have not strength to bring it down." "Let us see the chest first," replied Matilda, "and then we will consider of the other." She followed him into the back-kitchen, saw the chest, and its contents were soon tumbled into one corner. "Now, Joseph," said she, "I will assist you to bring the body down." "You, my lady!" cried he, staring at her. "Yes," rejoined she; "let us go up." She led the way and he followed; having unlocked and entered the room she could not help shuddering; yet took more observation of the gloomy apartment than she had been enabled to do in the morning; and recollecting what she had heard about inscriptions; she got upon a chair, and from thence to a kind of window seat very high from the ground: standing on this she examined the window; it looked out towards a sort of battlement, which surrounded the back part of the castle, the north wind blew full upon it, the only prospects were the walls and distant mountains. On the window she saw several lines apparently cut with a diamond; in one place she read.

I am dumb, as solemn sorrow ought to be;
Could my griefs speak, my tale I'd tell to thee.
In another place these lines were written;
A wife, a mother—sweet endearing ties!
Torn from my arms, and heedless of my cries;
Here I am doomed to waste my wretched life.
No more a mother—a discarded wife.
And again, in another place.

Would you be happy, fly this hated room.
For here the lost Victoria meets her doom
O sweet oblivion calm my tortur'd mind
To grief, to sorrow, to despair consigned.
Let gentle sleep my heavy eyelids close.
Or friendly death, the cure for all our woes.
By one kind stroke, give lasting sure repose.

Several other lines, expressive of misery though not of poetical talents, were written in different places, that proved the unhappy writer sought to amuse her painful ideas by her melancholy employment.

Poor Matilda concluded the wretched victim to some merciless man was sacrificed in that closet where the hand was deeply imprinted in blood on the floor; she viewed it with horror, and getting down from the window. Joseph had wrapt the body in the counterpane which lay on one side; he tried to lift it, and found the weight less than he expected, "I can carry it myself, my lady," and crept out of the room with it. Matilda, shutting the door hastily, followed him. They deposited the unfortunate woman in the chest, which was fastened down, and without speaking a single word returned to the parlour: here Matilda burst into tears, her resolution and spirits began to fail; the scenes she had witnessed, added to her own distresses, were indeed sufficient to wound and terrify a stouter heart than this young creature's; little acquainted with the calamities of life, she had flown from approaching danger, without the least idea of the miseries she might encounter in her journey! Joseph sympathized in her sorrow, and waited without speaking 'till she grew more composed: "Come, dear lady, let us leave this sorrowful place; I will take some oil and trim the lamps, for I shall come here every day, though, God knows, with very little hope of ever seeing my dear mistress again." Matilda, opprest and languid, rose from her chair; he followed her with the box to the apartment next hers, and having deposited it, returned to lock up the doors and trim the lamps in the passage, assuring her he would call daily at the post to seek for letters, as all came directed to him.

She threw herself on the bed after his departure, and gave her mind up to the most melancholy reflections; "Good heavens!" cried she, "what scenes of murder and atrocious crimes must have been perpetrated in this castle; how great is my curiosity to know more of the unhappy Victoria so recently the cause of joy and sorrow, and her unfortunate attendant, but their fate is enveloped in mystery and horror, what mine may be, heaven only knows."

When it grew near dark she went upstairs, but so altered by the agitations of her mind, that Bertha started and exclaimed, "Dear, my lady, are you ill." "I am not very well," replied Matilda; "I shall take an early supper, and retire to bed." The poor woman with great nimbleness prepared her supper, of which her guest ate but sparingly, and after sending for Albert, who appeared very sorrowful for her indisposition, she comforted him by an assurance of its being very trifling, and that she should be better after a night's rest; which was indeed verified, for having commended herself to the protection of the Father to the fatherless, she dropt into a soft slumber, and arose the following morning quite refreshed and composed.

For several days nothing particular occurred; her friends at the cottage called often to see her; Joseph visited the deserted apartments every day, all remained quiet; the uncertainty of the lady's fate gave them great disquietude, but there was no hope of obtaining any information of an event which seemed buried in obscurity. One day when Joseph returned from town, he whispered the lady to go into the garden; she walked thither it directly, he soon followed, and delivered to her the expected letter from the Marchioness; she made no scruple of opening it. After lamenting the unhappy situation of her sister, and expressing her wishes that she would quit her gloomy abode, she thanks her most cordially for her recommendation of the young lady, whose company will be highly acceptable to her, and assures her sister she will endeavour, by every kindness and attention in her power, to make the young lady's situation agreeable, and shall esteem her acceptance of their protection as a very particular favour. She admires her resolution in visiting the apartments in the castle, and is only sorry her sister cannot participate in the pleasures of society. She concludes with requesting the young lady may join them at Paris, soon as possible, within a fortnight; and assure herself that her old and faithful servant will be received and retained in the family with kindness and ease to himself.

This letter, so gratifying to the wishes of Matilda, was read with transport; she determined to set forwards on her journey within two or three days. Joseph undertook to procure her a carriage from the next town, and she intended leaving the horse for his use, and take Albert in the chaise with her. The next consideration was in what manner to account to the latter for her sudden intention of going to Paris, and his reception in the family of the Marquis: after some deliberation, she returned to the kitchen, and calling Albert aside, told him, by the most fortunate and unexpected intelligence she had heard of an asylum for herself and him, at Paris, in the house of a worthy family, where she hoped they should both meet rest and happiness; and that it was her design to proceed on her journey the third day from that. Albert stared with wonder, but never interrupted her 'till she stopt speaking, then, in a hesitating manner, "Paris is a long journey—I have no friends there; are you sure, madam?" "Yes, Albert," said she, "I am very sure we shall find friends there to receive us; I cannot explain everything to you now, some time hence perhaps you shall be informed of everything." "God bless you, my dear young lady!" cried he, "if you are satisfied I am sure I ought to be so, and will go with you when and wherever you please." She was affected by his love and confidence; she assured him, she never should forget the obligations she owed to him, and that his ease and tranquillity would ever be her first care. The old man hurried from her with tears in his eyes. Bertha was next informed of her intended departure, and was truly sorry, because, as she said, 'twas comfortable to have some kind body in that lonely place, and because the lady having plenty of money, they had very good living now, which, to say truth, she was sorry to lose. The day previous to her departure she sent for Pierre and Jaqueline: the honest couple were vexed to hear she was about to leave them. She gave them some money, and assured both families, whenever she had it in her power, she would remember their kindness and reward it in a more ample manner than she now could do They bestowed a thousand blessings on her, and declared she had made them rich for life.

After they had left her Joseph acquainted Bertha that a chaise would be there early the next morning, and desired she might have breakfast ready for the lady.

M atilda had but little rest; her journey, the circumstance of such an awkward situation, as a self-introduction amongst entire strangers, to one so little accustomed to company as she was, gave her much pain; yet on the other hand, she ought to consider that in her unfriended, unprotected state, an asylum, such as was now offered to her, must be desirable and advantageous; and that as in this life we seldom meet with pleasure or happiness, without some alloy, she ought to be thankful for the good, and submit to temporary inconveniences without murmuring. She arose early; her heart was depressed when she reflected on the uncertain fate of the lady to whose kindness she was indebted for her present hopes and expectations: "Ah!" cried she, "heaven bless you, dearest lady, wherever you are, and may Providence one day restore you to felicity and your friends." She quitted the apartment with a flood of tears, and coming, found the breakfast ready, and soon after a chaise at the gate; Joseph conveyed her portmantua and box to the carriage; Albert stared a little at the latter, but said nothing.

She shook hands with the worthy couple, tears running down their cheeks at parting with so gentle a lady, she having liberally rewarded their kindness, and previously concerted a correspondence with Joseph, if anything new occurred at the castle, and receiving advice from him how to manage at the post-houses about carriages and horses.

A few days after her departure, Joseph went to the neighbouring town, to procure a few necessaries, and, proud of his present, went upon the horse, instead of his old friend the ass. Whilst he was there, a gentleman came up to him, and, viewing the beast very attentively, asked him if the horse was his. Joseph answered in the affirmative. "Will you sell it?" demanded he. "No, Sir," replied the other, "I cannot sell it." "How long have you had it?" "Some time," said Joseph, roughly, and rode off, not liking the stranger's curiosity. He was however followed at a distance, and had scarcely put the horse into the stable, and entered the kitchen, before a knocking at the door was heard, and Joseph saw the same gentleman who was so inquisitive, with another, who had the appearance of a servant, enter the room. "Do not be alarmed," said the stranger, "I want to ask you a few questions, which, if you answer truly, no harm shall happen to you, else you must look to the consequence; tell me from whom you had the horse I saw you ride, and how long it has been in your possession? At your peril answer me with truth." Before Joseph could recollect himself to answer this demand Bertha fell on her knees, "O, Sir, do not hurt my poor husband, and I will tell you all." "Be quiet, wife," said Joseph, "I will answer for myself. I had the horse from a man, a friend of mine." "What was his name?" "Sir, I humbly think that is no concern of yours." "Villain!" cried the gentleman, "tell me this instant, or I will send you and your wife to prison, for the horse was stolen from me." "O, the Lord be gracious unto us," exclaimed Bertha, "the man's name was Albert, Sir; we are innocent indeed we are." "I believe it," said the other, very mildly; "you look like an honest woman, and I will reward you handsomely, if you speak truth. William, take care of the man, I will go into another room with this good woman." "Bertha!" cried Joseph, the stranger led her away into the parlour, she crying and begging no harm might happen to Joseph. He quieted her fears on that head, and then asked if Albert was in the house. "No, indeed, Sir," answered she; "he went away four days ago, in a chaise with the young lady." "Ah!" cried he, "that is the very thing I wished to know; and where are they gone, my friend?" "Alack, Sir, I believe they be gone to

Parish, or some place like that." "The devil!" exclaimed he, "to Paris. Well, and are they to return here?" "O, no, Sir," returned Bertha; "no such good luck to us, for to be sure she was as generous as an empress."

He then returned to the kitchen, where Joseph sat very sullen; "I tell you what, friend, I believe you may be innocent; but the lady you have had here is my niece, who has eloped from my care, and seduced my servant to steal the horse you rode today, and go off with her; I am now in search of her, and if I can find her, and she will return, I shall receive her with kindness and joy, and forgive everything; therefore, if you can tell me where she is, you will do her a great piece of service, I assure you; some wicked person has persuaded her to run away." "Sir," said Joseph, firmly, "I heard the lady say she was going to travel,—it was not my business to be impertinent and ask questions." "But you know where she is." "I do not, Sir," answered he, "I cannot tell where she is, nor the places she is going to travel through." "You know she is gone to Paris?" "Yes, Sir; but I heard her say she should not stay there, but travel further; and this is all I know. As to the horse, if you can prove it yours, give me a receipt, and you may take it." "No, my friend," replied the gentleman, "keep it for your use, but if you should ever hear from, or see Albert or the lady, and will let me know, I will give you a hundred crowns." "O, the goodness," cried Bertha, "bless your honour, you shall surely know." "What say you," said he, turning to Joseph. "I say, Sir, money would not tempt me to do a wrong thing, but as you say it will be for the young lady's advantage, to do her service I will obey you."

The gentleman appeared satisfied, and writing his address, whilst he desired Joseph to get a little wine and water for him, he whispered to Bertha, "Get everything you can out of your husband, and I will make your fortune; my man shall call again tomorrow." Having drank his wine, he took a civil leave, and, giving Bertha two crowns, rode off.

"Lord!" cried she, when he was gone, what luck attends us! What a kind gentleman; how sorry I am he didn't come before the poor lady went away." "So am not I," answered Joseph; "I don't like him at all; he has a smooth speech to be sure, but if he was good, neither madam nor Albert would have run away I dare say: however I shan't ride the horse any more, 'till I know to whom he does belong." Bertha tried every way to find if he knew where the lady was gone, but he evaded all her questions, and though he loved his old woman dearly, yet he knew she could not be entrusted with a secret; not that she would discover from ill-nature, but from a garrulity natural to old age, and a desire of obliging anyone who wanted information from her.

Joseph, in the early part of his life, had obtained a tolerable education, and had better expectations, but the wars had carried off his friends and little possessions; he was glad therefore, in a humble state, to earn his bread, and be contented with the situation Providence had ordained for him; but his sentiments were above his condition, and he prized his word, and kept it when pledged with much more exactness than a fine gentleman does his honour, when given to a favourite lady, or a humble tradesman: Joseph therefore persevered in his integrity, but thought there would be no harm in writing what had passed that day to the young lady, and take her directions how to conduct himself, for he had a perfect reliance on her truth, and thought only ill treatment could have induced her to quit an uncle's house, without a friend to help her.

The following day the gentleman's servant made his appearance, but to little purpose for though Joseph was in the garden, Bertha had gained no information; but she told all she did know of the lady's coming there, the ghosts disturbing her the first night, her subsequent courage, her kindness and sudden resolution to leave them, and that she heard her say something about going to travel to Parish, but she knew no more, and she was sure Joseph knew no more than she—how should he? he never spoke twenty words to the lady. He asked who was the owner of the castle, she told his name, and with a present of another crown he took leave. Bertha looked at the money, "Ah!" said she what a pity now I can't tell where she is; a hundred of these would make one happy for life."

A very few days after this the old couple were at dinner, when they heard the trampling of horses; they hastily opened the door, and beheld, to their great astonishment a carriage with three attendants, and in the carriage Joseph saw his master, Count Wolfenbach: struck with wonder, he forgot to tender his services, but stood staring at him until he alighted. Being conducted into the parlour, one of the horsemen with him, "Friend Joseph," said he, "I have sold this estate, and next month another family will take possession of it." "Good Lord!" cried Joseph, "what will become of me and Bertha?" "Don't be uneasy, friend Joseph, I shall take care of you; I have another estate in Suabia, a fine house and gardens, in perfect order. Bertha and you shall have the care of it, with a servant under her to keep it clean, and a man under you to work in the gardens—what say you to that?" "I am much obliged to your Lordship," answered the honest man; "tis rather late in life for me to travel, but I must obey your pleasure, and if you have not already got a man and woman there, I know a very industrious couple hard by, the only friends we have, who will be glad to go with us." "By all means," said the Count, eagerly, "but pray are you pretty quiet now; do the ghosts trouble you, as has been foolishly talked of?" "I am seldom disturbed, my Lord," answered Joseph; "I never saw nor heard any ghosts." "I believe not," said the Count; "the silly imagination of some people conjure up frightful fancies, and endeavor to impose them upon others as realities; but pray Joseph how soon can you leave this house? My man Peter will go with you to the other; you will find a much better habitation, and can take your friends with you." "In about a week, my Lord, I shall be ready." "Not sooner?" "I must speak to my friends; we must get our little domestic business put in order, and then we shall be fit to go comfortably, though 'tis a long journey for old folks, my Lord." "Nothing at all, nothing at all," said his Lordship; "Peter will see you safe. We shall be with you next week; use all the dispatch you can, for I have alterations to make in the house, before I give it up."

The Count and his attendants mounted their horses and rode off, leaving Joseph in great perplexity. Bertha, ignorant of the events which caused his uneasiness, was well pleased to change her abode for a better one, and was in a violent hurry to call on Pierre and Jaqueline, but Joseph requested she would wait another day, 'till he had considered the matter. He well knew that if the Count visited the other wing, he must be sensible that it had been lately inhabited. If he was innocent of his conjectures, and unconcerned in the late transactions he would judge unfavourably of Joseph; if, on the contrary, he had any hand in carrying off the lady and murdering her attendant, the removal of the body would convince him some person must have been there; his suspicions would naturally fall on himself, and perhaps he might be sacrificed also. These considerations greatly distressed Joseph; every way he saw perplexity and vexation, and was afraid to throw himself into the Count's power, though he saw no chance of avoiding it. He had been every day to the other apartments, except the preceding one, and found everything tranquil; but now that the Count was in the neighbourhood, he was afraid to go: yet he thought the only way to avoid suspicion, or impending evils, would be to replace the body on the bed, at all events.

Endeavouring to derive courage from necessity, he trembling ventured to the private passage, but, to his surprise and horror, the lamps were all extinguished; he knew they must have been put out, otherwise they would have lasted that day; he therefore hastily turned back, and regained the house. After a little deliberation he went up the staircase, and opening every apartment very softly till he came to the door which led to the gallery of the other wing, he found it fastened on the other side. This circumstance confirmed his fears: he listened some time, and plainly heard voices, but could distinguish nothing; he then retreated with the same care, locking up all the doors on the outside, for whether it was the Count and his servant, or a set of banditti, he thought his situation equally dangerous.

Poor Joseph could not communicate his fears to Bertha, and therefore his uneasiness passed off for indisposition, but he had a sleepless night.

The next morning he went to the post town, and, to his great joy, received a letter from Matilda. She was safe at Paris; and the Marquis and his Lady, under the greatest apprehensions for their sister; convinced she would never return to the castle, should she be alive, and grateful to their old friend Joseph, offered him and his wife an asylum at their house, thinking they might one day or other be sacrificed to the Count's revenge.

Scarcely had he read this letter, when he saw Peter, the Count's servant, coming towards him; he had the paper still in his hand, "So, Joseph, you have been at the post, I see." "Yes," answered he, with as much ease as he could assume; "I hear now and then from a sister of mine, who is in service at Paris; but is my Lord here in this town, Peter?" "Yes," replied he, "his Lordship is settling some business with his tenants." "Well," said Joseph, "next week we shall be ready to go, Peter." "Very well," cried the other, with a smile, and they parted.

On Joseph's return to his house, he began to consider of his removal; he was sure he could not depend on the Count, but how to get away without his knowledge was the difficulty; after much deliberation, he took his resolution and going to Bertha, told her the Lady Matilda was in Paris, and had sent for them to live with her. She was out of her wits with joy: "O," cried she, "that will be a thousand times better than living in the Count's house; yes, yes, let's go, the sooner the better, say I." "But," said Joseph, "you must not say a word to the Count, or anybody, for the world." She promised secrecy, and they began to contrive about taking away their little matters, and setting off in a day or two. That night Joseph thought to get some rest, though his fears still remained, and kept him waking for some hours: about midnight he dropt asleep, but was soon awakened by a great smoke and a terrible smell of fire. He hastily got up, and opening the door, the flames burst in upon him; he ran to the bed and called Bertha to follow him; she jumped out, as he thought, for that purpose: he got into the

43

court, and saw the other wing also on fire, and presently the building he came out of fell in. He called Bertha; alas! she was smothered in the ruins. The whole building was now in flames.

He ran to the stable, got the horse, and riding through the wood as fast as possible, a contrary way from the town, he stopt not till he came to the foot of a mountain; with difficulty he crept off his horse, and threw himself on the ground. "Bertha! my dear Bertha, I have lost thee for ever; I am now a poor forlorn creature, without a friend in the world: why did I fly,—why did I not perish in the fire with my wife? What a coward I am! O, that cursed Count, this is all his doings; I expected he would seek my death, but poor Bertha, she was unconscious of offence to the barbarian, yet she is gone, and I am left desolate who ought to have been the sufferer." Exhausted by grief and lassitude the wretched old man lay almost motionless for some hours when Providence conducted a carriage that way, with a lady and gentleman in it, and two attendants on horseback. Seeing the horse grazing and an elderly man lying on the ground, the gentleman stopt the carriage, and sent a servant to him: he explained his situation in a brief manner, which when the domestic informed his master of, he ordered he should be brought and put into the carriage, and the horse led on by the servant to their seat.

W e will now return to Matilda, who with her faithful Albert, arrived at Paris without meeting any accident. They soon found the Hotel de Melfont, and Matilda writing a short billet to the Marchioness, reposed herself a little after the fatigue of her journey.

In less than three hours the Marchioness arrived in her carriage, and entered the room with that delight in her countenance which plainly testified the pleasure she expected to receive in the company of her young friend; she flew towards her, and embraced her with a warmth that affected the grateful heart of Matilda to tears. "Welcome, a thousand times welcome, my dear Miss Weimar; the friend of my poor sister must be the friend of my heart! Charming girl!" said she, gazing on her, "that countenance needs no recommendation; what do I not owe my Victoria. Matilda, in returning her caresses, involuntarily started and repeated Victoria! "Yes, my love, that is my sister's name; you know her only as the unhappy Countess of Wolfenbach, I suppose: but let me see your faithful Albert, to whom I hear you are greatly indebted." "I am indeed madam," replied Matilda, "my whole life at present is and must be a state of obligation." "Dismiss that idea, my dear Miss Weimar, and feel that you have the power of obliging in your society those whose study it will be to convince you how grateful they are for the favour you confer on them." Matilda bowed and kissed the hand of the Marchioness, with an expression in her eyes that spoke volumes to the heart.

Albert now entered the room; "My good friend," said the Lady, "I hope you are well; I wished to see you, to thank you for your services to this young lady." "I humbly thank your ladyship," cried Albert, "but I have only done my duty, and when you know my mistress you will think so, for she deserves all the world should serve her." "I doubt it not," replied the Lady, "and after my first care to render your mistress happy, my second shall be to make the remainder of your days comfortable." Neither Matilda nor Albert could refrain from tears. "Come, come," said the Marchioness, "let us be gone; my carriage waits; the Marquis is impatient to see you, and I have a thousand questions to ask about my dear sister." All! thought Matilda, how shall I unfold the dismal tale—how must I wound a bosom so tender and affectionate! This reflection threw her into a melancholy reverie, as the carriage drove off. The Marchioness observed it, and taking her hand, "We are not strangers, my dear Miss Weimar; I have only been to meet my younger sister and introduce her to my husband, already prepared to love her." Matilda, overcome by a reception so kind, cried out, whilst sobs spoke the genuine feelings of her heart, "Dear madam, you oppress me with your generosity and goodness: O that I may be found, on further knowledge, to deserve your good opinion." "I am persuaded of it," replied the other, "and if you please," added she, with a smile, "here ends the chapter of favours, obligations, and such kind of stuff, as I have an utter aversion to."

By this time they were arrived at the hotel, and the Marchioness led her young friend to the saloon, where the Marquis sat expecting them. "Here, my Lord, permit me to introduce to you my younger sister; I bespeak your affection for her, and think you will find no difficulty in bestowing it." "You judge right, my beloved Charlotte: your sister claims a double share of my esteem from her own merit, legible in her countenance and your introduction." Having saluted and led her to a chair: "I am charmed," added he, "that our dear Victoria has procured us such a delightful companion; she must have sacrificed a great deal to give us pleasure, in losing your society." Matilda unable any longer to repress her feelings, burst into tears. Both were alarmed by the Marchioness, taking her hand, "Dear Miss Weimar, you have something in your spirits; tell me, pray tell me, did you leave my sister well? You have, I think, avoided mentioning her." "Ah! madam," she replied, "I am very unfortunate that my introduction to you must occasion pain and sorrow; yet I trust the dear lady will be the care of Providence, though alas! I know not where she is." "Not know where she is?" exclaimed the Marchioness, "Good heavens! Has she then left the castle?" Matilda then entered into a detail of every event that had happened at the castle, the death of the attendant, and the absence of the Countess. Perceiving the agitation and distress of her auditors, she added, "I have little doubt of the poor Lady's safety, from a persuasion that if any ill was intended towards her, they would have destroyed her, as well as the servant.' "You judge very properly, my dear Miss Weimar: be comforted, my Charlotte; your friend's observation is founded on truth and reason; I hope, e'er long we shall hear from the injured sufferer, or else," said he, raising his voice, "by heavens! neither oaths nor promises shall prevent me from publicly calling on the Count to produce her." This threat alarmed his Lady, and suspended her grief. "Tell me, my sweet girl, are you in her confidence— do you know my sister's story?" "Indeed, madam, I do not; Joseph, whom I have mentioned, is the only one acquainted with her woes, and he is bound by oath not to reveal them without her leave; unfortunately I postponed a recital which otherwise might have been a clue to trace her now." "Dear unhappy sister!" cried the Marchioness, "how severe has been your punishment! Another time, my beloved Miss Weimar, I will acquaint you with all I know relative to her situation: I trust heaven will protect her, and therefore I will not sadden your heart now, nor give you only sighs and tears for your reception, when we wish to make you cheerful and happy." With a deep sigh, which she endeavoured, though in vain, to repress, she conducted Matilda to the apartments appropriated for her, and embracing her, "You are dearer to me than ever; the child of misfortune, as you just now styled yourself, and the friend of my sister, has entire possession of my heart; love me but half as well as I feel inclined to do you, and I shall be very happy." Matilda replied in the most affectionate and grateful terms. The Marchioness insisted upon her taking a few hours rest, previous to their meeting at supper.

When she was alone she began to reflect on her situation; a recollection of past distresses impeded the satisfaction she must otherwise have felt for the fervent reception she had met with. An unhappy orphan, thought she, without a single claim on the world, from affinity or natural affection—a dependent on the bounty of friends, even for my daily subsistence, and of which I am liable to be deprived by a hundred accidents; is it possible any one can be more unfortunately circumstanced than myself? Yet, when I left my uncle's house, could I have hoped for such a protection as I am now under? O, I will not despair, heaven will preserve me, if I persevere in virtue and integrity; if I can acquit myself of wilful error, and dare appeal to the rectitude of my sentiments, when misfortunes and distresses befall me, I will kiss the rod of correction, and submit with resignation to the Almighty will.

Composed a little in her mind, she dropt asleep for above three hours, and then rose, refreshed and with recruited spirits. She was received by her good friends with the greatest and most flattering marks of kindness, and her grateful heart impelled her to return them by every attention in her power. The Marquis said, it was time, from Albert's age, that he should be laid up to rest; his honesty and affection to Miss Weimar deserves reward, I shall therefore allow him something above the wages he has had, and only request he will superintend my stables, and see that they take proper care of my horses, but on no account to take an active part in the business. Matilda most gratefully acknowledged this kindness to her old friend, whose welfare was very near her heart. The Marchioness told her they had intended leaving Paris in about ten days, now, said she, "I shall feel great reluctance to quit France without obtaining some knowledge of my poor sister's destiny; but as you expect to hear from Joseph, I will still try to flatter myself he will give you some information concerning her." Matilda encouraged the hope as it appeared to compose her, but she thought it a very slender one.

Two days passed swiftly away. The Marchioness carried her young friend round the city, pointed out every place worth observation, or that could afford amusement. Matilda was in a new world: the polite and sensible conversation she now enjoyed was so different from every-thing of the kind to which she had been accustomed, that she was mortified at her own deficiencies, and most assiduously endeavoured to profit by the good sense and elegant manners of her protectoress.

The third day after her arrival the Marchioness was to have an assembly. Matilda requested that she might not appear, as the cloaths she had were by no means suitable to such an occasion. "Indeed my love, I cannot excuse you; that objection shall soon be done away," said her friend. And presently some elegant silks, laces, linen, & co. were produced for her acceptance. "These things are for my younger sister; she must not presume to refuse a small testimony of affection from her elder one." Before Matilda could reply several tradespeople came in, and the Marchioness gave orders everything must be ready that evening; which was promised. When they were alone she kissed the hand of her benefactress. "O, madam, in what a gracious manner do you confer favours, without wounding the feelings of the person obliged." "A truce, if you please," said her friend, "to your—Oh! and Ah! the favour, if any, is conferred on me by your acceptance; but once for all, I beg it may be understood I acknowledge you as my sister by adoption; I have no children, therefore, in the rights of a sister, you have a claim to participate with me in everything; you must only bring yourself to submit to the commands of eldership, and let the words favour and obligation be blotted from your vocabulary." Saying this, she hastened from her, and left Matilda overwhelmed with grateful emotions. Before she had recovered Albert appeared. "Pardon me, madam, for coming up, but I longed to tell you what a blessed family we are got into; such kindness as I am treated with! such good servants, all doating on their Lord and Lady! O, it was a happy day when we entered the gates of Paris! I hope, my dear young lady, you think so too?" "I do indeed, my friend; I have a thousand obligations to this noble family; and 'tis not the least of them, that they have provided for you, to whom I shall always think myself indebted for every good I enjoy." Albert, overcome by this acknowledgement, hurried from her, tears of joy running down his cheeks.

In the evening Matilda's cloaths were brought home; the servant, who was ordered particularly to wait on her, drest her in the most fashionable style. When the Marchioness came into the room, she was charmed with her appearance. "My love," said she, "you will cause variety of emotions this evening; I foresee an abundance of admiration and envy, when I introduce my lovely relation, for such you are, remember; but there are two families I wish you to like; the Countess De Bouville and her daughter, and Madame De Nancy and her sister Mademoiselle De Bancre. You will receive a hundred professions of admiration and esteem from every one, but these ladies will speak from their hearts, and I trust they will thank me for the acquisition of a friend for their select parties." "You leave me nothing to say, my dear madam, but a repetition of the same words, and the same feelings for your uncommon goodness; I will study to deserve your recommendation, and to render myself agreeable to the ladies, as the only proof I can give of my sensibility."

The Marchioness conducted her to the saloon, and soon after a croud of ladies and gentlemen made their appearance; to whom she was severally introduced, and a buzz of admiration, with a hundred audible compliments circulated through the room; at length two ladies addressed the Lady of the house with an affectionate freedom that told Matilda they were the persons she was bid to love; nor was she mistaken. "My dear Countess," said the Marchioness, "for this young lady I bespeak your friendship; not only because she is a relation of mine, but because I am persuaded Miss Weimar has merit of her own to recommend her to your esteem, and that of your charming daughter." "You could not have paid us a greater compliment," answered the Countess, saluting Matilda; "this young lady's mind is legible in her countenance. Adelaide," said she, turning to her daughter, "I present you an amiable companion, whose esteem you must endeavour to merit." She joined their hands. "You could not, my dear madam," replied the young Lady, "have given me a command more agreeable to my inclinations." "You do me great honour, ladies," said Matilda, "in your approbation, it must be my care to merit the distinction which I already perceive will be necessary to my happiness." The young ladies were indeed mutually struck with each other. Mademoiselle De Bouville was an only daughter, and, contrary to the general fashion in France, had been educated at home, under the eye of a respectable mother, who, though she submitted to the frivolities, the gaities, and round of trifling amusements which engage the attention of that lively nation, yet found time to superintend and direct the education of her child, by which she avoided the stiff monastic air of a convent, and was equally unacquainted with the follies and vices which too generally prevail in those seminaries of education; for though they do not always incur general censure, yet it is extremely difficult to discriminate, as too often it is the punishment of profligacy to be confined in a cloyster; and what injury a person of that description may do amongst a number of young people, some with weak heads, and others with bad hearts, cannot be expressed nor thought of without horror.

Adelaide De Bouville had a very pleasing person, great sweetness of temper, and a cultivated understanding; she was near twenty, and had been for some time addressed by Monsieur De Clermont, son to the

Marquis of that name, an amiable and accomplished young man; and it was expected by their friends the union would take place when the young Count De Bouville returned from his travels; Adelaide being particularly fond of her brother, made a point of waiting till she could have his presence at an affair on which her happiness must entirely depend. She was charmed with the introduction of Miss Weimar to her acquaintance, and sought, by the most polite attention, to obtain her esteem. Matilda was equally delighted with her companion, and they soon after had an additional charm to their party by the arrival of Madame De Nancy and Mademoiselle De Bancre; the latter was near two and twenty, very handsome, a great share of good humour, and a most enchanting vivacity; her sister being sacrificed very early in life to an elderly man, every way unworthy of her, except by his immense fortune; he used her extremely ill, always out of humour and suspicious; she suffered under his tyranny five or six years; he then died, and left her mistress of a large independence, the expenditure of which did her great honour. Her sister, who had witnessed her bad treatment from an unworthy husband, determined never to marry; they resided together, equally beloved and respected.

Matilda was charmed with her new acquaintance; a swarm of beaus surrounded them, but she thought their conversation, their fopperies, and fulsome compliments truly disgusting, on a comparison with the sensible and elegant manners of her newly-acquired female friends.

W hen the company separated Matilda received numerous invitations, every one professing themselves delighted with the charming Miss Weimar; but those professions were not equally sincere. A Mademoiselle De Fontelle beheld her with envy and dislike: she was a young woman of family and large fortune, had been taken about two years from a convent, where she was placed on the death of her mother; and soon after that period her father also died suddenly, and left her solely to the care of an aunt, an old gay coquet, whom everybody despised, yet everybody visited, because she had large parties, elegant entertainments, and high play. Under the care, if it can be so called, of this ridiculous old woman, Mademoiselle De Fontelle had acquired all the follies and vanities incident to youth and beauty, when under no restrictions, no proper precepts or example. She detested handsome women, was desirous of engrossing universal admiration to herself, had a malignant heart, yet as far as a coquet's affections could be engaged, hers were devoted to the young Count De Bouville; but as her attractions were not powerful enough to detain him from pursuing his travels, she flirted with every one that came in her way, to the utmost extent that French manners and customs would allow among young persons, where there is certainly more reserve than in any other country (Spain excepted).

Therefore 'tis no uncommon thing for girls gladly to marry the man pointed out by the parents, if he is ever so old, ugly, or little known; the restraint laid upon them is so strict, and their conduct so narrowly observed, that to enjoy liberty they marry; from hence proceeds that levity for which the married ladies in France are so remarkable, and which has given rise to an almost general censure, which they do not always deserve: for those who have studied the characters and manners of the French ladies declare, there is more the semblance than reality of vice in them; and though many are profligate, like some of their neighbouring kingdom, who apparently carry more modesty and reserve in their outward deportments; yet there are very many amiable French women, who, under their national gaiety of heart and freedom of manners, are most truly respectable in every situation in life.

But the old aunt of Mademoiselle De Fontelle was not one of these, nor had she instilled any such sentiments of respectability in her niece; consequently the young lady ventured to the utmost bounds custom or courtesy would allow. She no sooner saw Miss Weimar than she dreaded and hated her; being a stranger, beautiful and engaging, she obtained universal admiration; but when she observed the decided preference and selection of Mademoiselle De Bouville for her companion, she was outrageous. The Count was soon expected home; he would doubtless be attracted by this hateful stranger—the idea was dreadful, and from that moment she was the declared enemy of Miss Weimar, though resolved to cultivate the most violent intimacy with her; consequently when the party broke up, she advanced and solicited the young lady's acquaintance, in the politest manner possible.

When the company had left the rooms Matilda thanked the Marchioness for the pleasure she had procured her, in the introduction to such charming young women as Mesdemoiselles De Bouville and De Bancre. "There was another lady, said she, "who paid me much attention, and invited my acquaintance." "Yes," answered the Marchioness, "Mademoiselle de Fontelle; but beware of her, my dear Matilda, she is far from being a desirable intimate—I neither like her nor her aunt, Madame de Roch; but I know not how it is, one meets with them everywhere, and cannot avoid seeing them sometimes in public, but they are never of my private parties, therefore let common civility only pass between you."

The young lady promised to observe her advice, and they separated to their respective apartments.

On Matilda's table lay a letter, which the servant placed there, not to disturb her whilst in company. She hastily broke it open; it was from Joseph: he related the incident respecting the horse, mentioned the gentleman's enquiries, and described his person. It was her uncle. She was terrified and shocked beyond measure, she sunk into a chair, and burst into a flood of tears: "Good heavens!" said she, "if he should trace me here yet so many days before him, I think I may be safe; Bertha was not in the secret, and Joseph I can, I know, depend upon not to betray me." Under the most painful reflections, she retired to rest, but sleep forsook her pillow; the dread of falling again into the power of a man so abandoned gave her the most poignant affliction "O, that we were in England," said she, "I should then, I think, be safe from his pursuit."

She past a restless night, and in the morning met her friends, with a pale countenance and uneasy mind.

"My dear child," exclaimed the Marchioness, "what is the matter, are you ill?" Matilda gave her Joseph's letter, and expressed her fears of being found in Paris by her uncle. Her friends requested she would compose her mind. The Marquis assured her of his protection. "You are not well enough, my love, to go out or see company this morning; we will retire to my dressing-room, and to amuse you from thinking of your own troubles, I will enter upon the story of my unfortunate sister, as far as I know it, for great part is involved in mystery, and she has taken, she says, the most sacred oaths never to divulge the rest, without permission of another person.

"My father, Baron Stielberg, inherited from his ancestors, a respectable name, a great share of family pride, and very small possessions, which by wars, and a struggle to keep up the family consequence, had been diminished greatly within the last fifty years. He had no son, a source of eternal regret to him, and two daughters, whom he determined should marry advantageously or not at all. Our mother died when I was about ten, and my sister eight years of age. We were placed in a convent for six years, at the expiration of which time we were sent for home.

"Our father seemed satisfied with our improvements. We had the good fortune to please, and it was the fashion to admire us. In a few months after our return to the world the Marquis De Melfort, who was on his travels, stopt at Vienna; we met at an assembly, and a mutual approbation took place; he was introduced to my father; and, in short, not to be tedious, his addresses were allowed, for though my father would have preferred a German nobleman, yet the amiable character of the Marquis, his very large fortune, and an earnest desire to see me settled in his life time, prevailed on him to accede to the advantageous proposals made for me, and in a short time I became the happy wife of one of the best of men. We remained near six months at Vienna, but the Marquis beginning to express a wish of returning to Paris, having been absent above two years. I requested my father would permit my sister to accompany me; but to this he peremptorily objected. I took leave of my friends and my country with tears and reluctance. The dear Victoria was ready to expire—it was our first separation, and we had lived in the most perfect harmony with each other: she was my father's favourite and therefore he did not feel that grief on my leaving him, which might have been expected. I had a consolation—I accompanied a beloved husband, and was received by his friends with the most flattering attention.

"My sister and I constantly corresponded. In about eight months after my residence at Paris she wrote me, that at an assembly she had met with one of the most amiable men in the world, a Chevalier De Montreville, a gentleman of a noble family, but small fortune, secretary to the French ambassador. The manner in which she described this young man convinced me she liked him: I was sorry for it, I knew he never would be countenanced by my father. She also added that Count Wolfenbach was her very shadow—that she detested him, notwithstanding his immense fortune and prodigious stock of love. In my answer, I cautioned her against indulging a partiality for the Chevalier, as I well knew my father never would approve of it. A short time after I received a very melancholy letter. 'Pity me, my dear sister, for I am miserable—I cannot deny my attachment to the most deserving of men; he has been rejected with contempt by my father, and yesterday I was commanded to receive Count Wolfenbach as my destined husband! I hate, I detest him—he is morose, savage, sneering, revengeful—Alas! what am I saying? this man may be my husband. O, my dear sister, death is far preferable to that situation.'

"These expressions filled me with extreme grief; my generous husband wrote my father immediately; he besought him not to sacrifice his child,—that if the want of fortune was his only objection to the Chevalier, he would gladly remove that deficiency, and he had both interest and inclination to procure him a handsome establishment; that from the affection he bore me and my sister, it was his earnest desire to see her happy, if at the expence of one third of his fortune.

"To this letter we received no answer within the expected time. I grew very uneasy, I wrote again to my sister. It was more than a month before I received any return. I have it now in my pocket book;" the Marchioness took it out, and read as follows.

COUNTESS OF WOLFENBACH, TO THE MARCHIONESS

MY DEAREST SISTER.

Just recovered from the jaws of death, the lost unhappy Victoria acknowledges the receipt of your kind letter: alas! the contents have almost broken a heart already exhausted by grief and despair. I have been a wife five weeks, near a month I was confined to my bed; but if I can, I will be methodical in the relation of what has befallen me. The letter your generous and respectable husband wrote, unfortunately was delivered by the servant in the same moment with one from the Chevalier. My father believed you acted in concert. Never shall I forget the fury of his countenance. 'This insolent Frenchman wants to degrade me into a dependence on him, and marry my daughter to his beggarly countryman.' 'Ah! my father,' cried I, 'do not judge so unkindly of my excellent brother, his views are for our general happiness.' 'And that,' said he, interrupting me furiously, 'can be accomplished without his interference; the Count has a noble fortune, high birth, a title, and is a German—not another word,' added he, seeing me about to speak, 'not a single objection; on Monday next you become his wife—see that you obey without the least reluctance.' Saying this, he left the room, and in a few minutes afterwards I fell senseless from my seat.

How long I continued thus, I know not, but on my recovery I found myself on my bed, and Therese with me; she was bathing me with her tears. 'Thank heaven, my dear young lady, you are alive still! O, what a dismal day for me to see you thus.' I thanked the poor creature, her kindness was of service,—I shed a copious flood of tears. Soon after my father sent to know how I did, and to tell me I was expected in the library. I obeyed the summons with trembling steps. The odious Count, I must call him so, was with him. My father advanced, and rudely snatching my hand,

'There, my Lord, I give her to you, your day shall be ours.' 'This day, this hour,' cried he, eagerly, kissing my hand, 'do not delay my happiness.' A sickness came over my heart—I sunk into a chair. 'Victoria!' cried my father, in an angry voice. I endeavoured to reply, but burst into tears. 'Foolish girl,' said he, 'receive the honour my Lord does you, in a manner more worthy of yourself and me.' He left the room. The Count approached me with a malicious air, 'Charming Victoria, am I so very hateful; has the Chevalier so many advantages over me, as to engross all your affection?' I started, but indignation rouzed my spirits,—'What-ever are his advantages, my lord, or whether he has any real supe-riority or not, for I make no invidious comparisons; yet if you suppose he is the object of my affections, surely I am unworthy the honour of being your wife; no man of spirit could bear a divided heart but if he engrosses all, which I neither affirm nor deny, your Lordship will do well, both for your own sake and mine, to renounce all thoughts of me.' 'No, madam,' said he, in the highest rage, 'your father has given me your hand, and you shall be mine, let the consequence be what it may.' He flung out of the room with a look of vengeance.

You may conceive, I cannot describe my situation. In the evening my father told me the Chevalier was gone to Switzerland. From the hour my father rejected him, I gave him up to outward appearance: I wrote and conjured him, if he valued my peace, to think of me no more. His answer almost broke my heart, 'but my commands were sacred, my peace all the good he sought for in this life.' When I heard he had quitted Vienna a momentary plea-sure seized hold of my heart; he would not be here when I was sacrificed to his rival, nor until I had left the city. Not to tire you, my dear sister, the Monday following I became a wife—spare me the repetition of the dreadful circumstances. The following day I was in a high fever and continued ill for a month; I received but little attention from the Count—there was more of resentment than tenderness in his manner when he came into my apartment, and involuntarily I used to shrink from his view. However it pleased heaven to restore me to health. I am gaining strength daily, but as yet keep my own apartment;—tomorrow I have engaged to meet our father downstairs to dinner. Pray for me, advise me, dearest sister; depend upon my honour, I will deserve your love whatever becomes of me. Heavens bless you and my dear generous brother.

VICTORIA WOLFENBACH

"You must suppose, my dear Miss Weimar," said the Marchioness, "that this letter made us extremely unhappy; I wrote however, and, fearful the Count might have meanness enough to insist upon seeing her letters, I took little notice of her complaints, but congratulated her on the recovery of her health, desired she would pay attention to it, for the sake of her husband and friends; in short, it was an equivocal kind of a letter, and I thought could give no offence. After this I heard from her but seldom, and then there was an evident restraint in her style, which hurt me, but which I dared not take notice of. She had been married about eight months, when the Marquis received a letter from the Count, acquainting us that my father was dead, after only three days' illness, giving an account of his effects, and inviting the Marquis over to see a proper division of them. I persuaded him to comply. He would not go without me, and I was not sorry for the opportunity offered me to see my sister. We got safe to Vienna. We met the Count and his lady, who had come from their country seat, about seven leagues from Vienna, for that purpose. We flew into each others' arms, with tears of mingled joy and sorrow. Alas! it was but the shadow of the once blooming Victoria. I surveyed her with surprise and distress: she took no notice, but introduced me to her husband; the cause of the alteration I observed was then explained. Never surely was there a man with a more ferocious countenance, he inspired me with horror the moment I examined him: I felt for my sister, but tried to receive his cold civilities with politeness for her sake.

"After dinner we were glad to leave the gentlemen to business, and

retire to ourselves. 'My dearest Victoria,' cried I, embracing her, 'tell me
—-tell me all: you are not happy, your fragile form too plainly speaks it.'
'I endeavor to be contented,' she replied; 'my dear father thought happiness must be connected with splendour and riches, he sought to aggran-
dize his children; I respect the motive, however he has been deceived.'
'The Count, I must own,' said I, 'is a disagreeable object.' 'My dear Charlotte,' she cried, 'do not think so meanly of me, as to suppose his want of
personal attractions weighs anything with me—I should despise myself
in that case; neither is it now any preference for another: I have never
seen or heard from the Chevalier since my marriage. I will strictly fulfil
every duty I have sworn to observe, perhaps time may do much for me;
it will either soften the severity of the Count's disposition, or habit will
enable me to bear with less feeling, evils I cannot prevent. Ask me no
questions, my dear sister, I am not at liberty to answer them; but if you
regard my peace, meet my husband with good humour and complaisance: and now tell me,' said she, 'of your comforts, your pleasures and
mutual happiness—in your felicity I will find my own.'

"I was drowned in tears, her manner was so solemn, so touching, so
resigned, that my heart was wrung with sorrow, and I could not speak.
'Dear Charlotte,' continued she, wiping my eyes, 'spare me those tears, I
cannot bear them: remember what I have told you, be cheerful when
you return to company, or I shall be the sufferer. I met you with tears of
joy, 'tis long since they were shed for grief. Here,' (putting her hand on
her heart), 'here my sorrows are buried, too deep for that relief but I
have done, dear sister let me enjoy pleasure now in your society.' She
attempted to smile, it was a smile of woe; I tried however to suppress
my emotions, and to divert her attention; asked a few questions relative
to our old acquaintance, and in about an hour we returned tolerably
composed.

"The Count examined my looks; I approached him with smiles,
chatted about our journey, and I observed his features grew relaxed, and
he behaved with great civility. We continued at Vienna a fortnight; he
never asked us to his seat. Victoria conducted herself like an angel; she
was attentive to every word and wish of his; her deportment was grave
but perfectly obliging so that it appeared more a natural disposition

than arising from any particular cause. When all our business was finished, the Count one morning took occasion to observe his presence was much wanted in the country; that he had lately purchased an estate in Switzerland, and should go there soon, consequently had many affairs which required his inspection. We took the hint, and finding I must part with my sister, I was very ready to leave Vienna.

"The day previous to our departure an old friend of my father's paid me a visit; after chatting some time, 'My dear Marchioness,' said he, 'I sincerely lament the unhappy fate of your charming sister; she has certainly the worst husband in the world; she is shut up, denied all society; he is jealous, cruel, and revengeful: I am sorry to grieve you, but I tremble for her life—she cannot long support such wretchedness. The poor Chevalier,' added he, 'has been absent from hence ever since her marriage. I am told he is now daily expected; he will hear most afflictive news, for her happiness is the chief wish of his heart.' I answered this worthy man, and told him my sister's reserve, as to her husband's treatment of her: he praised her prudence, and added, 'your father had two motives in obliging her to marry the Count; he was disappointed in both, for he was no stranger to her situation before he died.' 'And what, Sir, was his other motive?' 'An intention to marry a relation of the Count's, but she absolutely refused him, and married another two months ago. You know, I suppose,' added he, 'that the Count was a widower?' 'No, Sir, I never heard that circumstance.' 'Why, it is a black story, as it is reported: 'tis said about three years ago he married a young lady, an orphan, of good family, but small fortune, at Berne, in Switzerland; that he treated her so ill as to cause her death, and left two children, who were put to nurse, afterwards taken from thence, without anyone's knowing what became of them; however, your father told me the Count informed him they were both dead. Almost every person believes his wife and children came to an untimely end; but he is a man of such rank and large possessions, nobody chuses to say much. I hinted the affair to your father, but fortune and love was too powerful to be given up, he affected not to believe it; but after his own disappointment, he thought more of his daughter, and had he not been so suddenly cut off, I believe would have interfered; at least, I am sure, would have made some separate provision for her, independent of that bad man her husband.'

"You may conceive, my dear Miss Weimar, how much I was shocked at this relation. I trembled for my Victoria, in the hands of such a monster, but alas! we could do nothing. I entreated my good friend to watch the Count narrowly, and to give me information, from time to time, concerning her, who I considered a victim to a villain.

"The following day we took a heartbreaking leave. The Marquis entreated the Count to pay us a visit. 'In another year perhaps he might.' My sister, dear unhappy creature, never shed a tear. 'My Charlotte, my beloved sister, think no more of me,' said she, an hour before we parted; 'my pilgrimage will be short; the hour which gives birth to an unfortunate being (I had forgot to tell you she was with child) will, in all probability, give me everlasting peace: fortunate if the dear infant accompanies me to the grave, if not, O, my sister, consider it as the only remains of the wretched Victoria, who has, does, and ever will love you to her last hour.' I will not wound your heart, my dear Matilda, by any further recital of our conversation.

"When we parted, in presence of her husband, I could have struck a dagger to his heart. She embraced me with fervor. 'Heavens bless you, my dear and happy sister! and you, my generous my noble brother, may you both live to enjoy years of uninterrupted happiness.' 'Doubtless they will,' said the Count, with a malicious smile; 'surely you forget we are to meet again at Paris next year, and not taking leave for life.' 'True,' returned the Marquis; 'I thank you for the remembrance, Sir,—a few months hence, my valued friends, I hope to see you at Paris.' She tore herself from my arms, and I got into the carriage, more dead than alive. Not to enter into an unnecessary detail, we returned safe to Paris, and in a short time after I received a few lines from my sister, dated from their castle in Switzerland, telling me she was tolerably well, both in health and spirits, but hourly in expectation of an event which might affect both.

"Near three weeks after this letter we received two; one from the Count, informing the Marquis, that, to his inexpressible grief, he had lost both wife and child; the other from the medical gentleman who attended her, informing me of the same event, and that my sister, in her last moments, requested he would write to express her affection and wishes for my happiness with her departing breath. Though I had always apprehended this event, yet it caused me inexpressible misery; and there being no longer any ties to bind us to that detested Count, we never answered or took any further notice of him.

"About six weeks after the dreadful information we had received, a letter came to me, directed in an unknown hand; I opened it—judge what were my emotions in reading these words, deeply impressed upon my memory.

> Your sister lives, though dead to all the world but you; a solemn
> vow has passed her lips, never to disclose preceding events
> without permission—ask no questions, and you shall soon hear
> more, but more than one life depends upon your secrecy.

VICTORIA

"I flew to the Marquis with this billet; he was equally surprised and overjoyed, but naturally concluded we might have spies upon us, and that therefore we had better continue our mourning the usual time.

"It was upwards of a fortnight before I heard again, and I grew very impatient; at length I had another letter: this informed me she was confined, that she had reason to hope her child (a boy) was alive. Under that hope she lived, and, notwithstanding her confinement, was better in health than when I saw her last. I might write a few lines now and then, under cover to Joseph Kierman, in a vulgar disguised hand; that she perhaps might never see me more, and meet certain death if her secret was discovered.

"This letter, like the former, was in a different hand from hers. I answered it, and from that time, near eighteen years, we have corresponded about once in two months, never oftener, till our last epistles concerning you.

"The whole affair is certainly very strange: often has the Marquis vowed to apply either to the Count or courts of justice; but the letters we received were never written by her, we could adduce no actual proofs of his guilt, and she continually warned us to take no steps without her permission. Thus, in a most unaccountable manner we are prohibited from doing her justice, whilst all the world believes her dead: he lives chiefly at Vienna, a dissipated life; though from my friend I hear he is at times gloomy, and apparently unhappy: this gentleman however believes my sister and her child dead, nor dare I undeceive him.

"Thus, my dear Miss Weimar, you have before you all I know of this melancholy affair; what now is become of this hapless victim heaven only knows,—I cannot think of leaving Paris yet; the Marquis can scarcely be restrained from exerting himself, and, indeed, in a short time, if we gain no further information, I shall feel disposed to coincide with his wishes."

Matilda returned the Marchioness thanks for the trouble she had taken in giving this painful relation: she felt deeply for the poor suffering Countess, and could not help joining in opinion, that some step ought to be taken, if she was not heard of soon.

They both waited with impatience to have another letter from Joseph, as he promised to write again about the gentleman and his horse; and the Marquis and Marchioness requested Matilda to offer him and Bertha, in their name, an asylum at Paris, if they had any fears of remaining at the castle.

Three or four days passed, and nothing new occurred. Mademoiselles De Bouville and De Bancre had frequently called on Miss Weimar, also Madame Le Brune and her niece.

On the fifth morning the first mentioned young lady entered the house, accompanied by a very elegant young man, whom she introduced to Matilda as her brother. The Marquis and his lady were rejoiced to see him and gave him the most cordial welcome.

Matilda was uncommonly struck by his appearance; she thought him (and with justice), the most amiable man she had ever seen. The Count De Bouville was indeed deserving of approbation: he had all the

63

elegance of French manners, without their frivolities, an excellent understanding, and a desire of improving it which induced him to visit England, after his tour through Italy and Germany; he had gained knowledge from the different manners and customs of each nation, and returned a truly accomplished young man, with much good sense and polished manners, a strict integrity of heart, and the highest sense of duty and love for his mother and sister. He had always entertained great respect for the Marquis and Marchioness De Melfort, and that, added to his sister's warm eulogiums on Miss Weimar's perfections, brought him the morning after his return to make his compliments.

He had never seen a young woman like Matilda; she was in truth the child of nature; for, though accomplished and well informed, having been bred up in obscurity, never visiting nor being visited, a stranger to young men, to flattery, or even the praises of a chamber-maid, with a most beautiful face, and elegant shape, and many natural if not acquired graces; she was unconscious of her perfections—she knew not the art of displaying them to advantage—she had no vanity to gratify—-thought but humbly of herself, and received every mark of admiration and respect as favours to which she had no pretensions. A character so new to the world, which was easily understood in a short visit, from the frankness and naivete of her manners, could not fail of engaging the attention and esteem of the Count. Her person was charming; her conversation and unaffected sweetness insensibly gained upon the heart, and rendered it impossible to avoid bestowing that homage to which she made no claims.

When the visit was over and an engagement made for the Melfort family to dine the following day at the Bouvilles', Matilda, with her usual candour, warmly praised the young Count: her friends smiled, but coincided with her sentiments, and expatiated on his good qualities with all the warmth of friendship and esteem.

They were yet on the same subject, when a servant entered and delivered a letter to Matilda. "From Joseph," said she, looking at the address. "O, pray open it," cried the Marchioness. She did so, and perusing it hastily to herself was struck with horror at the contents. He was now at the seat of Baron Wolmar, from whence he writes an account of all the proceedings at the castle. He concluded with telling her the Baron and his niece have given him an asylum, but that the Count's story was still unknown; is desirous of receiving her commands, and bitterly regrets the loss of poor Bertha.

When she had looked it over, without a single comment she gave it to the Marchioness, but her looks prepared her friend for some dreadful intelligence. "Good heavens!" cried she, "what a villain! Everything now is past a doubt—most certainly he has destroyed my sister, and by burning the castle, sought to make away with the person privy to his transactions."

When the Marquis had read it, "By all means," said he, "let Joseph be sent for immediately, he will prove a material witness, and I am determined, if no news arrives from her shortly, to enter a process against the Count, and oblige him to produce her."

A servant was ordered to set off the following morning to bring Joseph, and the Marquis wrote to thank the Baron for protecting him.

Various and melancholy were their conjectures relative to the Countess, whose strange fate they all deplored. "I shall never forgive myself," cried the Marquis, "for not interfering in this business years ago. When I knew she was first confined, though we never understood so clearly the nature of that confinement till she wrote to us of the courage and resolution a young lady, driven by accident to the castle, had shewn in exploring the way to her gloomy apartments. At the same time she was cautious in withholding any particular information as to the nature of her situation. Maria, her attendant, always wrote for her, nor was any name signed on either side."

"Every circumstance," returned Matilda, "convinces me her life is not in danger, for had that been determined on so many years would never have passed, and left her in possession of it." "I hope and wish your observation may be verified, said the Marchioness. "But pray, madam," cried Matilda, "what became of the poor Chevalier after her marriage and the subsequent report of her death?"

"My friend at Vienna," replied the Lady, "informed me, he returned there soon after the Count carried my sister into Switzerland, and in a short time quitted the ambassador, and talked of visiting Asia, and remaining abroad some years; since which we have never heard of him, whether he is living or not."

Some company now broke in upon them; and an engagement in the evening prevented any particular conversation.

The following day they were to dine with the Countess De Bouville. Matilda, for the first time in her life, took some pains with her dress, and felt an anxiety about her appearance; yet, unconscious of her motives, she attributed them solely to a desire of pleasing the Marchioness. When they arrived at their hotel, the Count was ready to conduct and introduce them. The Countess received them with pleasure. "I know," said she, "my good friends, you rejoice with me on the return of my son. We are a family of love," added she, turning to Matilda, "therefore you must not be surprised to see us a little intoxicated with joy on meeting again after so long an absence." "Indeed, madam, such affectionate feelings do you great honour."

Adelaide was all transport, which was soon after rather checked by the introduction of the Marquis de Clermont and his son: the young men ran into each other's arms. "A thousand welcomes, my dear De Bouville, I impatiently longed to see you." "I believe it," returned the other, with a smile; "you had powerful reasons, and I have shortened my stay in England considerably on your account." "Apropos," said the Marquis; "how do you like England, my young friend?" "So well, Sir," replied the Count, "that I could be contented to pass my life there in the bosom of my friends. I consider the English as the happiest people under the sun: they are naturally brave, friendly, and benevolent; they enjoy the blessings of a mild and free government; their personal safety is secured by the laws; no man can be punished for an imaginary crime, they have fair trials, confront their accusers, can even object to a partial jury; in short, as far as human judgement admits can be deemed infallible. Very few, if any, suffer but for actual crimes, adduced from the clearest proofs. Their merchants are rich and respectable, the first nobility do not disdain an alliance with them, they are considered as the supporters of the kingdom: 'tis incredible to think of the liberal sums subscribed by these opulent, respectable, generous people, on any popular occasion, or private benefaction, without astonishment. The men of fashion are many of them admirable orators, great politicians, and perfectly acquainted with the government of different nations, as much as of their own. The young men, I believe, are the same every-where—fond of pleasure, expence, and intrigue; but the rock on which they most generally split is that spirit of gambling which pervades through almost all ranks of people, dissipates fortunes, distresses families, hardens the heart, depraves the mind, and renders useless all the good qualities they receive from nature and education. There are very strict laws against play, but those laws only awe the middling or poorer kind of people, the great infringe them with impunity.

"But I beg pardon," added the Count, "for falling into the common mode of travellers, engrossing the attention of the company to myself." "I desire you will go on," said the Marquis; "I am pleased with your observations." "And the ladies, dear brother," cried Mademoiselle De Bouville, "pray tell us something of the ladies." "I shall punish your curiosity," replied he, smiling, "by and bye. What I most admire in the English, is the great encouragement given to all manufactories, and to all useful discoveries; there ought not to be any poor, that is, I mean beggars, in England, such immense sums are raised for their support, such resources for industry, and so many hospitals for the sick and aged, that, if proper management was observed, none need complain of cold or hunger; yet in my life I never saw so many painful and disgusting objects as there are in the streets and environs of London. I admire the public buildings, the places of entertainment, and the performers at them; but sometimes, as will ever be the case, liberty degenerates into licentiousness, and the mob will rudely interrupt the performers, and carry their applause or censure in opposition to every effort of their betters: this certainly is an abuse of their freedom, but 'tis an evil they know not how to remedy in a land of liberty.

"As for the ladies, my dear sister." "Aye, brother, now for it;—I hate your English belles, they are such monopolizers when they make their appearance at Paris." "And yet, Adelaide, I assure you, it is not often you

67

see the most beautiful of them here, doubtless there are very many charming women among the first circles of fashion, who may dispute the palm of beauty with any court in the known world; but generally speaking, the middling ranks of people are by far the handsomest of both sexes, and I account for it in this manner. In fashionable circles they keep very late hours, play deep, enter into every scheme for amusement and dissipation, without regard to their health or complexions; hence they injure one, and destroy the other: no artificial resources can give brilliancy to the eyes, or health and vivacity to the figure; acquired bloom can never deceive, and the natural beautiful complexions of the English ladies are so delicate and transparent, that art may disguise, but never can improve them. Their ill hours, and deforming their lovely faces by the anxiety of avarice, envy, and passion, when at their midnight orgies, adorning and watching the effects of chance in their favour, destroys their beauty many years before age would have lessened their attractions; for I must confess," added he, smiling at his sister, "the English women, take them all in all, are more fascinating than any other nation I ever saw." "And yet," said she, "you are returned heart-whole, brother?" "That is begging the question, my curious sister; but where there are so many charmers, men's eyes involuntarily wander, and must consider it almost an insult upon the rest to select one, when there are such equal pretensions."

"The English ladies are much obliged to you, Count," said the Marquis de Melfort, "and we shall soon have an opportunity of judging if your picture is over-charged, as we design visiting England within this month."

This declaration conveyed no pleasure to any of the party. The De Bouvilles were already so much prejudiced in favour of Miss Weimar, that they were hurt at the idea of parting: the Count particularly felt uneasy, though he could not express it upon so short an acquaintance.

Matilda was highly pleased with Monsieur De Clermont, her friend's lover; he was polite, sensible, and intelligent; the Marquis, his father, lively, chatty, and attentive to the ladies.

The dinner hours passed very agreeably, and they regretted that an assembly in the evening must break in upon their party.

The young folks had an hour to themselves: the Count paid Matilda the most marked attention; congratulated his sister on the acquisition of such a friend, and hoped some event, favourable to his wishes, might prevent their tour to England, though he acknowledged the hope a selfish one. After chatting on various subjects, the Count accidentally enquired of Matilda, if she liked Paris as well as she did Vienna? The question confused her, and she replied, with some hesitation, she had never seen Vienna. "I beg your pardon, madam," said he, "I understood you came from thence." "No, brother, Miss Weimar resided in Switzerland." "At Berne, madam?" asked he. "No, Sir," answered she, still more confused. "I chiefly resided in the country." The Count saw by her manner he had been guilty of some impropriety, though he hardly knew of what nature; he was therefore silent, and she recovered from her embarrassment. In the evening the company began to assemble; amongst the rest that eternal gadabout Madame le Brune, and her niece, Mademoiselle De Fontelle. The Count was obliged to pay his compliments, and receive their congratulations on his return; which done, he hastily returned to the side of Matilda.

The envious De Fontelle could not bear this; she made her way to them, took the hand of Matilda, called her her sweet friend, assured her they must be violently intimate, she was quite charmed with her; with a hundred such delusive compliments, as meant nothing, and to which the other only replied with a cold civility. All at once, turning quickly to her, "Bless me, Miss Weimar, I forgot to ask if you have a relation of your name now in Paris?" The roses forsook Matilda's cheek, she trembled, and could scarce stand; every one observed her confusion; the Count caught her arm. "Bless me!" cried Mademoiselle De Fontelle, "has my question disordered you; I only asked because I was in company yesterday with a gentleman of your name, just arrived from Germany."

This was enough for the unhappy girl—down she dropt, and had not the Count been attentive to her motions, and caught her in his arms, she must have fallen to the ground. Everybody was alarmed, and crouded round her, the Marchioness particularly so; she was carried into another room, the Count still supporting her, and followed by his sister. It was some time before she returned to life. The first objects that struck her, was the Count holding her in his arms, the Marchioness on her knees, applying salts, and Mademoiselle De Bouville pressing her hand. "O, madam!" cried she, eagerly and trembling, "he is come, he is come." "Compose yourself, my love," said the Marchioness, "no one is come that can hurt you." "Yes, yes," answered she, hardly knowing what she said, "'tis he, he will carry me of, he will take me from you.'

Her friend still endeavoured to sooth and calm her spirits. The Count and his sister were surprised; they saw there was some mystery, but forbore any enquiries.

It was some time before she was perfectly restored: they urged her to return to the company—she felt a repugnance, "I fear that Miss—" "Fear nothing, madam," interrupted the Count; "you have friends who will protect you with their lives." She looked at him with an expression of gratitude, but said nothing. She arose, and with feeble steps attended her friends into the saloon.

Mademoiselle De Fontelle officiously came to congratulate her return. The amiable De Bancre felt real concern, and expressed it with feeling, and without exaggeration.

Matilda, sensible of the kindness of her friends, and ashamed of the observation she had attracted, tried to acquire new spirits; but it was an endeavour only; her eyes were incessantly turned towards the door, she dreaded every moment she should see her uncle enter, and nothing could exceed her joy when the evening closed and they were seated in the Marquis's carriage.

"O, madam! O, Sir! 'tis assuredly my uncle—he will know where I am, and tear me from you." "Do not afflict yourself, my dear Miss Weimar," answered the Marquis; "if it should be him, he shall prove his pretensions before he gets any footing here, much less take you from our protection."

Poor Matilda thanked him with a grateful heart, and retired to her bed, but not to sleep: her mind was greatly disturbed. "What a poor creature I am," cried she; "no father, brother, or protector, not even the cloaths I wear my own property; if this man, this uncle claims, who can dare detain me? What are the evils which may befall me—whatever becomes of me, I will not embroil my friends. Happy, happy Miss De

Bouville!" said she, "you have a mother, a brother to protect you! Such a brother! what an amiable man! O, I never knew my wretchedness 'till now, that I am humbled to the dust!" Under these melancholy impressions she past the night, and when morning came was in a high fever.

The servant who came to attend her was alarmed at her indisposition, and flew to inform the Marchioness, who instantly went to her apartment. She found her very ill. A physician was sent for, who ordered her to be bled and kept very quiet. About noon the Marchioness left her asleep, and had scarcely entered the parlour when she was informed a gentleman requested to speak with her; she ordered his admittance.

A middle aged man, of respectable appearance, politely entered the room. "I must apologize to your Ladyship for my intrusion, without sending in my name, which I now avow to be Weimar, and I am uncle, I may say father, to a young lady of that name now in your house. I fear, madam, you have been strangely imposed upon to afford her protection; it is painful to a person so nearly connected as I am to that unhappy girl." "I beg your pardon, Sir, for interrupting you, but I have no person under my roof that answers to your description; you are therefore, I presume, in all error as to the lady you allude to." "I believe not, madam," answered he rather haughtily; "I come here to demand my niece, Matilda Weimar, and through her to discover a servant with whom she went off, after robbing me." "Robbing you, Sir! Take care what you say; you shall bring proofs of your assertions, and then we will answer you: at present Miss Weimar is safe in our protection, and you will find, Sir, she has powerful friends to guard her, and expose those who are her enemies." "'Tis well, madam," replied he, "you will hear from me in another manner." He bowed and quitted the house.

She was glad he did not see the Marquis; at the same time she felt they were in an awkward predicament.

Soon after the Count De Bouville and his sister called on her. "My dear madam," said the latter, "how does our charming young friend? We have been quite unhappy for her indisposition." "You are very obliging, my dear Adelaide; she well deserves your solicitude and I am sorry to say she is really very ill this morning." "Ill!" cried the Count, eagerly; "O, madam, has she any advice—has she a physician?" "Yes," replied the Marchioness; "I hope there is no danger,—her spirits are hurried and she is a little feverish."

The Count walked about the room. His sister said, "Will you pardon me, madam, if I tell you the strange reports we have heard this morning?" "I shall thank you for the communication," replied the other. "This morning early Mademoiselle De Fontelle called on us, O heavens!" said she, eagerly, "no wonder Miss Weimar fainted last night; why she turns out to be an imposter, and a shocking creature." "Who, Miss Weimar," cried my brother, "impossible madam; go and circulate that envious tale somewhere else, there will be no credit given to it here." "You are very ready, Sir, to insult your friends, and take the part of strangers; but I assure you," added she, haughtily, "I have no cause to envy Miss Weimar, and should be extremely unhappy to be thought like her." Seeing my brother smile contemptuously, "Well," said she, "tis of little consequence to me if her uncle is come in search of her; if she run away from his house with a servant, and jointly robbed him of his property, and now has contrived to impose herself upon the Marchioness for a different person; perhaps she may elope with one of her servants next, the thing is nothing to me, only people ought to be careful how they introduce improper persons into a circle, though they are beauties and objects of envy—envy indeed! I shall never forget the pretty idea." She flung out of the room, leaving us almost petrified with astonishment. When my brother recovered, he said, "What I say now," cried the Count interrupting her, "that I will stake my life upon the honour and integrity of the young lady—that ingenuous countenance speaks a heart which never knew deception."

"You judge rightly, my dear Count, said the Marchioness: "I have not time to explain things now, but be assured she is truth and virtue itself; the servant, a worthy and very old man, who knew her from her infancy, is now in my house; he fled with her to save her from dishonour, from the wretch who now pursues her." "Heaven and earth!" cried the Count, "where is the miscreant, I will haunt him through the world for daring to asperse her character." "Softly, my good friend," returned she, smiling, "your interference will do no good; the Marquis and myself take upon us to do her justice; mean time you may pay him a visit, and your sister shall just step up and see my patient, provided she is very silent." "My best respects, Adelaide," said he. "O, doubtless," returned the Marchioness, "we shall make abundance of compliments and fine speeches, but it will be by dumb show, for I prohibit talking."

Being let blood had checked the fever, and Matilda lay tolerably composed when her friends entered; she rejoiced to see them, and held out her hand. "Yes," said the Marchioness, "we can take hands, but you are only to tell us how you are." "Much better, my dearest, best—" "Enough, enough," said the Lady, "that's all we wanted to know, so now kiss and part—by and bye you may meet again. My brother, dear Miss Weimar, sends his best respects." "Very well that is sufficient." "Heaven bless you, my love, go to sleep and compose your mind."

T he ladies returned to the parlour; the Marquis and Count were there, and expressed great joy to hear so favourable an account of Matilda's health. The Marquis entered into a little detail of her story, and strongly engaged the affection and compassion of the Count and his sister. "I tell you this in secret," said the Marquis, "remember it goes no farther; we have powerful reasons not to extend our confidence, nor withdraw our protection from a friendless orphan recommended to us by a valued relation." "I admire, I honour you," cried the Count, with earnestness; "do not give her up to this pretended uncle: but how shall we silence calumny, how stop the tongue of that malignant girl? We must act as circumstances shall require; I will call at Madame Le Brun's myself, and assure them there is a mistake in the affair, and warn them not to speak ill of my protégée, for I will defend her with my life and fortune."

They now separated; Mademoiselle De Bouville promised to return in the evening, and the Marchioness went out to pay a few visits, and see if the scandal was extended among her acquaintance; to her great mortification she was told of it everywhere, some condoled with her on being so greatly imposed upon, others affected to resent such a creature should have the assurance to get herself introduced into company, but all agreed, "They saw what she was, nothing but a little pretender, who was a stranger to good breeding; nobody was deceived but the Marchioness, for every one could see art and duplicity in her face."

Thus she, who the preceding evening was the most delightful, most engaging, most elegant girl in the world, by one stroke of slander, was deprived of every perfection, and admiration turned into contempt; so prone is the world to believe ill, and so little dependence is there to be placed on the breath of praise.

The Marchioness was exceedingly exasperated; she defended her young friend with warmth;—she congratulated the ladies on their ingenuity, in finding every virtue and every vice, every charm and deformity in the same person, within the space of eight and forty hours. "Their candour and good nature was highly commendable," she said, "and the compliments they paid her judgment were certainly very flattering."

In this ironical manner she treated the title-tattle of the envious and malicious; but, driving to Madame Le Brun's, she met her niece, just arrived before her, from circulating her scandalous tale: a malignant joy danced in her eyes, though she was a little confused when she saw the Marchioness. "I beg the favour of speaking to you Mademoiselle," said the Lady; and taking her seat, "I find I am to thank you for presuming to propagate reports to the disadvantage of my relation: you would do well to recollect, Mademoiselle, there is no character so truly despicable as the slanderer and tale bearer; you should also be well informed of the facts you relate, and of their origin in truth, before you asperse characters, or subject yourself to the mortification of being disappointed in your views, and of having the calumny retorted on yourself." "What views do you mean, madam,—-what is it to me whether Miss Weimar is the runway niece of Mr Weimar, or not?" "Your views," answered the Marchioness, "are pretty evident; but permit me to observe the Count De Bouville's esteem will never be obtained at the expence of veracity and generosity, and it would have been more becoming a young lady of liberal sentiments, in at least a doubtful case, to have suspended her judgement and have inclined to the good-natured side of the question; but I am now to inform you the whole tale you have, with so much avidity, related, is false; that Miss Weimar is as irreproachable as she is beautiful, and in a short time the Marquis will severely punish and expose those who dare assert anything to the prejudice of that young lady you will do well, Mademoiselle, to profit by the information.' Saying this, she arose, with a look of contempt, and returned to her carriage.

W hen she met the Marquis at dinner she repeated what she had heard, and her behaviour in consequence. The Marquis applauded her proceedings.

"When I left you this morning," said he, "crossing the street St Honore, I met Monsieur Du Versac, with another gentleman. 'This is the Marquis De Melfort,' said he, and immediately added, 'permit me to introduce to your Lordship, Mr Weimar; we were going to your hotel.' 'Has Mr Weimar any business, Sir, with me.' 'I have, Sir,' he replied, in a very calm tone of voice; 'I had the pleasure to wait on the Marchioness, but there was a misunderstanding took place.' 'Suppose we step home to my house,' said Du Versac. We agreed so to do. When seated, 'Now, Sir,' addressing Mr Weimar, 'I am prepared to hear whatever you please to say.' He then began a long story of taking Matilda from her infancy, after the death of her father and mother; the tenderness he had treated her with, the education he had given her, his design of giving her his moderate fortune; mentioned a variety of circumstances to prove his affection, and her subsequent flight with Albert, taking a horse from his stable, and deceiving him with false pretences. As her uncle, he had a right to claim her: her behaviour to him made her undeserving protection, but duty to his deceased brother called upon him to protect his child; and he would therefore forgive the error she had been drawn into, and receive her as kindly as ever.

"When he stopt, I replied, 'Sir, there is much plausibility, also, I believe, great truth in what you have related: you must not be offended if I also state facts exactly as Miss Weimar has related them to us.' I repeated her story; when I came to the circumstance of the conversation between him and Agatha in the summer-house, he started and turned pale, but quickly recovered. I added, that meeting accidentally with a relation of mine, she was recommended to our house as an asylum, which it was my determination to afford her, and I should suppose no uncle of hers could object to her situation with the Marchioness, who was desirous of considering her as an adopted daughter. 'I am no longer at a loss to account for her conduct,' replied he; 'and so far from blaming, I must applaud her adherence to those ideas of virtue and propriety I had always inculcated in her mind; but she ought not to have taken up things lightly, nor have proceeded to such lengths upon hearing imperfectly a desultory conversation which, if she had heard the whole, and its true meaning, she would have formed a very different judgement of; therefore, at the same time I applaud her discretion, I blame her precipitant decision; however, my Lord, I beg the favour of seeing my niece alone for an hour in your house, before I take any steps equally as disagreeable to myself as to her and your family. I told him I would consult Miss Weimar, without the least interference on my part, and transmit to him this evening her answer."

"This is indeed a very complex piece of business," replied the Marchioness, "but I really think she ought to see him, and I shall conceive it no breach of honour to be within hearing of their conversation; for although not a shadow of a doubt remains with me concerning her truth and innocence, yet I wish to have an investigation of the affair, that I may openly assert both, from a thorough conviction of it."

When dinner was over she went to Matilda's apartment. She was infinitely better, and proposed getting up in the evening. After a thousand expressions of kindness and assurances of protection, she mentioned the meeting between Mr Weimar and the Marquis, related the conversation that took place, and his wish to see her.

Matilda clasped her hands, "Oh! I cannot, cannot see him! I could not be mistaken. His words,—his actions previous to the scene I over-heard in the summer-house, leaves no doubts upon my mind; yet I ought not, I cannot involve my benefactors in trouble: instruct me, tell me, dearest madam, what I ought to do, and that I will do,—your opinion shall decide for me." "Why then, my dear Miss Weimar, I think you had best hear what he has to say." "Not alone, madam." "Mr Weimar is desirous of being alone with you." "No, my dearest lady, that cannot be; let me entreat the favour of your supporting presence." "Since you are so desirous of it," said the Marchioness, "and think you can see him tomorrow, I will appoint him to attend you in the library; the closet adjoining having a very thin partition, I can distinctly hear your conver-sation, and he will then have no restraint on his words or behaviour."

This plan being adopted, a note was dispatched by the Marquis to Mr Weimar, signifying that the young lady would be glad to see him the next day, at twelve, if her health would permit.

Poor Matilda dreaded the interview, and the power he might exert over her, yet it was a justice due to her character and friends, that she should confront him; she therefore endeavoured to reconcile herself to the meeting, though she knew it would be extremely painful to her.

M ademoiselle De Bouville paid her a visit in the evening: she was sitting up, and, from the quantity of blood taken from her in the morning, and the little hectic which the fever occasioned, she looked uncommonly delicate and beautiful. After saluting her in the most affec-tionate manner, she said, "I am charged with a thousand compliments from my brother; he has been extremely uneasy but if he was to see you this evening, I think he would have but little cause for it;—without any flattery, my dear Miss Weimar, you look quite enchanting."

Matilda smiled, but it was not a smile of pleasure. Ah! thought she, if the Count, if Mademoiselle De Bouville knew me, for what I am, a poor dependant, without friends of family—I should have few pretensions to their notice.

Adelaide took notice of her dejection,—"Come, my sweet friend, recover your spirits. My brother will be anxious for my return; you must enable me to give a good report, if you are desirous he should have rest tonight." "If I am desirous," replied poor Matilda; "is there anything I more sincerely wish than happiness to you and your amiable brother?" "Well then," answered Adelaide, "you must make haste to be well." "You are very obliging," returned Matilda; "I am much better, and should be very ungrateful to my friends if I did not exert myself against trifling indispositions."

Adelaide surveyed her with admiration and compassion, her generosity felt an increase of affection from the knowledge of her misfortunes, though she was cautious not to drop a word that might give the other any suspicion that she was acquainted with them.

They parted at night with mutual reluctance, and Matilda endeavoured to compose her spirits for the dreaded interview that was to take place the following day.

When the Marchioness entered her apartment next morning she found her dressing, and much better, which gave her great satisfaction; she encouraged and applauded the resolution she had assumed; but when the time came, and the name of Mr Weimar was brought in, she could scarcely keep from fainting. The Marchioness retired to the closet, and he entered; Matilda rose to receive him, he hastily advanced and embraced her, "My dearest child, I rejoice to see you, cruelly as you have used me, miserable as I have been from apprehensions of your safety, I am happy to see you under such respectable protection." He seated her and himself. "The Marquis De Melfort," said he, "has explained to me the cause of your absenting yourself from my house, therefore I am neither surprised nor angry; but surely you acted precipitantly, and on very slight grounds, the conversation you only partially heard and little understood." "I heard enough, Sir," said Matilda, with some spirit, "to inform me I was not in safety in a house with a woman of Agatha's principles." "You entirely mistook the affair," interrupted he, "but before I explain myself farther, tell me, Matilda, is

THE CASTLE OF WOLFENBACH

there no gratitude, no affection due to the man who has supported you from childhood, who took you, a helpless infant, without a friend to protect you from every evil incident to deserted infancy? Did I not treat you, love you, as a blessing sent from heaven?"

Matilda was drowned in tears at this representation of her forlorn state; with a deep sigh she answered, "Yes, Sir, all this I acknowledge, and heaven can witness for me how grateful I was for your kindness, until my delicacy was alarmed by freedoms I thought improper from our near connexion."

"One question more," said he; "should you have been offended at those freedoms (as you call very innocent attentions), had they been offered by a man who designed to make you his wife?"

Matilda started, "His wife! 'tis a strange question, but I answer, yes, Sir, I should; for confined as my knowledge of mankind was, nature and decency had taught me the impropriety of such behaviour."

"Perhaps," said he, "you carried your ideas of propriety too far; but doubtless you erred on the right side. But now, Matilda, I am going to disclose a secret, known only to Agatha, and which occasioned the conversation you misunderstood and misrepresented—I am not your uncle." "Good God!" cried Matilda, "who, or what am I then?" "That," replied he, "is a question I cannot resolve, I wish for your ease I could do so; but what I do know, I will repeat. One day I was in the garden, when Agatha came running to me with a bundle in her arms, 'Lord, Sir, the strangest thing; I am sure I am as innocent as the babe itself, where it came from, or to whom it belongs, but Lord, Sir, here is a child sent you from God.' Very much surprised, I uncovered a cloth, and beheld the most beautiful infant I ever saw. I asked her how she came by it: this was her account: she heard a knocking at the door, and going to open it, saw a man at a distance, running very fast and a bundle at the gate; the man was soon out of sight; she took up the parcel, and found the child, wrapt in a dimity petticoat, and two or three cambrick handkerchiefs, but no cloaths, and apparently just born; a bit of paper was pinned to the petticoat, on which was wrote, with a pencil, 'Look on this child as committed to your care by the hand of Providence; be careful of it, and you will not repent it.' I was very much struck," continued Mr Weimar, "by such an extraordinary circumstance, but resolved to do my duty: a nurse was provided in the house; I had it baptized and named it Matilda. I said it was my niece; having then no other servant but Agatha, and she being faithful to my wishes, as my niece the beloved adopted child was brought up, and had masters of every kind to instruct her. Years rolled away, no enquiry was ever made, and I began to see a thousand graces in this young creature, which insensibly warmed my heart, and taught it what it was to love, a lesson I had never learnt till then. When I returned from France my protégée was improved in beauty and state: she knew little of men and she was less known by them; I determined to acquaint her with the secret I have related, and to offer her my hand. I deliberated some time in what manner to disclose it, and was consulting with Agatha how to make the discovery when you overheard the conversation, mistook the purport of it, and in consequence of that mistake gave me inexpressible misery."

Here Mr Weimar stopt. Matilda, who sat almost breathless and stupified, fetched a deep sigh, "Then I am an outcast, a forsaken orphan, without friends or protectors! Gracious heaven! the offspring of guilt perhaps, for who but guilty wretches would give up their child to strangers?" A friendly burst of tears relieved her beating heart.

"Take comfort, my dearest Matilda, permit me to offer you my hand, my heart, I will be your protector through life; I consent that you shall consult the Marquis and Marchioness; you shall make your own terms for Albert, whom I shall value for his fidelity to you. If I have mentioned you in Paris as my niece, it was to avoid disagreeable questions, and keep your secret. The marriage may be private or public, as you like, no one will dare interfere with my wife. Think of everything; I will return to-morrow for your determination." He arose, he kissed her hand, and left her motionless in the chair.

The moment he quitted the room the Marchioness entered, and, embracing the warm statue, as she called her. "I have heard all, my dear Matilda, and am equally astonished with yourself: his tale is plausible, perhaps true. Whoever were your parents, I should suppose them dead, from their not making enquiries during so many years after their child. Some praise is doubtless due to Mr Weimar, for his care of you; his first motives were certainly benevolent ones; whether he latterly intended you honourable, or not, cannot be known; he offers to marry you now, in the face of your friends; 'tis possible you might mistake the tenor of the conversation you overheard—at any rate he seems now ready to act with honour. All this I say for Mr Weimar, justice demands I should be impartial; now, on the other hand, if your heart is repugnant to his offers; if you cannot be reconciled in your own mind to the account he has given you; if the gratitude due to his care of you in early life is effaced from your heart by his subsequent conduct, and you cannot overcome the disgust it inspired, never think of accepting his hand, to render both wretched. I have adopted you, I love you as a child, and will protect you; in me you shall find the mother you have lost: fear not therefore, my dearest Matilda, to decide as your heart and judgement shall direct; do nothing hastily, take this day and night to reflect and determine with your whole heart tomorrow. I shall, with your permission, inform the Marquis of this extraordinary story, and I am sure his affection for you will coincide with mine."

Whilst the Marchioness was speaking Matilda had time to recover herself from the astonishment she had been thrown into, and still more from the humiliating idea, that she was indeed a friendless orphan, and owed unbounded obligations to a man she had for some time past looked on with detestation.

When the Marchioness was silent the unhappy girl took her hand, and kissing it, with a flood of tears, "My dear, my generous benefactress, do you and the Marquis decide for me, I am incapable of judging for myself; I feel what I owe to Mr Weimar's humanity—I honour him for his benevolence and charity to a poor deserted infant; he is a good master, and beloved, as I have heard, by his tenants; I may have erred, I may have condemned him wrongfully, yet my heart, my judgment is not on his side. Condescend, dear madam, to direct me; I will take this day and night to reflect on everything I have heard; have the goodness to inform me in the morning of your own and the Marquis's opinion, and I hope I shall act so as not to forfeit the friendship you have honoured me with." The Marchioness embraced her with expressions of tenderness, and repaired to the Marquis, to whom she repeated the preceding conversation.

He was very much surprised and puzzled. "We cannot controvert any of the circumstances he has related, and his behaviour to her, from the moment she was thrown on his protection, deserves the greatest praise; one would scarcely believe a mind capable of such good actions could entertain designs so contrary to honour and the tenor of his former conduct; his offers now certainly prove his affection, but I own I should be sorry to see such a lovely young creature compelled to be sacrificed to a man older perhaps than her father: If there is a mystery in her birth, time yet may bring it to light; however, she must determine for herself, but let it be free from the idea of necessity, for on our protection she may rely."

The Count De Bouville, anxious for Matilda's health, and the result of the expected conference, made the Marchioness an early visit; as he had been informed of the preceding circumstances, they made no scruple to relate every particular that had taken place that morning. The Count was very much shocked; he scarcely knew the nature of the sentiments he entertained for Matilda; 'tis true, he admired and esteemed her, from the little observations he had found an opportunity of making on her character, but he possessed too much good sense to be violently attached on so slender an acquaintance; yet he could still less bear the idea, that she should marry Mr Weimar. A man of quality in France to marry an obscure young woman without even knowing the authors of her being, would, he knew, incur everlasting contempt; yet, were the Germans less proud?

But then Mr Weimar was an elderly man, accountable to no one, lived in the country, detached from the world, and could do as he pleased. In short, he saw insuperable difficulties attending an attachment to Matilda from himself, and the certainty of it gave him more pain than in prudence he ought to have indulged. He had forgot himself, his long reverie surprised his friends, the Marquis interrupted it by asking his sentiments on the story he had heard? He said it was impossible for him to form an opinion; the account, with respect to her birth, was uncommon, yet nevertheless it might be true, such things had happened, and were not impossible; but if Mr Weimar was just in every particular, although he had a claim upon her gratitude, he could not see he had any to her person, contrary to her inclinations.

The Marquis said, "Your sentiments exactly coincide with mine, therefore the young lady must determine for herself; for my own part I have little doubt but her birth is noble; her person, her figure, the extraordinary natural understanding she possesses confirms my opinion that so many graces seldom belong to a mean birth or dishonest connexions." "There may be some truth in your observation," said the Marchioness, "but we have seen and heard of many instances where a noble soul has been inclosed within a vulgar body, and honour, fidelity, integrity, and attachment are seen in a thousand examples among people of the lowest class, though I grant not in common to be met with; but then everyone has not had the cultivation nor accomplishments of Matilda." "Ah!" cried the Count, "your remarks are undoubtedly very just; but there are so many natural graces in this lady, that I think with the Marquis, they never could spring from a mean or improper connexion." "I think so too," replied she, "but be that as it may, she shall always command our friendship and protection."

She had scarcely said this before a servant entered with a letter, she looked with surprise at the post-mark, and withdrew to the window, she had no sooner opened it and perused two or three lines, than she exclaimed, "Gracious Heaven! in England, O, my Lord, the Countess is safe in England?" The Count De Bouville instantly took leave, nor did they attempt to detain him, but engaged his return in the evening, with his mother and sister, if they were disengaged. He had no sooner left the room, than she eagerly read the contents of her letter as follows:

My dearest sister will, I know, rejoice when I tell her I have
escaped from the worst of evils, perhaps from death, and am safe
in the protection of a charming English Lady, Mrs Courtney, at
her villa about three miles from London. The uncertainty

whether you have left France, or on your journey to England, prevents me from being more explicit; if you have not left France, write under cover to Mrs Courtney, Harley-street, Cavendish-square. If this letter is sent after you, hasten to me, dearest sister, —O, what happiness I promise myself in embracing my dearest friends. I hope Miss Weimar is with you; the uncertainty has given me great concern. Do not delay an hour to satisfy your affectionate sister and friend.

VICTORIA

"Good God! I thank thee," cried the Marchioness, "this is blessed news indeed." "I rejoice with you, my dearest love," said the Marquis, "but pray communicate the news to your lovely protégée." She hastened to Matilda; she was reclining on her arms, thrown across the table, and weeping bitterly. "My charming girl do not give way to sorrow, heaven, in its own good time, will send you relief; here is an instance to prove it" (giving her the letter). Poor Matilda raised her drooping head, and hastily looked it over, clasped her hand with joy, "O, my dearest madam, this is happiness indeed—let me not be so selfish to mourn on a day of joy like this." "Let this, my dear young friend, be a lesson to yourself, never despair; to misfortunes and contradictions to our best wishes, we are all liable, and all must expect; none are exempt from the calamities incident to human nature; to bear those inevitable evils with patience, to acquire resolution and fortitude under them, and to look forward with hope, that you may one day be delivered from them, will blunt the arrows of affliction, and enable you to support them with resignation."

"My beloved, my charming monitress," cried Matilda, "I will try to profit by your advice; the Countess and yourself shall be my great examples—dear lady, how kind to think of the poor Matilda; I wish I could see her, but alas!—" "No sighs," said the Marchioness, "you must and shall be cheerful this day; hope, my dear girl, and all may be well yet."

They descended to the parlour, and in the afternoon had the pleasure of hearing Joseph was just arrived with the servant. "Let him come in," they all cried, as with one breath. He entered; poor fellow, he fell on his knees and wept, it was difficult to say whether with joy or sorrow— he felt both; the sight of Miss Weimar remembered him of Bertha's dreadful fate, though he rejoiced to see her safe. The Marchioness and Matilda ran to raise him. "Welcome, my good Joseph," said the former, "you are come on a happy day." "My dear friend," said the latter, pressing his hand, "do not give way to grief; we have all our sorrows, but we have our pleasures too, and I have news for you, Joseph. Our good lady is alive, and safe from the power of her enemies." "Heaven be thanked," said the old man, wiping his eyes, "this is blessed news indeed; and to see you safe too, my dear young madam, makes me happy, though I can't forget poor Bertha: alas, your ladyship, she was a good and faithful wife; she knew nothing about my lady—poor soul, she kept no secrets from me." He seemed to feel a reproach for his secrecy.

"My honest friend," said the Marquis, "your kindness and fidelity to our dear sister deserves reward; in this house you may rest free from care the remainder of your days, and I will settle two hundred livres on you yearly besides."

Joseph again dropt on his knees, "God bless your honour! God bless the dear ladies!" And he hurried out of the room, tears of thankfulness running down his cheeks.

"Good creature!" cried Matilda, wiping her eyes, "may the rest of your life be peaceful and happy."

They now again recurred to the subject of the Countess and her letter. The Marchioness expressed her wishes to set off with all possible expedition to England, and within ten days it was fixed they should depart. Matilda heard this determination with a sigh, which did not pass unobserved, though they forbore to notice it; they concluded however she should be left to herself until the next morning, that their opinions might not appear to influence her. For herself, the idea of her obscure birth was a severe mortification; she considered her friends De Bouville and De Bancre as so much her superiors that she could no longer treat them with that easy familiarity she had been accustomed, though she little thought the former was acquainted with her whole story.

In the evening came the Countess of Bouville and her family, with Madame De Nancy and her sister. After the first compliments, "Bless me!" cried Mademoiselle De Bancre, "what in the world, ladies, have you done to Mademoiselle De Fontelle; I met her this morning, and pleading an engagement here as a reason for refusing her invitation, she flew into a violent rage, accused the Marchioness of treating her with rudeness unpardonable; and for Miss Weimar, she lavished such a torrent of abuse on her, that had I not known her fixed aversion to all handsome women, and a small predilection in favour of a certain person, whose attentions she is fearful of losing, I should have been at a loss to account for her acrimony."

"If the lady has any dislike, or fears respecting me," answered Matilda, with evident confusion, "she does me great injustice: 'tis impossible I should ever injure her, or clash with any views she has formed." "There is no saying what her views may be," said the Count, "but I will venture to assert, there can be no divided opinion concerning the merits of Miss Weimar and Mademoiselle De Fontelle; and the jealousy of a mean mind, when conscious of its deficiencies, is natural enough." "Come, come," said the Marchioness, "no scandal, my good friends: we cannot be hurt by malice, any more than we can be gratified by undue praises at the expence of others."

The uncommon spirits of the Marquis and Marchioness attracted observation, as well as the dejection of Matilda, which she attributed to ill health. The Count and his sister sympathized with her, and the former was so agitated for the event of the following day, that he did not dare ask himself why he was so much interested.

Matilda rejoiced when the evening concluded and she could retire to herself: she was far from well; her anxiety in what manner she should answer Mr Weimar distracted her mind; she felt the strongest repugnance to become his wife—she was sure she could not be happy with him; if she had wronged him, he never could, she thought, cordially forgive, nor should she ever look up to him with confidence. She past a restless night, and arose ill and unrefreshed. She entreated her friends to be present; they at first objected, but she was so extremely unhappy at their refusal, that they at length consented to come in after his appearance, if she sent for them.

His name was at length announced, and he absolutely started at the alteration in her countenance. "The solemnity of your air, my charming Matilda, gives me great uneasiness; how great will be my transport to remove every cause of sorrow from your heart, and see cheerfulness restored to your features. Have you acquainted your friends here with my communications?" "I have, Sir," replied she, endeavouring to collect some firmness, "but they decline giving any opinion; have you any objection to their being present now?" He hesitated; "I see no necessity for it—but as you please." She then rung the bell, and requested the Marquis and his lady would do them the favour of their company.

They entered, and after mutual compliments, and they were seated, Matilda addressed herself to Mr Weimar. "At the time, Sir, when you permitted me to believe I had the honour of being your niece, although sensible of your kindness, and conscious of my obligations to you, for the care of my infancy, I have often taken my heart to task, and upbraided its want of gratitude; what must I accuse myself of now, when I am informed that to your charity alone I am indebted for the advantages I possess. O, Sir, never, never can I return what I owe you— least of all, by becoming your wife; 'tis an honour I do not deserve—" "Pardon me for interrupting you, my dear Matilda: I disclaim the name of obligation; you owe me no gratitude but for my affection; consider how many years you have been the delight, the darling of my heart, and now, when my love is stronger than ever, am I to be thrown off at once; have you no feeling for the wretchedness you doom me to for the remainder of my life?" "Oh! Sir, what can I say," answered Matilda; "impressions once strongly conceived are difficult to eradicate; the conversation I overheard is ever present to my mind, and could I forget that, then my reverence for my uncle would return, and I should shudder at the idea of a nearer connexion. When I think of it, and indeed, Sir, I have endeavoured to think of it, an unaccountable repugnance makes the idea horrible to me; yet after all, if you persist in wishing me to become your wife, I do not think myself at liberty absolutely to refuse, but I tell you candidly, I never can love you, that though I will obey you, and do my duty, I know I shall be miserable, and in that persuasion surely 'tis impossible I can make you happy." "I am sensible," said he, "that my age is against me, I cannot expect to be loved like a young fellow, but my unremitting attentions to please will make me deserving your esteem." "Well, Sir," said Matilda, hastily, "it is fit you should prefer your own happiness to mine, I have no right to refuse, nor any way of discharging the obligations I owe you for the care of my early life, but by the sacrifice of the maturer part of it."

Unable any longer to struggle with the grief and horror that opprest her, she burst into tears. Her friends felt for her, but were as yet silent. Mr Weimar took her hand and kissed it, "Cruel Matilda, is this the return for all my tenderness; but I do not prefer my own happiness to yours; consider, pardon me if I say, consider your situation; with all the charms you possess, such is the cruel prejudice against those who have neither friends nor family to protect and provide for them, that in France you could not hope or expect any proper establishment." "Hold, Sir," said she, with indignation, "do not insult me; I know what I am, and since I am unworthy of an establishment in France, I never will have one in Germany. No, Sir, you have now convinced me, if I cannot honour you I ought not to degrade you. I will retire to a convent: I will become a lay sister, 'tis perhaps the line Providence intended for me; be that as it may, you have convinced me I ought not, nor I solemnly declare I never will be your wife." She spoke with a force and spirit as surprised them all. "Do not be rash, Matilda; I offer you a handsome fortune; you shall no longer be confined in the country, as my wife, you shall have a house at Berne, at Lausanne, or where you please; every pleasure shall attend you; the Marquis himself shall secure your future fortune: do not be offended for trifles, and what never was intended as an insult; trust to my love to create an interest in your heart." "No, Sir," answered she, "the die is cast; a little while since I thought, if you desired it, I ought to be yours; but if you can stoop to degrade yourself by a connexion with a friendless deserted orphan, I never will owe the obligation to any man, nor have the chance of being upbraided, that I belong to nobody. Pardon me, my good friends, the trouble I have given you, a few days hence I will hide myself for ever." She arose to leave the room. "Stop, madam," said Mr Weimar; "since nothing can prevail on you to accept my hand, at least permit me to tell you, you have no right to dispose of yourself without my permission; you were committed to my care, doubtless by your parents; you may one day be reclaimed; I am answerable for the trust reposed in me, and with me I shall insist upon your remaining till those to whom you belong appear to claim you."

Matilda sunk back in her chair, overwhelmed with horror; he looked furious with passion; the Marquis and his lady were perplexed and chagrined; at length the former said, "Without the smallest intent of contesting your rights, Sir, I have patiently attended to what has passed between this young lady and yourself; the Marchioness and I have been scrupulously exact not to give our opinion, much less advice on the subject; but now, since she has resolutely made up her mind, you certainly have too just a sense of what is owing to yourself, to persist in addressing her; taking that for granted, and that you think it improper she should become a Nun, I request it as a favour, that Miss Matilda may be permitted to spend a few months with us; should any person appear to claim her, I trust it will be no dishonour to have her found in my protection; and I pledge my honour she shall form no marriage or engagement under our care, but return to you as she now is." "My Lord," returned Mr Weimar, "I must consider of this request, and she will do well to consider and repent her rash determination; if she does, I will receive her with open arms. I trust her to your honour, and shall tomorrow wait on you with my decided opinion." With a polite, but general bow, he left the room.

The Marchioness was supporting Matilda's head upon her shoulder. "Look; up, my dear girl, be composed, he is gone." "Thank heaven!" said she, "but my head is very bad, and with your leave I will lay down an hour or two." "Do so, my dear," replied her friend; and calling the servant to attend her, she was conducted to her apartment.

When she left the room the Marchioness said, "Mr Weimar's conduct appears very strange, and unbecoming a man of his years; I know not what to think; had he not injudiciously mentioned her birth

89

she would certainly have accepted his hand, though I own it would have given me pain had she done so."

"For my part," answered the Marquis, "I marked him well during the whole scene; that he is excessively fond of her, I believe, but I am not perfectly satisfied, although I know not, what part to blame of his conduct; nevertheless she has now taken her resolution, and only force shall compel me to withdraw my protection from a friendless orphan, whose situation is really deplorable. If the circumstances he related of her birth are true, I have no doubt but one time or other a discovery will take place to her advantage; all I wish at present is, that she may accompany you to England." "Do you not think, said the Marchioness, "the Count De Bouville is very fond of her? "I fear so," replied he; "but you know Mr Weimar's observations with respect to the obscurity of her birth are founded on truth, I would by no means encourage a dangerous intimacy between them, which might be productive of misery to both; 'tis for that reason I should wish her to leave Paris whilst the liking which I think mutual is in its infancy."

During the conversation of her generous friends the unhappy Matilda gave herself up to extreme sorrow. If Mr Weimar chose to exert his right over her, she saw no one to whom she could appeal for redress; but determined as she now was never to become his wife, she was sensible she had little chance of becoming the wife of any other man; to engage her benefactors in disputes and controversies with him was equally repugnant to her inclinations, and without his consent it would be in vain to think of accompanying her friends, as he might pursue her everywhere. She knew she had many obligations to him, but she could not return them in the way he was desirous of, which must make her miserable, and of course give no happiness to him. "What then," cried she, weeping, "am I to do? There is no alternative but Mr Weimar or a convent; the latter is my preferable choice, and if he persists to-morrow in exerting the authority he claims over me, I will fly to that for protection."

Having now made up her mind, she dropt asleep, but her slumbers were broken and disturbed; and in about three hours she returned to her friends, very little refreshed, but was much gratified by their peculiar tenderness and attention, and an increased respect in their manner proved they wished to restore her self-consequence, and make her at ease with herself.

This is true benevolence; 'tis the mode of conferring favours that either obliges or wounds a feeling heart. Many people are generous, but they forget how painful it is to ask favours, and think it quite sufficient if they give, let the manner of giving be ever so ungracious, and their superiority ever so ostentatiously displayed. Not so the Marquis and his lady—they endeavoured to persuade her, they were the persons obliged by her acceptance of their little civilities, and entered into all her concerns with the affection and anxiety of her nearest relatives.

Matilda's grateful heart overflowed; speech indeed was not lent her, but her tears, her expressive looks forcibly conveyed the language she could not utter.

In the meantime Mademoiselle De Fontelle was not idle; scarce a person the Marchioness was acquainted with, but knew she had taken a girl under her protection, who had robbed and run away from her uncle, with a young handsome footman; and during two days' circulation of the story Miss Weimar was detected by her uncle in several low intrigues, which he kindly forgave, 'till quite abandoned and incorrigible, she had taken away all his gold and jewels, and came to Paris with this fellow, whom the Marchioness herself had taken into the house.

"Ciel," cries one, shrugging her shoulders, "a pretty story indeed; this is the discreet, the admirable Marchioness De Melfort, held up as a pattern to all the women in Paris." "Yes, I thought she was a wonder," said another; "abundance of art, to be sure she has; for I'll answer for it, this intrigue with a footman is not the first by many; but, poor woman, her charms are in their wane now, so the man is a substitute for the master." "What," cries a third, "has the Marchioness herself an intrigue?" "Lord, didn't you hear that? Why this girl is only a cover to her own amusements." "Well," said a fourth, "I saw both the other night at Madame De Bouville's, and I am sure they are both ugly enough, notwithstanding the men made such a fuss about them."

'Twas thus the scandal of Mademoiselle's fabricating was increased and magnified among their generous and charitable acquaintance: like Sir Peter Teale's wound, it was in all parts of his body, and by a variety of murderous weapons, when the poor man was unconscious of having received any himself, and could scarce obtain credit when he appeared in perfect health: so unwilling is the good-natured world to give up a story that is to the disadvantage of others. It was in vain the Countess De Bouville, her son and daughter, Madame De Nancy and her sister, attempted to stop the scandalous tales; like lightning it flew from house to house, and everyone who had no character to lose, and others of suspected reputation only rejoiced to level an amiable respectable woman with themselves.

The Count De Bouville was distracted; he flew from a set of envious wretches to the Marquis De Melfort's; when he entered the room he met the eyes of the lovely dejected Matilda, with such an expression of grief and softness in them, that it pierced his heart: she blushed, and withdrew them, with a sigh she could not suppress. The Marquis had left the room, the Marchioness was holding her young friend's hand with an affectionate tender air.

After the usual compliments he enquired particularly after Matilda's health; she could not trust her voice just then to speak, the Marchioness answered, "She is better, only a dejection on her spirits, which you must assist in removing: I was trying to persuade her to accompany me in a carriage to pay a few visits." The Count, alarmed at the intention, replied, "Paying visits might possibly be too fatiguing, but an airing would surely be of service." "Well then," said the Marchioness, forgetful of her Lord's caution, "you shall accompany us." The carriage, which was in waiting, drawing up, he gladly escorted the two ladies to it, and took his seat very quietly opposite to Matilda, who had hitherto observed a profound silence. He contrived however to draw her into a little conversation, and was charmed with her good sense and sweetness of manners. The languor that pervaded her fine features, powerfully engaged the heart, and the Count could not help thinking how happy that man must be who was destined to possess so great a treasure! This reflection caused a sudden alteration in his countenance; he grew thoughtful and uneasy, when he was disturbed in his reverie by an exclamation from the Marchioness, "Good heavens! what insolence." "What's the matter, madam?" "Bless me, didn't you observe the two carriages that past, in one was Madame Remini and her two daughters, in the other Madame Le Brun, her niece, and two others of my acquaintance. As the carriage past, I bowed and kissed my hand; they one and all returned a slight bow, and laughed in each other's faces: upon my word I never saw such rudeness." The Count who could too well account for this behaviour, was however very much vexed. "Dear madam," said he, "such impertinent women are scarce worth your notice, and only deserving contempt." "That's true, Count," replied she, "and henceforth I shall treat them as they deserve."

As neither of the parties were in high spirits, their airing was not a long one, and they returned to the house as the Marquis entered it.

After they were seated the Marchioness was expressing her wishes to be in England. "Does Miss Weimar accompany you?" asked the Count. "I hope so," replied the Marchioness. The Marquis giving the Count a glance, they retired to the library, where the conversation of the morning, between Mr Weimar and Matilda, was repeated. The Count felt indignation, pity, and resentment; he was delighted with Matilda's spirit, yet most sincerely felt for her unhappy situation. "Good God, my dear Marquis, what is to be done for this amiable girl?" "I hope," he replied, "we shall prevail on him to leave her with us,—tomorrow will determine; but take it how he will, I have this day made several persons acquainted with his being the guardian of Matilda, and his offers of marriage in my presence: the circumstance of a young lady's flying from her guardian is nothing extraordinary, and will, I hope, do away the scandal that has been propagated at her expence." "You are very good," returned the Count, "and I am sure she merits the esteem of all the world." He took his leave under such a contrariety of sentiments, and so much real concern for the unfortunate Matilda, that when he returned to his sister she was quite alarmed, and asked a thousand questions relative to her friend. When he had explained everything, the gentle Adelaide felt equal concern, and lamented that her troubles were of a kind that placed it out of the power of their friendship to afford her any consolation or relief.

Whilst they were expressing mutual regret Mademoiselle De Fontelle was announced; she was received with a coldness that would have mortified any other person, but putting on a gay air, "Ah! Count, so soon returned from your party; I did not expect to find you here." "Perhaps, madam, had I known your intended visit, I might have been elsewhere." "Very polite, upon my word," said she, colouring deeply; "your brother, my dear Bouville, has acquired the English roughness of manners, by his tour to that country." "I hope, madam," replied he, significantly, "I have acquired the sincerity of that nation, at least, to speak as I think; and as a proof of it, were you not my sister's guest, I should be free enough to say, I so much detest the fabricators of scandal, that I heartily rejoice when they are mortified by being obliged to hear the object of their envy is as much superior to them in every amiable quality of the mind, as she is in the beauty of her person, and that it will be her own fault only if she is not established in a more brilliant situation than her enemies can boast of."

With these words he left the room, with a look of scorn she could not support, but burst into tears. "Your brother has cruelly insulted me," said she. "I am sorry for it, and for the occasion," answered Mademoiselle De Bouville; "but indeed you have been too unguarded in your reports to the disadvantage of Miss Weimar." "Name her not," cried she, "I hate her." "That may be," returned the other, "nevertheless I hold it my duty to do her justice." She then briefly mentioned Mr Weimar was only her guardian, and that he was come after her to solicit her hand, the only thing for which she left him, his offers before the Marquis and his lady, and the very great justice he did her character. The malicious girl was ready to burst with spleen, but carried it off with an air. "Upon my word," said she, "Mr Weimar was himself the person who first mentioned the affair to her disadvantage; and I suppose there is some point to carry, or some mystery in an affair where there are such contradictions, which I do not comprehend, and which, I dare say, will deceive nobody, though I would venture to swear, hardly any person will concern themselves about the Marchioness's little protégée, or whether the German is uncle or not to one whom nobody knows." She arose, and desiring her respects to her very polite brother, flounced out of the room.

Neither her resentment nor absence was a subject of regret to Adelaide, who only visited her in compliance with the fashion of the times, which is to go everywhere with the rest of the world, and assist in forming a croud, without knowing or caring for three fourths of the company.

M eantime the remainder of the day was spent at the Marquis's in the most affectionate endeavours to console Matilda, and the warmest assurances of love and attention to her interests. They all anxiously expected the return of Mr Weimar next morning, as the crisis on which her future destiny appeared to depend.

At the appointed hour Mr Weimar sent in his name; her friends had persuaded Matilda to receive him alone, and send for them when she thought it necessary. She had tried all the morning to reconcile herself to his displeasure, but she was resolved to persevere in the resolution she had formed of retiring to a convent, if he made it necessary.

He entered the room with an air of kindness and complacency took her hand and kissed it. "Let me flatter myself, dearest Matilda," said he, "that you are in better health and disposition than when I left you yesterday. I have passed many uneasy hours lately, indeed I may say truly, from the day you was committed to my care, every hour of my life has been spent in anxiety on your account." "Do not, Sir," said she, "for heaven's sake, do not crush me with the weight of obligations I owe you: a poor forlorn being, without family or friends, as you have justly told me, is entitled to no one's consideration; I am therefore beyond all possibility of return at present; indebted to you for everything, for the life I enjoy, hard is the task upon me to refuse anything you request, but as this meeting is to decide once for all, pardon me if I say I cannot marry you, but this deference I owe to your fatherly care of me, I solemnly declare, that unless the authors of my being claim my first reverence, I never will encourage any man without your permission; this, Sir, is all I can, or ever will promise in your favour." "Ungrateful girl!" cried he, raising his voice, "and is this all, this all you owe to a man who preserved your life, and bestowed his time and fortune to make you what you are?" "Oh! that I had died," cried Matilda, in an agony, "rather than to live and be thus upbraided for favours I never can return; but my mind tells me you will one day be repaid for all;—yes, I have a pre-sentiment I am no base-born unworthy offspring; one day, Sir, I may yet have the power to prove my sense of the obligations you reproach me with, and it will be the happiest moment of my life." She had spoken with such vehemence as precluded interruption; he was surprised; "You are warm, Matilda," said he, very calmly. "I cannot help it, Sir, you have made me desperate; I will seek peace and quietness in a convent. You will not permit me to accompany the Marchioness," said she, softening, and tears running down her cheeks, "and I think I owe you that respect not to go without your leave; therefore I have no other asylum but a convent to hope for." "Have I not a house, Matilda?" "Yes, Sir; I might have resided in my uncle's house, but I cannot, with propriety, in yours, when I have no such claim to boast of." She arose and rang the bell; "Desire the Marquis and his lady to favour me with their company." When the servant retired, "You are then determined, madam?" "I am, Sir." "Then so am I, and you may take the consequence."

Her friends now entered; after they were seated Matilda spoke, "I took the liberty to request your presence, that you might be witness to my declaration for the last time, That I never will be the wife of Mr Weimar, nor without his consent, unless commanded by my parents (alas! how unlikely at present that hope) never to marry any other man. It would be the joy of my heart to have been permitted to accept the honour of the protection you have offered me, but as I fear that cannot be, I will retire into a convent, 'tis the only place of refuge for a poor unfortunate, friendless being, without family, friends, or even a name." She wept aloud, pronouncing those last words. The Marchioness sympathized with her, and addressing Mr Weimar, "Come, Sir," said she, "let me prevail on you to accede to our request, we ask it as a favour; permit Miss Matilda to be in our care for six months; I engage my honour she shall return by that time free from every engagement." He made no answer.

"Shall I entreat the favour of a few words in private, Sir," said the Marquis. They arose and left the room. Within a short time they returned. Mr Weimar, advancing to Matilda, "I have consented to oblige you, too ungrateful girl; I permit you to remain with the Marchioness, but conditionally, that you write me constantly every occurrence, nor presume to enter into any engagement without my acquiescence." "To these conditions," cried she, her eyes sparkling with joy, "I most cheerfully subscribe." He looked full of resentment at her, but taking a polite leave, declined an invitation to stay dinner, and hastily withdrew.

The moment he left the room Matilda arose, and throwing her arms round the Marchioness, her grateful heart overflowing into tears, "Oh! my dearest, my generous protectress, how shall I ever return your goodness?" "By loving me, my precious girl, as affectionately as I do you," answered she, embracing her. Observing the Marquis seeming musing, "May I ask, my Lord, what occupies your thoughts?" "Yes," replied he; "it is fit you should know; to be plain then, I don't like Mr Weimar; I suspect he means to deceive us." "Good God," cried Matilda, alarmed, "how is that possible?" "Be it as it may," answered the Marquis, "we will guard against any sinister design; let our young friend retire this night to some place of safety." "You do not surely apprehend he will apply for a lettre de cachet?" said the Marchioness. "I should not be surprised at it," returned he. "Then," said she, "we will set off instantly on our journey; Louison and Antoine can attend us; Marianne shall take care of all our baggage here, and follow us, with Pierre, in a day or two, or come with you." "'Tis a hasty, and rather an inconvenient scheme," said he, "but I have no other to offer at present." "O, what trouble I occasion to my friends," cried Matilda. "Go to your apartment, set about packing, my dear girl; we must take a few necessaries with us, and set off immediately after dinner." She obeyed. The Marquis set about the arrangements for their journey, and promised to follow in four or five days.

Poor Joseph and Albert deplored their fate, in being too old to accompany the ladies, and were the only domestics left in the house, who knew to what place they were going.

Everything being settled in a few hours, it was given out in the family, they were going into the country for a short time; even Marianne and Pierre knew no more for the present; and the ladies, attended by Louison and Antoine, set off, with all expedition; fortunately, Antoine had been in England once before, with a former master; he was therefore acquainted with the roads and accommodations, and consequently extremely useful.

The Marquis found the following day he had been right in his conjectures. Two men came to his hotel, armed with authority, to demand a lady commonly known by the name of Matilda Weimar, with a description of her person, then under the protection of the Marquis De Melfort. The Marquis was not at home; the men were informed the young lady was gone, with their mistress, into the country. They searched the house, and being disappointed, waited till the Marquis returned; he gave them the same information, and drew up a paper, signifying, that having taken the young lady under his protection, by the consent of Mr Weimar, who called himself her guardian, she had accompanied the Marchioness on a visit to some friends; that he pledged his honour for her safety, also to answer any charges that could be brought against her. With this declaration the men departed and returned no more; but a person was observed to watch the house for some days after.

The Marquis made no secret to the Bouville family of the past transactions, and though they felt great regret for the loss of their friends, they acknowledged the event had justified their prudence in the steps they had taken.

The Count felt more than he dared express, yet tried to subdue his feelings, from a consciousness of their impropriety to be indulged. His sister was to be married the following week to Monsieur De Clermont, and her establishment engrossed much of his time and attention.

The Marquis very soon arranged all his affairs, and within five days after the ladies left Paris, he followed them.

T he Marchioness and her friend pursued their route, arrived at Calais, and crossed over to Dover, without meeting a single accident; here they determined to rest, and wait for the Marquis. They were exceedingly fatigued with the expedition they had used, and were glad to sit down comfortably.

The Marchioness understood the English language perfectly well, and spoke enough to make herself comprehended in common matters; Antoine did the same, but as to Matilda and Louison, they knew not a single word 'till the Marchioness taught them to name a few necessary articles, and write down common words.

Much sooner than they expected, they had the pleasure of embracing the Marquis, and then learnt the danger Matilda had escaped, and the duplicity of Mr Weimar. She shuddered to think how near she had been to misery, and her affection and gratitude to the worthy pair, who protected her, was proportionably increased.

The following morning they left Dover, and by easy journies arrived at the Royal Hotel in Jermyn-street. A card was instantly sent off to Harley-street, The messenger returned, with a line only, from the Countess, that they should follow the bearer with all speed and within ten minutes after the coach drew up. The Marquis hastened down to receive and conduct the ladies. The Countess was almost breathless with joy; she flew upstairs, and in a moment was in her sister's arms. Their mutual joy, their tears of affection and transport excited sympathy in everyone. The Countess, recovering, led her sister to Mrs Courtney, "The two dearest friends I have on earth," said she, "love each other for my sake now, you have congenial hearts." She then warmly embraced Matilda. "This is the first day of my life," cried she, putting her hand to her heart; "I have all that I love in the world about me, at least, all that I know," added she, with a suppressed sigh.

Matilda, whose grateful heart expanded with delight, to see all her friends happy, expressed her feelings with such a warmth of satisfaction as engaged all their affections. She was introduced also to Mrs Courtney: and when the first tumults of joy were over, the Countess, taking that lady's hand, said, "Behold, my dear sister and brother, the preserver of Victoria's life; to her goodness I am indebted for all the happiness I now enjoy, a vast debt of gratitude, never to be repaid." "You neither do me nor yourself justice," answered Mrs Courtney; "if you do not think I am a thousand times overpaid for any little services, I have been so happy to render you, by the pleasure of your company, and the honour you have procured me, of knowing your respectable friends." They all gratefully bowed to this compliment, and then began to talk of their future residence. The Marquis wished to have a ready furnished house, in the neighbourhood of Mrs Courtney. She contended for the pleasure of accommodating them in hers; but this, for several reasons, they declined; and after a long and friendly contest it was decided, a house should be procured for them in her neighbourhood, but that they should spend every other week at Mrs Courtney's villa, and until a habitation was fixed on they would remain at the hotel, where they all supped together that evening.

"I know," said the Countess, "you must all be very anxious to understand by what means I obtained my present happy situation, and I am equally curious to know how my dear Miss Weimar conducted herself from the time we last met; but we will suspend curiosity for the present, nor cloud our happy meeting with a recital of painful events." "You are right, my dear Countess," said Mrs Courtney; "we are now all happily met, and 'tis of little consequence by what means it came about at present."

They passed a most delightful evening, and parted with reluctance, after engaging to spend the following day in Harley-street, and Mrs Courtney promising to search the neighbourhood for a house to accommodate them.

"What a charming woman is Mrs Courtney," said the Marchioness.

"Ah!" cried Matilda. "I wish I understood English. I should like to speak to that lady in her own language." "You shall learn it, my love, when we are settled; but as the lady speaks French remarkably well, you have no cause for regret."

They retired to rest, and the following morning had some trades-people with them, who are always on the watch to attend foreigners at the hotels. They purchased a few trifles, but chose to have Mrs Courtney's judgment before they bought anything of consequence.

The Marquis, who had letters of credit on the house of Sir Thomas Herries, attended by the master of the hotel, went out to get cash, whilst the ladies attended to the business of the toilet, as they had engaged to be with their friends at a very early hour.

Soon after his return they drove to Harley-street, and were received with that affectionate cordiality, a thousand times more desirable than distant civility and respect: they met like old friends, with congenial minds, to enjoy the pleasures of society. Mrs Courtney told them, she hoped she had already succeeded in her endeavours to procure a residence for them; "and, fortunately," said she, "only three doors from hence; if you are inclined, we can now look at it." The proposal was accepted. The house and furniture, which had been all new within the twelvemonth, and belonged to Lord G—, who found it convenient to go abroad for his health; was now to be let for a year certain, at 400l. per annum. They were extremely well pleased with the house, and readily agreed to the terms. Within two or three days it would be ready for their reception.

This being settled, they returned in high spirits, and spent a most delightful day in a quiet family party.

The next day was appropriated to shopping and excursions round the town; and indeed, except sleeping hours, they passed their time solely together; Mrs Courtney having shut her doors to all company 'till they were settled in their new abode for the same reason the Marquis deferred sending all his letters of recommendation or waiting on the French Ambassador.

The fourth day after their arrival in England they took possession of their house; and having been fortunate enough to obtain a respectable woman, who was perfectly conversant in the French language, as house-keeper, they agreed to spend the following week in the country, previous to their being publicly announced in town.

Nothing particular occurred until their arrival at Bellvue, Mrs Courtney's little paradise: they were quite delighted with its situation, and charmed with its polite and friendly owner. The second morning after their residence here, the Countess entered the Marchioness's dressing-room; Matilda was with her. "Mrs Courtney has just got two or three neighbours with her; my presence not being necessary, I have seized the opportunity, to make our respective communications: I am sensible you must be very curious, but I wish to hear my dear Miss Weimar's story taken up from the visit she promised me, and I suppose intended paying me." Matilda very readily gave an account of every event at the castle. The Countess shuddered, and heaved a sigh to the fate of poor Margarite, but did not interrupt 'till she came to the letter received from Joseph, of the fire in the castle, Bertha's miserable fate and his escape. "Good heavens!" cried she, "of what atrocious wickedness is that man capable! Poor wretch, what a long account has he one day to make—God grant him repentance!" Matilda proceeded, and related every circumstance until their safe arrival in London.

The Countess embraced the lovely girl, who had betrayed a sense of mortification in recounting the particulars of her birth. "I thank, my beloved sister," said she, "for the attention she paid to my request, and I am persuaded your charming society has amply recompensed her for the favour she did me." "You judge right, my dear Victoria; I am indeed the obliged person: but come, pray begin your narration, and take it up from the time you married that brute whose name you bear—" "But which I do not assume here," answered the Countess; "I pass for a Madame Le Roche, and as we neither go to court nor attend any public galas, I have never been particularly introduced, and am known among my dear Mrs Courtney's friends, as a widow of some fashion, but small fortune, on a visit to her, and not very desirous of much company; therefore you must get your lesson by heart against we return to town.

"Now, as to your request, you may possibly think I am too observant of my word towards an inhuman monster, when I declare that the sacred vows he drew from me still bind me to secrecy, as to what occasioned my being shut up in the castle, and permitting the general belief of my death." "Good God! sister," cried the Marchioness, "vows forced upon you, under such circumstances, have no power to bind; and you have sufficiently proved your truth and honour, by preserving them so many years from your dearest friends;—I am sure our confessor will absolve you." "May be so," replied Madame Le Roche, "and on our return to town I will consult him, 'till when I shall take up my story from the day Matilda left me.

"Charmed that I was likely to procure an asylum for her, as I doubted not of your acceding to my request, I retired to bed at an early hour, but could not sleep; about midnight I thought I heard an uncommon noise at the outward doors; I listened, and, convinced it was not fancy, I called on Margarite; the noise had alarmed her, she ran to me in the same instant that we heard the door in the kitchen burst open, and the Count appeared with an ill-looking fellow. I was out of bed, and had thrown on a wrapping gown about me; I trembled from head to foot; he came up to me furiously; 'Wretch,' cried he, 'you have broken your oath with me, and therefore mine is no longer binding—prepare to die.' Despair had given me courage—I was no longer the poor weak creature he had entangled some years before; my spirits returned, 'Strike, barbarian, and complete your crimes, I fear not death, it will free me from all the miseries you have heaped upon me; but I will not suffer under imputed guilt—I have broke no vows, I have kept the fatal oath you extorted from me in the hour of terror.' 'How dare you persist in falsehoods,' cried he; 'you have had a woman here—you see and converse with Joseph daily; dare you deny those charges?' 'I do not,' answered I, 'but still I have preserved my faith; the woman came here by accident, unawed by the terrors Joseph and I endeavoured to inspire, but she knew not who I was, nor any thing relative to my situation, and goes from hence in a few days: as to Joseph, the poor fellow, when he brings my provisions, enters into a little chat with Margarite, and sometimes I speak to him, and where is the mighty crime? You must know your diabolical secret is too well kept, or I need not be here in your power.' He paused a few minutes, then withdrew to the window, and spoke to the man in a low tone; they came again towards me, and I expected instant death, but they locked the doors, and stopping the mouth of poor Margarite, dragged her out of the room, still locking the door after them.

"The apprehensions I was under for that poor creature overcame the courage I assumed, and I swooned; how long I was deprived of my senses, I know not, but I recovered by cold water they threw in my face. 'O, what have you done with my poor nurse?' 'She is safe from betraying secrets,' replied he; 'come, madam, put on your cloaths, and I shall bestow you safely too.' 'If you design my death,' said I, 'let me die here.' 'Do as I command,' cried he, furiously, 'or I shall carry you off as you are.' I threw on my cloaths, as well as my terror would permit; meantime he broke the locks of my cabinet, although he could have had the keys, took out what valuables belonged to me; and then taking me between them, they led me through a long subterraneous passage, till we came out through a thicket to the skirts of the wood; it was but faint star light; I saw two horses fastened; I was immediately put upon one, though I made some resistance expecting they intended carrying me into the thick part of the wood, and murder me there,—and I still think it was so designed. The man held me fast; we passed a small cottage, but all was quiet, and soon after entered another part of the wood, when suddenly the Count's horse fell and threw him over his head; he lay motionless; the man who held me rode up to him; he did not move. 'I must see what hurt he has,' cried he; and jumping off, left me on the horse; at the same instant I gave him a kick, and the animal set off full speed through the wood. I must inevitably have been killed, had it pursued its way through the thickets, but providentially he made towards the road, and being tired, slackened his pace. Unable any longer to support the fatigue; my head giddy, and dreadfully galled with the saddle, I slipped off on a small hillock, on one side, and lay quite exhausted, expecting every moment to be overtaken and murdered.

"I had been there but a few minutes before a carriage appeared, with two or three horsemen; I uttered a cry; the carriage stopt—a servant came up/ 'Who are you—what is the matter?' said he. I replied, feebly, 'An unfortunate woman, escaped from being murdered, for God sake save me.' The man went to the carriage, it drew up, the door was opened, and I was put in. The sudden joy added to the terror and fatigue I had gone through overpowered my senses, and I fainted; I was soon restored by the help of the lady's salts; I was able to look up, by my side sat the charming Mrs Courtney, supporting me; opposite was a middle aged gentleman, and a young one about seventeen or eighteen; I tried to speak, and kissed her hand. 'Be composed, dear lady,' said she, 'your spirits are already too much exhausted' (seeing me look with terror then on one side and then another). 'you fear being pursued,' she continued; 'we shall stop very soon, but as the day appears the blinds shall be drawn up.' This was accordingly done: 'tis needless to tell you our conversation. My heart expanded with gratitude to heaven for my deliverance.

"I was unable to give a satisfactory account of myself, only so far as related to my escape from the wood; I mentioned you, my sister, and your intended journey to England, and the uncertainty how soon you might depart, and therefore my wishes to join you. Mrs Courtney told me she was immediately going there, and as I was apprehensive of being known, it would be much better to accompany her, and write my sister from England. Before I could reply to this obliging proposal, we stopt at the posthouse, changed horses, and pursued our journey with rapidity 'till about noon, when we drew up to a very fine old castle, which I found belonged to a friend of theirs, and where they proposed passing the night.

"I was shocked at my appearance; my cloaths thrown on in a hurry, discomposed by the flight of the horse, and not one article about me calculated for travelling. My amiable preserver requested I would make myself easy; 'Fortunately,' said she, 'we are nearly of a size; I have another habit in my trunk, with which I can accommodate you, and my woman will soon make your appearance decent, and reconcile your feelings, which I see are much opprest.' The moment we alighted, 'My friend has been ill,' said she, 'and is in dishabille, will you shew her an apartment, that she may alter her dress?' The lady's woman instantly attended me to an elegant room, whilst Mrs Courtney's got the trunk opened and procured me necessaries. I was soon equipped; my charming friend came to conduct me to the company; I was received with kindness and attention by an elderly gentleman and lady, the owners of the castle, and passed a comfortable night.

"The next day we pursued our journey, though much prest to stay, and arrived at Lausanne. I found the gentleman with us was uncle to Mrs Courtney, and was come over to place his son at Lausanne, to finish his education; but having formerly resided some years in Switzerland, he had been paying a few visits to his friends, and was returning from one of them, when I was so fortunate to obtain their protection. We stayed a week at Lausanne. I kept very close in my apartment, in a constant dread of being discovered; I was heartily rejoiced when we pursued our journey, much more so when we arrived in England. Mrs Courtney's kindness cannot be described; she treats me like her dearest sister, and her uncle, who lives not far from us in Cavendish-square, appears to make no difference between us; he is a nobleman, a widower, about forty; has an only son, and is one of the most amiable men I ever knew. Judge how much happiness is now my lot with such friends, and blest with the company of my dearest relations. Sometimes," continued she, "I thought it possible the Count might have been killed by his fall; at other times, that he might be only senseless; in short, I had a hundred conjectures about him, but 'tis plain he was not much hurt, since he could return to the castle and contrive more mischief. Now, in this land of liberty should he ever appear to persecute me again, I shall make no scruple to open the whole scenes of wickedness he has been guilty of;— there is one corroding care that hangs about my heart, but of that hereafter." She arose in visible emotion, "Come let us take a ramble in the garden after my tedious narrative." They accompanied her.

"I think, my dear sister," said the Marquis, "'tis a justice you owe yourself and friends to institute a process against this monster." "I shall think of it," said she, "but I have many objections; at present let us drop the subject." They acquiesced.

Mrs Courtney joined them in the garden; "Lord bless me!" said she, laughing, "how eager and persevering is curiosity; here I have had three ladies dying to see the French family with me; asking ten thousand questions about their dress and their persons, their fashions, and many other matters equally important. They made a most tedious visit, and as I discovered the motive, I was at length obliged to inform them my Parisian friends saw no company until they had been introduced in town: this effectually did the business,—they rose all together, made their congeés, and put an end to their tiresome enquiries."

A week was spent at Bellvue, in all the delights of love and friendship, in little excursions round the neighbourhood, and in viewing the delightful prospects the Surrey hills afforded them.

Persons of good sense, like the present party, were never at a loss for rational amusement when at home, and on their return to the metropolis they separated with reluctance, though so near to each other.

Two days after their arrival the Marquis received a letter from the Count De Bouville, informing him of his sister's marriage, and that three days subsequent to an event which had given them so much joy, they had been exceedingly alarmed by the sudden illness of their respectable mother, who continued in a dangerous way, which was the reason Madame De Clermont had not written to Matilda, whose health they were extremely anxious to hear of; he further said, he had made some secret enquiries about Mr Weimar, and learnt, that after remaining in Paris near a week, he had disappeared, but whether returned to Germany or not, they could not tell; that great prejudice was still entertained against Matilda, in consequence of which their family had declined seeing Madame Le Brun and her envious niece.

The Marquis communicated this letter to his friends, but as Matilda was ignorant of the scandal circulated at her expence, what related to Mademoiselle De Fontelle was omitted. She shuddered at the name of Mr Weimar, and dreaded lest he might have pursued her to England. But this (the Marchioness said) was by no means to be apprehended, as it could answer no purpose.

The Marquis and his lady now prepared for their presentation at court, and had sent their friend's introductory letters to several persons of fashion.

O n Thursday they were at the drawing-room with the French Ambassador, and returned highly gratified with the politeness and affability of the king and queen, and equally charmed with the princesses. The following day they received abundance of visits from the nobility, both English and foreign, and very readily coincided with the sentiments of the Count De Bouville, as to the attention and charms of the English ladies.

They were now obliged to be in public, and both pay and receive a number of visits; consequently Matilda spent most of her time with Madame Le Roche and Mrs Courtney. Both ladies were extremely fond of her; they sometimes accompanied her to the play, and as she studied the language with care, she hoped in time to have her ears equally gratified with her eyes.

Lord Delby, Mrs Courtney's uncle, was always of their parties, and his great partiality and admiration of Madame Le Roche was evident to the whole family; she was sometimes rallied about it; the subject gave her pain. "Compassion is the only claim I can have to his Lordship's notice," said she, one day; "do not, my dear friends, suggest an idea which would make me very miserable." "I see not, answered the Marquis, "why you are to give up every pleasure in life, and compel yourself to refuse the blessings of love and friendship, through any dread of a villain who deserves the severest punishments; but I will send another person talk with you tomorrow, for I really will not permit you to live in a situation so unworthy of yourself and friends."

The following day Doctor Demouriez, the Ambassador's Chaplain, called at Mrs Courtney's, and had above three hours' conversation with her. He returned to the Marquis. "I have heard a tale of horror," said he; "and having subdued all your sister's scruples respecting her compulsatory vows, she has confessed everything to me, and will this evening, she says, repeat each circumstance to you, after which we must consult what steps will be necessary to pursue."

They all anxiously expected the hour of meeting in the evening and after they had dined, and retired to the drawing-room, the Marchioness eagerly claimed her sister's promise. "I will obey you, my dear sister, though you little think what it costs me to make such a painful relation.

"You well know the reluctance with which I married the Count, my subsequent illness and recovery. When my health was restored I began seriously to consider my situation, and the sacrament I had vowed to observe: I determined to do my duty; and if I could not love the Count, at least, to esteem and oblige him, I was then a stranger to his real disposition; I thought him severe and stern, but I soon found he was gloomy, suspicious, and revengeful. Whilst my father lived he observed some little decency towards me, but after his death, and you had quitted Vienna, my sufferings, from his causeless ill-humour, cannot be described.

"I was now far advanced in my pregnancy, an event I looked forward to as the end of all my troubles; for I had lost my spirits, my strength, and appetite. One day he went to Vienna, he returned at night in a most horrid temper. 'Prepare yourself,' said he, 'for a journey to Switzerland, the day after tomorrow.' 'Good God, to Switzerland, in my situation?' 'Yes,' he replied, 'you can bear the journey very well, and Margarite, who is to be your nurse, shall attend you.' 'Indeed I am very unable to travel so far,' said I. 'I know better,' he replied; 'but the reasons you have for declining, madam, make me the more anxious for it.' 'Well, Sir, I have no more to say, but to obey you.' 'You do well, madam; for anything you could urge will have no effect upon me.' I was silent; I withdrew, and passed a wretched night. The next day poor Margarite and I were employed in packing our cloaths and other necessaries, and the following day, soon as it was light, we set off on our journey.

"We at length arrived at the old castle which Matilda has described to you. My blood chilled when I entered the gates. I was conducted to the right hand wing, which had then a door into the court, though it was afterwards bricked up. The furniture was handsome, but antique even then. 'This, madam, is your apartment, and I think the Chevalier will have good luck to obtain entrance here.' 'Chevalier! What Chevalier?' repeated I. 'Your Chevalier, madam; don't suppose I was ignorant of his return to Vienna, and sauntering about my grounds.' 'I don't know, Sir, what you mean; there is no Chevalier belongs to me, nor do I know of any man sauntering, as you call it, in your grounds. My heart justifies me, that ever since I became your wife, I have strictly fulfilled the duties of that situation.' 'Your conscience, madam, is mighty convenient to your wishes, I don't doubt; but I am not to be duped by either. This is your habitation; the other parts of the house are not so good, but with them you need have no communications; they are occupied by the gardener.' My bedroom was the horrid one where Miss Weimar saw poor Margarite murdered, and very gloomy it was then, though without iron bars. I wept almost incessantly; my nurse was still more miserable, but she had been brought up from a child in the Count's family, and was obsequious to his will.

"I had been in the castle about three weeks, when, one evening, as I was sitting in my room, at the close of the day I heard a little noise at the window. I was startled, but recovering myself, I took a chair and got upon the window seat; I saw the figure of a man. I shrunk down; again the window rattled, I recovered and looked up; presently I distinctly perceived a man, who, with a diamond, was cutting a small strip out of a pane of glass; he accomplished his work, thrust a letter in, and disappeared behind the battlements in a moment. I secured the letter, with a beating heart, and on opening it, found it came from the Chevalier De Montreville. I was surprised and agitated; I perused this fatal letter; it was filled with the tenderest expressions of regret at my unhappy fate. His own misery he could have borne, he said, had I been happy; but to see the woman he adored treated so unworthily, was more pain than he had philosophy to support; he entreated I would write a few lines, to tell him in what manner my husband behaved to me, and if there was a possibility of his doing me either service or pleasure. I shed floods of tears over this epistle: I found, though I had suppressed, I had not subdued my affection for him; yet what would it avail to encourage a correspondence I felt was improper: I hesitated,—-I considered for some time whether I should write or not; at length I took up my pen.

"I acknowledged myself obliged for the interest he took in my happiness, but at the same time assured him any attentions of his never could do me service; on the contrary, I had reason to believe the Marquis was very jealous of him, and that possibly all his motions might be watched, I therefore besought him to return to Vienna, and leave me to my destiny. The following day, nearly at the same hour, I heard the noise at the window repeated; trembling for fear of interruption, I hastily got up, and slid my answer through, resolved at the same time to run no such risks, nor receive any more letters,—happy had it been could I have kept my resolution. The next evening I did not go to my room 'till accompanied by Margarite. I trembled every moment, lest the signal should be repeated, but I heard nothing. The next day I was peevish and dissatisfied; the Count gloomy and sullen. After dinner, as usual, he went out among the people he had at work in the wood: involuntarily I hastened to my apartment; I will own the truth, I wished, though I dreaded hearing the signal.

"Towards the close of the day the sounds at the window were repeated: scarce knowing what I did, I got on the window-seat, and secured the letter: fancying I heard footsteps coming up stairs, I too hastily stept back on the chair, which gave way, and I came with violence to the ground; at the same instant my door opened: I had received a dreadful blow on the side of my head, though it did not altogether deprive me of life, yet I was unable to speak. The Count ran to me, he snatched the fatal paper from my hand, and then rang for assistance; Margarite came up. With his help I was placed on the bed;

she bathed my head, gave me drops and water, and I was soon restored to sense and misery. He ordered the nurse out of the room, and then coming up to me, 'Wretch!' cried he, furiously, 'behold a proof of thy guilt and falsehood: I could sacrifice thee to my vengeance, but I will have more exquisite satisfaction, and complete revenge, such as shall strike thee with remorse and endless sorrow.' I besought him to hear me; I repeated what I have told you, and added it was the last I ever intended to receive. He smiled with disdain, 'Doubtless it was, and I take upon me to say it will be the last you shall ever receive from him.' He never left me the whole evening, but used every cruel malicious expression it was possible to conceive. I continued very ill and agitated that night and great part of the day.

"In the afternoon my persecutor left me, but Margarite remained; I got up, and was under the most dreadful apprehensions of what might happen; my eyes were continually turned to the window; I suffered the most agonizing terrors, when in a moment they were realized beyond whatever I could conceive of horror. A violent noise was heard on the stairs, like persons struggling, and in a moment the door was burst open; the Count and his man appeared, dragging in the Chevalier, with his mouth bound, his hands tied, and every mark of cruel treatment; I screamed, and clasped my hands, but could not speak; he made several desperate efforts to free himself—alas! to little purpose. Let me hasten over the dreadful catastrophe. 'Now,' said the cruel Count, 'you have your minion where you wished him to be, in your bed-chamber, nor shall he ever quit it alive.' I tried to speak, I threw myself on my knees, 'Spare, O spare!' was all I could say, and fell senseless, but I was soon recovered by the officious Margarite, to still greater horror. 'We have waited your recovery,' said the barbarian; 'I would not deprive you of so great a pleasure as seeing your lover's last breath expire for you.' He was then dragged into the closet opposite to where I sat, and immediately repeated stabs were given with a short dagger, by the Count, through several parts of his body; his blood flowed in torrents, and with groans he fell on his face and expired. Great God!" cried she, "here the scene never will be absent from my remembrance. I sat like one petrified; I neither spoke, shrieked, or groaned, but with my eyes fixed on the closet I appeared insensible to everything.

"The inhuman Count was not satisfied; he came and dragged me to the closet, and seated me by the side of the body, the blood flowing round me. 'Now,' said he, 'clasp your beloved Chevalier—now despise the old and cross looking Count,'—words I had once said in his hearing, long before I was married—'and now enjoy the company of him for whom you despised your husband.' Saying this, he ordered Margarite and Peter to leave the room; and finding I was still unable to speak or move, he pushed me farther into the closet, locked the door, and left me.

"How long I continued in this state, I know not; I believe I swooned, for it was daylight when I found myself on the floor, my cloaths covered with blood, and the unhappy murdered Chevalier dead before me. 'Tis impossible to describe the horror of that moment; I found myself seized with violent pains; I began to think the monster had poisoned me—the idea gave me pleasure, and I endeavoured to bear my pangs without a groan; nature however asserted its claims; I became so very ill, I could be silent no longer, I groaned, I cried aloud. Presently the door was unlocked,—the Count and Margarite appeared; they saw me in agonies; 'I am dying, barbarian; you will be satisfied, you have murdered a worthy man who never injured you—you have killed an innocent wife.' I could say no more. Margarite cried out, 'My Lord, my dear mistress is in labour, for God's sake assist her to her apartment.' He seemed to hesitate, but she urging her request, between them I was conveyed to the bed, and without any other assistance than hers delivered of a boy.

"When a little recovered, the Count entered the room, Peter with him. 'I do not design to destroy you; no, you may live a life of horror, but dead to all the world; yet your infant shall be sacrificed.' I screamed, I cried for mercy to my child and instant death to me. He paused and I expected the welcome stroke at last; 'On one condition you child may live.' 'Oh! name it,' I said; 'any conditions.' 'Remember what you say: you shall join with these two persons, in taking a solemn oath, with the sacrament, that without my permission, you will never reveal the transactions of this night and day—never mention the Chevalier's name, nor ever presume to contradict the report I shall make of your death to the world.' I shuddered, but alas! there was no alternative; he fetched a prayer-book, and making the two poor creatures kneel, we all joined in the solemn oath, and received the sacrament from his polluted hands. Methinks at this moment I tremble at the impiety of that horrid wretch.

"My child was delivered to me; Peter was ordered to assist Margarite in making a fire and getting necessaries for me. How I survived such horrors is astonishing! The curtains were drawn, and that night the body was removed, but where it was carried to, heaven only knows, for Margarite never was informed. A coffin and every necessary for a funeral was bespoke and brought home. It was given out I had died in child-bed, and therefore in decency my own women only could attend me. A figure or bundle, wrapt in a sheet, was placed in the coffin (Margarite used to think it was the Chevalier's body) and the whole ceremony took place without any one's presuming to doubt the truth. Judge what must have been my feelings, and what an excellent constitution I must have had, to bear such dreadful scenes without dying of distraction.

"In a few days I was removed to another room, and, as I heard, the fatal closet was cleaned out by Peter; the rooms locked up, and orders given no one should enter them. The Count never appeared before me until I was up, and able to walk about the room; one morning he entered, just as I had done breakfast. I forgot to tell you I had no sustenance for my poor babe, consequently it was brought up by hand. The dear infant was laying on my lap; I started with surprise and terror. 'Come, madam,' said he, with a look that made me tremble, 'come and view your former apartment.' 'God God!' I cried, 'why must I return there?' ''Tis my pleasure,' answered he; then bidding Margarite take the child, he ordered me to follow him. I tottered across the gallery, and on entering the room saw the windows barricaded with iron bars, the pictures and toilet taken away, and the whole appearance gloomy to excess. 'This is once more your bed chamber; no more Chevaliers,' said he, with horrid grin, 'can convey letters here—here you are to reside for ever.' 'Oh! kill me!' I cried, 'rather than shut me up here—death is far more desirable.' 'That is the reason I chuse you shall live, to repent every hour of your life the wrongs you have done me: and now hear me—your child you will see no more.' At these words, overcome with the unexpected shock, I dropt senseless on the floor; I was soon recalled to life. 'Your oath,' I cried; 'O, spare my child!' 'I do not mean to hurt its life; I will have it properly taken care of, but the indulgence is too great for you to enjoy. I here swear, that as long as you remain confined in this castle, and observe your oath, never to reveal the Chevalier's murder, nor undeceive the world respecting your fate, so long your boy's life is safe; I will take care of him, and one day or other, there is a possibility, you may see him again; but if you ever escape from hence, or divulge these particulars, without my permission, instant death awaits you both, for I shall have a constant spy.' To these conditions, dreadful as they were, I was compelled to subscribe.

"Margarite was ordered into confinement with me, for he found she was my friend. That night the child was conveyed away: dear and precious boy! Alas, heaven only knows whether I shall ever see him more; unconscious he has a mother, if he lives, we may remain strangers to each other! We were locked in, and for three days the Count himself brought our scanty fare; the fourth, he entered with Joseph, who was the under gardener. I was startled to see a stranger,—he appeared equally shocked at seeing me. 'Here you both are, remember your oath, madam, for on it more than one life depends. And you,' said he, turning to Joseph, 'tremble, if you dare break your solemn vow, never to let any person know this woman is alive, never to suffer her to pass from these apartments, without my permission, to hold no conversation with her, but when you bring her food, and in fine, to obey every command of mine and not hers.' 'I will obey your Lordship,' cried the man, trembling. ''Tis well, then you will preserve her life, and gain my favour. No strangers must be permitted to remain here, should chance or inclination engage any one to visit this castle. Remember this side of it must never be seen, 'tis haunted—do you understand me?' 'I do, my Lord,' answered Joseph, 'and I promise you, these apartments shall never be looked into.' 'On that depends her existence and yours.' They now quitted my room, and left me scarcely able to breathe.

"The following day the Count and Peter left the castle. Every other day Joseph came with necessaries, and Margarite was permitted to go

ELIZA PARSONS

down, accompanied by Joseph, to carry up and down water and other
conveniences. In this state I lived two years, if living it could be called,
having no other consolation than now and then hearing from my sister;
for I had so far gained upon Joseph to permit Margarite's letters, after
shewing them to him, to pass under cover to him, and as he found I
carefully preserved my secret from others, the poor fellow granted me
that indulgence. At the expiration of two years, the Count unexpectedly
made his appearance. I shrunk from his sight; he viewed me some time
with great emotion; 'I am satisfied with your conduct,' said he, 'and am
come to extend my indulgence to you.' 'O, my child!' I cried out. 'No,'
answered he, 'that cannot be granted; but you shall have permission to
live in the rooms below, and if you swear to enter the garden only at
night, the door into it shall be opened.' I joyfully agreed to this, and was
once more led to the rooms below. Peter was still with him; a bed was
brought from another room, and placed in a small parlour, also one for
Margarite. The apartments above were again locked up.

"I tried to soften the Count; he sometimes appeared moved and
affected, then again stern and cruel; he staid near a week—the day he
left the castle he came to visit me. 'Once more I leave you, but as there is
some danger that strangers may come here, I charge you, by everything
that is sacred, by your child's life and your own, should any person sleep
in this castle, that you go to the gallery or next apartments, rattle a chain
I shall leave for that purpose, groan, and make such kind of noises as
may appal those who come here, and drive them hence, under an idea of
the castle's being haunted. I have already sworn Joseph, do you promise
the same?' 'Ah! Sir,' cried I, 'why all these oaths. why all these persecutions, which must give you a world of pains, to punish an innocent
woman?' 'Because,' said he, furiously, 'because I prefer revenge to my
own quiet; because I will be feared, and make your destiny hang on my
pleasure.' I could say no more, I wept bitterly, but nothing could soften
his heart; he made me renew my vows, still threatening the life of my
child, if I failed—he told me it was well, and carefully attended. I was
compelled to acquiesce with his request, or rather command, and he
once more left me. He regularly came once in two years, for some time,
but latterly it was above four years since I had seen him, till the fatal

116

night he carried me off. 'Tis plain he was well informed of everything, and knew of Matilda's being at the castle.

"I dragged on a wretched existence, in a daily hope, that from his own words, 'There might be a possibility I should see my child again'; and that time might soften his heart, or death deprive him of all power over me. Margarite, who at first hardly brooked her confinement, grew more reconciled, and awed by the dreadful oaths we had taken, we submitted to what we could not prevent, being always in terror of being watched, and that nothing in the castle passed unnoticed. This was our situation when Matilda came. Joseph came to me late in the evening, the day she arrived at the castle, acquainting me with the circumstance, and in consequence of our vows we were obliged to conform to our orders, —he to give hints of what might happen, and myself and Margarite try to frighten her from thence—you know the consequence. Had Joseph been at home, probably she would hardly have obtained permission to sleep in the castle, but Bertha knew nothing of me, and was prevented by her fears from ever venturing through the apartments.

"The rest you know. I intended to have placed a confidence in Matilda, as far as being brought to the castle, but beyond that I dared not violate my oath. At your request, my dear brother, I consulted our good Dr Demoureiz, and he absolved me from my vows, which were compulsatory, and made under such horrid circumstances; I have therefore complied with your wishes, and now pray tell me what I can do, or what I ought to do? I cannot disclose to the world what I have related, without bringing the Count to condign punishment, for the death of the unfortunate and ever-lamented Chevalier, and perhaps may irritate him never to inform me whether my child exists or not—Alas! Every way I turn is replete with difficulties and horror."

Here the Countess stopt, leaving her auditors overcome with astonishment and terror.

"Good heavens!" said the Marquis. "I never could have supposed it possible a man should carry jealousy and revenge to such frightful guilty lengths, and the whole story appears incredible and almost impossible, that he should proceed so far, trust so many with his secret, and that you should remain such a number of years a victim to his diabolical passions, when there was always, open to you the means for escaping and appealing to your friends."

"Consider, my good brother," said she, "the difficulties, the oaths I had taken never to leave the castle without his permission, the fate of my child, the certainty that every step I took was known, otherwise I could have offered Matilda an asylum with me, but he assured me I was constantly watched, and therefore any attempts I might make to free myself, would, too probably, accelerate the events I dreaded, and my life (as I doubt not was intended, when he carried me to the wood) would have been the sacrifice. If you look back, you will observe his cunning: when he afterwards came to the castle and saw Joseph, he did not mention my name, and to be sure expected that he would have told him of my being carried away by some banditti, as he doubtless intended Joseph should believe, but the old man being silent, he supposed he was suspected as the author of the outrage, and therefore determined to put that witness out of the way—"

"What a villain!" cried Mrs Courtney, "and what a wretched life that man must have endured, with such fears of detection, and conscious of such complicated wickedness."

"It is ever the fate of villainy," said the Marchioness, "to plunge deeper into vice, and suffer tenfold the miseries they inflict, from the apprehensions of a discovery, which they know seldom fails at some time or other to overtake them, and Providence has so ordered it, that we generally see the very means they take to hide their crimes from a knowledge of the world, are productive of such events as lead to their detection. I sincerely lament the fate of the poor Chevalier—"

"Ah! sister," cried the Countess, "never shall I cease reproaching myself on that account; had I with firmness refused to receive his second letter, and avoided going to that room alone, perhaps his life, and all my subsequent miseries would have been spared: I failed in the duty I owed my husband and myself, in permitting a clandestine correspondence, although I did not intend to continue it; and one false step, you see, brought on irreparable evils and eternal remorse!"

"I will not pretend, my dear Victoria," answered the Marchioness, "to exculpate you, as entirely free from blame, but if we consider the ill-treatment you received from the Count, previous to the Chevalier's attempts to see you, and the sudden surprise of the moment, when the first letter was conveyed to you, doubtless some allowance ought to be made in your favour; and had you positively refused to receive a second, you would, 'tis possible, have escaped much bitter reflection; but the worst that can be said of you, in my opinion, is, that, in your difficult and unpleasant situation, it was an error in judgment, for I am well assured in you there was no depravity of heart."

The poor Countess was drowned in tears. "Be comforted, my dearest sister," said the Marquis, kissing her hand, whilst the ladies tenderly embraced her, "you are, thank heaven, and that good lady, restored to your friends; I will consult Dr Demouriez, as to our future proceedings, for I will do nothing rashly, and for your sake, would avoid dragging your husband's crimes into public view."

VOLUME TWO

The ladies proposed an airing to divert the Countess from dwelling on past events, and Matilda from apprehensions of future ones. The carriage was ordered, and they drove as far as Hampstead. The evening was uncommonly beautiful, and when they returned, the moon, which was in its meridian, shone with all its splendour. Just as the carriage stopt in Harley-street, Matilda, who sat next the door, saw two gentlemen pass slowly and look into the coach; she plainly perceived one of them was Mr Weimar: she met his eyes, and he turned his hastily from her; she gave a faint shriek, and hid her head behind Mrs Courtney. Her friends were alarmed, but hastened her into the house; she ran into the dining-parlour, and, in inconceivable terror, cried out, "He is come—he is come!" "Who, who?" exclaimed the Countess. "Mr Weimar," answered she; "did you not see him" "No," replied the Marchioness, "and I hope your fears deceived you." "Too sure they did not," said Matilda, "and I am convinced also that he knew me." "Fear nothing," said Mrs Courtney; "you are in the power of your friends; he must prove his right to you before he can take you from us: here are no lettres de-cachet, the laws will protect you from injury; compose yourself, therefore, my dear girl—in England no violence can be offered to you in any shape."

This kind and seasonable assurance calmed the terrors of the trembling Matilda; but when she retired to rest, and reflected on her cruel destiny, she shed floods of tears, and passed a sleepless night.

The following day was appointed for their return to Mrs Courtney's villa, to spend a week or two, previous to the preparations for the birthday, after which the whole party, with Lord Delby, proposed going to Scarborough.

The Countess and Matilda bore evident marks in their features and pale looks, of the uneasy state of their minds; their amiable friends fought to raise their spirits, and they felt too much gratitude to their kindness not to make the effort, though their smiles were clouded with sorrow.

They had a pleasant excursion to Mrs Courtney's house, and its delightful situation, with the cheerful hospitality of its charming owner, could not fail of making those happy who had the honour of her friendship.

The Countess, who was known in public only as Madame Le Roche, and by which name her friends always called her in company, found in the sympathy of Matilda more consolation than the conversation of strangers or any amusements could afford her; they generally contrived to steal from company and ramble in the gardens, relating past sorrows, and mutually endeavoring to inspire each other with hopes of happier days, though despairing of any to themselves.

A few days after they had been in the country, the Marquis received another packet from the Count De Bouville, enclosing a letter from Madame de Clermont, to Matilda. They learnt, with much sorrow, that the Countess died three days after the Count's first letter; that their affliction had been very great, and preyed much on the spirits of her affectionate daughter, in consequence of which she had been advised to visit Aix, and from thence to the Spa; their departure was fixed for the end of that week—Madame De Nancy and her amiable sister De Bancre were going with them. Madame De Clermont requested the correspondence of Matilda, and charged her to take great care of her brother. This charge Matilda did not comprehend, until the Marquis congratulated the party on the agreeable addition they might daily expect from the company of the Count De Bouville, who had written to him, that his sister having a party of her own going to Aix, he had no inclination to visit that place, and therefore should gratify his wishes, by returning to England for a few months, and hoped to enjoy additional satisfaction by the pleasures of the society.

Every one appeared gratified by this information, except Matilda. She felt her heart flutter at his name; she was convinced he was more interesting to her than any other man, and that in her circumstances she ought not to indulge a preference which never could be returned. Ah thought she, where is the sorrows that can equal mine? Scarce a wretch that breaths but has some connexion, some relation to own them and sympathize in their troubles, I alone am destitute of family, or fortune; I can carry only disgrace to the arms of a husband, and am therefore an outcast—a being without any natural ties, and must despair of procuring any other protection but what charity and benevolence affords me! She felt the full force of these melancholy reflections, and it threw such a sad impression on her features that everyone was touched with compassion, though they knew not the cause, and sought by kindness and attention to render her more cheerful.

Within three days after this letter, which had occasioned so much pleasure and pain to different parties, the Marquis, by a note, was informed of the Count's arrival in London. Mrs Courtney entreated the honour of his company, and Lord Delby offered to accompany the Marquis and escort him to their friends. This offer was too obliging to be declined; they set off that evening, and the following morning returned with the Count.

Matilda spent the intermediate time in laying down rules for her behaviour. She still suffered under the apprehensions that Mr Weimar had pursued, and would occasion more trouble to her; she therefore resolved to avail herself of that fear, keep as much in her apartment as possible, and avoid mixing in all the little pleasurable parties where the Count might make one.

The company received the Count with the politest attention. His amiable person, his polished manners, and enchanting vivacity, could not fail of engaging the esteem of every one who had taste and discernment. After he had been introduced to the lady of the mansion, to the Marchioness, and to Madame Le Roche, whom he knew not, he advanced to Matilda; she trembled; he took her hand, and bowing on it, "I am charged," said he, "with a thousand expressions of kindness and friendship from my sister and Mademoiselle De Bancre, to the charming Miss Matilda; but you must take them upon trust now, and permit me to express my own happiness in seeing my lovely friend well, and situated in the midst of a society so delightful as this." She attempted to speak, her voice, her powers failed her; "Your Lordship does me honour," was all she could utter. The conversation became general and sprightly, but she had no share in it; the day appeared uncommonly long, and she rejoiced when night came, that she could escape to her apartment and enjoy her own reflections.

The Count, who had observed her emotions, her silence and melancholy air, felt himself much concerned for the unfortunate girl; he thought her more lovely, more interesting than ever: the soft melancholy which pervaded her fine features could not fail of touching a susceptible heart; and the Count soon found the tender interest he had formerly taken in Matilda's misfortunes, revive with more solicitude than ever. He seized an opportunity the following morning, to enquire some particulars respecting the cause of her distress. The Marquis told him of her alarm on seeing a gentleman she believed to be, and possibly, said he, might be, Mr Weimar. "I am really," added he, "unhappy about this charming young woman; we all love her exceedingly; beauty is her least merit; she has every amiable quality, joined to an excellent understanding, that can adorn a human being; I could not love my own child better; but she has too much sensibility to be happy—she feels her dependent and unprotected state too keenly,—it preys upon her mind and injures her health. Consulting with the Marchioness on this subject last night, I intend this day to write, and order a deed to be drawn, agreeable to our design of making her independent, at the same time, I wish not to burthen her feelings with too high a sense of obligation, by settling any very large sum on her: four hundred a year, English money, paid her quarterly, will enable her to live genteelly, should she ever wish to separate from us, and will be a handsome provision for pocket expences, if she does us the favour of continuing under our protection."

"Will you permit me," said the Count, eagerly, "to add another two hundred to her income?" "Indeed I will not," replied the Marquis; "I think myself as much the guardian of Matilda's honour and delicacy as of her person: no young man shall boast any claims upon her, nor shall she be humbled by receiving favours, which, if known, might subject her to censure—say no more, my dear Count," added he, observing he was about to reply, "the Marchioness will not have her protégée under any obligations but to herself." "Shall I be sincere with you, Marquis?" demanded the Count. "Doubtless, my Lord, you may, and assure your-self of my secrecy, if necessary." "Well then," resumed the Count, "I confess to you, that with the Marchioness's protégée, as you call her, I should be the happiest of men: I feel, and acknowledge, that she has more than beauty—she has a soul; she has those virtues, those amiable qualities, which must render any man happy: but, my dear Marquis, her birth—the scandalous stories promulgated of her in Paris: ah! what can do away these objections which rise hourly before me, and bar me from happiness and Matilda?"

"Since you do me the honour of your confidence, my Lord, 'tis my duty to be candid and explicit. That I entertain the highest opinion of Matilda, is most certain that I think whoever the man is, who is honoured with her hand, will be a happy one, I also acknowledge; but, my Lord, family and society have great claims upon us; we ought not to injure the one, nor disregard the other. Could you bear to see your wife treated with contempt, as one whom nobody knew, as one who had no claims to distinction, but what your very great friends might allow her? Could you support the idea that she, whose genuine merit might entitle her to the first society, should be refused admittance among such, as in real worth she very far surpassed? No; I know you would feel such a degradation most painfully; and, though young men, in the moment of passion, think they could sacrifice everything to the object of it; yet, believe me, passion is but short-lived, and though your wife may yet retain your love and esteem, you will regret the loss of society—you will feel the insults offered to your wife, and you will both be unhappy."

"Ah! my dear Marquis," cried the Count, "say no more. How happy are Englishmen! Free from all those false prejudices, they can confer honour on whom they please, and the want of noble birth is no degradation where merit and character deserve esteem; but we are the victims to false notions, and from thence originates all that levity and vice for which we are censured by other nations." He walked away with a melancholy air: the Marquis felt for him, but national honour was in his opinion of more consequence than the gratification of a private individual, how great soever the merit of the object.

The Count walked into the garden, his arms folded, his mind distrest, unknowing what he should, what he ought to do. Turning into a small alcove, he beheld Matilda, her head reclining on one hand, whilst with the other she dried the tears which fell on her face: they both started; she rose from her seat; he advanced, prevented her going and seated himself by her. Both were silent for moment, at length Matilda, making a second effort to rise, exclaimed in a faint voice, "Bless me! I dare say I have made the family wait breakfast," and attempted to pass him. "Stay, Miss Weimar, I beseech you; tell me why I behold you a prey to sorrow and grief?" "Because, Sir," said she, withdrawing her hand, "I am the child of sorrow; I never knew another parent; poor, forlorn, proscribed, and dependent, I never can belong to any one." She snatched her hand, which he endeavoured to retain, from him, and flew like lightning towards the house; the Count followed, full of admiration and grief. He entered the breakfast-room; everyone was seated, and rallied him on his passion for morning rambles: his natural vivacity returned, and he tried to make himself agreeable and pleasant.

They had scarce finished breakfast when the Marquis received a letter from the French Ambassador, requesting he might see him in town immediately, on an important affair. The Marquis was surprised, but gave orders for his horses to be ready. The Countess trembled, Matilda was terrified; each thought herself concerned, and when the Marquis quitted the house, retired together.

"Ah!" cried the Countess, the Count has discovered me!" "No, no, madam," replied Matilda, "'tis I am discovered and shall be torn from you." Both burst into tears, equally for herself and friend.

The Marchioness, who saw him depart, now entered the room; "As I supposed," said he, "you retired to frighten each other, but that I shall not allow, so ladies, if you please, throw on your cloaks; I have made up two parties this morning for an airing: in my coach goes Lord Delby, the Count, my sister, and Miss Matilda; I accompany Mrs Courtney, in her chariot; so pray hasten directly, the carriages wait."

She withdrew on saying these words, and left them no power to frame excuses, and consequently they were obliged to follow, though with aching hearts.

They were disposed of according to the Marchioness's arrangements, but for some minutes after the carriage proceeded all were silent. Lord Delby first spoke, and regretted the party did not seem to accord with the wishes of the ladies, if he might judge from their averted looks. "Indeed, my Lord," replied the Countess, "you do me particular injustice; I entertain the highest respect for every person here; to your Lordship I owe obligations never to be forgotten; I infinitely esteem the Count, as a friend, and this young lady I love with the affection of a sister. I have been a little agitated by the sudden departure of the Marquis, and my uneasiness has communicated itself to my friend; we beg your pardon, and will endeavor to be better company." After this the conversation became more general and amusing.

The Marquis proceeded to town, and instantly waited on the Ambassador. "I am sorry, my dear Lord," said his Excellency "to have broken in upon your retirement, and must mention the visit I received yesterday as my apology. A German gentleman, who sent in his name as Mr Weimar, requested permission to wait on me; he was consequently admitted: he entered upon a long story of an orphan he had preserved from perishing, of a paper fastened to the child, deputing him the guardian of it 'till claimed by its parents; and in short, that despairing, from the number of years past, that those parents had any existence, he resolved to marry the young lady, that he might provide for her without injury to her reputation; that, from what motives he knew not, she had been induced to fly from his house, seducing a servant of his to go with her; and she was now detained from him by you, notwithstanding he had a lettre de-cachet, which he produced, commanding you to give her up; consequently, by virtue of that order, he requested I would compel you to deliver the young lady to his care. Now, my dear Marquis, I am prepared to hear you on the subject, for it is a delicate affair, and I am convinced you would be sorry it should be noised abroad." "No otherwise, Sir," replied the Marquis, "than as it might wound the young lady's delicacy to be publicly talked of. I am obliged to your Excellency for your communications, and must trespass on your patience to elucidate the affair properly." He then recapitulated the whole of Matilda's story, concealing everything relative to the Countess at that time; and having deduced it down to the present period, he besought his Excellency to protect an amiable young woman, under the most unfortunate circumstances.

"I am really," he replied, "much interested for her, and perfectly disposed to comply with your wishes, but the whole affair is replete with so many extraordinary circumstances, that I think we had best consult the German Ambassador before anything can be determined on."

The carriage was ordered, and his Excellency took the Marquis with him. They most fortunately found the German Minister at home, and after some deliberation it was settled Matilda should remain under the protection of the Marquis for one year, he to be answerable for her; during that interval advertisements should be sent to the different kingdoms, in quest of her parents; and if in the course of one twelvemonth no such persons appeared, Mr Weimar was the natural protector of the young lady, but could not oblige her to marry him—neither could he prevent her retiring to a convent, though she might be accountable to him for her choice of such a retirement.

The Marquis was obliged to be contented with this decision, and returning with the Ambassador, he said, "I shall in all probability have to trouble you again soon, on a still more extraordinary affair, and relative to one more dear and nearer to me than this young lady." "Upon my word, Marquis," replied the Minister, smiling, "you are quite a knight-errant, to protect distressed damsels." "A very honourable employment," answered the other, in the same tone; "but though these are not the days of romance, yet I have met with such extraordinary incidents lately as carry much the face of the wonderful stories we have heard of former times but as the development of this business will be attended with serious consequences I must consider a few days before I make the discovery." "Very well, said his Excellency; "you have excited my curiosity, and, if I am not too old to join in a Quixote-like expedition, behold me ready to assist in the defence of the fair." The Marquis smiled, thanked him, and declining an invitation to dine at his house, got into his own carriage, and drove back with all speed, rightly conceiving everyone would entertain uneasy conjectures.

The party were but just returned from a long morning's drive when the Marquis arrived; every one met him with anxiety in their looks—he accosted them with a smiling countenance; "A truce to interrogatories at present," said he, "I have good news for all, but I am really faint for want of refreshment; order something for me; and then I shall give an account of my proceedings."

Every one flew to the bells, and in a moment he had chocolate, jellies, wine, and biscuits set before him.

"Ah!" said he, laughing, "nothing like giving a little spur to curiosity, I see; this is an excellent lesson for me how to be well served."

When he had taken his repast, which he maliciously prolonged 'till the Marchioness in a pet rang the bell, and declared he should eat no more, the things taken away, and the servants withdrawn, "Now listen, ladies, and thank me for having procured, in the person of our gallant Ambassador, a Don Quixote, ready to fight in your defence." He then, in a more serious tone, repeated the particulars which have been already related.

Poor Matilda felt but a gleam of satisfaction; "A twelvemonth," cried she. "A twelvemonth," repeated Mrs Courtney; "why, do you consider, my dear girl, how many strange events may happen in that time?" "Yes," answered she, sighing, "I consider and hope death will free me from his power long before that period expires."

The Count de Bouville rose and left the room to conceal his emotions.

"I will not forgive you, my dear child," said the Marchioness "if you indulge such desponding ideas; depend upon it happier days await you —trust in Providence, and rejoice you are now free from anxiety: equally under the protection of the ambassadors and the Marquis, Mr Weimar will not dare to molest you."

The ladies all congratulated Matilda; and, the Marchioness taking her hand, "Come with me into the garden, I must chide you, but I will not do it publicly, though you deserve it." She led her to a little temple, at one end of the garden, and when seated she said to the still silent Matilda, "You do not consider the advantages we have gained." "O, my dear madam," cried the other, interrupting her, "how sensible I am of that kind we have gained!" "Well, well," resumed the Marchioness, "hear me out. We can now take public methods to enquire, if there yet exists a being who has any claim to you, without fear of Mr Weimar; a twelve-month may make great alterations in his sentiments; should it appear you have no particular relations, he has no legal claim upon you, but from his expenditure for your maintenance and cloaths—let him bring in his bill, he shall be paid to the uttermost farthing; you are my adopted child; consider yourself as such, and dare not refuse that trifle for your future expences;—if you utter any ohs! or ahs! if you ever talk of obliga-tions, I will never pardon you: to be cheerful and happy is the only return you can make or I accept." She then placed the deed mentioned by the Marquis, with a fifty-pound note, upon the lap of the astonished Matilda, and hastened away to the house.

It was some moments before she recovered herself enough to examine the papers. The contents overwhelmed her with gratitude; she burst into a flood of tears, the papers in her hand, when unexpectedly the Count stood before her. "Good heavens!" he cried, "what means this distress, these tears?" "O, my Lord," answered she, "they are tears of sensibility and gratitude." "I rejoice to hear it," replied the Count, "heaven forbid they should ever flow from any other cause." He seated himself by her, she dried her eyes, and put the papers in her pocket. "I congratulate you, madam," resumed he, "on the happy turn in your affairs, which the Marquis has informed me of." "You know me then for an unhappy deserted orphan?" said she, blushing and mortified. "I know you," replied he, eagerly, "for the most amiable of your sex; no adventitious advantages of birth or fortune can add to those claims your own merit gives you to universal esteem." "Ah, my Lord," said she, "to generous spirits like yours and this family's, misfortunes are a recommendation to kindness and attention, but with the generality of mankind I have not to learn it must be otherwise. Stranger as I am to the manners and customs of the world, I am sensible birth and fortune have superior advantages, and that without them, though with liberal minds we may obtain compassion, we can never hope for consideration or respect." "Pardon me, madam," replied the Count, "if I presume to say you judge erroneously; she who with merit, with good sense, delicacy, and refined sentiments can command respect, is a thousand times superior to those whose inferiority of mind disgraces a rank which the other would ennoble." "You are very kind, Sir," said Matilda, rising, and unable to support a conversation which she feared might grow too interesting for her peace; "you are truly friendly, in endeavouring to reconcile me to myself; and I have no way of deserving your favourable judgment, but by constantly remembering what I am, that I may at least preserve my humility." She courtesied and walked fast towards the house, and to the apartment of the Countess.

That lady was alone, her head resting on her hand, and seemed buried in thought. Matilda would have withdrawn, the other entreated her return; "Come in, my dear girl," said she, "my own thoughts are the worst company you could leave me in at present." "I come to tell you, my dear madam," cried her young friend, "that my heart is bursting with gratitude: the Marchioness will not hear me, but I must have vent for my feelings, or I shall be opprest to death." She burst into tears. "My dear April girl," said the Countess, "no more of those showers,—you have too much sensibility; I know what you want to tell me, therefore spare yourself the trouble, and let me acquaint you, that I am indebted to my generous brother, for a settlement of treble the value of what he has given you, yet I make no fuss about the matter." "But, dear madam," cried Matilda, "sure there is great difference in our situations, you have a natural claim—" "A natural claim," repeated the Countess; "the best claim to a generous mind, is being unfortunate with merit that deserves a better fate. I think little of those favours which are bestowed from claims of affinity only; since family pride, the censure of the world, and many causes, may unlock a heart to support their own consequence in their connexions, but the truly benificent mind looks upon every child of sorrow as their relation, and entitled to their assistance; but when beauty and virtue suffer, from whatsoever cause, believe me, dear Matilda, they receive a superior gratification that have the power of relieving sorrows, than the receiver can in accepting the favours." "I believe, my dear madam," replied Matilda, her heart warmed by the idea, "I believe you are right; for if there is a human being I could envy, it would be the one who can raise the desponding heart to hope and peace."

"With that conviction," resumed the Countess, "feel as if you conferred a favour, without the oppressive notion of having received one; and now pray listen to me. My brother and sister hourly importune me to prosecute the Count: you know my objections,—God only knows whether I have a child living or not—the doubt gives me a thousand pangs; as to the murder of the poor Chevalier, Peter only was a witness beside myself, and he is a creature of the Count's; then to accuse one's husband, what an indelible reproach! I never can submit to it: tell me, advise me, dear girl, what I must do?" "Impossible madam," replied she; "I am incompetent to advise,—your own good sense, and the opinion of your friends, are more capable of it than one so little conversant in the world as I am." "Well," resumed the Countess, "I will be guided by Lord Delby and Mrs Courtney; my own relations are too warmly interested in my favour to give an impartial opinion:—but pray, my dear, what do you think of our Count, is not he a charming youth?"

A question so mal-a-propos, when poor Matilda's heart bore testimony to his merit, threw her into the greatest confusion, she was unable to speak.

The Countess observed her emotion, but was too delicate to notice it; she therefore added, "'Tis a needless question; I see your sentiments correspond with mine; but your spirits are low, child—in truth mine are not high, so let us seek for better company." She arose, and taking Matilda's passive hand, led her to the drawing room, where the company was assembled.

Matilda could not see her benefactors without being visibly affected, which the Marchioness observing, "Come, ladies," said she, "give me your votes, I am collecting them for a party to Windsor tomorrow." "O, doubtless you may command ours," replied the Countess; "novelty has always its charms for us females." "Very well," said the Marquis, "then it's a settled business."

The excursion to Windsor, and several other places, in the fortnight they staid at Mrs Courtney's, jumbled the Count and Matilda so frequently together, and he had so many opportunities of admiring her strong understanding and polished manners, that his affection was insensibly engaged beyond all power of resistance, and he determined to brave the censures of the world, and marry her, if he could obtain her heart. From the moment this resolution took place, he treated her with that insinuating tenderness in his voice and manners, which seldom fails of communicating the infection to a susceptible mind. Matilda's feelings alarmed her; she was conscious of the impropriety of indulging them, and felt the necessity of avoiding the Count as much as possible. He quickly observed the alteration in her behaviour, and was determined to come to an immediate explanation; justly conceiving nothing could be more wounding to a delicate mind than suspence under such circumstances.

She so carefully shunned him, that it was not easy to find her alone; but the morning when it was intended to return in the evening to London, chance afforded him an opportunity. The Marchioness, Matilda, and the Count were in the garden; the Marquis came to them and requested to speak a few words to his Lady; she disengaged her arm from her companion, and went with him to the house. Matilda turned with an intention to follow; the Count took her hand, "Let me entreat you, madam, to pursue your walk; I wish to speak a few words, on an affair of consequence, that will not detain you long from your friends." She trembled, and without speaking, suffered him to conduct her to an alcove at the bottom of the garden. They were both seated for a minute before he could assume courage to speak, at length, "I believe from the first hour I had the happiness of being introduced to you, my admiration was very visible, but it was that admiration which a beautiful person naturally inspires, I knew not then it was your least perfection. Your story, which the Marquis related, convinced me you had every virtue which should adorn your sex, joined with a courage and perseverance, through difficulties which might do honour even to ours. Since I have been admitted a visitor in this house, I have been confirmed in the exalted opinion I entertained of your superiority to most women, and under this conviction I may justly fear you will condemn my presumption, in offering myself and fortune to your disposal."

"How, my Lord," cried Matilda, recovering from her confusion, and interrupting him, "do you consider who and what I am? "Yes, madam," replied he, "I have already told you, I think you one of the most perfect of your sex, and as to any other consideration 'tis beneath my notice: if you will deign to accept of me, it shall be the study of my life to make you amends for the injustice of fortune, who blindly bestows her favours on the unworthy." "You will pardon me, my Lord," said she, "for interrupting you a second time, but I cannot suffer you to proceed in error; I entreat you, therefore to hear me with patience, and believe that the sentiments I express are the genuine feelings of my heart, from which no persuasions, no temptations shall ever make me depart. I acknowledge, with a grateful mind, the honour you offer me is far beyond any expectations I can ever form in life, and such as affords me both pride and pleasure, that I am not deemed unworthy your esteem. At the same time, although you can generously resolve to forego the respect you owe to yourself and family, my duty to myself obliges me to remember it: without family and connexions, without even a name—perhaps the offspring of poor, or still worse, of infamous parents, brought up and supported by charity; shall I intrude myself into a noble family, contaminate its lustre, reflect indelible disgrace on the author of my undeserved elevation, and live despised and reproached, as the artful creature who had taken advantage of your generosity and compassion? No, my Lord, permit me to say on such terms I never would condescend to be the wife of a prince. I shrink at my own littleness; I am in a state of obligation for my support, but I never will incur my own contempt, by deserving it from others. My mind is indeed, I hope, superior to my situation: I will preserve a rectitude of principles under every evil that may befall me; those principles impel me to avow, with the greatest solemnity in the face of heaven, that under the disgraceful circumstances in which my fate seems enveloped, I never will be yours." "Hold, hold, madam," cried the Count, endeavouring to interrupt her, "great God! What have you vowed!" "What duty to myself and you required of me," said she; "and now, my Lord, let this subject never be renewed. If it can afford you any consolation," added she, softened by the disorder and distress of his appearance, "be assured, my Lord, that as I never can be yours, I never will be another's; and if my happiness is as dear to you as yours will ever be to me, you will from this moment cease to think of me but as an unfortunate girl, deprived of all power to return obligations, and therefore with too much pride and spirit to receive them, but from this worthy family, where I conceive it no disgrace to hold myself dependent."

As she ended these words she rose. "Stop one moment, madam," exclaimed the Count; "unless you would drive me to madness, afford me one gleam of hope, distant as it may be: your cruel vow precludes me from bliss, yet tell me, too lovely Matilda, that you do not hate me, that if—"

"Ah! Sir," said she, involuntarily, "hate you! Heaven is my witness, that did my birth and rank equal yours, it would be my glory to accept your hand; but as there exists not a possibility of that, I beseech you to spare me and yourself unnecessary pain; from this instant determine to avoid me, and I will esteem you as the most exalted of men."

Without giving him time to reply, she darted like lightning towards the house, leaving him overwhelmed with admiration, grief, and despair.

"What are the advantages of birth and rank," cried he, "which this sweet girl does not possess? A dignity of sentiment, a rectitude of heart; —how greatly superior to that wretch Fontelle, whose malicious stories have so much injured her reputation, and whose birth and fortune only render her the more despicable; as mine must be to me of no value, when considered as bars to happiness and Matilda."

He walked slowly to the house and met the Marquis. "Dear Count," said he, "what have you done or said to my amiable protégée; I met her running upstairs, out of breath, and tears trembling in her eyes?" The Count, without the least reserve, repeated the preceding conversation. "And did you really make such an offer," cried he, "and did she refuse it?" "'Tis very true," replied the Count. "Why then," said the Marquis, "you are two of the noblest creatures under heaven; that you, my worthy friend, should step beyond the prejudices of your country—that you should resolve to brave the censure, the malevolent whispers and contemptuous neglect of your equals, and support the insolent derision of your inferiors, in favour of a young woman under such peculiarly distressing circumstances, excites my wonder and admiration but I scarce know any words that can do justice to my sentiments, when I reflect that this very young woman, without friends or fortune, from a sense of rectitude, and a loftiness of sentiment which would do honour to the highest rank, could peremptorily refuse a situation and prospects so brilliant—do violence to her own heart, and prefer a dependence her soul is much superior to, rather than incur self-reproach for your degradation. Indeed, my Lord, I know not any language sufficiently expressive of my feelings: you must admire her more than ever." "Doubt not," answered the Count, in a melancholy tone, "of my more than admiration—my adoration; but, alas! she is inflexible—she has sworn never to be mine—she has charged me to see her, to think of her, no more." "Do her justice my Lord and obey her; prove your esteem for such an extraordinary exertion of virtue and prudence, imitate an example so deserving praise, and be assured the trial, however severe at present, will afford you satisfaction hereafter, in subduing love, though your highest esteem she has a right to challenge." "Say no more, Marquis," cried the Count; "I must cease to think of her before I can cease to love, for this day has riveted my chains more firmly than ever. I will not however be an inmate of your house; though I cannot relinquish the charms of her society altogether, yet I promise you I will indulge in no more dangerous tête-à-têtes but I must see her sometimes." "Ah! Count," said the Marquis shaking his head. "Trust my honour and discretion," replied he, to his significant looks; "you may, for that angelic girl will never put them to the proof."

They proceeded to the house, and the carriages drawing up, the party was collected together. Matilda contrived to accompany the Marquis, his Lady, and Mrs Courtney. The two latter kept up a sprightly conversation with the Marquis, and but once or twice broke in upon her reveries; yet she appeared easy and cheerful; in truth, the delight of being dear to the amiable Count, and a consciousness of having performed her duty, gave that peace and serenity to her mind which never fails of communicating itself to the countenance.

O n their arrival in Harley-street the party separated, and the Count was compelled to accept an invitation from Lord Delby, to reside with him. "The Marquis," said his Lordship, "has his family party, but I am alone, and therefore you will do me particular honour and pleasure in complying with my wishes."

As the Count could not reside with the Marquis, this was certainly the next best situation, for his Lordship was himself too fond of the "family party" to be long absent from them; he therefore gladly accompanied him to Cavendish-square.

They had been now near a fortnight in town, enjoying its variety of amusements, and preparing for their journey to Scarborough, which was now to take place in four days. The birthday being arrived, the Marquis, his Lady, and the Count proposed paying their compliments at court, with Lord Delby: the Count had been previously presented. The Countess (still known even by the Count only as Madame Le Roche) Mrs Courtney, and Matilda, contented themselves with attending the ball, at night, in the Lord Chamberlain's box. They were accordingly accommodated with an excellent situation, and were extremely charmed with the beauty and splendour of the British court.

Matilda's eyes were so intently fixed on the Royal Family, she had scarce thought of looking round her, until some audible whispers in French reached her ear; turning her head quickly, her eyes met those of Mademoiselle De Fontelle. A stranger to the malice of that young lady, she bowed with a smile, being rather too distant to speak; the lady gave her a look of contempt, and speaking low to the person next her; before Matilda could recover from her surprise and confusion, she observed three or four persons look full at her, with scorn and disdain strongly marked in their features. Shocked beyond measure at this to her unaccountable behaviour, she turned sick and faint, was obliged to have recourse to her salts, and heard a laughing whisper on one side of her, whilst the Countess on the other was eagerly enquiring the cause of her illness. Her salts, and natural dignity of mind soon enabled her to recover. She evaded the curiosity of her friend by complaining of the heat, and declaring herself better. She then turned her head towards Fontelle and her companions; she viewed them with a steady air of the highest contempt and indifference, 'till even the eyes of that malicious girl fell under hers, and she was evidently confused. Matilda then returned to the amusements below her, and, though her mind was not easy, she appeared to enjoy uncommon satisfaction.

When the Royal Family had withdrawn, and they were about to quit their seats, they perceived Lord Delby and the Count making way to assist them in getting out. The latter had no eyes but for Matilda, 'till a sudden exclamation, and his name, caught his ear in the moment he had presented his hand to her; quickly turning, he saw Mademoiselle De Fontelle and her aunt Madame Le Brune. Surprised and vexed, he darted at them a look of scorn, and with an air of the highest respect and attention, assisted Matilda into the room, joined her friends, and they were safely conveyed through the croud to their carriage,—Lord Delby and himself following in theirs.

When they alighted in Harley-street, Matilda, who had suppressed her feelings in the ballroom, and had been likewise deeply affected by the Count's attentions, scarcely entered the drawing room before she fainted: everyone was alarmed, but the Count as distracted; his behaviour discovered the secrets of his heart to all the company, and when she recovered, she saw him on his knees, holding one of her hands, whilst his air of distraction was but too expressive of his feelings; she withdrew her hand, and he arose; she apologised to the company, and imputed her disorder to the heat of the room, and the sudden chill she felt in getting out of the carriage. Her friends, glad to see her recovered, enquired no further, but the Count drew the Marquis out of the room, and in much agitation, cried out, "That persecuting fiend, in a female form, is the cause of her illness." "Who do you mean?" demanded the Marquis. "Who should I mean," answered he, warmly, "but that malicious Fontelle; I saw her not far from Matilda, and I dare say she insulted her; but, by heavens! if she propagates her infamous falsehoods here, she shall repent it, however she may trust to my honour."

The Marquis was a little surprised at this sally, but without appearing to observe it, said, "You know, Count, we shall leave town three days hence, and consequently be out of her malice. I wonder what brought her to England." "Spite and envy," replied he; "but does the amiable girl know how much Mademoiselle De Fontelle is her enemy?" "No, certainly," answered the Marquis; "you do not suppose we would wound her feelings, by repeating the disagreeable reports spread among our acquaintance at Paris." "I am glad of it," said the Count, "yet I cannot but think the other affronted her." "We shall know tomorrow, but let us return and eat our supper now."

They went down to the supper-room, and were much pleased in beholding Matilda cheerful and perfectly well.

When the company separated, and she was retired to her apartment, she gave way to her own reflections; she could not otherwise account for the impertinence of Mademoiselle De Fontelle, but by supposing she was acquainted with her birth; "Ah!" said she, "I doubt not but Mr Weimar published it at Paris, from motives of revenge and she, who as a relation to the Marchioness, received a thousand civilities, is now despised as an imposter; an orphan, and a dependent on charity; nay, even my benefactors may suffer in the opinion of their friends for introducing me! Good heavens!" cried she, "why should I continue in the world—why assume a character and appearance I have no pretensions to? What blameable pride, what meanness, in accepting gifts which draw upon me contempt and derision—I will no longer support it."

Tormented all night by the distress of her situation, she arose unrefreshed, pale, feeble and agitated.

The Marchioness, alarmed at her appearance, insisted upon sending for a physician; the Marquis was going to pull the bell. "Stay, my dear friends," cried she, "I beseech you; 'tis my mind, not my body, that is disordered, and you only have the power to heal it." "Speak your wishes, my dear child," said the Marchioness; "be assured, if in our power, you may command the grant of them." "On that promise, my dearest benefactress, your poor Matilda founds her hopes of peace." She then repeated the affronts of the preceding evening, and her own conjectures upon it. "I am humbled, my dearest madam, as all false pretenders ought to be," added she: "I can no longer support the upbraidings of my heart; a false pride, a despicable vanity induced me to lay hold of your sentiments in my favour, which, after the discovery of my original meanness, I ought to have blushed at your condescension, and sought some humble situation, or retired to a convent, where, unknowing and unknown, I might have pursued the lowly path Providence seems to have pointed out for me. I have been punished for my presumption and duplicity—it has made me look into myself; doubtless, out of this family, every one beholds me with the scorn and contempt I have justly incurred from Mademoiselle De Fontelle, and all who know my doubtful origin. O, my beloved friends," cried she, wringing her hands, tears running down her cheeks, "save me from future insults, save me from self-reproach! complete your generosity and goodness, and let me retire to a convent. My poor endeavours to amuse you as a companion are no longer necessary; the Countess is restored to you, and I have only been a source of vexation and trouble ever since the hour you first condescended to receive me;—a convent is the only asylum I ought to wish for, and there only I can find rest." Here she stopt, overwhelmed with the most painful emotions.

The Marquis was affected, the Marchioness drowned in tears. "My dear, but too susceptible girl," said she, when able to speak, "why will you thus unnecessarily torment yourself; what is Fontelle and her opinions to us? We are going to Scarborough; you have friends who will protect you from every insult,—who will treat you with increased respect, from a conviction that your mind is superior to all the advantages which birth and fortune has given to Mademoiselle De Fontelle, or a thousand such: besides, depend upon my assertions,—you sprung not from humble or dishonest parents, the virtues you possess are hereditary ones, doubt it not, my dear Matilda; if nobleness of birth can add any lustre to qualities like yours, you will one day possess that advantage."

'Tis impossible to express the agitations of Matilda, on hearing such kind and consoling sentiments; but her resolution to retire from the world was unconquerable; she found her heart too tenderly attached to the Count she knew the impossibility that she should ever be his; she was convinced her story was known, her friends had not attempted to deny it; in whatever public place she might visit, it was very possible to meet persons who had heard it, and she might be exposed to similar insults, which her spirit could not brook.

The Marquis and his lady made use of persuasions, arguments, and even reproaches, but she had so much resolution and fortitude, when once she had formed a design, approved by her judgment, as could not be easily shaken; and though her heart was wounded with sorrow, and her mind impressed with grief, in being obliged to resist the kindness of her friends, yet she still persevered.

"Well, Matilda," said the Marchioness, in a reproachful tone, "since you are inflexible to our wishes, I must insist upon your going with me to Mrs Courtney's: what will she, what will my sister think, but that I have treated you ill, and you can no longer remain with one you have ceased to love."

"Kill me not," cried she, in an agony, "with such reproaches; let me fly to the Countess and disclose my reasons—ah! surely she will do more justice to my heart: oh! madam, that you could see it—that you could read the love, the admiration, and respect indelibly imprinted there, with your image, never, never to be erased whilst it beats within my bosom."

Overcome with these sensations, she wept aloud; the Marchioness embraced and soothed her.

The carriage was ordered, and they drove to Mrs Courtney's, the Marquis setting them down, and going on to Lord Delby's.

It is needless to repeat what passed at Mrs Courtney's, since it was only a repetition of every argument and persuasion which her protectors had before used in vain. Nothing could shake her resolution; and all the favour they could obtain was to permit Louison and Antoine to accompany her to Boulogne, and remain in a convent there, 'till her friends returned to France, and the twelvemonth expired Mr Weimar had allowed her to remain under the care of the Marquis.

Whilst every countenance spoke pity, grief, and admiration, the gentlemen suddenly entered the room, the Count with an air of wildness and distress. The moment Matilda saw him she trembled violently, and could with difficulty keep her seat. "Ah! madam," said he, "what is it I hear—is it possible you mean to abandon your friends, to distress the most affectionate hearts in the world, to give up society, and, from romantic notions, bury yourself in a convent? Hear me thus publicly," cried he, throwing himself at her feet, with a frantic look, "hear me avow myself your lover, your protector, and if you will condescend to accept of me, your husband; yes, that is the enviable distinction I aspire

141

to; plead for me, my friends,—soften the obdurate heart that would consign me to everlasting misery. Oh! Matilda, cruel, unfeeling girl, has a proud and unrelenting spirit subdued every tender and compassionate sentiment.—has neither love nor friendship any claims upon your heart?" His emotions were violent.

The ladies, 'till now strangers to his sentiments, sat mute with wonder.

Matilda had covered her face with her handkerchief; when he stopt she withdrew it; it was wet with tears: he snatched it from her trembling hand, kissed it, and thrust it into his bosom. "I beseech you, Sir, to rise," said she, when able to speak, "this posture is unbecoming of yourself and me. The resolution I have formed is such as my reason approves, and my particular circumstances call upon me to adopt; I ought to have done it long ago, and blush at my own folly in delaying it." "But, good God! madam," interrupted the Count, "can the ridiculous behaviour or unjust prejudices of one worthless woman weigh against the affections, the esteem of so many respectable friends? What have we done to deserve being rendered miserable through her envy and malice?" "Could the warmest love, gratitude and respect, which I owe to everyone here," answered she; "could the arguments of the most condescending kindness, deeply imprinted here"—putting her hand to her heart—"could these avail to alter my purpose, I might not be able to withstand your persuasions; but, my Lord, when I have had fortitude sufficient to deny those who are dearer to me than life, you cannot be offended, that 'tis impossible for me to oblige you; and here, in the presence of those who have been witnesses to the honours you have offered me, I release you from every vow, every obligation your too ardent love has conferred on me, and from this hour beseech you to think of me as a friend, zealous for your honour and happiness, for your fame, and the respect you owe to your family; but equally jealous of every duty I owe myself, and therefore determined to see you no more." She rose quickly from her chair, and ran into Mrs Courtney's dressing-room, giving way to a violent burst of tears. The astonished Count, who had not the power to prevent her departure, threw himself into a chair, without speaking. The Countess had followed Matilda.

"This is really," said Mrs Courtney, "the most extraordinary young woman I ever met with; I wonder not at your attachment, my dear Count, but after this public declaration, you have nothing to hope for: imitate her example of fortitude and self-denial, and suffer not your mind to be depressed, when it is necessary you should exert man's boasted superiority of reason and firmness." The Count replied not.

The Marchioness looked with a little surprise at Mrs Courtney, who she thought appeared less affected than she ought for her young friend.

Lord Delby was warm in her praise, and offered to be her escort to Boulogne, as he thought it highly improper she should be accompanied by servants only.

This offer was thankfully accepted by the Marchioness. "She has absolutely prohibited the Marquis and myself," said she, "but I hope will make no objections to the honour you intend her."

The Count, making a slight apology, withdrew, and every one joined in pitying the necessity for a separation of two persons so worthy of each other. "Was fortune the only obstacle her delicacy could raise," said the Marquis, "there are those who would rejoice to remove it; but when we consider the particular disadvantages of her situation—the disgrace and insults which would attend the Count, from her want of birth, however great her merit: unjust as I know those prejudices are, yet I confess it would have given me pain, had she acted otherwise. I applaud, I admire, I love her more than ever, but I do not wish to see her the Count's wife, unless those bars could be removed, which now appear next to an impossibility." "No!" cried the Marchioness, briskly, "no! I will not believe merit like Matilda's is born to wither in the shade; I will hope to see her one day in a conspicuous point of view, that may reflect honour on all who are connected with her, either by blood or friendship."

"You are romantic, my dear madam," said Mrs Courtney, with a smile; "but suppose we go to your young favourite, and see how the poor thing does after her heroics."

This was said with so little feeling, that the Marchioness was surprised; and a sudden idea darting into the mind of the Marquis, he could not suppress a smile, whilst Lord Delby looked offended with his sister's light manner of speaking.

Under these different impressions they entered the dressing-room, and found poor Matilda reclining her head on the Countess, and both weeping. "Fie, fie, my good friend," said Mrs Courtney, "is this the way to comfort the young lady for the sacrifices she has made to honour and principle." "I adore your sensibility, madam," cried Lord Delby, hastily; "in my opinion, whoever loves Miss Matilda does honour to their own heart."

Both ladies bowed to his lordship, though unable to speak; but endeavouring to recover themselves, the Countess said, "This dear obstinate girl proposes setting off the day after tomorrow." "Well, and if she is so determined, what hinders us from all taking a trip to Dover, previous to our Scarborough journey?" said Lord Delby.

Everyone agreed to the proposal, after which they sought to amuse their minds by talking on different subjects.

The Countess and Mrs Courtney accompanied the Marchioness home to dinner, but Lord Delby excused himself, that he might attend to the Count. On his return to Cavendish-square he was informed his guest was in the library. He found him writing, and would have retired; the Count requested he would sit down: the conversation naturally turned on the recent occurrences in Harley street. "Don't think meanly of me, my dear Lord," said the Count, "if I cannot help gratifying a little malice and revenge; I have just finished a few lines to Mademoiselle De Fontelle; I will, at least, make her remember she is in my power, and tremble every moment, lest I should put my threats in execution; I will plant a thorn in her bosom, if she is capable of feeling, though, alas! I can never draw the one from my breast she has been the cause of transfixing there for life! I shall send to the Ambassadors, to procure her address, as doubtless from old acquaintance Madame Le Brune has been to pay her respects to his lady, and that is the only clue at present, I have to find her."

When Lord Delby acquainted him the day was fixed for Matilda's departure, and their intended jaunt with her, "Ah!" said he, "how hard, that the person most interested in that event should be precluded from being a witness of it, though I know I could not stand the shock." "If my sister does not accompany us, which I rather doubt, as one coach cannot hold them, and I intend going on horseback, there being no necessity for great expedition I shall consign her to your care, my dear Count, in our absence." "If Mrs Courtney will accept the attendance of such a spiritless being as myself," answered he, "I shall be honoured by permission to wait upon her."

Not to dwell on the melancholy circumstances of parting, when nothing new or particular occurred, 'tis sufficient to say both parties were overwhelmed with grief, and Matilda submitted, with much reluctance, to Lord Delby's going in the packet with her; but her friends all protesting, if she refused, everyone would go, she was obliged to acquiesce; and embracing the two ladies a thousand times, with streaming eyes, she tore herself from them and embarked.

The wind was fair; they reached Boulogne in seven hours; and whilst they partook of some refreshment at the hotel, Louison and Antoine walked to the Ursuline Convent, in the high town, and having acquainted the porteress with their errand, found, to their great mortification, they took no ladies in chamber, or high pensioners. They were directed to the Annunciate Covent, and there soon procured admission, and accommodations for Matilda, and Louison, who gladly attended her, thinking it would be only for a short time, 'till her lady came from England.

Within a few hours Matilda was received and settled. She took leave of Lord Delby, with tears of gratitude. "Ah!" said he, much moved, "not one word of remembrance to my worthy guest?" "Yes, Sir," said she, raising her voice, "tell him I admire, I esteem him—that his happiness is the first wish of my heart. Take care, my dear Lord, of the worthy Count; teach him to forget me, and if ever he should be united to an amiable woman, deserving and possessing his affection, I will then boldly claim his esteem—'till then we must be forever separated."

She entered the gates, unable to say more, and when they were shut upon her, Lord Delby, overcome with pity and admiration, returned to the hotel; that same evening re-embarked for Dover, and joined his friends before nine the next morning.

S piritless and unhappy, they arrived in Harley-street the following evening, and sending a messenger to Mrs Courtney, that lady shortly after entered the house, the Count with her; she cheerful and lively, he looking pale and dejected. She enquired, with an air of indifference, the particulars of their journey, but seemed little interested in it; not so the Count, he asked a thousand questions. "I have a message to you from the amiable Matilda," said Lord Delby. "For me," said the Count, eagerly; "O! why have you delayed it?" His Lordship repeated her last words. "Sweet angelic girl!" cried he, "is my happiness dear to her! But why should I doubt it? She is truth and goodness itself; my esteem, my love, must ever be hers, for no other woman shall ever possess that heart she condescended to prize, and never will I marry, if Matilda cannot be my wife." "Lord bless me!" exclaimed Mrs Courtney, "let's have no more dismals; I declare these last five days have vapoured me to death: I hope our journey to Scarborough will teem with more pleasant incidents than yours to Dover seems to have produced." "I am sure so," answered the Count; "the world does not abound with characters like Matilda's to lament.'

No more was said; supper was announced, and more general conversation introduced during the remainder of the evening, though everyone appeared absent and uneasy.

After the company had left them the Marchioness took notice of Mrs Courtney's behaviour. "Surely she has taken some pique against Matilda," said she. "Yes, replied the Marquis, "the pique natural to a jealous woman." "Jealous! repeated the Marchioness, "why, surely you do not think she is fond of the Count?" "Indeed, but I do," replied he;

"nay, I am certain of it, from many observations I lately made on her conduct." "Bless me!" returned she, "why, Mrs Courtney is seven or eight and thirty, the Count only two and twenty." "That's true," said he, smiling, "but my love, ladies have various ways of concealing their age, and the depredations of time; besides, vanity never forsakes them; and to do Mrs Courtney justice, she is an agreeable woman." "Yes, and a sensible woman," returned she; "I never can suppose her guilty of such a weakness; I rather think her prejudiced against Matilda, by some falsehoods or other." "Very well," replied the Marquis, "be it so: I am always more gratified by your favourable opinion of your own sex, than a readiness to condemn them; the one shews a generous mind, free from guile itself—the other, a malignant spirit, desirous of acquiring merit from the deficiencies of others." "But, pray," said the Marchioness, "how will you account to Mr Weimar for the retirement of Matilda, should he hear of it, and apply to you?" "By the simplest truth," replied he, "except what relates to Bouville. He must thank himself for all the stories Mademoiselle De Fontelle has repeated to her disadvantage, and from whence originated her sudden determination. She is now safe; the letter I procured from the Ambassador, addressed to any convent, at least, the superior of it, will always protect her, since mine is the only claim she is subject to."

Tranquillised by this, the Marchioness recommended her young friend to the care of Providence, and retired to rest with a virtuous heart, and an easy mind, which could not fail of producing quiet and refreshing slumbers.

The Count, Lord Delby, and Mrs Courtney, were not equally happy. The former, more sensible every hour of Matilda's worth, cursed the pride of birth, which stood between him and happiness, and determined to live only for her. Lord Delby had been many years a widower; he had only one son, whom he carried to Switzerland, at the time the Countess so fortunately obtained his protection: he was then extremely struck with her appearance; beauty in distress has a thousand claims upon a susceptible mind; but the Countess had good sense, sweetness of temper, and delicacy of manners to recommend her; and though the first bloom of beauty was worn off, she had sufficient charms both of mind and body to procure for her the admiration of any man. Lord Delby conceived a very warm affection for her, though he knew it was entirely hopeless, unless death should rid her of her persecutor; he was therefore condemned to silence on a subject nearest his heart, and felt the restraint very painfully. Mrs Courtney, from the first moment she beheld the Count, was charmed with his person and manners. She had been a widow four years: when about three and twenty, at the request of her father, Lord Delby, and the temptations of a very capital fortune, superb carriages, fine jewels, and those other avenues to the heart of a young and fashionable female, she gave her hand to Mr Courtney, who was struck with her person, and thinking it right to have an heir to his immense possessions, suspended for a time the delights of Newmarket, and his favourite sprightly, to attend the laws of Hymen; but in a very few weeks his former propensity returned; his young bride was forsaken for the pleasures of the turf, Newmarket, its jockies, its tumultuous pursuits, deep bets, and jovial companions, engrossed all his time and attention.

His lady, happily for her, was not doatingly fond of her husband; she was possessed of every appendage proper for a female in fashionable life, and outshone two-thirds of her acquaintance in jewels, plate, carriages, and dress; she was therefore extremely easy about the absence of her husband, and whilst he neither contracted her expences, nor deprived her of the amusements she liked, she was perfectly disposed to shew him the same complaisance. This very modish pair lived some years together, without feeling either pleasure or pain, from their different engagements. Mr Courtney was at first much disappointed by not having an heir, but time reconciled him to an event he could not remove; and having determined to make a distant relation, who was to inherit his estate, take his name by Act of Parliament, he ceased giving himself any further concern about the matter. They had been married upwards of ten years, when unfortunately taking cold, after very hard riding, a violent fever terminated his life in six days, and his disconsolate widow was left to undergo all the forms and ceremonies of deep mourning, and to wear odious black for three months. This state of mortification being rubbed through, she found herself mistress of all her former finery, and a very noble jointure, to live as she pleased.

Mrs Courtney was good-natured, not from principle but constitution; she hated trouble of any sort, therefore bore anything, rather than have the fatigue of being out of humour; she was polite and friendly, where she had no temptation to be otherwise; in short, she had many negative virtues, without any active ones. Such was Mrs Courtney, when she appeared in this book first. All men were indifferent alike, 'till she saw the engaging Count; a few interviews decided her fate; she found she loved to excess, and hated Matilda in proportion; she discovered his partiality in her favour, long before it was publicly known, and fought to recommend herself to his notice, by paying attention to his favourite; but finding all her endeavours ineffectual, she began to dislike the innocent object of her jealousy, and was casting about in her mind how to get rid of her, when Matilda unexpectedly declared her intention of going into a convent.

The Count's subsequent behaviour, his public declaration and protestations, were mortifying circumstances, 'tis true, but she depended upon time, absence, and her own endeavours, to conquer a passion he could not but look upon as hopeless. The Countess, so many years secluded from the world, at first felt only the warmest gratitude to Mrs Courtney and her brother, for their generous protection; but the polite attention, the mark'd kindness of Lord Delby, inspired her with the most perfect esteem for him,—and though, from the melancholy circumstances which attended her early prepossession, her heart was dead to love, she yet experienced all that partiality in his Lordship's favour which her heart was capable of feeling.

Such was the state and sentiments of the party, now about to set off for Scarborough. The day previous to which, after a consultation between the Marquis, his Lady, and the Countess, on the entrance of the Count, to pay his morning compliments, the Marquis led him to the Countess, "My dear friend, you have hitherto known this lady only as Madame Le Roche, the name she bears in England; I now introduce you

149

to her as our dearest sister, the Countess of Wolfenbach, whose death you have heard us often lament."

The Count started with surprise; "Good heavens!" said he, after saluting her, "how is this possible?"

The Marquis gave him a brief recital of her confinement, and promised him the particulars another day. "I could no longer keep our secret from you, but she must still retain her former name, until the whole affair is brought forward. The Ambassador was made acquainted with it yesterday; he will take some private steps, at first, if possible, to do us justice; and when we return to London for the winter, we shall use decisive measures; mean time, I have written to a friend, as has likewise my sister, to procure Joseph's testimony, as far as his knowledge extends, lest, as he is old, we should lose a witness of some consequence."

The Count entered warmly into the business; his life and fortune was at the service of his friends: they embraced and thanked him The following day they left town, after writing the most affectionate letters to their beloved Matilda, whose absence they most sincerely regretted.

M atilda, on her first residence in the convent, found it replete with many inconveniences she did not expect. For the first week she cried incessantly, and poor Louison, not happier, continually prest her to return. "Ah, mon Dieu!" cried she, "if my good master and lady, if the dear charming Count de Bouville knew how miserable you are, they would fly to bring you out again. Ah! the good Count, the morning before we came away, gave me ten English guineas; the tears were in his eyes; 'Take care of your charming mistress, Louison,' said he, 'and I will always be your friend':—Dear, dear gentleman! O, that he was but here!"

This little anecdote, which one might have supposed would have added to Matilda's grief, proved a most salutary remedy for it: she instantly dried her eyes. "Amiable, generous man!" said she, "shall I repine, that I have devoted myself to retirement to preserve a mind like his from repentance and self-reproach, and from the disdain of those low-minded people, incapable of the nobleness of heart which would prompt him to forget his own dignity, to raise a friendless orphan. No; I will at least prove deserving of his esteem, by my own self-denial; I will support every inconvenience, every trial with resignation—happy, if, in sacrificing the trifling amusements the world affords, I can promote his peace, and secure his future happiness."

Fortified by these generous sentiments, she no longer wept or sighed; she sought consolation in the practice of her religious duties, which strengthened her mind and composed her spirits: she found in the uniform observance of piety, charity, and compassion towards the sick and unfortunate, that peace which the world could not give, and that serenity of mind which no recollection of misfortunes could deprive her of.

She became the admiration of the whole community; everyone was desirous of her favour, but Matilda, blest with uncommon penetration, and capable of the nicest discrimination, was at no loss to distinguish the selfish and fulsome attentions of the officious, from the approbation of the worthy and humble few who looked on her with eyes of kindness, but never intruded; from these few, to whom she paid particular civility, her heart selected Mother St Magdalene; she was about eight and twenty, and had been a nun nearly ten years; she was one of those very elegant forms you cannot behold without admiration; her face was more expressive than beautiful, yet more engaging than a lifeless set of features without animation, however perfect or blooming, could possibly be; she was pious without ostentation, kind and affectionate to her sisterhood, and courteous, without design or meanness, to the pensioners.

This charming woman soon attracted the notice of Matilda,—she sought her company and conversation—she received her attentions with particular complacency.

Mother Magdalene was sensible of her civilities—she plainly comprehended the value of them, but from peculiar notions of delicacy, and to avoid giving umbrage to the sisterhood, she rather repressed than encouraged her particular kindness. Matilda, however, would not be repulsed, and Magdalene was at length compelled to be her "Dear Mother".

They were frequently together, and by her example Matilda was encouraged to the perseverance in every moral and religious duty. Letters from her two friends, the Marchioness and Countess, were the only things she permitted to break in upon them, and those letters were a continual stimulation to a sense of gratitude and generosity, which she found herself called upon to exert. Whilst Matilda had thus happily reconciled her mind to her situation, her friends were enjoying the amusements that Scarborough afforded.

T he Count was always the attendant on Mrs Courtney; and though his passion was as fervent as ever, and his regrets as powerful for the loss of Matilda, he could not be always in company with an amiable woman, who paid him such particular attention, without being gratified by it, and sometimes shewing those little marks of gallantry which all women expect.

The Count, though he had a more than common share of solidity and stability, with the most refined understanding and integrity of heart, yet he was still a Frenchman—still possessed a natural gaiety of heart, the greatest politeness and attention to the fair sex, and some-times fell into the hyperbolical compliments so natural to his country-men, when addressing the ladies. Mrs Courtney, too ready to believe everything to be as she wished, gave him every encouragement, and contrived frequently to draw him into situations and expressions which were rather equivocal, but by which he meant nothing, though the lady thought otherwise.

They had been near three weeks at Scarborough; the ladies had heard twice from Matilda, but as she requested her name might never be mentioned to the Count, but from necessity, they only answered his eager enquiries, by saying she was well, and appeared to be much pleased with her situation. He saw there was a reserve in their manner, and justly supposed it owing to her restrictions: he did justice to her greatness of mind, which only served to increase his love and regrets.

———

One morning Mrs Courtney, entering the Marchioness's dressing room, flung herself into a chair, "Bless me! said she, "what shall I do with your friend, the Count? he has drawn me into a pretty scrape,— I never intended marrying again, but he is so pressing, so irresistible—" "Who," cried the Marchioness, surprised, "the Count? he pressing?" "Why, yes," answered she; "surely you must have observed his particular devoirs for some time past." "Not I, upon my honour," answered the Marchioness; "I never supposed his attentions to you wore the face of particularity." "Then you can have observed nothing," said she, peevishly. "Pray, what think you, my dear madam?" turning to the Countess. "Upon my word, I am equally surprised," replied she; "but if you can settle the matter agreeably between yourselves, I shall certainly rejoice at it, because I am very sure Matilda will keep her resolution, in refusing his addresses."

Those last words, which were spoken undesignedly, piqued Mrs Courtney a good deal. "I do not think 'tis of much consequence," said she, haughtily, "whether she keeps her resolution or not;—I believe by this time he is very sensible of the impropriety of his offer—but I forget, I appointed him to meet me at a friend's, in the next street,—bon jour, ladies," said she, with a forced gaiety, and ran out of the room, leaving them looking at each other with astonishment.

"Can this be Mrs Courtney?" cried the Countess, "my God, what a change!" "But is there, can there, be any truth," said the Marchioness, "in the Count's attentions?" "Heaven knows," said she, "but if it is so, I shall never depend upon man again."

Some company coming in, prevented further conversation; but at dinner, when they all met, the ladies observed the Count appeared to be thoughtful and uneasy, Mrs Courtney gay and lively, Lord Delby rather attentive to both; in short, it was the first dinner in which the party seemed collected within themselves, and forgot their friends, except

Mrs Courtney, who behaved with remarkable politeness and sweetness to all.

When the ladies retired to the drawing-room the Count addressed the Marquis in the following manner. "I believe, my dear Sir, you are sufficiently acquainted with me, to know that I am equally incapable of a dishonourable thought or action to any one, much less towards a lady for whom I entertain the highest respect, and the sister of my hospitable entertainer." "For heaven's sake," cried the Marquis, "what is all this,— who dares accuse you?" "A misapprehension only, I hope, said the Count, in a calm tone, "not an accusation. Both you and all our friends are perfectly acquainted with my attachment to the amiable Matilda,— an attachment," added he, raising his voice, "that will be as lasting as my life, for I never shall love any other woman but unhappily the respect and attentions I have paid to the merits of Mrs Courtney, have been misconceived; I have been upbraided with seeking to gain her affections, and with having given colour to suppose mine were also devoted to her: the highest respect, nay, even admiration of her many amiable qualities, I have undoubtedly expressed, but not one word beyond what friendship would warrant, from a man who made no scruple to own his love for another, though perhaps that other never can be his. My heart, my honour, does not reproach me with the least duplicity or mean design. Can you, my dear Marquis, from the whole tenor of my conduct, suppose I could be a trifling coxcomb, much less a deliberate villain, for I must hold any man as such who could seek to gain the affections of an amiable woman, to gratify his vanity only?" "I am equally surprised and concerned," said the Marquis, "that such misapprehensions should have taken place—" "And I," interrupted Lord Delby, "equally displeased and mortified, at being made a party in the business; but there is no accounting for the vanity of women, and how very readily they entertain ideas they wish to indulge. I am very sorry, Count, I have been drawn into this foolish affair, for I observed at first it was very unaccountable, that a man should make his court to one woman, and avowedly profess his admiration of another; I shall however talk to my sister, and I beg the subject may drop and go no further". "I feel myself extremely at a loss how to behave," said the Count; "I think I had better leave Scarborough." "By no means," said his Lordship, hastily; "behave as usual to Mrs Courtney, in public, but avoid tête-à-têtes;—if she is wise, she will herself approve this method, to escape observation."

The Count reluctantly submitted, knowing after what had passed, he must appear very awkward in his civilities, which had been so misconceived.

They attended the ladies in the drawing-room, and it being proposed to go to the theatre, the Count, as usual, offered his hand to Mrs Courtney, though with a look of confusion and reserve; she accepted it with a polite and tender air.

Lord Delby, not knowing she had exposed herself to the ladies, requested the Marquis would not mention the affair to them.

T he evening past off very well, and at supper they were more cheerful and talkative than usual. The following day however Mrs Courtney appeared with a new face; she looked pensive and unhappy, complained of a pain in her breast, ate little, sighed frequently, and in short, engaged that particular attention we naturally pay to those we love, and see indisposed. The Count looked the image of despair; he addressed her one moment, with an air of tenderness, the next he studiously seemed to avoid her; his behaviour was unequal, confused, and evidently perplexed. Things continued in this state for some days,— Mrs Courtney more melancholy, the Count more distressed; when one day, as they were at table, the Marquis received an express from London. Everyone was alarmed; it came from the German Ambassador, requesting the Marquis would instantly come to town, the Count of Wolfenbach being there dangerously ill, and desirous of making all possible reparation to the Countess.

This news suspended all the new schemes. The Countess could scarcely be kept alive; she was apprehensive of some fresh plots, and dreaded the idea of being again within his power. "Fear not, madam," cried Lord Delby; "the monster shall never see you without your friends to protect you." "Besides, sister," urged the Marchioness, "the Ambassador is himself a pledge of your safety, and tells us he is dangerously ill, —perhaps the poor wretch cannot die in peace without your pardon." "O, my God!" said she, starting up, "let me go this instant!—alas! he has need of forgiveness; his crimes are great, yet if they were the consequence of his love for me, 'tis my duty to speak peace and pardon; grant heaven!" cried she, lifting up her hands, "I may not come too late! I will set off this very hour." "Be composed, my dear sister," said the Marquis, "we will go this evening; the Marchioness and I will attend you." "And I," exclaimed the Count. "We will all accompany you," said Lord Delby. "Ah! my Lord," answered the Countess, "why should I so suddenly call you from the amusements of this place: you proposed staying three months, we have only been here a little better than one." "Wherever my friends are," replied Lord Delby, "is to me the desirable place; I have no local attachments without their presence; and I dare answer for my sister, she has no objections, as I think the air of Scarborough has been of little use to her health." "You judge very right, my Lord, I shall certainly accompany our friends," said she, in a languid tone, adding, "their happiness must constitute mine."

The Count, who took everything literally which betrayed generosity of sentiment, could not help saying, "Tis impossible to doubt Mrs Courtney's concurrence in every scheme productive of pleasure to those she honours with her esteem." This compliment made her eyes dance with pleasure.

Their women were called and desired to set about packing immediately. Everything was hurried on, and at five the next morning they were all on their return to London.

About a week previous to this Matilda received a letter from an unknown hand, and without a name, signifying that the Count De Bouville was paying his addresses to Mrs Courtney; that he was extremely fond of her, but that she hesitated on account of his vows to Matilda, which made him very unhappy.

She read this letter with composure,—she felt some pangs at her heart, she tried to overcome them: "Why should I be uneasy," said she, "have not I wished the Count might make a suitable alliance?—did I not release him from his vows? Alas! I have neither claims nor expectations,

—let him marry, I can then renounce the world, and settle here for life, —when lost to him I have only this asylum to bury myself in forever." The tears would flow, but she quickly dried them. "From whence this sorrow," said she again, "had I any hopes O, no! all is despair and bitterness on my side, but I will rejoice in the happiness of the amiable Count, whatever befalls myself.'

Within three days after this, she received a letter from Mrs Courtney; these were the contents:

MY DEAR MISS MATILDA.

Honour, sentiment, and generosity impel me to address you; I am well acquainted with the nobleness of your heart, and can confide in its integrity. You have refused the Count De Bouville, publicly refused him: was there a shadow of hope you ever could be his, I would have been silent; but as I deem that impossible, I trust to your generosity and fortitude, when I tell you, he has for some time past paid his addresses to me, with the warm approbation of all our friends. I at first made objections on your account; he pleaded, you had publicly rejected him; and, as I did not feel satisfied, he offered to write you, and procure his release but knowing men have great duplicity, when they wish to carry a point, I declined his offer and chose to write myself; and I conjure you, my dear Matilda, to believe I will not consent to what he calls his happiness, without your permission. If you have any hopes or expectations; if you think his love may ever return to you, and that different situations may give a countenance to his addresses, and admit of your claims upon him, depend upon it I will dismiss him, however unhappy he may be; for I would not wound your peace, by acceding to his wishes, be the consequence what it may. Your friends, who are mine also, chuse to be entirely silent on the subject; nor will they take notice of it, until settled between you and me. Look on me as your friend, dear Matilda,—be explicit—do not consider the Count or myself; speak your wishes, your hopes, and be assured that your felicity

is my first wish, whatever it may cost me. I am my dear Matilda's
sincere friend and obedient servant.

MARIA COURTNEY

P repared as Matilda had been, by the anonymous letter, to expect
such intelligence, no words can express her feelings at receiving
this letter; overcome with grief, she retired to her apartment and gave
loose to the painful emotions that opprest her. After a little time she
grew more composed: "Is a heart like his worth regretting?" cried she.
"Could he, if his love had been founded on esteem, so soon have offered
his addresses to another? O, no! it was only a transient affection, not
imprinted on the heart, but vanished with my person: how fortunate
then our hands were not joined; how miserable should I have found
myself, if united for life to so fickle a disposition."

Whilst this impression was strong upon her, she took up her pen and
wrote the following answer:

DEAR MADAM.

Accept, I beseech you, my warmest acknowledgements for your
very friendly and obliging letter: your candid communications
and consideration for my peace, I feel in the most sensible
manner; but I beg leave to assure you, madam, neither my happiness nor peace depend now upon the Count De Bouville. I shall
always think myself obliged for the affection he offered me, but
as it is impossible we should ever meet on those terms, I hope
reason has entirely subdued an improper sentiment, and if we
ever should meet again, which is not likely, we shall behold each
other with the indifference of common acquaintances. I am
exceedingly happy here, and, if at the expiration of the twelve-
month Mr Weimar allowed me, my friends will accede to my
wishes, and permit my stay in this convent, I trust I shall be

happy for the remainder of my life. I hope this will prove satis-factory to your very friendly offers respecting the Count, who has my sincerest wishes for his happiness, with any other woman but her who is, my dear madam, Your much obliged humble servant,

MATILDA.

After she had sealed and sent off this letter her spirits grew more tranquillised; she tried to conquer her feelings, and consider only the fickleness of men's dispositions. "Yet why should I upbraid him," thought she; "he has a family, a name to support, and ought to marry: Mrs Courtney is amiable, has a large independent fortune, respectable friends, and a noble origin to boast of;—what am I in a comparative view with her? Ah!" cried she, bursting into tears, "the retrospection humbles and subdues both my pride and regret: what have I to do but to submit to the lowly state I am placed in, and bless at a distance those generous spirits that have enabled me to procure such an asylum as this."

Mother Magdalene entered as she was wiping the tears from her cheeks; taking her hand affectionately between hers, "My dear young lady, why those tears? Spare me the pain of seeing you unhappy; remember this is but a short and transitory life; our pilgrimage through it is painful, no doubt thorns are strewed in our paths, sorrows planted in our bosoms; but if planted and strewed by others, where is the sting to afflict our own hearts? Believe me, dear lady, reason can subdue every affliction but what arises from a condemnation within; with a self-approving conscience we can look forward with hope; and if turbu-lent and ungracious spirits are too powerful for us to contend with here, we can trust to our Heavenly Father, that our sufferings and patience will meet with a recompence hereafter, far superior to the brightest expectations that can be formed in this life." "My dear friend and comforter, said Matilda, kissing her hand, "be you my monitress if I grieve for temporal evils; yet, alas! my misfortunes are not common ones." "You think so,' answered Mother Magdalene; "we are all apt to magnify our own troubles, and think them superior to what others feel; but, my dear child, you are yet a novice in affliction; when you know more of the world you will know also that there are varieties of misery which assail the human frame,—and 'tis our own feelings that constitute great part of our distress.'

Matilda sighed, and after a little pause, "That I may not appear impatient, nor grieved at trifles, I will unbosom myself to you, and perhaps from you obtain that consolation I have hitherto sought in vain."

She then related every part of her story, except the name of the Countess and situation of the castle.

Her gentle friend sympathized with her, and confessed, for so young a woman, her trials were very great. "But still, my dear lady," said she, "I bid you hope; you have a Father and Protector, trust in him, and you will one day assuredly be happy. Another time you shall know my sad story, and will then confess, of the two, I have been most wretched; and, though I cannot entirely exclude a painful remembrance sometimes, yet I am now comparatively happy—my troubles no longer exist, and religion has restored peace to my mind. Adieu, my dear child,—take hope to your bosom and compose your spirit." "Yes," cried Matilda, "I will at least try to conquer one cause of my distress, and in destroying this fatal letter of Mrs Courtney's, lose all remembrance of the Count: surely after having so solemnly renounced him, I have no right either to complain of him or grieve for myself,—tis an unpardonable folly, for every way he is dead to me." She threw the letter into the fire and walked into the garden.

In the evening she received another visit from her good mother, who was much pleased to see her so tranquil. Matilda reminded her of her promise to relate her history.

"My story, my dear child, is not a long one, but replete with many melancholy circumstances. My father was a merchant at Dunkirk; he married a very amiable woman, and had a numerous family—five girls and four boys; few people lived more respectable than they did, but they were not rich; a large family, liberal minds, and hearts always disposed to relieve the wants of others, precluded affluence, though they had a decent competence. The failure of a very capital house in England, with whom my father was materially connected, obliged him to go over, without loss of time; he embarked from Dunkirk. Alas! My dear child, we saw him no more! A storm overtook them, as 'tis supposed, and all on board perished, for the packet was never but once seen or heard of after. When this dreadful news arrived, my mother was weeping over a letter just received from a friend in London, with the intelligence that the house which had failed could not pay a shilling in the pound, and from some particular connexions between them and my father, all his effects would be seized, and he was likewise declared, or included in the bankruptcy. One of those unhappy gossiping persons, fond of telling everything, without considering the consequences, called upon my mother, as she was in an agony over the contents of this letter; 'Ah! My dear madam,' cried she, 'I see you have received the fatal news?' 'Yes,' answered my mother, wringing her hands, 'we are all undone forever!' 'But who,' said she again, 'could write you about it, for only the boat that is just come in saw the packet go down.' 'What packet?' cried my mother, starting. 'Why, the packet your good husband was in.'

"She heard no more, but fell senseless on the floor. I had been out upon business, and entered the room just as this officious newsmonger and the servants were trying to raise and recover my wretched parent. A stranger to all the circumstances, I was frightened to death almost, and teased everyone to know what had happened; no one answered. It was some time before she was brought to life. With a look of horror I shall never forget, she cried, 'Hermine, you have no longer a father, a friend, nor a home!' 'Great God!' I exclaimed, 'what is all this?' ''Tis misery in extreme,' said she, still with a fixed look and a dry eye; 'your father is drowned, and I hourly expect everything to be seized. Well,' cried she, rather wildly, 'let it be complete! Ruin should not come by degrees.' Two or three of the younger children came into the room; the moment she saw them she gave a violent shriek and fell into convulsions. Scarce in my senses, I flew about the house, and by my screams drew several persons to me. We got my mother up to her apartment, a physician was sent for, but it was many hours before she was restored; she lay three days at the point of death, the fourth the fever abated, and hopes were entertained of her life. This day a person came and took possession of the house and all our effects. By the interposition of a friend we were allowed to remain in it ten days. Judge, my dear young friend, what must have been my situation; a father dead, a mother scarcely alive, our whole property seized,—eight children younger than myself, I only fifteen, and all unprovided for—obliged to be the comforter, the supporter of all.

"Out of the numerous set of acquaintances we had, two only appeared as friends in our distress; one an old gentleman of small fortune, the other a young merchant, who had for some months paid particular attention to me, young as I was. These two persons interested themselves a good deal for us. My mother grew better, but her nerves were so shattered, that a kind of partial palsy took effect upon her speech, she spoke thick and scarcely intelligible; a sort of convulsive cry succeeded every attempt to talk; in short, her situation was most truly deplorable. Within a few days we were removed to the house of the old gentleman, without any one thing we could call our own, but cloaths. This good and worthy man placed out my sisters in a convent, put my brothers to school, raised a subscription for their support, his own fortune being insufficient to maintain us all, and in fine, did everything a father and friend could do, for the whole family.

"Not one of my mother's former gay acquaintance ever concerned themselves about her; she was poor and afflicted with sickness, 'they could not bear to see a woman they esteemed in so miserable a situation, and therefore were obliged to give her up'. Oh! My dear lady, of all the worldly evils that can befall us, surely there is nothing so painful to support as the ingratitude and contumely of those who once thought themselves honoured in your acquaintance: mere butterflies of the day! They bask in the sunshine of your prosperity, but when night shuts in and sorrows assail you, they fly elsewhere, in search of those sweets you can no longer afford them, and despise what they once coveted and admired. Young, at that time, almost a stranger to mankind, I felt indignation and astonishment when I met any of our former friends— friends! Let me not profane the name of friendship! I mean intimates

and companions; my civilities were repressed with scorn; my appearance glanced over with a look of contempt, and 'poor souls, they are
supported by charity, I pity them to my heart', said aloud in my hearing,
with features expressive of everything but pity.

"I will not dwell on things so common as ingratitude and hardness of
heart; stings which you, my young friend, have never yet experienced,—
heaven grant you never may, for 'tis a bitter cup to taste of. We lived in
the manner I have described for near eight months, my poor mother so
ill and helpless I could not leave her. The young gentleman I have
mentioned paid me the same attention, and scrupled not to acquaint
our good friend, it was his design, in a short time, to make me his wife.
'If you do,' said he, one day, 'you shall have a father's blessing with her
when I die; whilst I live I will support the children: but Hermine is a
good girl—she who can, at her time of life, give herself up to the care of
a sick parent, and find delight in her duty, will make a good wife.'

"One morning, when the old gentleman was in my mother's room,
he was suddenly seized with an apoplexy and dropt senseless from his
chair: my screams soon brought assistance—a surgeon was sent for;—
alas! he was gone forever. My mother was, in consequence of her fright,
taken in a shivering fit, which in a few moments turned to a stroke of
the palsy, and deprived her entirely of speech and the use of her limbs
on the left side. That I preserved my senses at such a time, was wonderful. I sent for my lover, in an agony no words can describe; the news
flew through the town, and two or three of our late friend's relations
hastened to the house; they were rich and wanted nothing; however,
they began to assume an air of authority; when my lover interfered, told
them he was convinced there was a will, and that I was the appointed
heir. This enraged them greatly; the will was eagerly called for, and by
all parties earnestly sought for: alas! no such thing was to be found. The
unfeeling women ordered me to remove my mother and my trumpery
the following morning.

"My lover was almost beside himself with vexation and disappointment: I was stupid with sorrow; I hung over my almost lifeless parent,
without speaking, and unable to shed a tear. After some time, those
women quitted the room, leaving orders with a woman servant, to

watch me, that I took nothing but my own, and to take care I quitted their house next day. When they were gone, this poor woman in circumstances, but rich (oh! how much richer than her employers!) in goodness of heart, approached the bed, and, gently raising me, she gave me some drops and water that rouzed me from the stupor which had seized upon my faculties, when, looking round the room for my departed friend, and then on my helpless parent, I burst into a flood of tears. 'Thank God!' said the good creature, 'that you can weep: don't be unhappy, my dear Miss, Providence will provide for you: I have a sister, who lives in a very humble style indeed, and keeps a little shop; her husband was formerly an under clerk to your father; he loves the whole family dearly, and I dare say, if you will condescend to stay under their mean roof 'till you are better suited, they will wait upon you with joy.' 'Ah! where is Mr.—?' meaning my lover. 'I know not, madam,' answered she, 'but I think he followed the ladies.' 'Good heavens!' I cried, 'could he leave me under such a complication of horrid circumstances; this is bitterness indeed, if deserted by him,—but it cannot be,—he is doubtless gone to fetch a physician.' In this vain hope I passed several hours, no lover, no physician appeared; I was in a state of distraction: the servant sent for her sister and brother; they came, and offered me their services with a heartiness which spoke their sincerity.

"I was incapable of determining; I sent to my lover, 'he was particularly engaged, but would see me some time tomorrow'. 'O, let me begone!' cried I, in a frenzy, 'I will take my dear mother in my arms— we will die together.' With difficulty they separated me from her: the dear saint was sensible, though incapable of speaking; her eyes told me all she felt—O! the expression in them can never be forgotten,— what a night was that! In the morning my dear mother was put into a kind of litter, and we were conveyed to the humble dwelling of this charitable pair. She was laid in a decent bed and dropt asleep: I was kneeling at the side of it when the door opened, and the man who called himself my lover appeared before me. I felt undescribeable emotions; he took my hand, and placing me in a chair, still unable to speak, he said, 'I came to you, my love, the first moment of leisure; last night I was engaged; but you shall not stay in this poor place, I will take a decent lodging for you and your mother, and will be answerable for all expences; I will daily be y our visitor, and I hope in a little time you will recover your spirits.' At first my heart bounded with joy at his kindness; then again I thought there was a something wrong, though I hardly knew what; at last, 'I think,' replied I, 'that I ought not to put you to such great expences, nor would it be proper you should maintain me, unless—' There I stopt. 'Unless what?' said he, earnestly. 'Unless I had a claim to your protection,' said I, blushing. 'I will be very sincere with you, my dear Hermine: had your old friend performed his promise, and left you his fortune, though but a small one, I would have married you; but I am young, and only entering into life; a wife without a fortune, a mother in such a situation, and a family of young relations would soon ruin me, and of course you: I must prove my love another way; an old rich widow has been recommended to me; I will marry her; I shall then be enabled to support you all in affluence, and have no ill consequences to dread. What say you, my dearest Hermine, may I hope your sentiments concur with mine?' You will wonder, my dear child, at my patience and silence during this proposal; in truth I wondered at myself; heaven, no doubt, supported me, and gave me, at that trying moment, superior resolution. 'Of my opinion, Sir, and of the sentiments you have avowed, you must collect my thoughts, when I tell you, that so far from living a life of obligation with such a man, were you this moment possessed of millions, and would offer to marry me, I would prefer poverty and want—I would starve, with this dear insulted woman, before I could condescend to marry a man of such infamous principles!—Leave me, Sir, forever; presume not to enter the habitation of virtuous poverty, and blush at your own littleness, when you enjoy the house of wealth and magnificence.' He attempted to speak. 'I hear you no longer, Sir; you are more mean and contemptible in my eyes than the poorest reptile that crawls upon the earth.' I stampt with my foot, and Mrs Bouté came up. I never saw a countenance so expressive of wonder and disappointment when she entered. 'I am sorry to say, madam, you do not know your best friends; but should your mind alter upon consideration, you know where to find me, and I shall be always happy to attend your commands.' I gave him no answer, but a look of contempt, and he left the room.

"The spirit and indignation which had supported me through this scene, now subsided; I shed a flood of tears. I saw no one being to whom I could look up with any hope or prospect of comfort. Mrs Bouté, who sympathized with me, said, 'Ah! madam, if Madame De Raikfort, if Madame De Creponier were acquainted with your sorrows, I am sure you would find friends; they always assist the unfortunate, and particularly persons like you, born to higher expectations.' I took my resolution immediately; I wrote to both, describing my past and present situation.

"From the latter lady I received an almost immediate visit: she condoled with me; she entered into my concerns with a kindness and delicacy peculiar to herself, as I then thought; I knew not that the principles of charity and benevolence were the same in every well informed mind and good heart. I received the same kind attentions from the other family: Madame De Raikfort sent me every comfort and convenience I could want for my poor mother. In short, to those good ladies I was indebted for my chief support during her existence.

"A fortnight, exactly, from the death of our good old friend, she expired. There was no apparent alteration till within a few hours of her death; and she went off without a sigh or groan. Though the shock was dreadful, yet I had so long expected it, and in her melancholy situation it was rather to be wished for, that I found myself, though grieved at my irreparable loss, yet rejoiced that she escaped from the evils of this life, to awake in a blessed immortality. The benevolent ladies I have mentioned, did not forsake me; they paid the last sad duties to my parent; they undertook to educate and place my younger brothers and sisters to get their living decently; they asked what were my views and wishes? I frankly answered, 'To be a nun.' Had I any choice of a convent? I named this; a young lady, a friend of my juvenile days, previous to my misfortunes, had professed here. The ladies told me I should enter upon my noviciate, but on no terms to be persuaded to assume the veil; it was by no means their wish; and the first summons from me they would take me out and provide for me in the world: that they rather complied with my wishes than their own inclinations—which would be more gratified in my residence with them. I thanked my generous benefactresses, but persisted in my desire of quitting the world. The day before I intended leaving Dunkirk, I received a letter from my quondam lover, expressing regret for his behaviour, and an unequivocal offer of marriage. I put his letter under a cover, with these lines: 'The man who presumes to insult the feelings of a virtuous female, and when he fails in his purpose, condescends to solicit pardon, and offers to raise that ill-treated woman to a level with himself, lowers her more, by such an offer, than the bitterest poverty can inflict: but the person to whom this letter is addressed is fortunately beyond the reach of insult or indigence; she therefore rejects the proposal with her whole heart, and with the highest contempt.'

"Having seen my brothers and sisters safe under the protection of those worthy ladies, and received from them every pecuniary assistance I could want, with letters of warm recommendation I arrived here; and here, in a short time, recovered tranquillity and ease: leaving nothing in the world to regret, I studied the duties of my situation, and, at the expiration of the time allowed to consider, I gave my decided choice of a monastic life, and took the veil. I hear often from my generous friends. Two of my sisters are well married; the rest of my family have every prospect of success. Now, my dear young lady, I have related my history, tell me candidly, have your troubles ever equalled mine?"

"Oh! no," cried Matilda; "I am ashamed of my own impatience and inquietude. Good heavens! If such are the evils to be expected in life; if misfortunes are so frequent, ingratitude and malignancy so prevalent, men so abandoned, and the good and benevolent alloted so small a share in the proportion of the world, the only asylum for the unfortunate is a convent." "Not always," answered Mother Magdalene; "there are situations and difficulties in life, from which even the unfortunate may extract hope and comfort: yours is such: 'tis possible you have parents still living, who may one day fold you to their bosoms; 'tis likewise not impossible you may one day be united to the man you prefer. In short, your situation is not hopeless, like mine: I saw the downfall of every expectation I could form, and had no one hope or engagement to the world; you have many: you have no right to dispose of your future destiny, whilst there is the least probable chance you may be reclaimed. Reside here as a boarder, my dear child; but under your doubtful circumstances, never take the veil, for the mind should be entirely disengaged from all worldly hopes, before it can renounce it properly."

From this day Matilda grew entirely resigned; she derived wisdom and comfort from her good mother's conversation, nor suffered antici-pation of evils to disturb her serenity.

T he Scarborough party were now arrived in London. The Marquis immediately waited on the Ambassador. His Excellency told him the Count Wolfenbach was alive, out past all hopes of recovery. "He knows you are hourly expected, and is anxious to see you."

The Marquis, taking his address in Dover-street, hastened thither and sent up his name. He waited some time for the servant's return; at length he was desired to walk up, and on entering the room, scarce could he trace any recollection of the object in the bed before him. It was some years since he had seen the Count; he was not then young; but age, anxiety, and conscious guilt, with the disorder that now opprest him, had indeed greatly altered him. When the Marquis drew near, he was for a moment silent; then, addressing him, "I am told, my Lord, you requested my presence." "I did," replied the Count. "Pray, is your sister with you?" "Not in the house," answered the Marquis, "but she is in town, and will soon attend, if it is your wish to see her." "Yes," said the Count, "let her come; I can tell my story but once, 'tis fit she should be present." The Marquis instantly dispatched a messenger for his wife and sister. In the interim the Count desired to be informed in what manner the Countess effected her escape through the wood and got to England. The Marquis recounted every particular. "There was a fate in it, no doubt," said the Count; "Providence intervened, to prevent me from the commission of crime I intended, and preserved her life."

Word was brought up that the Countess and Marchioness were below. They were desired to enter. When they came into the room the

Countess involuntarily shrunk back. "Approach, madam, do not fear; the discovery is now made, and in a very short time I shall have nothing to hope for, nor you anything to dread." The Countess advanced, trembling, and seated herself by the bed. "I now," said he, "entreat your forgiveness of all the wrongs my cruel jealousy heaped upon you; say, speak, can you pardon me? Tell me that, before I begin my narrative, lest I should be cut off e'er I have finished." "I do indeed," replied the Countess; "I pardon you from my soul, and may the God of mercy pardon you likewise." "I am satisfied," said he, "and now attend to my confessions.—I was well aware, before I married, of the affection subsisting between Victoria and the Chevalier; I was not blind to the difference in our persons and ages, and hated him in proportion to the advantages in his favour. I was resolved to carry my point, to gratify both passions; her father seconded my wishes, and she became mine. From that hour I never knew a peaceful moment. I doated on her to distraction; jealousy kept pace with love. Her conduct gave me no right to complain; yet she loved me not, and I feared the Chevalier was the object of her partiality and regret. My temper, naturally impetuous and furious, grew daily worse; for what hell can give torments equal to what a jealous man feels? One day I had been at Vienna, and was informed of the Chevalier's return: desperate and alarmed, I came home.

"In the Park I met Peter. He had lived some years with me, was blindly devoted to my service, and had been employed by me to watch the Countess. He told me a gentleman had been walking round the park, examining the house, and on his going to him, and enquiring who he wanted, he only asked if the Count and Countess of Wolfenbach were there; and Peter answering, yes, he walked hastily away. This information was a dagger to my soul: I resolved to carry her to my castle in Switzerland, secretly. I pursued my design. I had been there but a short time before I heard a man, disguised, had been about the grounds, who made off when any person came near him; I concluded 'twas the Chevalier, and resolved to have him watched, determined he should die; at the same time that I thought it impossible he should come at the Countess in her apartment. One day going to her room, I heard a sudden noise, found her on the floor, with a paper in her hand, and saw a figure glance from the window. I was struck with rage and astonishment. After confining and upbraiding her, as she may inform you, I closeted Peter, and by promises of present reward and future prospects, he took a solemn oath to assist in my revenge, and to be secret.

"We took our stand the following night by the wall, and saw him advance to climb up the battlements; we sallied out, knocked him down, bound and gagged him, and, determined to have complete revenge, we dragged him to the Countess's apartment." "Spare the repetition of what passed there," cried she; "it was a scene of horror; repeat only what were your transactions out of my sight." "You shall be obeyed," answered he. "It was in vain she protested innocence; I gave no credit. My first intention was to murder both; and when I locked her in the closet with the dead body, I hoped terror and fright would have done my business. In the morning we heard her groans; we entered; the sight of her agonies for a moment disarmed my rage, and I consented Margarite should assist her. After she was delivered, and the curtains fastened, Peter and myself took the body and carried it to one end of the subterraneous passage, dug a hole in the earth, on one side, and threw it in. I now grew irresolute with respect to my wife s death; my revenge cooled, but I knew it was impossible but she must hate and detest me. One day I went to her, uncertain whether to destroy her and the child or not, to prevent a discovery. She knows what followed. I felt a thousand soft emotions at the sight of the child, and both loved and hated her to madness. I resolved at last to confine her for life, and to preserve the child. Joseph, the under gardener, the only man who lived in the castle, I was obliged to confide in. I told him my wife had been detected in an intrigue, and I had intended to murder her, but she recovered of her wounds, and now I should only confine her for life. I swore him to secrecy, and vowed, if ever he betrayed her place of residence, or life, to any one, I would murder both. The poor fellow swore faithfully to obey me. The rest she can inform you."

"But my child! my child!" cried the Countess, eagerly. "Is alive, and an officer now in the Emperor's service." "Great God! I thank; thee!" said she, falling on her knees; "and in this posture, when I return thanks to my Heavenly Father, for his preservation, I also forgive and bless you, for the care of my child; may every evil deed be forgiven, and may you enjoy peace in your last moments, and everlasting happiness hereafter!"

The hard heart of the Count was softened into tears by the warmth of her expressions: he held out his hand; she kissed it, in token of peace. "May your prayers be heard," said he; "but I have more vices yet to confess. I took the child to Vienna, brought it up, as the son of a friend, very privately. At a certain age he was placed in the military school, and about six months ago I procured for him a commission. But to return. Once in two years I generally visited the castle. Her resignation and obedience to my orders sometimes moved me in her favour, and every visit my heart grew more and more softened; yet I dared not liberate her, her death had been so universally believed for many years; how could I account for my conduct, or her appearance, without incurring suspicions against myself? Distracted in my mind, I neither enjoyed peace nor rest;—alas! there is neither for the wicked, however we may disguise our crimes to the world however we meet with respect and approbation from mankind, the man conscious of his wickedness, with doubt and terror gnawing at his heart, is the most miserable of human beings: we may swear to secrecy, we may silence everything but conscience—there is the sting that for ever wounds—there the monitor no bribes can suppress. Life became a burthen to me, yet I feared to die; I feared daily a discovery of my crimes; I resolved to forbear my visits, but to send Peter every six months, to gain intelligence and see all was safe.

"On his return from his last errand of that kind he informed me, that, calling at a woodcutter's cottage near the castle, who knew him not, from a curiosity to hear if they were acquainted with Joseph (of whose fidelity he was always doubtful) the woman told him a story of a young lady's coming there, being recommended to the castle; and that she had so much courage as to go to the haunted rooms (for I had taken care to have it supposed that wing was haunted) and that very day was there several hours. Alarmed at this intelligence, Peter flew to me, then on a visit about seven leagues from the castle, frightened out of his senses. After a little consultation we resolved to go in the night, break open the doors, if locked, and murder both Victoria and Margarite, and after that fall upon some method to silence the young lady and Joseph in the same manner. We succeeded in our attempt: we dispatched Margarite, and came down to do the same by her mistress, but Providence, who counteracts the designs of wicked men, and turns those very measures we take to secure ourselves to our destruction, suggested to me to take her into the wood and destroy her, that Joseph, if he came in the morning, might think it was a gang of banditti who had carried them off; for which reason, I thought my being concerned would never be suspected. This foolish concerted scheme we pursued; the Countess remembers I was thrown from my horse, and she took that opportunity to escape.

"When I recovered my senses I found I had some bruises on my head and shoulder. I looked round, 'Where, where is the Countess?' 'Ah!' cried Peter, 'I fear we are undone; the horse flew away with her as I alighted, and your horse also run off.' 'Villain!' I cried, 'find her this moment, or I will murder you.' ''Tis impossible to pursue her on foot; 'tis most likely she may be dashed to pieces in the wood; mean time, Sir, creep, if possible, to the town, have some assistance; I will borrow another horse and make all possible search.' I had no alternative; distracted with pain and horror, I got with difficulty to the town, and was put to bed very ill. Peter rode off immediately; he was wanting a day and a night. I suffered a thousand tortures; I began to think he had betrayed me. 'Tis the curse attendant on villains always to be suspicious of each other: for what vows or ties can bind a man you know would commit the most atrocious crimes for money. In my conjectures; however, I wronged Peter; he returned. He had searched the wood, and every part of the adjacent neighbourhood, without gaining any intelligence, but that two or three persons had seen a horse saddled, galloping furiously in the wood: he had called at the cottage—nothing had transpired there. In short, we began to hope, as our only security, that she was killed somewhere in the road, and the body carried away by passengers.

"In a few days I got well, determined to visit the castle, and either destroy Joseph, or decoy him away to some remote place. In short, my schemes were so many and unsettled by fear that I fixed on no positive plan. We arrived at the castle; we saw no appearance of any lady; but Peter, taking an opportunity to speak to Bertha, was informed there had been a lady, but she had left them three or four days. This was another stroke: the lady, we knew, had seen the Countess; she might betray the secret, where could she be gone, or who was she? Peter enquired again, Bertha knew only that she talked of going to Paris. We were now distracted; the sword seemed suspended over our heads, and we every moment feared detection. That night we met in the Countess's apartments and searched thoroughly; in a drawer we found a purse with some money, and a paper signed Matilda, giving an account of sundry articles taken from the drawers. This convinced us we had reasons for our apprehensions: the death of Joseph would rid us of one witness—I secretly determined to destroy another.

"We went to the town the following morning—I procured from the different medical persons some laudanum. We agreed the best way would be to get Joseph and his wife to my other castle, and destroy them there, where they were unknown. I deceived Peter by this foolish scheme, having taken a different resolution. I told him we would return that night to the castle, take the remaining valuables, money, & co., which should all be his, previous to our departure. He joyfully consented. I took an opportunity to give him the opium in the evening; by the time we got to the apartment he grew very heavy, and during his search among the drawers, dropt down in a heavy sleep; I put him upon the bed, fastened every window and door, set fire to the curtains and counterpane, and went out, locking the door after me; I then hastily proceeded to the wood-house which joined Joseph's kitchen, and soon had that in a blaze; bringing some dry stubble, I lighted it against the door and window shutters, and seeing the whole take fire in both wings, I went to the stable, took my own horse, which was there fastened up, ready saddled, as we left them, and riding off to the town, went to the inn I had been ill at, and waited patiently for news.

"Within a few hours I was called up: my castle was discovered by some woodcutters to be in flames, and before assistance could be procured was entirely destroyed. I pretended great vexation and distress; rode to the spot; it was a dreadful sight; my soul shuddered—I was in agony. The people imputed it to a different cause. I asked, had nobody seen Joseph nor his wife. No, was the general answer, and the fire imputed to their carelessness. Some of the neighbouring gentlemen rode over; every one condoled with me, and offered me accommodations; I returned with the gentleman to whom I had first been on a visit.

"When retired to my apartment, a retrospection of all my crimes forced themselves on my remembrance. I tried to sleep, alas! there was no sleep befriended me; ten thousand horrid images swam before my sight; I threw myself out of bed; it was moonlight; my room commanded a view of the distant wood, I shrunk at the sight—there lies my wretched wife! then the Chevalier, Joseph, Bertha, and Peter, all seemed to walk before me; great God! what were my sufferings that night, never to be effaced from my memory. When daylight came, I went down stairs to the garden; here I first thought of destroying myself —my boy shot across my mind—I took my resolution at once. I set off that day for Vienna. On my arrival I sent for Frederic, and after some preparation acknowledged him as my son, acquainted him his mother died in child-bed, and I had particular reasons, immaterial to him, for not owning him sooner; I made my will, secured my whole fortune to him, by proper testimonials, that I acknowledged him my son, and then resolved to retire from the world, repent of my sins, and try to make my peace with heaven.

"All Vienna was astonished at my resolution; my son sought every argument to divert me from my purpose, his tenderness, goodness, and virtue were daggers to my heart; I fell very ill, and earnestly prayed for the hour of death; heaven thought fit to spare me, that I might receive some comfort before the fatal hour arrived. I began to get better, though weak and declining, when, to my inexpressible surprise, I received a letter from our Minister in England, with a brief account of the Countess, the deposition of the Marquis, and requesting I would acknowledge the lady, and not permit such black transactions to appear before the public as the Countess said she had the power of disclosing. At first I thought this letter was all illusion; but when I considered the possibility of her escape from death, and the application of the Marquis to the Ambassador, I was convinced the whole was founded on truth. What a mountain was taken from my bosom! I wrote immediately, I would follow the letter. In three days my strength mended greatly, yet I was obliged to take very easy journies, and by the time I arrived in England fatigue had quite exhausted me.

"His Excellency sent off an express to you. I now thank heaven that both you and Joseph are alive, and adore the ways of Providence, who extracts good out of evil, and made the very crimes I intended to perpetrate the means of deliverance to you both. The death of the unfortunate Chevalier I bitterly repent, and can only observe here, that when a man gives himself up to unrestrained passions of what nature soever, one vicious indulgence leads to another, crimes succeed each other, and to veil one, and avoid discoveries, we are drawn insensibly to the commission of such detestable actions as once we most abhorred the idea of: for, although my temper was not good, and my passions always violent, had not love and jealousy urged me to desperation, and deprived me of reason, my soul would have shrunk at the thoughts of murders, which grew at last necessary for my preservation."

Here the Count stopt, exhausted and fatigued; indeed he had made several pauses in his relation, from weakness, and it was very visible he had not many days to live.

The Countess could not restrain her tears. "Ah!" said she, "I have been the unhappy cause of all—" "Do not reproach yourself," cried he, hastily; "I am now convinced of your innocence; indeed I long believed it, even when I designed your death the second time; only innocence could have supported you to bear my cruelties, and your horrid confinement with resignation: I knew too well the terrors of guilt; for let not the unhappy wretch, who forgets his duties towards God and man, who gives himself up to the indulgence of his passions, and wrongs the innocent, think, if he escapes detection, he can be happy: alas! remorse and sorrow will one day assail him; he will find he cannot hide his crimes from himself, and his own conscience will prove his bitterest punishment."

The Countess extremely rejoiced to find him so sensible of his guilt, said everything in her power to ease and calm his mind.

After he had a little recovered, he turned to the Marquis. "I sent for you, my Lord, not only to hear my confession, but to direct me in what manner I must do my wife justice; if it be your pleasure, I will repeat my story, or at least assent to a drawn up confession before witnesses." "By no means," answered the Marquis; "it will be perfectly sufficient if one part of the story, nearly what relates to her confinement, so as to authenticate her person, is related." After some consultation the Marquis attended the German Minister. A paper was drawn up, signifying the jealousy of the Count, without naming any particular object, in consequence of which he shut up his lady in the castle, after her delivery, and gave out a report of her death; that he had brought up her son, now an officer, who was lately acquainted with his real birth, and to whom his estates were secured: that the lady, after many years confinement, had found means to escape to her brother and sister, with whom she resided. The Count having accidentally heard of her residence, was come to England, with a view to obtain her pardon and do her justice; that he acknowledged her innocence in the strongest terms, and desired, in case of his death, she might enjoy every advantage settled on her, when married to him, in the fullest extent.

This paper was signed in presence of the Ambassador, his Chaplain, and all the friends of the Countess,—Lord Delby among the rest.

Not a word was said relative to the Chevalier, Margarite, or Peter: the former had been so many years given up, as dead by his relations, though they never guessed in what manner he died, that it would have been the height of cruelty to have awakened sorrow so long dormant, had it ever been necessary, but as no such occasion appeared to demand an investigation, everything relative to him and the other victims was buried in oblivion.

T he Count survived nearly a week after their arrival in town, and then expired with more resignation and composure than could have been hoped for. Two days previous to his death he wrote to his son a few lines, referring him to the testimony he had given the Countess, and requesting he would, by his duty and tenderness, atone for the cruelties of his father; bid him remember the awful lesson placed before him, and restrain those passions, the indulgence of which had brought sorrow and shame on his guilty parent, whom, nevertheless, he had the comfort to tell him was a truly penitent one. The Marquis, taking upon him to direct everything for preserving the body, and having it carried into Germany within a fortnight, a few days after the necessary orders were completed, told the Countess he thought it highly proper she should go in person to make her claim. She, who was impatient to see and embrace her son, received the proposition with joy. The Marchioness, Lord Delby, and Mrs Courtney accepted an invitation to accompany her with pleasure. The former had written to Matilda the late unexpected and agreeable turn in the affairs of the Countess, and again prest her return to them. The latter, Mrs Courtney, still perse-vered in her soft melancholy, her tender looks, and attentions to the Count, who, when he found the party fixed for Vienna, excused himself from attending them, but promised, if the Marquis and his family did not return to France before Christmas, he would join them early in the spring.

This declaration was a thunderbolt to Mrs Courtney. She seized an opportunity of speaking to him alone. "How, my Lord," cried she, "is it possible you can think of separating yourself from your friends,—will you not go to Germany?" "It is not in my power, madam," answered he. "Say rather not your inclination," said she, warmly: "you pique yourself on speaking truth, you know." "I wish to do so always," replied he, "but the ladies will not always permit me." "I beg your pardon, Sir, for contradicting you; I, at least, gave you credit for truth and sincerity, when you unpardonably fought to gain those affections you have since cruelly trifled with." "Such a charge from Mrs Courtney," said he, "has too much severity in it, not to call for a serious answer; I therefore protest, madam, I never sought—I never wished to gain the affections of any woman but Matilda: my love for her is no secret to my friends,—I glory in it. For you, madam. I entertained the highest respect; I thought it my duty to shew you every possible attention, a man of politeness was bound to offer to an amiable woman; more I never intended—I never could be thought to intend, with a heart avowedly devoted to another."

"And do you call this politeness?" cried she, highly enraged. "I must tell you, Sir, you have (if you please to call it so) trifled too much with my peace, by your gallantry; and was I not completely revenged by the entire indifference of your idol, I should resent it in a very different manner. There, Sir," tossing Matilda's letter to him, "there see how much you are beloved or regretted by an insensible paltry girl." The Count had caught up the letter, and in his eagerness to read, scarcely heard her last words. He devoured every line with his eager eyes; and when he came to the conclusion, "happier with another woman". "O, Matilda! never, never! You may indeed forget me; mine is a common character, but there are few like yours in the world." Then looking at it again, and turning to Mrs Courtney who looked full of fury and malice, "May I be permitted to ask, madam, on what occasion you wrote this young lady, and of what nature those offers of service were, made in my name by you." Mrs Courtney blushed, and was in the highest confusion. "Shall I interpret your looks, madam?" asked he again. "No, Sir, I can speak their language myself. I wrote to know her sentiments, at the time you were amusing yourself at the expence of my folly, as I had too much honour to give you encouragement, if she had any hopes of you." "So then," said he, in a rage, "she believes I was paying my addresses to you, madam." She smiled contemptuously. "No wonder she renounces me; if such ideas took possession of her mind, she must think me the most contemptible of men." "And of what signification are her thoughts to you? Are there not insuperable difficulties to a connexion with her?" asked she. "Not on my side, madam; this hour, this instant, I would receive her hand with gratitude and transport; her dignity of sentiment, her true greatness of mind are the bars to my happiness." "Well, but if there are bars—" "I beg pardon for interrupting you, madam; I know what you would say; and it is far from my design to be rude to any lady, but you must permit me to declare, I am resolved to wait weeks, months, or years, to have a chance for the removal of those impediments; and if I do not succeed at last, in all probability I shall never marry at all." As he ended this speech he withdrew, with a respectful, but reserved air. "Heavens! said she, peevishly, "is this the gallant, polite Frenchman! I see 'tis all over; I can make nothing of him, and I will gratify his vanity no longer; on the contrary, treat him with levity and contempt." Pride stepped in to her aid, and produced that change of sentiment which reason, honour, and good sense had failed to do: so true is the poet's observation.

Pride saves men oft, and women too, from falling. She determined, however, not to accompany her friends; being so lately returned from the Continent, she had no inclination to revisit it, without a powerful inducement, such as she had no chance of. The Count's motives for refusing were of a similar nature.

The Marchioness had heard from Matilda. She declined being of their party, and entreated to remain in the Convent 'till that lady returned to France. She wrote a letter of congratulation to her dear Countess, on the great change in her situation, but gave, what she thought, very satisfactory reasons for not going into Germany. Lord Delby, however, could not resist his desire of attending the Countess, though so recently returned from thence. He entreated the Count to accept his house, but he had previously accepted a similar offer from the Marquis.

In a few days the party separated: the Marquis, his Lady, the Countess, and Lord Delby for Germany: the Count, to avoid attendance on Mrs Courtney, went to Bath, and that lady soon after accompanied a party of friends to Tunbridge.

F rom the time that Mr Weimar had agreed, before the Ambassador, to permit Matilda's residence twelve months with the Marquis, her friends had sent advertisements to all the different courts in Europe, describing the particular circumstances attending her birth, without mentioning names. No intelligence arrived, nor enquiries had yet been made on the subject, though they still entertained hopes of one day meeting with success. As to the young lady herself, she had none; resigned to her misfortunes, her only wish was to remain in the convent, free from the persecutions, and exempt from the temptations, of the world. She heard of her friend's unexpected restoration to her family and fortune, with real delight; and no mention being made of the Count or Mrs Courtney, in the letter she received from the Marchioness, she concluded they were either married, or soon to be; and though a few sighs would follow the idea, she supported herself with fortitude and resolution.

She was one day sitting in her apartment, and ruminating on past events, when the superior of the convent came in, and with a look of regret, "Ah! madam," said she, "I am grieved to be the messenger of ill news to you, and sorrow to the whole community." "Bless me!" cried Matilda, "what is the matter?" Alas! my dear child, I have received an order from the King to deliver you to a Mr Weimar, and another gentleman, waiting to receive you."

The unhappy girl repeated faintly the name of Weimar, and fell back, almost senseless in her chair. The good mother ran to her assistance; she soon recovered. "Oh! madam," said she, "save me, keep me here; I wish to be a nun—I will not go into the world again. "Would it were possible for me to protect you," answered she, shrugging her shoulders "but we have no power to retain you from the King's order; you must go, we dare not keep you."

At this moment entered St Magdalene, all in tears.

"Well, madam," said Matilda, endeavouring to collect fortitude from despair, "have the goodness to inform the gentlemen I will presently wait on them." The superior appeared rather unwilling to leave her with her favourite, but however she withdrew.

Her good mother advised her instantly to write a few lines to the Marquis, and likewise to the Countess at Vienna. "Give me the first letter," said she, "I will endeavour to have it conveyed; take the chance of leaving the other at some inn on the road: but make haste, for we have no time."

Poor Matilda, more dead than alive, soon executed her task, and the other assisting in packing, she was just ready when a messenger came to hasten her. With a resolution that astonished her friend, she followed the persons who came for her trunks, and went down to take leave of the community. Everyone was affected, for she was generally beloved; but when she kissed the hand of her good mother both burst into a flood of tears. "Farewell, my dear, my amiable friend," said she; "farewell, my good mother: if my wishes were gratified, and I have ever any power over my own actions, I will return to reside with you forever." "To the protection of heaven I leave you," said mother Magdalene; "persevere in virtue and goodness, truth in God, and doubt not of being the object of his care; for he is a Father to the fatherless, and will never forsake the virtuous.

With streaming eyes Matilda followed her conductor. The porteress opened the gates; there stood Mr Weimar and his friend. He seemed at first to shrink from her view; but recovering himself, advanced and took her hand. "Well, ungrateful run-away," said he, you are once more in the custody of your true and natural protector." She made no answer, nor any resistance; she was placed in the carriage between them. Mr Weimar was hurt at her silence, "You are sullen, you are ungrateful Matilda." "No, Sir, I am neither: I am grateful for past benefits, and if I do not speak, 'tis because my sincerity or sentiments cannot be pleasing." "You are mistaken," said he; "I wish you to speak with sincerity; to tell me why you forsook the friend of your youth, the man who offered to make you his by every holy tie, to fly with an acquaintance of a day, and who, after all his professions, at last placed you in a convent?" "It was my own voluntary choice, Sir, and very distressing to my friends, that I persisted in choosing a retirement from the world. To the first part of your question 'tis not necessary for me to answer: you know my motives for quitting your house, and for the subsequent offer of your hand, if you really were sincere, I must confess I think circumstances more than inclination prompted you to it. How you mean to dispose of me, or by what right you assume to yourself to be master of my destiny, I know not; but of this you may be assured, no force shall prevail upon me to act contrary to my own inclinations and judgment; and since I am not your niece, you have no legal authority over me."

Weimar looked confounded at her spirit, the other stared with surprise; all were mute for some time, at length he said, "You have taken up unjust prejudices, Matilda; but you will find I am still your best friend." "Then," replied she, "I shall truly rejoice, for it is grievous to me to think ill of any one, much more of him, whom, for many years, I was accustomed to think my nearest relation and protector. If you are sincere, permit me to write to the Marchioness that I am in your care, to dispel the anxiety she will naturally feel on my account." "We will think of that, said he, "when we are settled."

This evasion proved to her, she had not much favour to expect.

She was entirely ignorant of the road they took; she knew it was different from the Paris route, and had no opportunity of asking a single question, much less of dropping her letter, as the chaise being their own, they sat in it whilst they procured horses at the different post-houses, and at night stopt at a miserable hut, where they got only a few eggs and a little milk, no beds were to be had, and they were obliged to remain four hours in the chaise, until they could enter the next town. The distress of mind, with fatigue and want of rest, overpowered Matilda; as they were changing horses, she fainted. Weimar was frightened; he had her taken out of the carriage, laid upon a bed, and every method used to restore her. It was a long time before she recovered, and then she was so weak and exhausted, that he was at a loss how to get her on. Some wine and toasted bread was given to her, and he quitted the room a moment, to order refreshments into the chaise: she seized the opportunity; taking the letter and a louis d'or out of her pocket, "If you have charity," said she, "let that letter be sent to the post." The woman, surprised, took the letter and money, and going to speak, Matilda heard his footsteps; she put her finger to her lips; the other understood, and thrust both into her bosom. Joy and hope gave her spirits, and when he told her she must pursue her journey, she arose with difficulty, but without speaking, and was rather carried than walked to the chaise. When they drove off she recollected she had forgot to ask the name of the town; she put the question to him. "Faith I have forgot," was his answer. She said no more.

The two gentlemen talked of indifferent matters, which afforded her no information; she therefore resigned herself to her own contemplations until they arrived at a sea-port town.

She was astonished when he told her they were to embark on board a vessel. "Where are you going to carry me to," said she, trembling. "To Germany doubtless," replied he. "By water?" "Yes, by water: but ask no questions, Matilda; I am once more your uncle during this voyage, to preserve your character." "And do you think, Sir," said she, assuming courage under a palpitating heart, "do you think I will give a sanction to your falsehoods, and permit myself to be made a slave of?" "You will find," answered he, "you can have no voice to alter my determinations; but I will now make you a fair proposal, If you will consent to marry me, I will, in this very town, receive your hand, and without scruple then carry you to join your friends: if you refuse I will not part with you, but where I propose carrying you, shall be entire master of your destiny. The old story is propagated by my servant, that you are my niece, and I am saving you from a shameful marriage with a footman." "Good God!" cried she, "is my character thus traduced? And do you suppose such methods will oblige me to become your wife? No! Sir; I will die first." "Very well," answered he, calmly, "you have had your choice—I shall pursue mine."

Presently they were informed the vessel was ready. She was lifted out of the chaise, and notwithstanding her resistance, and cries for help, she was carried on board and down to the room below.

"You are now safe in my possession," said he. "I am sorry you made force necessary; but you must be convinced 'tis now in vain to contend with me." Matilda sat stupidly gazing at him; but the vessel beginning to move, she turned very sick: without any female on board to assist her, she was compelled to let him place her on the bed; and then requesting to be alone, he retired, and left her to her own very painful reflections.

All hope of assistance from the Marquis was now at an end; she knew not the place of her destination; she saw no probability of escaping from Mr Weimar; yet she felt an unconquerable repugnance to become his wife—a man capable of such duplicity and cruelty; "O, no!" cried she, weeping, "sooner will I plunge into a watery grave than unite myself for life to a man I must hate and despise." She continued extremely sick and ill. They had been two days at sea, when she was alarmed by an uncommon noise over her head; voices very loud, and everything in much agitation: soon after she heard the firing of guns, and Mr Weimar entered with an air of distraction. "I am undone," cried he, "unfortunate girl; you have been my ruin and your own, but I will prevent both." He instantly drew a large case knife, stabbed her and then himself. At the same instant a number of strange men burst into the cabin, Weimar's friend with them. The Turks (for they were taken by a Barbary Corsair), highly enraged with the bloody scene before them, were about to dispatch Weimar, who lay on the floor, when Matilda faintly cried, "Spare him, spare him." One of them who understood French, stopt their hands: he ordered him to be taken care of, and approached Matilda, who, growing faint with loss of blood, could with difficulty say, "My arm." The cloaths being stript off, it was found the wound was indeed through her arm, which being laid across her breast, received the blow which he was in too much confusion to direct as he intended. The humane Turk soon staunched the blood; and having with him necessaries for dressing wounds, he sent on board his own ship for them, and a person who could apply them. He requested the lady to make herself easy, no insult should be offered to her person. Meantime Weimar was carried on board the Turkish vessel, and carefully guarded. His wound was a dangerous one, and the person who drest it gave but little hopes of his life; it continued however in a fluctuating state 'till their arrival at Tunis.

Matilda was out of all danger, but a prey to the most dismal apprehensions of what might befall her.

O n their arrival she was taken on shore to the captain's house, where a very amiable woman received her with complacency, though they could not understand each other. Weimar was likewise brought on shore; and his situation growing more desperate, he requested to know if there was any hopes of his recovery, and being answered in the negative, the poor wretch, after many apparent convulsive struggles, asked if there was any French or German priest in the city? and being informed there was none, he requested to see Matilda, in presence of the captain and his friend, but that friend had been carried to a country house, to work in the gardens; the captain and lady however attended him. When he saw her he groaned most bitterly, nor could she behold the man to whom she had owed so many obligations in her juvenile days, reduced to a situation so wretched, without being inexpressibly shocked. He saw her emotions, and keenly felt how little he deserved them. "Matilda," he cried, "I shall soon be past the power of persecuting you myself, but when I think where and in whose hands I leave you, I suffer torments worse than death can inflict." "Let not the situation of the lady grieve you," said the generous Turk; "though I pursue an employment I am weary of, I never injure women; if she has friends, they may recover her." "O, Matilda!" said the dying man, "I will not deceive you, your death would to me have been the greatest comfort; I cannot bear the idea, another should possess you. Swear to me," added he, eagerly, "that you will become a nun—that you will take the veil." She was terrified by his vehemence; and though she both wished and designed it, hesitated. The captain said, "How dare you, so near death, compel an oath foreign to her heart; no such vow shall pass in my hearing, be your affinity to her what it may." "No, Mr Weimar" answered she, "I will not swear, though it is at present my intention so to do." "Then I am dumb," said he; "I will not be the victim to procure happiness for others."

It was in vain Matilda and the Captain urged him to speak, he was resolutely silent. The Turk whispered her to withdraw; she obeyed; and in about half an hour was desired to return. "I am conquered, said Mr Weimar; "this man, this generous enemy has prevailed. Prepare to hear a story will pierce you to the heart. I am your uncle, but not a German, nor is my name Weimar." "O, tell me," cried Matilda, "have I a father, have I a mother living?" "Not a father," answered he, sighing, "perhaps a mother you may have, but I have not heard for many years." She clasped her hands and burst into tears. "O, tell me—tell me all, for I am prepared to hear a tale of horror," "Horror, indeed!" repeated he, "but I will confess all. Your father, the Count Berniti—" "My father a Count!" cried she, in all accent of joy. "Yes; but do not interrupt me. Your father was a Neapolitan nobleman, I was his younger brother; he had every good mild amiable quality that could dignify human nature. From my earliest remembrance I hated him; his virtue procured him the love of our parents and the esteem of our friends; I was envious, malicious, crafty, and dissipated. My parents saw my early propensity to wickedness, but entirely taken up with their darling boy, I must say that they neglected to eradicate those seeds of vice in my nature, which an early and proper attention might have done; but given up to the care of profligate servants, never received but with frowns and scorn; my learning, my dress, my company, all left to myself, and treated in general as a disgrace to the family, I soon grew hardened in wickedness, and hated my relations in proportion to their neglect of me.

"Parents would do well to consider this lesson: unjust, or even deserved partialities, visibly bestowed on one child, whilst others are neglected, too generally creates hatred to that child, and a carelessness in performing their duties, which they see are little attended to. It lays a foundation for much future misery in the family; creates every vice which envy and malice can give birth to, and the darling object is generally the victim.

"But here I will do my brother justice; the only kindness I ever received was from him, and often with tears he has supplicated favours for me, which was the only ones that ever met with a refusal, all others he could command. I grew at last so desperate that I formed an association with the most abandoned youth of the city, and was universally despised. About this time my father died, leaving his whole fortune to my brother. Except a very trifling pittance, weekly, to me, disgrace affected me beyond all bounds of patience. My brother sent for me; with a heart bursting with rage, I went. The moment I appeared, he rose and embraced me, with tears. 'My dear brother,' said he, 'I have now the power to make your life more comfortable; evil minded persons set my father against you, nor could I ever remove the prejudice: henceforth we are brothers, more than ever; use this house as your own; give up your idle acquaintance—I will introduce you to the good and worthy, and those only shall be my friends that are my brother's also.' A reception so unexpected for a few moments warmed my heart to virtue, but the impression soon wore off; I accepted his offer, nevertheless, and for some time endeavoured to keep within bounds, and to be as private in my vices as possible.

"I found it easy to deceive my brother; whilst I preserved a semblance of goodness before him, no suspicion entered his breast. I had so long accustomed myself to behold him with hatred and envy, that every proof of his kindness, which carried with it an obligation, I could not support; rendered him more hateful in my eyes, because I knew it was undeserved. One morning the Count asked what I thought of the Count Morlini's daughter? (At that time esteemed the most beautiful woman in Naples, and whom I had long looked at with desiring eyes.) I spoke my opinion freely. 'I am glad,' returned my brother, 'your sentiments correspond with mine; she is good as well as beautiful, and I hope in a short time will become my wife.' This was a dagger to my heart: I knew she never could be mine, and therefore had suppressed my wishes, but the idea of her being my brother's wife threw me into a rage little short of madness; I hastened from him to vent my passion alone.

"Every plan which malice could suggest, I thought on, to prevent the marriage, but my plots proved abortive, and the union took place. The day previous to the marriage, my noble brother presented me with a deed, which secured a handsome annuity to me for life; assuring me his house was still my home, his country seat the same, but he chose to make me independent. From that day I was truly miserable: I adored the Countess, I hated my brother. She treated me with sweetness and civility, which increased my passion. In short, I grew so fond of her, that I neglected my old associates, and lived almost at home for ever. The deluded pair were delighted with my reformation, and behaved with redoubled kindness. Here I must pause," said Mr Weimar, "for I am much fatigued."

Matilda, whose eager curiosity could ill support any interruption of the narrative, hastened to give him a cordial, and some drops to recruit his spirits.

"Before I proceed any further," said Mr Weimar, "'tis fit an instrument should be drawn and signed by me and proper witnesses, proving that I acknowledge Matilda to be the only child and heiress to the late Count Berniti's estates, which I have unjustly withheld; let this be done, lest the hand of death should cut me off, as I every hour expect."

The generous captain lost no time in procuring the instrument to be drawn and properly attested. Matilda withdrew mean time to reflect on what she had already heard, and in trembling expectation of what was to follow. A painful thought obtruded itself. "Ah! had I known," cried she, "some time ago, that my birth was noble, happiness might have been my portion—it is now too late!" She was soon recalled to the sick room; and everything being settled as the unhappy repentant Weimar desired, he lay a short time composed and then resumed his narrative.

"For some months I lived in the house, a torment to myself, and concerting schemes to ruin the happiness of others. The Countess advanced in her pregnancy: my brother was overjoyed—I affected to be the same. There was at this time a young woman in the city whom I had seduced and who was likewise with child; I knew I could bring her to any terms I pleased; I laid my plan accordingly: she went to live near my brother's country house, and passed for a young widow, greatly distressed. We contrived my sister should hear of her; the consequence was, as we expected, she was sent for, and told a plausible tale; was relieved, and engaged as a nurse for the Countess's child. She was brought to bed three weeks before that lady, of a girl. The Countess was delivered of Matilda. Agatha, for it was she, Matilda, whom you well remember, attended her and received the child. As soon as the Countess could be moved with safety, we all went to the house in the country. It was close to the sea, and at the back a beautiful wood, where my brother frequently amused himself by having little vistas cut. It was in this place I designed to execute the horrid plan I had long concerted.

"I had privately procured a disguise, which lay concealed at one part of the wood. I knew he generally walked in the evening, and proceeded accordingly. Taking a horse one morning, I pretended to go into the city: I did so; and returned about the hour I supposed my brother in the wood: I fastened my horse at the entrance of it, changed my dress, put a mask on my face, and crept on towards the lower part; I distinguished him through trees—let me hasten from the remembrance!—I suddenly came upon him, and by repeated stabs, laid him dead at my feet.' Matilda uttered a cry of horror. "I do not wonder at your emotion,' said he, "since at this moment I tremble at my own crimes! I rifled his pockets of everything valuable, to make it believed he had been dispatched by robbers. I returned and dug a hole at a distant part, where my horse was, hid the cloaths, mounted the beast, returned to the public road, and came on horseback to the door; previous to which I had thrown his watch and money into the sea. I had executed a few little commissions for my sister, in the city, and appeared before her in good spirits, with the trifles she had sent for.

"We waited for my brother's return, at the usual time, to supper; the hour elapsed—she grew alarmed. I made light of her fears for some time; at length I joined in her apprehensions, and calling the two manservants, proposed to search for him. She thankfully accepted the offer. We went to the wood, calling on him aloud, and for some time I pursued a contrary path to the one I knew he laid in; at last we came to the dreadful spot, where we all stood aghast; I made most moving lamentations. We found he had been robbed and murdered. The poor fellows took up the body, and we proceeded to the house. I bid them go the back way, whilst I prepared my sister. Villain, and hardened as I was in wickedness, I trembled at this talk, and the agitations of my mind, on entering her room, told the dreadful tale for me. 'O, heavens!' cried she, 'what is become of the Count? He is dead! he is dead!' she repeated, as I was silent to the question. I drew out my handkerchief, and turned from her. She gave two or three heavy groans and fell to the ground."

Poor Matilda again gave way to the most lively emotions of grief Weimar seemed much affected, and was some moments before he could proceed.

"I will not dwell on a scene so horrid. An express was sent into the city, search made for the murderer, but no traces appeared that could lead to a discovery. My sister continued very ill for many days, and my brother was universally regretted. My melancholy was observed by everyone, and kindly noticed by the Countess who desired I would act for her without reserve: this proof of her confidence gave me great credit, and not one suspicion, I believe, ever glanced on me. It was my first intention to have destroyed the child, but the deed I had done filled my mind with such horror, I could not imbrue my hands a second time in blood. I was some time unresolved in what manner to act. The Countess still kept her bed, in a very languid state. One morning, going to Agatha's room, I found her in tears; her child had died that night, in convulsions; it was in the cradle, and the features much distorted. A thought darted instantly into my head, to change the children: I proposed it to Agatha, and promised her great rewards; she readily agreed to everything I proposed; the dresses were changed in a moment, and the children being only six weeks old, had been little seen. I left the room. Soon after, a servant came to the Countess's apartment (where I then was, to pay my morning respects, a custom I always observed) and requested me to step out on business. 'O, Sir!' cried she, 'we are all undone—the poor nurse is frantic—the sweet child, the young Countess, is dead! expired an hour ago, in convulsions, whilst poor Agatha thought it in a sweet sleep.' I pretended to be most exceedingly shocked; exclaimed against the nurse, sent for a physician—would have the body examined, I did so; I ran to Agatha's apartment the other end of the house, abused her for her carelessness; she, who was really grieved for the loss of her own child, shed torrents of tears.

"The physician came; he examined the child; he said, it was really sudden convulsions had carried it off and no fault in the nurse, the disorder being common among infants. This satisfied every one; nobody troubled themselves about Agatha's child. I sent off to the Count Morlini's, who had left us the day before, intending to return the following one. He came immediately; I detained the physician. The Count made very minute enquiries, and was, or appeared to be contented with the physician's deposition. 'Alas! my Lord,' cried I, 'who shall break this melancholy accident to the Countess I cannot, I dare not do it. Unhappy lady!' I exclaimed, 'how great are your sorrows! My own share in them is lost, when I consider yours.' The Count shook my hand in a friendly manner but spoke not. He went from me to his daughter; I retired to my own apartment. I was now my brother's heir to his title and estates; everything promised to give me an undisputed right; and I enjoyed, by anticipation, the pleasures which fortune and rank would bestow." Here Mr Weimar stopt. "I cannot proceed now I am fatigued and exhausted." He was quite faint, and they were obliged to give him a respite for the present, and administer cordials. He promised to proceed and finish his story in the evening.

Matilda withdrew overwhelmed with grief, horror, and a painful curiosity for the subsequent events which might have befallen her unhappy mother. Sometime after she was in her apartment, the captain came in. "The surgeon," said he, "has just examined Mr Weimar's wound, and makes a much better report of it than in the morning. This last dressing has abated the inflammation, and the fever is not so violent." "If his repentance is sincere, heaven grant he may recover," said she.

In the evening, at Mr Weimar's request, Matilda and the captain went to his apartment: he appeared much more easy and composed after recollecting himself a little, he went on as follows:

"The Count took upon him to acquaint the Countess with the loss of the child; but notwithstanding all his precautions, it had a dreadful effect upon her. She was for some weeks deprived of reason, and when recovered, the disorder turned to a settled melancholy nothing could remove. Having some relations at Florence, the Count proposed taking her there to change the scene. What had been secured to her by marriage, was of course hers. From an affected generosity, I presented her with the house and furniture in the city; and under a pretence I could no longer stay where such melancholy accidents had taken place, and having no relations living, I disposed of my estates, and said I should travel into Turkey and Egypt, without assuming any title.

"In truth, I was ever in fear some unforeseen events might bring my evil deeds to light: for 'tis the fate of villainy never to be secure; and the constant apprehension of detection embitters every hour of their lives who once plunge into guilt. I had persuaded Agatha, with the child, to embark on board a French vessel, bound to Dieppe, and there wait for me; having engaged the captain to take care of her, though I secretly wished the waves might swallow them up; at the same time I had not resolution to destroy them. After the vessel sailed, I set off from Naples, glad to escape from a place I could not behold without shuddering. Whether any suspicions were entertained of me, I know not; for I kept up no correspondence there. I travelled into France, and arrived at Dieppe, where I found Agatha and the infant. I had a great inclination to settle in Switzerland, and determined to go through the country, and find a habitation. Leaving the woman at Dieppe, I went first to Paris, invested great part of my property there, in the name of Weimar; and from thence I went through Germany and Switzerland. Between Lausanne and Lucerne, I heard of an estate to be sold. I saw and liked it; the purchase was soon made, and everything quickly settled. I sent for Agatha: she came part of the way by water, the rest, to Lausanne, by land; there I met her, and conducted her to my house. We now resumed our former intimacy, but she had no more children. I endeavoured by my care of Matilda to atone for the crimes I had been guilty of, in destroying her father, and robbing her of her fortune—a fortune I was afraid to enjoy, and a rank I dared not assume, always apprehensive my villainy would be discovered. I kept but little company. Agatha, who was my housekeeper, and directed everything, many times I was tempted to destroy, but fear preserved her life.

"As Matilda grew up, I became passionately fond of her; my love increased with her years, and I determined to possess her. Agatha had too much cunning not to perceive my inclination; and having long ceased having any particular attachment to me, she blindly fell in with my desires, and encouraged me to proceed. The conversation you over-heard, Matilda, was such as you apprehended; she persuaded me to say I was not your uncle, and the story I told you in Paris, was the one we had fabricated to deceive you. I did not at first intend marrying; I had an aversion to that tie, and therefore a different plan was proposed, which, overhearing, drove you from my house. 'Tis needless to tell you what ensued on discovering you had left me: I resolved to find you, if possi-ble, and traced you to Paris. I thought to have deceived the Marquis; he was too cunning for me: but I obtained knowledge of your being in England through the means of Mademoiselle De Fontelle; a servant of hers having met the Marchioness and you at Calais. I still followed you.

"You know the concession I made to the Ambassador, which I never intended to observe, having intelligence the Count De Bouville was your lover. I had every step watched, and no sooner found you were at a convent than I repaired to Paris, told my own story, and obtained an order for your delivery. I found letters at Paris, from my steward, informing me of the death of Agatha, almost suddenly. This was a most agreeable piece of news; there was now no one living that could accuse me. Blind, infatuated mortals! we forget there is an all-seeing eye, that sooner or later brings us to justice, when most we think ourselves secure! I went to Brest, I hired a vessel to carry me to Venice, determined to reside there with you. With the order in my pocket, and a person who had attended me, more like a confidential friend than a servant, I came to Boulogne, and obtained your delivery to me. The rest you know. It was my intention to have married you, unless you rejected me—in that case you must take the consequence. When I saw the Turkish vessel I gave all up for lost; and when they boarded us, expecting you would be sacrificed to their desires, and myself made a slave, I resolved to prevent both: Providence preserved you—what I have suffered, and the near prospect of death, determined me to confess all my crimes—crimes that have embittered every hour of my life, and which have led me into a thousand inconsistences, from fears and terrors, only created by guilt. Thus it is with the wicked; early plunged into vice, they proceed from one bad action to another; afraid to look back, unable to repent, they go on to fill up the measure of their crimes, 'till their best concerted schemes prove their ruin. Had not the hand of death overtaken me, this confession never would have been made; yet even at this moment I adore Matilda. Pardon me, dear unhappy girl, the evils I have caused you; let me die forgiven by you, and join in supplicating that mercy I have so little room to hope for, but from Divine goodness to the truly penitent."

Matilda assured her of her forgiveness, and implored heaven's mercy on him. "But tell me, Sir," said she, "did you never hear of my mother?" "Only once, and by accident, eight years ago; she was then at Naples, with her family." "Grant heaven!" said Matilda, "she may be there still; O, what happiness, if I should ever embrace a mother!" Tears stopt her utterance; her uncle was affected. "O, Matilda! leave me; I cannot bear your tears, they reproach me too deeply; and I have much to repent of before I leave you forever."

She quitted the room, opprest with the most painful sensations: the tragical end of her father, the melancholy situation of her mother, the crimes of her uncle, and her own present distressed and forlorn state, altogether gave her unutterable pangs: yet a gleam of joy darted through the gloom that pervaded her fate—she was of noble birth; no unlawful offspring, no child of poverty: then she thought of the Count—"Ah!" cried she, "he is now the husband of Mrs Courtney; in all probability I shall never see him more." A sigh followed the reflection, which she strove to place on another score.

She was soon after joined by the captain. "The surgeon came in as you left the room, madam; and notwithstanding the sick man's agitation, in telling his story, he says, he is undoubtedly better, and he begins to entertain hopes, if no change happens for the worse." "I am glad to hear it," replied she, "may he live to repent." "Meantime, madam," said he, "if you wish to write your friends, I will take care your letters shall be conveyed by the quickest dispatch possible."

She accepted his generous offer, and retired to write the Marchioness and Countess what had befallen her; but recollecting that she could not wish to be in France until she had visited Naples, she left her letters unfinished, to consult the captain the following morning. She retired to rest, but the agitations of her mind precluded sleep: alternate joy and sorrow, hopes and fears, created such different ideas, that she passed the night without closing her eyes, and arose, at break of day, resolved to write and address a letter to her grandfather with her story. "If he lives," said she, "he will be overjoyed; if not, if I have no such relation, no dear mother alive, some one of the family will doubtless write and inform me."

When the captain came to breakfast, she imparted her different thoughts to him. She had no way of paying court to his amiable wife, but by kissing her hand, whilst the other prest hers to her bosom, with tender affection, her husband having related the lady's story to her.

The Captain, after some deliberation, said, "I told you once, madam, the employment I am, or rather was engaged in, by no means suited me. I was not originally accustomed to this kind of life; my wife's father always was; he persuaded me to follow it. I sailed with him three years; we made a good deal of money. He died six months ago. This last voyage was the first I ever made for myself. I am disgusted at the service, and mean to quit it: my wife wishes me to do so; she is a good woman; we have enough; I do not want a plurality of wives—I am content with her. My mother was an English woman—I imbibe her sentiments. I have not disposed of my vessel; I will take you to Naples, or even to France, if you wish it, under neutral colours, which I can procure. This will be better than engaging your friends to come here. I have no enemy but the Russians to fear, and those I can provide against." "You are very kind, Sir," said she; "I really am at a loss how to proceed, and will consult Mr Weimar" (she could not reconcile herself to call him uncle). She did so: he approved of the Captain's advice, but thought she had best write her friends of her safety and situation, also of her intention to go to Naples, from whence they might expect to hear her decisive plan; previous to which the Captain could write to some persons, to know if any of her relations were living. This being agreed upon, as the best methods to be taken, Matilda resigned herself to patience 'till answers could be obtained, which must necessarily take up some time.

W e must now return to the Countess and her friends, who arrived at Vienna without meeting any accident.

Their first step was to deliver the German Minister's letters to the English Ambassador, his Excellency having sent dispatches to his own court of this extraordinary affair.

The Countess found but little difficulty in being acknowledged, and put in possession of her rights. Her story engrossed the public attention at Vienna, and she received a thousand visits and congratulations from every person of distinction. Though abundantly gratified by their civilities, she was too anxious to see her son for her mind to be at ease. A messenger had been sent to his quarters, by the Marquis, with leave from the Emperor for his return, and preparing him, by degrees, for the agreeable surprise of finding some near and dear relations. The youth had been apprised of his father s death, but not having read the Count's letter, was a stranger to all the circumstances relative to it. He made no difficulty of obeying the order, and set off for his father's seat directly.

One day, when every heart beat high with expectation, a travelling carriage was seen driving through the park. "My son, my son!" cried the

Countess starting up. The Marquis ran out to meet him. In a moment a tall elegant youth, about sixteen, entered the room, with looks of eager expectation. The Countess flew towards him, threw her arms round him; attempted to speak, but overpowered by tender emotions 'till then a stranger to her breast, she fainted in his arms. The young gentleman, alarmed, and equally agitated, assisted, in silence, to convey her to a seat; and whilst the Marchioness was busy in her endeavours to restore her sister, he kissed her hand eagerly and cried to the Marquis, "Tell me, Sir, who is this dear lady?" "It is—" said the other, with a little pause, "she is your mother, Sir." "Mother!" repeated he, dropping on his knees. "Great God! have I a mother? my own mother!" "Yes," replied the Marquis, "she is indeed your parent, for very many years believed to be dead." Young Frederic was now in a state very little better than the Countess: surprise, joy, the soft emotions that at once assailed him, rendered him speechless and immoveable.

It was some time before they were both sufficiently recovered to be sensible of their felicity. The Countess embraced him with tears of expressive tenderness; he, on his knees, kissing her hands with ardour. "My mother! my dear mother!" was all he could utter for a long time. The Marchioness at length separated them. "My dear Frederic," said she, "you have other duties to pay, besides your present delightful one—I claim you as my nephew; this gentleman is my husband, consequently your uncle." He flew and embraced both. "Gracious heaven!" cried he, "what happiness. A few months ago I supposed myself without family or friends, dependent on the Count's bounty; then I was agreeably surprised with being acknowledged as his son, then suddenly separated, and only ten days since informed of his death—again I was an orphan, and knew not what claims I could or ought to make; but now this unexpected tide of joy and happiness—to find a mother! O, the blessed sound! to find a mother, uncle, aunt, all dear and honoured relations! Great God, I adore thy bounty, make me deserving of thy favours." He again threw himself at the feet of the Countess, who had hung with rapture on his words, and now embraced him with the highest delight.

After this tumult of pleasure was a little subsided, he eagerly enquired the particulars of her story; which the Marquis repeated, as had been agreed upon, glossing over the Count's crimes, as much as possibly could be done, to exculpate the Countess. No mention was made of the Chevalier's death; but the youth heard sufficient to comprehend his mother had been cruelly used, and his features bore testimony of his emotions. "Dearest madam," cried he, "how great have been your sufferings! henceforth it shall be the study of my life to make you forget them in your future happiness."

Lord Delby, who had been rambling in the park, now entered the room. Young Frederic was introduced to him, and the foregoing scene slightly described by the Marchioness. "I am glad," said his Lordship, "I was not present; for though I adore sensibility, such a meeting would have been too much for me."

Growing more rational together, his relations were delighted with the young officer. "It must be confessed," said the Marquis, "the Count paid particular attention to Frederic's education." "Yes, my Lord," answered the youth, "it would have been my fault, if I had not profited by the instructions I received; but I thought my debt of gratitude so great for such uncommon kindness from a stranger, on whom I had no claims, that I strove to exert my small abilities, and by diligence and application, evince my sense of his favours, as the only return in my power." "The deception, as far as related to you," said the Marchioness, "proved a happy one; it laid the foundation for virtue, humility, and gratitude, which perhaps happier circumstances and legal claims might never have called forth. Thus sometimes good springs out of evil."

The following day, when the happy party was assembled, and projecting pleasurable schemes, the Marquis received the letter which the good Mother Magdalene had found means to send off from Matilda. He started, with an exclamation of surprise. All were eager to know the contents. "Prepare yourselves for some regret, on account of your young friend," said he. "What! Matilda?" cried both in a breath. "Yes, I am sorry to tell you she is again in her uncle's power; he has again claimed her as his niece." He then read the letter, and all were equally grieved at the unfortunate destiny of this deserving young woman.

Frederic, with the warm enthusiasm of youth, cried out, "Is there no clue to trace them—I will myself pursue them." "Alas! my son, answered the Countess, "'tis impossible to say where he may have carried her to; but let us hope, as she found means to send this letter, she will find an opportunity to write again; at all events, she has a protector, to whose care we must trust her, until we can obtain further intelligence."

This letter threw a damp on the general joy.

Her story was repeated to Frederic, whose ardour was again raised to deliver the unhappy girl from her persecutor.

The Marquis, who was that day writing to the Count the happy event of their journey and meeting with his nephew, could not resist throwing in a postscript. "My dear Bouville," added he, "we are thrown into the greatest consternation by a letter from Matilda. She is again in the power of that villain, Weimar, who, contrary to his engagements has procured an order from the King, and carried her off, we know not where. We wait with impatience to hear further."

This letter from the Marquis found the Count De Bouville at Bath; where he vainly sought amusement, to remove the anguish which preyed upon his mind, arising from the impossibility of ever calling Matilda his. He viewed the gay females of fashion, with birth, beauty, and accomplishments to boast of, with perfect indifference. Ah! thought he, where is the modest retiring sweetness of Matilda? Where those unaffected charms—those natural graces of her deportment? Never shall I meet with a woman that I can admire or love, after knowing that lovely girl, whose very virtues preclude my happiness. He was in one of these reveries when the letter from the Marquis was delivered to him. The happiness of his friends gave him infinite delight; but how changed were his emotions on reading the postscript: his rage exceeded all bounds; he determined to leave Bath instantly. "I will hunt the villain through the world," cried he; "I will find her, if she is on earth, and no power shall ever take her from me again. O, Matilda! too scrupulous girl, you have undone us both, and ruined my peace forever." He called his servants, and ordered the necessary arrangements for leaving Bath that night. He went out to call on some friends he had formed an engagement with, and to whom he thought more than a card was due. Crossing the parade, he saw, coming towards him, Madame Le Brune, Mademoiselle De Fontelle, and Mrs Courtney, who had arrived from

Tunbridge together the preceding evening. Nothing could have happened more unfortunate than this meeting. His temper irritated before, at the sight of the two ladies together, both of whom he considered as enemies to Matilda, his passion increased beyond the bounds of politeness to restrain. "I congratulate you, ladies, on an intimacy, minds like yours naturally create. For you, madam"—turning to Mademoiselle De Fontelle, who was pale with fear, observing his violence—"you were never an object of my esteem, and long since of my aversion and contempt: your diabolical falsehoods have deprived me of happiness forever; but vengeance will one day overtake you—I promise you it shall," said he, in a voice that made her tremble and unable to go on. "For you, madam," turning to Mrs Courtney—"I have still some respect: you have many good qualities; but your malice and dislike of an unoffending and excellent young woman is inexcusable, and very evidently pursued, by attaching yourself to one you know all your and her friends despise; malice only is the cement of your intimacy. Take my advice, madam,—break it off, and entitle yourself to the respect and esteem of those who are the friends of yourself and Lord Delby."

He was going to leave them, but Mrs Courtney, struck by his manner and words, still partial to him, cried out, "Stop, my Lord,—tell me how long you remain in Bath?" "This night I leave it," said he, "and a day or two hence I shall quit England." "For heaven's sake!" cried she, "let me see you for five minutes, an hour hence;—do not deny me, 'tis the last favour I will ever ask." Seeing he hesitated, "At No. 11, on the South Parade—I will expect you."

She hastily followed her companions, who had gladly removed a few paces from them, and left the Count irresolute, whether he should oblige her or not: but recollecting the civilities he had received at her house and Lord Delby's, he thought gratitude and honour required his obedience.

He called on his friends, and at the appointed hour attended Mrs Courtney. When introduced, she was alone, and very melancholy, but rose to receive him with evident pleasure. "I thank you for this visit," said she, "which I scarcely dared flatter myself with receiving, from your abrupt behaviour to me this morning." "You saw me, madam, very much ruffled; and the company I saw you in was not calculated to put me in better humour. You will pardon me, if I behaved any way rudely; but I really have too much respect for Mrs Courtney, to whose hospitality and kindness I am under so many obligations, to see her in company with a dissolute woman, whose want of chastity is perhaps her least crime; she is unprincipled, in every respect, with a base and malignant heart." "Good God! Count, cried Mrs Courtney "I did not know Mademoiselle De Fontelle, was charged with any other faults than a dislike to Matilda." "That of itself," replied he, "would to me be a sufficient proof of a bad mind; for only those who dislike virtue and goodness can be enemies to her: but independent of that, Fontelle is a profligate young woman, and by no means a fit companion for a lady of your respectability, though, being unknown, she may be received into company. I hope, madam you will deem this an apology for my abrupt behaviour; and now favour me with your commands." "Commands!" repeated she, "dear Count, are you obliged to leave Bath so very soon?" "I am, madam; and I will frankly tell you the cause." He repeated the Marquis's letter. "The amiable Matilda ever was, and ever will be dear to me; tho' her superior greatness of mind will not permit her to accept my hand, I neither can nor will marry any other woman, nor shall she, if I can help it, be subject to the power of any man earth." "But," said she, "without knowledge even of the road they travelled how can you pursue them?" "It matters not," answered he, "I will not rest till I do obtain information." "This is really a Quixote expedition," said she; "travelling the world through to deliver distressed damsels." "It may appear so," replied he, gravely, "but don't let me think Mrs Courtney possessed of so little feeling, as to be indifferent about the fate of an amiable girl, who esteemed and respected her. But have you any commands for me, madam—I am really hurried at present." "Well, Sir," answered she, "if you are determined to go, I must own I wish to preserve your esteem, at least, and therefore I promise you I will profit by your advice, and give up the French ladies." "You will entitle yourself to respect, madam by so doing. Every French woman is not a Marchioness De Melfort, nor, I hope, a Mademoiselle De Fontelle; but 'tis necessary ladies should discriminate in their acquaintance."

Then rising and kissing her hand, "Accept, madam, my grateful thanks for the favours you have honoured me with. If I ever return to England, I shall again pay my respects to you, if you will permit me; and, if I am ever happily settled in France, I shall think myself highly honoured by a visit from Mrs Courtney, and her worthy uncle, Lord Delby." Mrs Courtney's pride forsook her at this polite address, she burst into tears, "Adieu, my dear Count; may happiness attend you, though you leave me a prey to regret and sorrow." He hastened from her with some emotion. That woman, thought he, has many amiable qualities, but she wants steadiness and respect for herself: an imbecility of mind makes her resign herself up to her passions, from the want of resolution or fortitude to subdue them; she has naturally a good and generous heart, but she is easily led aside by others more artful than herself. He thought however he had done his duty by warning her against Mademoiselle De Fontelle; and returned to his lodging with satisfaction to himself.

Everything being ready, the Count quitted Bath that night, slept a few hours on the road, and arrived in town the next day.

He pursued his route to Dover, and from thence to Boulogne. He went to the convent, to gain intelligence; the porteress very readily answered his questions, but that afforded him not the least clue to guide his search, as she knew nothing of the road taken. She told him that Matilda had left money to convey Louison to Paris, who had been gone upwards of a fortnight.

Although the Count scarcely supposed Weimar would carry her to his own house, yet he determined to go there. He wrote the Marquis, and proposed being at Vienna, should he prove unsuccessful in Switzerland.

It would be tedious to follow the Count thro' his journey. He made all possible enquiries through the different towns, without obtaining any information. He arrived at Mr Weimar's; they had not heard from him since he left England. Disappointed and mortified, he went from Switzerland to Vienna, and from thence to the villa of the Countess. He was received with transport. The Countess eagerly exclaimed, "She is found, we have a letter—O, such good news!"

The Count had hardly patience to go through the ceremony of introduction, before he begged to know the good news!

The Marchioness had two days before received the letter Matilda had written from Tunis—she gave it him to read.

Matilda had briefly given an account of her voyage and arrival at Tunis, the civilities of the captain, and dangerous state of Mr Weimar. She mentioned, that she had reason to suppose she was descended from a noble family, in Naples; that a short time would relieve her doubts; and, at any rate, she would write again, if not join them, in a very little while.

Lovers, who are ever industrious to torment themselves, would perhaps, like the Count, have conjured up a thousand fears to distract their minds. "Is this all your good news?" cried he, "alas! I see little to depend upon here; 'she has hopes' she belongs to some noble family,—a scheme of that villain Weimar's, to keep her easy 'till he recovers; besides, what dependence can be placed on a corsair? Ah! if these are all your hopes of safety, they are small indeed." "Upon my word, Count," said the Marchioness, "you are very cruel, to destroy the pleasing illusion we entertained of her safety; for my own part, I see no cause to doubt the kindness of the Captain, who, 'tis plain, must have permitted her to write; and for the other, he can have no power, in his circumstances, whether ill or well." "I hope, madam," replied the Count, "your conjectures are founded on truth and reason,—I shall rejoice to find my fears are groundless; but, be that as it may, I am determined to go immediately to Tunis." "You are right, my dear Sir," cried the young Count, Frederic; "could I disengage my mind from superior duties, I would, with pleasure, accompany you." "Ah! the knight errantry of youthful folks!" said the Marquis, smiling, "but I assure you, my good friend, we are all here equally interested in the fate of Matilda, and equally desirous of promoting any plan conducive to her safety." "I am sure of it," answered the Count, "and therefore hope you will not take it ill, if I leave you tomorrow, for I am resolved to go to Tunis, if a vessel can be hired."

They saw it was in vain to oppose his resolution, and were therefore silent.

He was delighted with the warmth of the young Count, and praised his spirit in the most lively terms.

He took leave of them the following morning, to pursue his plan, with the earnest good wishes of the whole family.

Meantime everything succeeded at Tunis, to Matilda's wishes. Mr Weimar daily grew better. At first his recovery seemed rather a matter of regret to him; but when she assured him of her entire forgiveness, that she never would betray the secret of her father's death, and that the restitution of her estates would sufficiently prove his penitence for the intended wrong done to her, he grew more reconciled, and by degrees, her sensible and pious observations wrought such a change in him, that he determined, when he got well, the Captain giving him his liberty, he would enter into a monastery for the rest of his days. Matilda encouraged him in the design.

The Captain, who was present at many of their conversations, said, one night, that his dislike to the cruel business he had been engaged in was considerably strengthened by Matilda's dissertations on virtue and vice; he was resolved never to make another voyage; and, though he could not but think the faith of Mahomet the true faith, yet, for her sake, he would always respect Christians; because the two best women he knew, exclusive of his wife, were both Europeans and Christians.

Matilda impatiently expected an answer from Naples. The Captain at last received one. The good Count Morlini had been dead three years; the Countess, his daughter, was alive, though in a languid state of health, and was gone, with another family to Nice, to stay two or three months.

This intelligence was delightful to Matilda: she was anxious to set off as soon as possible.

Mr Weimar was now well enough to bear the voyage. He made a deed of gift to his niece, of all he possessed; having greatly improved the original fortune, from a fear of exciting too much notice and enquiry if he had lived otherwise; and told her, his intention was to enter into the order of poverty, as the proper retribution for his inordinate desire of wealth, which had induced him to commit such horrid crimes. She would have persuaded him to have chosen an order of less severity; but nothing could alter his resolutions.

The Captain having hastened his preparations, the day was appointed for sailing.

Matilda could not take leave of the Captain's amiable wife without feeling a very sincere regret; for, though they did not understand each other's language, yet the expression, of the heart was comprehended by both, and engaged mutual esteem and tenderness. The friend, or rather confidant of Mr Weimar, was sent for from the country, his liberty given him, and Matilda, at her uncle's request, promised to pay him the sum agreed upon in France, for his assistance to carry her off.

They set sail with a prosperous gale, but with hearts very differently agitated.

Much about the same time the Count De Bouville had taken leave of his friends; and having hired a vessel at the first sea-port, he proceeded on his voyage to Tunis, and, without any accident or interruption, safely arrived there six days after Matilda had left it. He was soon on shore, procured an interpreter, and hastened to the Captain's house. His heart beat fast with hope, fear, and expectation; but who can describe his emotions when informed of their departure for Nice. He asked a thousand questions could scarcely be persuaded but some sinister design was again practised against her, and it was with much difficulty he at length grew more reconciled and satisfied with the account he received.

He had nothing now to do but to follow her to Nice; but as water and some provisions were wanting for the vessel, he was obliged to bridle in his impatience, and remain there three or four days, which were ages in his calculation.

Matilda, meantime, safely arrived at Nice. Mr Weimar instantly left the place, promising to write his niece, under cover to the Marquis De Melfort, soon as he was settled in a monastery.

The Captain conducted Matilda to a hotel, and they consulted how to act. It must be confessed her situation was a very distressing one; no female companion, no one to introduce her, she might be supposed an impostor, notwithstanding the testimony of Mr Weimar, signed before the Captain. In short, they found themselves at a loss how to proceed. The first step was to know if the Countess Berniti was there; of this they were soon informed she was, accompanied by the Count and Countess Marcellini. After much deliberation the Captain proposed waiting on the Count, telling him a lady just arrived from Tunis, requested the favour of seeing him, to enquire after some very particular friends and relations she had at Naples. This scheme was adopted and put into execution. The Count was surprised at the message, but curiosity carried him immediately to the hotel, and he was introduced to Matilda. He was extremely struck with her figure and appearance. She trembled, and for some moments was incapable of speaking; but endeavouring to collect fortitude from necessity she thus addressed him, "The liberty I have taken in requesting the honour of seeing your Lordship here requires many apologies, but I am in a very singular and distressing situation. Will your Lordship permit me to ask you how long you have known the Countess Berniti?" The Count started at the question. "Almost from a child, madam; we were brought up in an intimacy from our youth." "You knew her unfortunate husband then, and his brother," said she, "and possibly may recollect it was supposed the infant daughter of the Countess died in convulsions?" "Supposed!" repeated he, "good God! What can you mean, madam?" "To recall to your mind, Sir, those circumstances on the developing of which my future happiness depends. Save your surprise, my Lord, and to elucidate my meaning, I must entreat the favour of you to peruse these papers, the confession of a dying man once brother to the late Count Berniti." The Count took the papers with the most eager curiosity.

Matilda, affected with hopes, doubts, and fears, could not suppress her tears: on this important moment her fate seemed suspended .

The Count made two or three exclamations, but when he came to the murder of his friend, he smote his breast, "Unparalleled wickedness and ingratitude!" cried he. Hastily proceeding in the narrative, he no sooner came to the exchange of the children, than throwing his eyes on Matilda, "My heart, and your striking resemblance to the charming Countess, tell me, you are her child."

"I am! I am!" replied Matilda, weeping, and strongly agitated, "if she will vouchsafe to own me!" He folded her to his bosom, "Own you! O, what transport to recover such a daughter! Compose yourself, my dear young lady; I am little less affected than you are,—but let me finish this interesting confession of a miserable wretch." He went through the whole without any further interruption.

At the conclusion, the Captain related the events at Tunis, and the result of their enquiries at Naples, which had brought them to Nice.

"Doubt not, my dear lady, but all your troubles are over: behold the hand of Providence in every event; had not your wretched uncle taken you from France; had you not fallen into the power, perhaps of the only man who would have treated his captives with honour and compassion, unknown in general to people of his profession,—forgive me, Sir, the observation"—the Captain bowed—"had not the dread of death and everlasting punishments terrified the guilty wretch; had not all these singular events happened, through Divine permission, you might, to this hour, have been ignorant of your birth, and my amiable friend deprived of the joy and transport that await her in your arms."

The Count again warmly embraced her. He paid a thousand polite compliments to the Captain; and though he regretted leaving them, he was anxious to consult his lady in what manner to convey this delightful intelligence to the Countess.

When he returned to his lady she saw he was greatly agitated, and knowing the message he had received, was very curious to hear the result of his visit. She fortunately happened to be alone; he therefore related the whole story, read the papers, and spoke in raptures of Matilda's person, and engaging manners. Nothing could equal the astonishment of the Lady Marcellini. She anticipated the joy of her friends, yet was at a loss how to inform her of an event so entirely unexpected. They knew it must recall to her mind the horrid circumstances of her husband's murder, which neither time nor reason had ever reconciled her to support with any fortitude. "Yet," said the Count, "to recover such a child; to have a hold, a connexion in life so desirable and so unlooked for, must surely greatly overbalance the affliction of a painful remembrance, at least weakened, though not subdued."

They went to the apartment of the Countess. She was at her toilet. Her woman, being dismissed, "Well Count," asked she, "have you seen the lady from Tunis,—is she a Turkish woman?" "No, madam, she was brought up in Germany; she is a charming young creature, and you may be proud of the compliment," added he, smiling, "when I assure you she very strongly resembles your ladyship." "You are very polite, my good friend," answered she, in the same tone, "but I am neither young nor handsome, and you say this lady is both; but, pray, is she acquainted with any of our friends?" "Yes, but by name only; she has no personal knowledge of any one in Naples; she was very particular in her enquiries after you." "Of me!" said the Countess, surprised; "how could she know anything of me?" "You remember the Chevalier N—, who went abroad so many years since?" "Ah!" said she, with a sigh, "I do indeed remember him; is he alive,—does this lady belong to him?" "He is not living," answered the Count, for Matilda permitted him to suppose he was dead, without asserting it; "this young lady was in some degree related to him, but I think more nearly so to your ladyship." "Heavens! my dear Count, you surprise me! I know not of any female relation I can possibly have." "She is certainly a near relation, however," replied the Count, "and you must prepare yourself for a most agreeable surprise, as I am convinced you will love her dearly." "Indeed, my good Count," exclaimed the Countess, "you have given me violent emotions; my heart palpitates, and my whole frame trembles; for God s sake, do not keep me in suspence—who can this lady be?" "Before we answer you, my dear friend," said the Count's Lady, "let me persuade you to take a few drops, in water, the agreeable flutter of your spirits will require them." "All this preparation terrifies me; I will take anything, but pray be explicit at once." "Then, my dear lady, bear the joyful recital, I am about to give you with resolution."

He took up the story, at a French vessel, captured by the Corsair, and a gentleman on board, attempting to destroy himself and a lady, described the subsequent events, and then began the narrative. When in his address to Matilda, he said, "The Count Berniti was your father," the Countess started from her chair, "Gracious God! what do I hear; but no, —I can have no interest in it." She was silent. He proceeded, whilst she hung her head, drowned in tears at the mention of her husband whose death he slightly passed over, 'till he came to the circumstance of the children. She gave a shriek, and throwing her arms around her friend, "If this is true, great God! if this is true, I may yet have a child. O! say," cried she looking wildly at him, "tell me at once, have I child?" "You have," said the Count, approaching her, "you have a daughter, my dear Countess, whom heaven has preserved to bless the remainder of your days." "'Tis too much, too much, said she, putting her hand to her bosom and instantly fainted in the arms of her friend. Having drops and water at hand, she was soon recovered; and after a few sighs, that removed the oppression from her heart, she said, "Tell me, if it is the illusion of my senses only, or if indeed I have a child?" "No, my dear lady, you are not deceived—we have told you truth." "Then, where is she?" cried the Countess, eagerly, "let me see her—I die with impatience!" "Recover your spirits," answered the Count; "collect your fortitude, and I will immediately fetch her to your arms." "O, hasten! hasten!" cried she, dissolving in tears, which they were glad to see. And the Count, with joy, flew to the hotel, where poor Matilda waited in all the agonies of suspence. "The discovery is made, my dear young lady; your mother is impatient to receive and bless you.'

This intelligence, though so anxiously wished for, gave her inexpressible agitations; she got up and sat down, two or three times, without speaking, or being able to move; and at length, with trembling knees, was conveyed to the carriage, the Captain, at the request of the Count, accompanying them. When arrived at the house, and conducted to a room, she had a glass of wine to raise her spirits, whilst the Count announced her arrival. In a few minutes he returned, and took her hand. The Captain wished not to be present at the first interview. With a tremor through her whole frame she gave her hand; the door opened; she saw a lady, at the top of the room, who appeared to be in tears. Matilda saw no more, she sprung from the Count, threw herself on her knees before her, and without uttering one word, sunk into insensibility. The friends hastened to her relief. The Countess sat stupid, gazing wildly on her, without moving. When Matilda's senses were a little restored she looked up, she exclaimed, "My mother! O, have I a mother?" That word recalled the Countess to sense and feeling; she clasped her in her arms, "Blessed! blessed sound!" she cried, "my child, my dearest daughter! heaven be thanked." She dropt on her knees and lifted her hands and eyes to heaven, then again embraced her child, whose soft and tender emotions were too powerful to admit of speech, nor is it possible to describe the tumultuous joy of both for many minutes. The unhappy widow, the childless parent, dead to every hope of comfort, to embrace a child, adorned with every grace, to feel those delightful sensations to which her breast had been a stranger, and which mothers only can conceive,—a blessing so great, so unexpected, no language can describe. What then must be the feelings of Matilda, after suffering such a variety of sorrows, to find herself in the arms of a parent? O, sweet and undefinable emotions! when reciprocal between a mother and a child! who can speak the rapture of each tender bosom, when parental and filial love unites!

A fter the first transports were a little abated, the Captain was introduced. The Countess welcomed him as the preserver of her child. He was struck with the perfect resemblance between the mother and daughter, and extremely gratified by the affectionate attention of every one present.

In the evening Matilda promised to relate the particulars of her whole story, and the following day to write to her friends.

The Count now pursued his voyage to Nice, still doubtful of Matilda's safety, and the sincerity of Mr Weimar's repentance.

The wind was not favourable to his impatience, and the passage was a tedious one; at last, however, he was landed at Nice, and, after many enquiries, learnt there was a Turkish vessel on the point of sailing. He flew to the ship; the Captain was on board; without reserve the Count acquainted him with his errand, and search after Matilda. "Indeed, Sir," said the Captain, "I pity you; tis peculiarly unfortunate, that they have quitted Nice three days, on their way to Vienna."

The poor Count was struck dumb with vexation and disappointment; the Captain, however, related to him the whole story, as he recollected, in Matilda's narrative, he was mentioned as a particular friend. "When," added he, "the Countess was acquainted with the extent of her daughter's obligations to the ladies in Germany, she instantly proposed going to Vienna, which being correspondent to Matilda's wishes, their friends consented to accompany them, and the happy party set off three days ago. Me," said the Captain, "they have rewarded with unbounded generosity much beyond my wishes or deserts; I shall now return, to live in the bosom of my family, and give up the sea forever."

The Count applauded his resolution; and taking a ring from his finger, of value, "Wear this, my dear Sir, as a testimony of my esteem for the friend of Matilda, and remember, that in the Count de Bouville you will ever find one, upon any future occasion."

The Captain could not refuse so polite a compliment, though he was already amply gratified for the services he had done.

Thus we see a just and generous action scarcely ever fails of being properly recompensed.

The Count had now nothing to do but follow his mistress. He remembered Mrs Courtney telling him he was going on a Quixote expedition. What would she say now, thought he, how exult at my disappointed knight errantry? Then, when he thought of the discovery of Matilda"s birth, "Ah!" said he, "should I no longer be dear to her, of what use is my pursuit? She will now be introduced to the great world, and my pretensions may be distanced by a thousand pretenders of more merit and superior fortune! Nevertheless, I will not give her up until from herself I receive my doom." Accordingly the following morning, a little recovered from his fatigue, he set off for Vienna.

Meantime the Countess, her daughter, the Count and Countess Marcellini, with their attendants, were safely arrived at Vienna, from whence Matilda wrote to her beloved friends, and earnestly requested the favour of seeing them.

'Tis impossible to describe the transports which her letter occasioned. They lost no time in setting off, and that very same evening their names were announced, Lord Delby and the young Count restraining their impatience 'till the following day.

The mutual joy, congratulations, and expressions of obligation which took place on their meeting may be easier conceived than described. The Countess Berniti was never weary of pouring forth her acknowledgements to the friends and preservers of her child, whilst they, on the other hand, could not help admiring the wonderful chain of events which had gradually led the way to such a happy discovery both for her and the Countess of Wolfenbach.

"Tomorrow," said the Marquis, "we shall beg leave to introduce our friend Lord Delby, and the young Count, my sister's son. I assure you," said he, addressing Matilda, "when we first heard of your being forced from the convent, our young Frederic, though only sixteen years old, had the gallantry to offer himself as your champion to pursue and deliver you." "Can I wonder at his generosity and heroism, my dear Sir," answered she, "born of such a mother, and possessing doubtless the virtues of his family? No; I am already prepossessed in his favour; I know he must resemble my charming Countess."

She forebore speaking of Lord Delby, that she might not be obliged to ask for the Countess, his sister, as she concluded the marriage must have taken place long ago.

They spent a most delightful evening together, and engaged to accompany the Countess of Wolfenbach to her seat, in three days from the present; that lady next day sending orders to prepare for the reception of her noble guests.

Matilda longed to see young Frederic, and her ideas of him were all confirmed when she beheld him: his elegant form and polished manners, in some measure, reconciled her to his late father, for having done his son so much justice in his education. Everyone was charmed with him; and Lord Delby was received with all the respect due to his rank and merit.

As both the Countess Berniti and her daughter were silent respecting the Count, the others were equally cautious not to name him, lest they might say more than Matilda chose to have known; and there being no opportunities for private conversation, the Marchioness earnestly wished to be in the country, that they might enjoy a few uninterrupted tête-à-têtes.

At the appointed time they all quitted Vienna, and arrived at the Countess's villa.

They were just seated at the dinner-table when the Count De Bouville's name was announced. The Marchioness gave a cry of joy; the knife and fork dropt from Matilda's hand, and it was with difficulty she kept her seat when he entered the room. The Marquis introduced him to the strangers as his particular friend: as they had never heard his name mentioned, they received him with the politeness due to that recommendation only: but when he advanced to Matilda she changed colour, and trembled so violently as to attract her mother's observation, although she was too attentive just then to speak, for the Count's agitations were visibly greater than hers; he bowed upon her hand and said a few words, but they were not intelligible. The Marquis hurried him through the rest of the company, and then placed him between Lord Delby and himself, saying, "Now, if you please, let us have our dinner; I put a negative to all compliments and question for this hour to come —'tis plain we are all very glad to see each other."

In consequence of this seasonable order the conversation became general, and the Count and Matilda had time to recover themselves. She wondered indeed no one asked for his lady, nor that she appeared to be of the party. He cannot help being a little confused, thought she, and did not expect to find me here, I suppose: well, I must try to exert my fortitude, and, amidst so many blessings, I ought not to repine that one is withheld from my possession. Occupied by these reflections, she ate very little, nor attended to the conversation.

THE CASTLE OF WOLFENBACH

The Countess, her mother, who had been an attentive observer both of the Count and her daughter, said, "My love, Matilda, you eat nothing." She almost started, but replied, "I beg your pardon madam, I am doing extremely well."

Bouville, who had been at no loss to discover Matilda's mother, as well from the likeness as the tender looks of the latter, now paid that lady particular attention.

***

When the dinner and servants were removed, the Marchioness complained of a trifling head-ache, and said she would go for a few minutes into the air. "Will you step out with me, Matilda?" "With pleasure, my dear madam," answered she, rising quickly from her chair, and glad to escape.

The two friends walked to the garden. "My dear Matilda," cried the Marchioness, "I could rein in my impatience no longer; I was eager to congratulate you on the arrival of the Count, and on your happiness, in having now all your friends about you." "You are ever good and kind to me, my dear madam. I have indeed met with so many great and undeserved blessings, that my heart bounds in gratitude to heaven for its goodness towards one who, a short time since, thought herself the most unhappy of her sex." "You will remember, my dear," said the Marchioness, "it was my constant lesson to you, never to despair. Providence has now brought you out of all your troubles; a reliance on its justice and mercy, and an humble and grateful heart for the blessings you enjoy, will henceforth make your happiness permanent. But, my dear Matilda, I can perceive your confidence in your charming mother has not been quite unreserved; I plainly see she is a stranger even to the name of the Count De Bouville; how comes that to be the case?"

"As all possibility of any connexion between the Count and myself was at an end, I conceived there would be an indelicacy in mentioning his former offers to my mother; yet perhaps I was wrong, and ought to have done justice to the sentiments he then honoured me with, as they proved his generosity and nobleness of mind. If I have been wrong," said she, with a sigh, "'tis not too late to repair the fault, though it can be of no consequence to him now." "Your words astonish me," cried the Marchioness; "what has the Count De Bouville done to have forfeited your esteem?" "Nothing, madam," replied she, confused; "he has done nothing to lessen his merit or virtues in my estimation." "I think indeed," resumed her friend, "you must be strangely altered. If it should be so, for I thought you always an enthusiast in gratitude, and surely the man who made you an unreserved offer of his hand, and though rejected, still preserved his affection through many temptations—who has traversed lands and seas in search of you." "Of me, madam!" exclaimed Matilda, surprised; "pardon my interruption, but did you say the Count had been in search of me?" "Doubtless I did," replied her friend; "can that surprise you; could you suppose we did not inform him, you were in the power of Weimar? or that he knowing it, would not range through the world to find you? I am sorry you do him so little justice, Matilda, for certainly he is entitled to your warmest gratitude, if your heart no longer speaks in his favour." Astonishment overpowered the senses of Matilda for a moment. "He is not then married to Mrs Courtney?" said she, faintly. "To Mrs Courtney! good God! no; how came you to entertain such a ridiculous idea?"

Joy, transport, and unexpected relief from the painful thoughts she long had entertained were now too powerful for her feelings: with difficulty she tottered to a seat, and leaning her head on her friend's shoulder, burst into a flood of tears, which preserved her from fainting.

"My dear Matilda," cried the Marchioness, "I now clearly comprehend the whole; but, at the same time that I give you joy of your doubts being removed, I could beat you for presuming to wrong my amiable friend by entertaining them; see that you excuse yourself well, or depend upon my displeasure."

Matilda, after taking some time to recover her spirits, mentioned the anonymous letter; also, nearly as she could recollect, the contents of Mrs Courtney's, written to her whilst she was in the convent; she repeated her answer. "After which," added Matilda, "your journey taking place, when you kindly sent to invite me of your party, the Count was not mentioned; I therefore naturally concluded he was married, and remained with his lady, and that, from considerate motives you declined giving me the information." "How industrious some spirits are to torment themselves," exclaimed the Marchioness, "yet I own you had some little cause for your conclusions; but I am most inconceivably surprised Mrs Courtney should have taken such a step; that she was very partial to him, I believe, and might wish for a return from him, is also very probable, but I am convinced the Count never did make, nor ever thought of making the smallest pretensions to her favour, any more than common politeness required; and so, my little credulous, jealous friend, I desire you will return to the company, make the Count one of your best courtesies, and pay him the highest attention otherwise I will certainly put him out of the pain that now oppresses him, by telling the whole story."

Matilda, who felt her heart uncommonly light, readily promised to behave very well, and requested the Marchioness would take an opportunity to acquaint her mother with the Count's generosity and affection for her.

This being agreed on, the ladies returned to the dessert, with so much satisfaction in their countenances as excited the attention of their friends.

"I do not ask after the head-ache," said the Marquis, smiling, "a tête-à-tête seems to have driven it away." "You are right," answered his lady, in the same tone; "it sometimes cures both the head and the heart; but come, give us some fruit, it must be confessed you have done pretty well in our absence."

The Countess Berniti was delighted to see her daughter look cheerful; and as the Count De Bouville had engaged her in conversation, Matilda joined in it now and then with great complaisance towards him, which elevated his spirits to the highest pitch; and everything relative to her being full in his mind, he observed what an uncommon generous Turk the Captain of the corsair was.

"Why, do you know him, my Lord?" asked the Countess.

He was struck mute; Matilda hung her head, evidently confused. "Ah! Count, Count," said the Marquis, "when men get tipsy, whether with wine or joy, out pops all their secrets; but I see you are dumb—I will answer for you. Yes, madam," added he, addressing the Countess, "I believe the Count does know the Captain, for he has been taken a prisoner too." "Indeed!" cried she, "what, at the same time my daughter was?" "I will not take upon me to say," answered he, smiling archly at Matilda, "that it was exactly at the same time, but I believe it was pretty nearly so."

The Marchioness and her sister could not help laughing at this equivoque which added to the confusion of Matilda.

"Come, come," cried the Countess, her friend, "none of your pleasantry my Lord; the Count shall tell his own story to the ladies another time, and I will assist him where he fails to do himself justice."

The Count bowed; "You are very good to me, madam; I am only afraid I shall have occasion for troubling you and the Marchioness to prove your partiality for me, at the expence of your judgement." "Very well, Count," said the Marquis, "I am thrown out, I see. Faith, you are in the right; a young handsome fellow seldom fails of engaging the ladies, whilst no such dust is thrown in our eyes, to blind our judgement, or obtain a partial testimony." "Be quiet, Marquis," said his sister; "you are really malicious."

The company arose soon after, and going into the garden, divided into little parties. The Marchioness and the two Countesses went towards an alcove; the lady of the house, with Matilda, the Count, Lord Delby, and Frederic took another path; the Marquis and Count Marcellini strolled into a different one.

Matilda now took an opportunity to atone for the omission she had been guilty of, by asking Lord Delby after Mrs Courtney and his son. Meantime the Marchioness explained to the Countess the sentiments of the Count De Bouville; his early affection for Matilda, his repeated offers of marriage, and her noble refusal openly, grounded on the uncertainty of her birth, since she did not deny a preferable esteem for him. She also repeated his long and tedious searches after her, as far as she knew of them, and concluded with observing, his rank and fortune, elevated as both were, fell far short of his merit and amiable disposition. When she had finished, "I own to you, madam," said the Countess, "your relation has broke in upon my favourite plan. I hoped to have carried my daughter to Naples, and to have seen her married and settled there for life. "Ah!" said she, "to what purpose did I find her, if we are to be separated again?" "But where is the necessity for a separation?" said the Countess Marcellini, "cannot you alternately visit each other every year?" "No," replied she; "when she marries there will be many things to prevent it. Indeed," added she, in tears, "good and amiable as the Count is, I wish Matilda had never known him." "Possibly, madam," answered the Marchioness, very gravely, "she might then never have seen the convent, never have been carried off, and you still ignorant you had such a daughter living, whose generous self-denial deserves some praise as the Count's disinterested and uncommon passion is entitled to some consideration: but I beg your ladyship's pardon; I have only done my duty in making this communication; the Lady, Matilda, will doubtless conform herself to your wishes."

The Countess struck with her words and manner of speaking them, caught her hand, and kissing it, "Pardon me, dearest madam," said she, "if I have appeared petulant and ungrateful, my heart is not so, but consider how natural it is for a mother, just in possession of a treasure so long and painfully regretted as entirely lost, to be jealous of a superior attachment, and unhappy at the idea of parting from an object so entwined about her heart." "It is natural, my dear madam," answered the Marchioness, "and if I did not hope some method might be found out to obviate the objection, I believe the Count would have little chance of succeeding with—" "Your and my Matilda," said the Countess, eagerly. "That 'Lady Matilda' struck me to the heart." "She is indeed mine," replied the Marchioness, "my adopted child; and had the want of fortune only prevented her union with the Count, we offered largely to remove it; but her objections proceeded from an elevation of soul, a greatness of mind, that would not disgrace the man she married, whilst the Count thought she would dignify any rank, and honour any man to whom she gave her hand." "Amiable, good young people!" said the Lady Marcellini. "O! my dear Countess they ought not be separated." "Nor shall they," answered she, "if I find their affection is still mutual: I will have a private conversation with Matilda tomorrow, and you, madam, shall immediately know the result." They now walked towards the house, and were soon joined by the rest of their party.

Notwithstanding every one wished to appear pleasing, the evening was not a gay one. The Countess Berniti seemed collected within herself, Matilda was confused and apprehensive; the Count De Bouville distracted with doubts, drew unfavourable omens from the looks of the mother and daughter, and therefore was very silent. They separated at an early hour, and sought in sleep a forgetfulness of care.

T he following morning, the Countess and Matilda being alone in their dressing-room the former said, "How comes it, my dear child, that, in relating your story to me, you never mentioned the particular obligations you owed to the Count De Bouville, for his generous offers?" "Because, madam," answered Matilda, blushing, "I thought it would appear to give myself a consequence I did not wish to arrogate, for merely doing my duty in declining them. Another reason was, I had been misled into a belief, that the Count had married an English lady, a sister of Lord Delby's; and therefore supposing he never could be anything to me, I judged it of no consequence, for the present, at least, to say anything about him." "You have answered with candour and sincerity," said the Countess "and I expect the same to the following question: Do you love the Count De Bouville?" "If, madam," replied she, hesitating a little, "to prefer him to any other man I ever saw; if to confess that I think him deserving of the highest esteem from every one he honours with his acquaintance; if this is to be called love, I must answer in the affirmative." "You are not quite so ready and explicit in this answer," said the Countess, with a smile, "nevertheless I believe your sentiments in his favour are pretty decisive; and if my conjectures are right what part am I to act, and how be expected to give a sanction to your union, which, in all probability will part us forever." "Never, my dear mother," answered she, in a firm tone, "never; no power on earth shall part us again: how great soever my affection for the Count may be, be assured my duty, my love for you will greatly over-balance it; and if the alternative must be to part with one, behold me ready to give him up, without the least degree of hesitation." "Now, my dear Matilda," said the Countess, extremely moved by the firmness of her voice, and the expression in her eyes, "now you have found the way to subdue me at once: you shall make no such sacrifices for me, my child; and I will think of some method to reconcile your duty and inclination to my wishes." Matilda kissed her mother's hand with the warmest affection, and some of their friends coming into the room precluded further conversation.

She went in search of the Marchioness. She was told that lady was in the garden, and thither she repaired, when, coming to an alcove, she saw her seated in earnest conversation with the Count De Bouville. She would have turned back, but the Count ran, caught her hand, and led her to the Marchioness. "I am rejoiced to see you," said she, "my dear child; do, pray, take this troublesome young man off my hands, for I declare he has been making down right love to me." "Who, I?" said the Count. "Yes," answered she, "you know you have—as a proxy; and, as I am quite tired of being only a substitute, I leave Matilda to supply my place for the present." She got up and walked away, Matilda being too much confused to have the resolution to prevent her.

The Count seized this moment to know his doom. He besought her attention for a few moments, briefly ran over the affair between Mrs Courtney and him, as a mere bagatelle, without wounding the lady's consequence. His distress and pursuit of her through France, Switzerland, Germany, from thence to Tunis and back again. He described the fervency of his love and the tortures of suspence; called upon her in the tenderest manner, to remember the time when she had said, "If her rank and fortune equalled his, she would, with pleasure, give him her hand." "And now, madam," added he "that hour so much wished for by you, though of little consequence in my estimation, when thrown into the scale with unequaled merit and dignity of mind; that hour is arrived, deign, my beloved Matilda, to tell me, if I still can boast a share in your esteem; tell me, if I may presume to hope, that, however changed your situation, your heart, faithful to your other friends, has not withdrawn itself from him who lives only for you, and depends on you for happiness or misery in extreme?"

Matilda endeavoured to assume a composure she did not feel, for after the conversation with her mother she thought she was not at liberty to act for herself. Being silent a few moments she replied, "Believe me, Sir, my heart is still unchanged, still the same grateful and affectionate sentiments predominate in my mind: the Count De Bouville possesses my esteem, if possible, more than ever, for my obligations to him are increased; but—I have a mother; no longer mistress of my own destiny, she must determine for me. I will not scruple to confess, that it will be to me the happiest moment of my life, if my duty and affection to her coincide with your wishes."

The Count, transported with joy, kissed her hand in expressive silence, whilst Matilda rose from her seat and hurried to the house, rejoiced that this interview was over. She returned to her mother's apartment. The ladies were with her. The Marchioness smiled a little maliciously at her, but observing she looked rather agitated, she asked, "What is become of the gentlemen this morning? Have you seen the Marquis and his friends, my love?" "No, madam," replied she, "I suppose they are rambling in the grounds."

Just then the Marquis entered. "Ah! ladies," said he, "I am happy to see you together: I have undertaken to bring a cause before your tribunal today, against one of your coterie, and I expect an impartial judgement. What say you, ladies, dare you promise to be just and sincere?" "Your impertinent question is so affronting to us," replied the Countess, "that I think we ought to decline hearing your cause." "Conscience, conscience, my dear sister," cried he, smiling, "nevertheless, I will open my brief. A gentleman of rank, fortune, and unquestionable merit"—here Matilda trembled—"has, for some time, entertained the warmest affection and respect for an amiable woman. When first he knew and admired her she was in a situation that precluded hope, he was therefore condemned to silence; that situation is changed; he has no obstacles to combat but the lady's over-strained delicacy: she owns a preferable esteem, but—she cannot approve of a second marriage." Here all eyes were glanced at the Countess, who was confused. Matilda began to respire. "Tell me, ladies," resumed the Marquis, ingenuously, "should so futile an objection preclude her from making a worthy man happy, gratifying her own partiality in his favour, and giving a dear and valuable additional relation to her friends? You see I put the case simply and plainly. Will you, madam"—addressing the Countess Berniti—"have the goodness to speak first?" "I am not an advocate, Sir," she answered, "for second marriages; on the contrary, I think there are but very few cases that can justify them. If a woman is left with a family she is anxious to provide for, and has an eligible offer, that will enable her to do so, duty to them should make her accept it; gratitude to the generous man, should render her a good and affectionate wife. If a woman has had a bad husband, who has used her ill, and unworthy of her merit, I conceive she owes no respect to his memory, but may, without any imputation whatever, reward the affection of a deserving object, and find her own happiness in so doing." The Countess Marcellini, said, "My sentiments exactly correspond with my amiable friend's." "And mine, also," cried the Marchioness, "only I must be permitted to add, that if a woman so situated declines the offer, from over-delicacy, which is no delicacy at all, and by so doing renders a worthy man wretched, and refines away her own happiness at the same time, I think her quite inexcusable, and deserving reproach from her friends." "Thank you, my love," said the Marquis; "and now, sister, your opinion, if you please." "Mine," answered she, in some confusion, "you are no stranger to, otherwise whence this appeal? But to convince you I am neither obstinate nor perverse, but open to conviction and the advice of my best friends, I will frankly subscribe to the opinion and judgement of these ladies." "Now," said the Marquis, "you have redeemed my love and esteem. I will not apply to our sweet Matilda here; she is unqualified, at present to judge; and I fear her trial is not far off from an accusation something similar, though not on account of a second marriage; however, I shall now rejoice my client with intelligence, that he has gained his cause." He bowed with a smiling air, and left the room.

"My dear sister," said the Marchioness, "accept my congratulations:

Lord Delby is a most worthy nobleman, and offers to reside in whatever country you please; wherever you are will be his home."

The ladies all congratulated the Countess.

"I own," said she, "I have a very preferable regard for Lord Delby, and am, in all probability, indebted to him for my life and present happiness: it shall henceforth be my study to return those obligations."

This matter being settled, the ladies retired to dress; and, after a little hesitation in her voice, Matilda informed her mother of the preceding conversation, between herself and the Count. "I have referred him to you, madam, and I beg previously to observe, I will implicitly, and without a murmur, abide by your decision. I never will be separated from you; and if my union with the Count must be attended with so great a sacrifice, no consideration whatever shall induce me to marry him. I have already shewn I can resign him, when I think it my duty to do so." "You are an extraordinary good girl," answered the Countess "but I will make no promises; when I have heard the Count, I shall be the better able to determine what I ought to do."

T his day a cheerfulness pervaded through the whole party. Young Frederic, extremely attached to Lord Delby, was delighted with the prospect of a nearer connexion. He was charmed with the Count De Bouville; but his young heart felt a little degree of envy when he considered him as the favoured lover of Matilda, whom he admired so exceedingly, that his extreme youth only prevented him from being a formidable rival.

In the evening, when they took their usual walk, the Count requested the honour of a quarter of an hour's conversation with the Countess Berniti, and they retired to an alcove.

Matilda, who was leaning on the Lady Marcellini's arm, trembled so exceedingly, that she prest her hand, and said, "Fear nothing, my good girl, and hope everything." This a little reassured her, and they pursued their walk.

The Marquis suddenly joined them, and observing her companion engaged in chat, drew her gently aside, "There is a letter for you, under my cover, and I suspect, from Weimar." They walked aside, and Matilda, hastily opening it, found it was really from him. He had entered among the Carthusians, at Paris. He pathetically laments all his past crimes, and acknowledges the justice and mercy of God: calls upon her to forgive and pray for him; cautions her against the allurements of the world, and takes an everlasting leave of her; meaning, from the hour he receives one line from her, to inform him, that she has recovered a mother, and is happy in her present prospects, to shut up his correspondence and connexion with the world for ever.

This letter affected Matilda greatly; she remembered the care he had taken of her youth, though she shuddered when she considered him as the murderer of her father. "Unhappy man," cried she, "may God afford him penitence and peace in this life, and endless happiness in the world to come!" She promised the Marquis to write an answer the following morning, and he undertook to enclose it.

She joined her friends; but the letter had given so melancholy a turn to her thoughts, that everyone took notice of her dejection; and judging it to arise from another cause, everyone was anxious to dispel it, and raise her spirits.

At supper they all met. Matilda glanced her eyes once towards the Count, and observed joy seemed to animate his whole frame; from thence she derived hope, that he was not very displeasing to her mother.

When they retired for the night, the Countess was silent; Matilda of course asked no questions.

The next morning the Countess held a long conversation with her two Neapolitan friends; at the conclusion of which, the Count and her daughter was sent for. They attended, both visibly agitated. After they were seated, the Countess addressed herself to her child: "My dear Matilda, the Count has done you the honour to express a warm attachment to you, and has requested me to authorize his addresses, without which permission you have refused to listen to him. I expect you answer me with sincerity; will my consent, my sanction to his addresses meet your wishes? or, can you renounce him, and follow me to Naples, if I desire it?" "Certainly I will, madam, there, or anywhere you command;

at the same time, I should make a very poor return for the obligations I owe the Count De Bouville, if I hesitated to own, that had his addresses been favoured with the approbation of my mother, I could have preferred him to all men living; but no preference whatever shall militate against the superior obligations I am under to a parent." "Come to my arms, my dear children," cried the Countess, extending them, "I know not which is most dear to me."

They threw themselves at her feet: she blessed them with tears of joy and joined their hands. Both were speechless, but language was not necessary to prove their mutual transports. She raised them, and presented them to her friends, "Love my children," said she, "I think they deserve it."

When a little recovered from their joy, and seated by her, "Now listen to me," said the Countess; "I will not repeat the conversation I had with the Count last evening, 'tis sufficient to say his offers were beyond my hopes or expectations: he frankly of himself requested my daughter and self should never be separated, for he would settle in Naples. That intention of his did away the only objection I could make. I consented to his wishes, but reserved to myself the pleasure of telling Matilda so. Last night, when I came to reflect on the sacrifice the Count was about to make, of his country, his friends, the injury his fortune must sustain, and the uncommon affection he manifested for my daughter, in paying me so great a compliment, I felt myself little in my own eyes for my acceptance of his generous offer. Dissatisfied and uneasy I said nothing to you, my love, of our conversation. This morning I consulted my friends; they were equally struck with myself at the Count's attention to my happiness; their opinion coincided with my own—that it became my character not to accept such a resignation." "My dear mother!" exclaimed Matilda. "Patience, my love; those generous friends, I presume to flatter myself, decided against their own inclinations. In one word, they approved that I should renounce Naples; that your country," —turning to the Count—"should be my country; and that the satisfaction of entertaining the friends of my youth, who offer to pay me a triennial visit, should be the only favour I ought to ask, or you consistently can grant. Yes, my dear children," added she, "I will accompany you to France, and end my days under your roof."

Never was delight equal to what the Count felt at this unexpected turn in his favour; for it could not be supposed he could renounce his country and friends without a pang; on the contrary, only his superior love for Matilda, and respect for the feelings of her mother, could have induced him to offer so great a sacrifice. He thanked her, in transports of joy. He embraced the Count and Countess. "Complete your good-ness," cried he, "and add to my obligations, by making this your first visit,—go with us to France, and let there be no drawback on my happiness."

The Countess and Matilda, urging the same request, they consented to spend three months with them.

"Now, young folks," said the Countess, smiling, "you may take a walk and congratulate each other, conscious that you deserve the happiness that awaits you, from nobleness of mind, and a generous self-denial, which preferred the satisfaction of others to your own gratification."

The Count availed himself of this permission, and led Matilda to the garden, whilst the delighted mother sent for the rest of the family and repeated the preceding scene.

Pleasure shone on every face—all were equally happy; and even Frederic, with a repressed sigh, said, "They were deserving of each other."

Within a week from that day the Countess of Wolfenbach gave her hand to Lord Delby at Vienna, after a mutual agreement, that they should divide their time equally between Germany and England, with sometimes a visit to their friends in Paris, which was promised on all sides, should be reciprocal.

The Count De Bouville wrote to his sister, Madame De Clermont, who was returned to Paris, with restored health, on the happy turn of his affairs, and requested she would make every magnificent prepara-tion for the reception of his guests, the Count and Countess Marcellini; the Countess Berniti and Matilda accompanying the Marchioness until proper arrangements should take place for their marriage, which all were desirous should be publicly performed at Paris, to confute the odium Mademoiselle De Fontelle had thrown upon Matilda's character.

Lord Delby and his lady had written to Mrs Courtney, of the different events which had taken place, and requested a visit from her to Germany; the Marchioness and Matilda wrote, also, and entreated the same favour.

These letters a little discomposed her at first; but as she had given up all hopes of the Count, and was not of a disposition to fret herself long on any subject, being naturally of an easy temper, she answered their letters with perfect good-humour, congratulated them on the happiness before them, and promised to visit all parties the following Spring.

The parting of the friends from the Countess and Lord Delby was very painful: they were strongly entreated to accompany them, but Frederic having only another month's leave of absence, to remain with his mother, the time was too short to admit of his going to Paris, and the Countess could not be persuaded to leave him; they were therefore obliged to be contented with the assurance of an early visit to the Count De Bouville, in the Spring, when they would come to meet Mrs Courtney.

The Paris travellers, though much affected by taking leave, as they proceeded on their journey, recovered their spirits, and arrived without meeting any accident at Paris.

Madame De Clermont, her husband, Madame De Nancy, and Mademoiselle De Bancre waited to receive them. Great was the joy of all parties: a thousand embraces and felicitations passed between the Count's sister, Mademoiselle De Bancre and Matilda; and when the latter called to her remembrance the difference of her feelings now, and when before she had felt herself humbled by their caresses, as passing upon them in a false light, she bent herself, with a grateful adoration, to the Divine Being, who had protected her, and by such unforeseen, and apparently untoward accidents, brought her to such unexpected happiness.

The Count Marcellini waited on the Neapolitan Minister, who came and paid his compliments to the ladies, congratulating the Countess on the recovery of such a daughter, and requesting he might have the honour of introducing them at court.

Three days after the Marchioness gave a superb entertainment: all the foreign ministers were invited, an extensive circle of friends, and among the rest, Madame Le Brun and her niece, who were just returned from England. Conscious as they were of their ill conduct, they had not the resolution to refuse being present at an entertainment where all the great world was invited, and appeared with much effrontery. When they entered, the Marchioness led them to the Countess Berniti, "The Countess Berniti, ladies, mother to the Lady Matilda, whom you had the honour of seeing with me a few months ago, as my relation." They bowed, paid their compliments, in a confused manner, and hurried on; but the Marchioness had not done with them; she observed the Imperial and Neapolitan ambassadors were conversing with Matilda; they rather shrunk back; "Nay, ladies," said she, "you must pay your respects to the queen of the day." Mademoiselle felt extremely confused, yet resolved to put a good face on the matter; she assumed a gay and affectionate air as she advanced. The Marchioness having introduced Madame Le Brun, "And now," said she, to Fontelle, "let me present you to Lady Matilda Berniti, one of the first families in Naples, as his Excellency can bear witness; and to your Ladyship I beg leave to say, this is Mademoiselle De Fontelle, the envious traducer of your character; the despicable young woman, who, incapable of practising virtue, from the depravity of her own mind, naturally hates the good and exalted characters of those who entitle themselves to the respect and admiration of the world, and who now meets with that contempt and mortification worthless and censorious characters like hers deserve."

The struggles of Fontelle, to free her hand from the Marchioness, and the elevated voice of that lady, had drawn a large circle round her. "Go, Mademoiselle," added she, "leave the presence of those you can never see without self-accusation; and may your example teach others how cautious they ought to be in judging of persons and appearances from the malignancy of their own hearts. Candour and good nature," said she, smiling "will give beauty to the most indifferent faces, whilst envy and malice will render the most beautiful persons truly contemptible."

Matilda, who had not expected this denouement, was extremely confused, and felt for the mortified Fontelle, but the numbers who crouded round her, and expressed their satisfaction, though it in some degree abated her regret, induced her to think there was little dependence on the applauses of the multitude: these very people, thought she, a few months ago encouraged the persons they now reprobate; let me not be vain of respect which only circumstances create!

Matilda thought justly; since every day's experience must convince her, fortuitous circumstance will engage the shew of esteem and respect, which the next moment of misfortune will as assuredly deprive us of, among those who are not capable of discriminating, and attach themselves only to persons gifted by fortune, and are incapable of giving merit, if in obscurity, the praise it deserves.

The two ladies having left the room, boiling with rage and indignation, and leaving a useful lesson to the envious and ill-natured, harmony was restored; everyone exerted themselves for the entertainment of others, and everyone agreed it was the most delightful evening they had ever spent; though many of them called on Mademoiselle De Fontelle the following morning, expressed their sorrow for the ill-treatment she suffered, and assured her it was the most horrid entertainment; the Lady Matilda, the idol of the evening, the most vain, impertinent, conceited creature they had ever seen.

Such is the progress of envy, such the hatred of virtue, in bad minds, and such you meet with in all public circles.

In less than a fortnight after their arrival in Paris, the Count De Bouville, who had been indefatigable in his endeavours to hasten all the elegant arrangements he had projected for the reception of his bride, had the pleasure of seeing everything in proper order, and by the approbation of all their joint relations and friends, received the hand and heart of his Matilda, who all acknowledged was the only one deserving the entire affection of the accomplished and respectable Count De Bouville.

Thus, after a variety of strange and melancholy incidents, Matilda received the reward of her steadiness, fortitude, and virtuous self-denial. A consciousness of performing her several duties ensured her happiness; and when she wrote her beloved Mother St Magdalene the happy conclusion of her adventures, "From you," said she, "I learnt resignation, and a dependence on that Being who never forsakes the virtuous; from you I learnt never to despair; to your precepts and prevention I am indebted for not taking the veil; and I trust, called into an elevated situation, I shall ever remember the unfortunate have claims upon the hearts of those whom God has blessed with affluence; and that, through your means, reserved to experience every blessing of life, I shall feel it my duty, by active virtues, to extend, to the utmost of my abilities, those blessings to others less fortunate than myself.

THE NECROMANCER

OR, THE TALE OF THE BLACK FOREST

LAWRENCE FLAMMENBERG

EDITOR'S NOTE

When I think of gothic literature, I think of the nights I spent in New York watching double features in the Village. After reading an article about vintage double-feature paperbacks, my head went straight to horror and gothic. I thought about what stories would pair well together, and the Northanger Horrid Novels came to mind. These seven stories are bound by their inclusion in Jane Austen's gothic-spoof *Northanger Abbey*, when Catherine (the protagonist) is given a list of must-read gothics. This list, once thought to be fabricated, includes seven rediscovered tales. I decided to create this double-feature volume including two of the seven Northanger Horrid Novels.

I wanted one of the stories to be a clear example of the types of stories Jane Austen is satirizing in *Northanger Abbey*. The first work in the volume, *The Castle of Wolfenbach*, includes many of the tropes mirrored in Austen's tale.

For the second work, I wanted something different. While researching each of these pieces, I came across *The Necromancer; or, The Tale of the Black Forest*. I quickly realized that this story was very strange.

The Necromancer was originally written in German by Karl Friedrich Kahlert, under the pseudonym Ludwig Flammenberg, before being translated by Peter Tuethold (the pseudonym of Peter Will). Many scholars originally believed that Tuethold had not, in fact, translated the story but had claimed a German origin for his original tale to give the work authenticity. When it was later discovered that the German source material did exist, it became apparent that Tuethold's "translation" had deviated quite a bit from the original. A large portion seems to have been plagiarized from another work entirely. Many attribute the odd structural choices in the novel to Tuethold confusing his differing source materials. The translation was so unusual some scholars speculated that the resulting tale was meant to discredit German literature.

I found it intriguing scholars had believed that attributing the tale to a German author might make the story more believable. While the source material did actually exist, the following preface is evidence that Tuethold considered believability to be very important. It is often assumed that as a story is passed from person to person it loses credibility, but the opposite seems to be true of ghost stories. The best horror tales always come from a friend whose friend's cousin's friend knows the person it "really" happened to. Instead of degrading in veracity, ghost stories are enlivened by each person who passes the tale along. Each iteration adds a bit of the teller's essence, making the ghosts more and more real.

The structure of the novel made me particularly interested in including the story in this double feature. Not only is *The Necromancer* a translation by a pseudonym of a pseudonym, but it's also told in a Russian doll-style sequence of framing narratives situated one inside another. Editing the work was an intense exercise in punctuation. When one character, telling a story to another character, quotes a third character as they read a letter from a fourth character that includes dialogue from a fifth character, it's easy to lose track of the quotation marks.

The Necromancer is a strange and baffling tale of complete absurdity, making it perfect for the second half of this Northanger Double Feature.

—Ann Marie Hormeku
Athens, GA, 2022

PREFACE OF THE TRANSLATOR

The wonderful Incidents related in the following Sheets, not being made up of tiresome Love Intrigues, repeated again and again in almost every new Book of Amusement, will, as I flatter myself, not be quite displeasing to the reader, on account of the Novelty of the Subject. The strange mysterious Events which occur in this little Performance are founded on Facts, the authenticity of which can be warranted by the Translator, who has lived many Years not far from the principal Place of Action.

If the Subject of the following Tale should be thought interesting and amusing, the Public may expect a speedy Publication of a still more intricated and wonderful one, exhibiting a long Series of similar Frauds, perpetrated under the mysterious Veil of pretended supernatural Aid.

The Publisher being sensible of the manifold Defects of his Translation, will acknowledge with Gratitude the gentle Corrections of the dread Arbiters of Literary Death and Life, and Promises carefully to avoid, in a future Publication, the repetition of any slips the Critick's Eagle Eye shall discover in the following Sheets.

THE NECROMANCER

PART ONE

I

The hurricane was howling, the hailstones beating against the windows, the hoarse croaking of the raven bidding adieu to autumn, and the weather-cock's dismal creaking joined with the mournful dirge of the solitary owl;—such was the evening when Herman and Elfrid, who had been united by the strongest bonds of friendship from their youthful days, were seated by the cheering fireside. Thirty long years had elapsed since they were separated by different employments; Herman having been called to distant countries, whilst Elfrid (leaving the University where their mutual friendship had begun) hastened home to his parents, to ease the burden of their old age, and to cheer the tempestuous evening of his dear progenitor's life.

On his journey homewards, he rambled over some of the most charming parts of Germany; yet he sought in vain after pleasure, separated as he was from the dear companion of his youthful days. At length he found in the circle of his family, what he had been seeking in vain abroad. The pleasure which his venerable parents felt, in again beholding the offspring of their mutual love, soothed the disquiet of his mind; the joy sparkling in their eyes at the sight of the supporter of their declining years, tinged his cheeks with the rosy hue of content-ment, and filled his soul with inward bliss. After ten years of congenial happiness, his aged father died, closing a well-spent life in his seventy-second year. The guardian angel of virtue carried his unspotted soul to the cheerful mansion of everlasting peace; the gentle smile of a good conscience sat still on his wan lips, when his sainted spirit arrived in heaven, hailed by millions of holy angels.

Twelve years longer Elfrid soothed the sorrows of his mother, and supported her under the heavy load of ever-increasing infirmities, until she was re-united to the dear companion of all her earthly joys and cares. He dropt a tear of filial affection on her tomb, and now directed all his care and tenderness towards the promoting his only sister's happiness; who as well as himself remained unmarried; and some years after, in order to disperse the clouds of gloomy fancies, the usual companions of bachelors, he determined on taking a journey, and left the care of his house to his maiden sister.

He was so fortunate as to meet on his journey with many friends of his earlier days, companions of his academical studies; at length he also traced out his dear Herman, the most beloved among his youthful friends.

He found his worthy friend a favourite of fortune, blest in the lap of sweet contentment and unmixed happiness.—A loving wife crowned the favours which fortune had so abundantly blessed him with; providence had also surrounded him with a circle of promising children, two of whom were happily married, and had blessed him with two grand-daughters and three grandsons—Heaven's greatest blessings smiled upon him wherever he went, contentment and joy sat upon his reverend brow, and peace of mind had taken her abode within his heart.

"Good God!" exclaimed he, as soon as he could find words to give vent to the rapture of his soul, "do I then behold, once more before I die, the dear companion of my youthful days? Heaven be praised for that unexpected happiness! Now all my wishes are fulfilled—Oh, Elfrid! The separation from thee, the apprehension of seeing thee no more, was the only bitterness mixed in the cup of bliss which providence has kindly administered to thy friend. Thou art alive—I have nothing else to wish than that my end may be as happy as this hour."

After the first ecstasy of meeting was over, Elfrid related how anxiously he had ever been inquiring after his dear friend; told him how many letters he had written to get information of his abode, and was going to chide him for his negligence, when Herman fetched a letter from an old acquaintance of his, who had written to him, that "Elfrid had left the service of the Muses, enlisted under the banners of Mars during the Seven Years' War, and had fallen a victim to his martial spirit."

Elfrid was satisfied with this explanation.

"Brother," he exclaimed, "let us forget our age and live together, as long as I can remain with thee, as if the thirty years since we have seen each other had never passed, and be as merry as we have been in our youthful days."

Herman's cheek glowed with pleasure, and he squeezed Elfrid's hand. Six days passed in mutual joy. Herman resided at a country seat, situated on the banks of the Elbe, and enclosed by an ancient forest, which made it a pleasant abode to Elfrid, who was passionately fond of hunting. Every morning they rambled through the woods, and the two friends pursued the fleet game with almost juvenile ardour, till the dinner bell summoned them to a substantial meal and a bottle of old Rhenish wine. When the cloth was removed, the goblet went cheerfully round, and the two happy friends drank and talked of the achievements of their younger days, and what had happened during their separation. Thus days rolled on like hours, and Elfrid did not yet think of departing.

The gloominess of the weather, on the day when this narrative opens, gave their conversation a serious turn. They began to discourse on the calamities of war; of the dangers they had formerly undergone, and of the many distresses and sufferings they had experienced in the early part of their lives. As night advanced, the tempest grew more furious, the flame in the chimney was wafted to and fro, and began to die away by degrees, when Herman fed it with dry wood, stirred the ashes, and it began again to blaze.

"Brother," said Elfrid, "brother, dost thou believe in apparitions? Dost thou believe in spirits?"

Herman, smiling, shook his head.

"I also," Elfrid went on, "do not believe in apparitions; yet, when travelling through Germany, I have met with adventures which I still am unable to unriddle."

Upon Herman's requesting an explanation, Elfrid began as follows:

The great fair was just beginning when I arrived at F—; the bustle of the buyers and vendors, the meeting with a number of dear friends, and the many different amusements, promised to afford me a great deal of pleasure, and I resolved to stop a few weeks at that town.

The inn where I had taken lodging was crowded with travellers: an aged hoary man amongst them was particularly noticed by everyone, on account of his remarkable appearance. His looks were reverend; his dress, though very plain, was costly; he appeared to be a rich nobleman, and occupied the best apartments. A coach and six, with four servants richly dressed, carried him frequently out; he was seen at all the public places, was present at all amusements, yet, what raised my curiosity, he was constantly alone and in profound meditation. I often remarked, that wherever he was, he did not take the least notice of what was doing around him, and, as if a prey to grief and inward sufferings, seemed to be insensible of all the objects that surrounded him. He was also continually alone when in his apartment, the door of which was always bolted. He rode out as soon as dinner was over, and commonly returned very late at night.

I questioned the landlord about this strange man, but he shrugged up his shoulders and could tell me nothing. "But," exclaimed I peevishly, "you certainly know where he comes from, could not you ask his servants?"— "The servants," answered he, "are as mute as their master. He is supposed to be an English lord, that is all I know."

I was of the same opinion when I first saw him; having met, on my travels, with many Englishmen who had behaved in the same sullen and reserved manner. His melancholy mood I fancied to be the effect of the spleen, and I did not trouble myself any more about him.

I had not been above three days at F— when I lost my purse. At first I fancied I had dropt it somewhere in a shop, or my pocket had been picked in the street, and determined to be more careful in future; but, in spite of all my precaution and care, I suffered a second loss the next day, missing a diamond ring, with a miniature picture of my deceased mother; I was sure that the preceding night I had pulled that ring from my finger and put it on the table when I went to bed; I questioned the waiters, but they appeared to be offended at my inquiries—in short, the ring was gone.

A few days after, I went to the play; I had a snuff-box, of very little value, in the right pocket of my coat; a gentleman who was sitting by me, at the left, begged me to give him a pinch of snuff, but I could not find my box. That insignificant theft made me smile. I was only glad that I had left my purse at home.

The play was over, and a boy with a lighted torch went before me to an adjacent tavern; I wanted to see what hour it was, but my watch was also gone. "Cursed misfortune!" exclaimed I. The boy reminded me of his money, I gave it him, and entered the supper room. An acquaintance of mine took notice of the paleness of my countenance, inquiring whether I was ill; I denied it, and took my seat at the table. I hurried down my supper without noticing my neighbour, and determined to depart the next morning, being persuaded that some cunning rogues had singled me out to try their skill with me at the expense of my property. As I was pushing back my chair, somebody close by me asked me what o'clock it was. I did not answer, because that question, by reminding me of my loss, had vexed me, and was going to leave the room.

"Sir, what o'clock is it?" exclaimed somebody once more, tapping me on the shoulder. "I do not know," I replied, without looking back, and paid my bill.— "Have you no watch with you?" exclaimed the same person again. Now I turned round in great vexation, and, guess my surprise, the troublesome inquirer was my neighbour at the inn, the very same gentleman who had excited my curiosity so much some days ago.

He stared me in the face, as if expecting an answer.

"Sir," said I now, "my watch—"

"Has been stolen," interrupted he quickly, "I have caught the thief, there it is." So saying, he put my watch into my hand. I was stunned with amazement, and could not help wishing to know the thief, that I might recover the other things I had lost, for I was sure that the same person who had robbed me of my watch had also pilfered what I had lost before; but, ere I could signify my wish, the mysterious gentleman had vanished.

I went home, struck with astonishment, but the stranger was not yet arrived. At length he came, as usual, at midnight; I rushed out of the door when I heard him coming upstairs, made a respectful bow, and begged him to give me leave to ask a question; but he passed me hastily, without taking notice of me, absorbed in melancholy thoughts, took the candle from the servant, and bolted his door.

All my attempts of speaking with him were fruitless. When at home, his door was bolted, in the hall he took no notice of me, and in public places he shunned me. Vexed at this rude behaviour, I would not make another attempt to get acquainted with that queer fellow.

Meanwhile three days more elapsed, and that strange accident had made me forget my departure; but now I renewed my resolution of setting off as soon as possible, and determined to leave F— the next day. I put everything in order, had my trunks packed, and was obliged to find out a banker who would take a bill on a person at Leipzig, which I had brought with me.

Towards evening I met with a reasonable man; joyfully now did I put my hand into my pocket to take the pocket-book out of it, but I could not find it. "For God's sake," exclaimed the merchant, when he saw me pale and trembling, "what is the matter with you?"— "Nothing, nothing at all," stammered I, rushing out of the house.

A faint ray of hope was still glimmering within my soul; I fancied I had left all the remainder of my little fortune at the inn, though I was certain that I had taken the pocket-book with me. I arrived, trembling, at my lodging, and was hardly able to unlock my door; I entered slowly, as if I wanted to avoid the terrible blow that threatened me; I minutely searched the room, but alas! all my property was gone.

I could not believe the reality of my misfortune; I emptied my trunk more than ten times, and more than a hundred times did I search every corner of the room, thinking it impossible that the bill and the pocket-book should not be there, however I could find neither of them.

It grew late, and I was still sitting on my trunk, half-distracted; at length I resolved to go next morning to some of my acquaintance, and endeavour to get some money advanced. That terrible evening was followed by a more terrible night; morning dawned and I still could not sleep—my pride revolted against the thought of borrowing money, but the idea of want staring me in the face, got the better of it, and I went. Every one whom I applied to was sorry for what had happened to me, railed against the villain who had robbed me; but nobody would lend me money—the scarcity of cash, the backwardness of debtors; these and a thousand other obstacles prevented my friends from assisting me. I went home in a melancholy mood, and did not know what to do. It struck one, the dinner was on table, but I could not eat. I was standing in my room with a downcast look, and musing on my distress, and I cannot tell how long I had been in that desponding situation, when a gentle knock at my door roused me suddenly from my reverie: I exclaimed in an agony, "Come in!" The door opened, and I was thunderstruck when I beheld the unknown gentleman before me. I ran almost frantic with joy towards the stranger, clasped him in my arms, and exclaimed, "Have you, have you found it?"

"I have not!" answered he.

"No!" groaned I. "Gracious heaven! how unhappy am I."

"Patience, young man," he replied, "although the thief may have made his escape, yet I am here."

I gazed at him with astonishment. He took his pocket-book, opened it, and gave me two papers. "There, take them," said he, "there is as much as you may want at present, the mail will set off tomorrow for your native country. I wish you a happy journey."

Then he laid the papers on my table, and hastened out of the room; a strange sensation fixed me to the floor, and fettered my tongue. I neither could thank my benefactor, nor inquire how I was to repay him. I felt veneration for this singular man, admired his humanity, and yet I could not help feeling some inward sensations of horror; I was for a considerable time as motionless as a statue. Having recovered from my

amazement, I went to the table, took up the papers, and saw, with astonishment, that each of them was a draft for a hundred dollars payable at F
—. It grieved me to be obliged to accept a present from a stranger. But
what could I do? How could I get access to him? Perhaps (thought I) he
will send his direction, but I waited in vain for it. He got into his
carriage and drove away.

I also left the house and returned late, the stranger was not yet come
home; however, I determined to await his return, and as soon as he
should enter the house, hasten to his apartment, and insist upon his
taking a bond for his money, and if he refused, force him to resume his
present. This resolution, however, I could not execute, for he did not
return.

Night being far advanced, I laid myself down upon a couch and
began to doze. Nodding, I heard a noise at my door; I got up, and all was
silent. I fancied the noise I had heard was the effect of those early
dreams which sometimes amuse our fancy when sleep is coming on, but
soon after I heard the same noise again. I once more got up from my
couch, and all was silent again. Listening attentively, I heard the same
noise repeated; it grew now louder and louder, and resembled the
tapping of somebody who could not find the latch. I was going to open
the door, but before I got to the middle of the room saw it move on its
hinges. I stopped, the door opened slowly, and now I could distinguish
my visitor. It was a strange figure, tall and emaciated, clad in a white
garment. As it entered the room, it advanced towards me with slow and
solemn steps; I staggered back, and a chilly terror trembled through my
frame. The apparition moved towards the table in awful silence. It took
up my watch, looked at it, gave a hollow groan, and laid it down again. I
was thunderstruck. The phantom now moved slowly back, and I looked
at its face as it was passing the table where the candle stood. Merciful
heaven! How was I chilled with horror when I beheld the features of my
deceased mother! My knees shook, a cold sweat bedewed my face, and
my strength forsook me.

Meanwhile the apparition had come to the door without having
turned its face; it opened the latch gently, and, when on the threshold
turned round, staring me in the face with a ghastly look, and lifting up

its emaciated hand, thrice made a threatening gesture and disappeared.

I fell senseless back upon my couch, and when I could recollect myself again, I fancied I had been haunted by a bad dream. The clock struck one as I was going to look at my watch.

Vexed that the stranger did not come home, I went to bed and slept till it was broad day. When the waiter brought my breakfast, I asked whether my neighbour was come home. He said no. Then I asked if he had left F—? The waiter answered, "It may be, he always pays his bill after dinner, he carries no trunks with him, and none of his servants lodge in our house."

I went with the waiter to the apartment which the stranger had occupied. The key was in the lock, we walked in, all was empty.

I returned to my room, took up the drafts he had given me, and would have destroyed them, if I thus could have disencumbered myself of the obligation which I owed him. It suddenly came in my mind that they perhaps might be fictitious, or the name of the merchant who was to pay the money not known. This thought afforded me pleasure, though I could expect nothing but misery if it should prove true.

I hastened to the host and shewed him my drafts, under the pretext of wanting to know the direction of the merchant. He described the house and the street where he lived. I was frightened and went that same morning to the merchant. He looked slightly at the paper but very seriously at me, and his eyes seemed to denote astonishment and pity. I expected joyfully that the bills would be protested; however, I was mistaken. He opened, sighing, his drawers, and counted down two hundred dollars, still looking at me with astonishment. I put the money in my pocket, and being convinced that he pitied me for being obliged to that stranger, I took the liberty of asking him by whom he was to be repaid; upon which he appeared disconcerted, shrugged his shoulders, muttered some unintelligible words, and left me suddenly. I went away under the greatest apprehensions, and the weather being fine, was tempted to walk to a public garden. The beautiful morning had assembled there a great number of foreigners, and of the inhabitants of F—; I went into a remote bower, and ordered some chocolate. Retired from the noisy bustle of company, I could now muse on the strange accidents which I had experienced during my short stay at F— I also recollected my dream, and reflected on it more seriously than before. Though I was very much tempted to deem it something more than a delusion of fancy, yet I was still disinclined to ascribe that strange incident to a supernatural cause, being strongly prepossessed against the belief in apparitions, and found myself bewildered in a maze of irksome fancies. I struggled hard with my imagination, striving to forget what had made me so uneasy; but all was in vain; the dream, or rather the apparition, continually returned to my remembrance, in defiance of my reasoning, and the horrid spectre hovered still before my eyes.

Tired and wearied with the struggle between reason and fancy, I endeavoured to ease my soul of her heavy load, by a loud exclamation, and, without recollecting where I was, I suddenly broke out in the words, "No, it was a deluding dream?"

"It was no dream!" exclaimed a well-known voice on a sudden. I looked up. Imagine my surprise at beholding the mysterious stranger standing before me!

"Young man," said he, without giving me time to utter a single word, "young man, do you wish for an explanation of the apparition of last night?" I gazed at him in dumb silence. "If you wish to have unfolded that incident," he resumed, after a short pause, "then await me this evening by ten o'clock, at the town gate, next to the inn." The stranger pronounced these words with a friendly, courteous mien, made me a bow, and disappeared amid the crowd.

The waiter brought the chocolate, but I could not swallow a single drop. In vain did I now roam all over the garden in hopes of meeting the stranger; in vain ask all my acquaintance and the waiters, describing minutely the stranger to every one; nobody had seen him.

I hastened home, awed and terror-struck. I entered my apartment; the door of my chamber seemed to be in constant motion, and the figure of my mother haunted me without intermission. I could not get rid of the gloomy reflection on her threatening looks, and left the house. I now rambled about in great uneasiness from the coffee-house to the promenade, from thence to the museum, from the museum to the tavern, from the tavern to the exhibition of wild beasts, and at last to the playhouse, but I could nowhere find tranquillity.

It was growing dark when I left the playhouse, my soul was disturbed by strange sensations, and I was consulting with myself whether I should go or not. Doubt and apprehension suspended my resolution for a considerable time, and overwhelmed me with agony.

Shall I go or not? Prudence asked, "What hast thou to apprehend?" I could give no answer, and fears and doubts still continued keeping up a most distressing conflict. Curiosity on a sudden raised her bewitching voice, driving away every doubt, and bidding defiance to the wise counsels of prudence. "Thy departure is fixed, tomorrow thou art going to leave this town;" thus the charming seducer whispered in my ear; "and today thou canst get rid of every teasing doubt. Thou wilt repent it if thou refusest to go. Courage, man, courage, don't be such a coward as to fear an old man;" and thus my pride added, "thou canst inform thyself how to pay the notes."

I was determined to go. "I will repair to the place of rendezvous," said I, and was instantly disencumbered of a load of uneasiness. I returned to my apartment with composure, called for a light, and began to write some letters. Having continued that occupation till eight o'clock, I went downstairs to amuse myself a little, and spent two hours at the table d'hôte. When supper was over, the landlord desired to speak to me in private. As soon as we were retired to another room, he said, "I bring you happy tidings." I listened attentively. "You have lost several things during your residence in our town?"— "I have," replied I, with surprise. "Your loss has given me great uneasiness, on account of the reputation of my house."— "To the point," exclaimed I, with impatience. "You have lost a purse, a snuff-box, a ring, and a pocket-book."— "You know exactly what I have lost," answered I with amazement.

"You will find every article in your room." I staggered back. "An unknown person brought all your things an hour ago."—"An unknown person! Was it that strange gentleman? But it cannot be him, you know." — "Whom do you mean?"—"My neighbour."

The landlord shook his head smiling, he was called away, and hastening to my room, I found everything as the landlord had told me.

The bill of exchange was in the pocket book, and I was lost in dumb amazement, not doubting that this was a new trick of my unknown benefactor. "But why did he not wait till ten o'clock?" said I to myself, "why not return my things at our appointed meeting? Has he doubted my coming, or been obliged to depart suddenly?" The last was the most likely proposition, but at the same time the most disagreeable to me, as it would deprive me of the means of returning him his money, and paying my debt now I had recovered my property. But how could I be certain that he really was departed, since all his proceedings had been so strange and eccentric? How could a gentleman like him, a pattern of honesty, a friend to human nature, how could he be guilty of transgressing the first duty of an honest man? How could it be possible that he would break his word? He had appointed me to meet him at ten o'clock, and the landlord had not said anything to the contrary.

I went down to the supper room, requesting a few minutes' hearing of the landlord, and asked him if the unknown person, who had brought my lost property, had left no message for me. He replied in the negative, adding, that the messenger merely said, "there are the things Mr. Elfrid has lost," and without giving him time to question him any farther as to by whom he had been sent, he went away.

I looked at my watch; it wanted fifteen minutes to ten. I fetched my hat and greatcoat and walked slowly towards the town gate. The night was exceedingly fine, the moon shone bright, and was surrounded with millions of sparkling stars. It struck ten when I stood on the appointed spot, I took every passenger for the stranger, ran towards several of them, and began to speak, but I was always disappointed. It was now forty-five minutes past ten, and I began to get tired, and to conclude that my apprehension that the stranger had been obliged to depart suddenly was correct.

"I will wait till it strikes eleven!" said I to myself, "and then return home, if he should not be here." The bell of the adjacent steeple tolled eleven, and the stranger was not yet come.

"I will stay fifteen minutes longer, and then return to the inn." These fifteen minutes likewise expired without his making his appearance. The stillness of midnight surrounded me. I proceeded on my return.

I had not gone ten steps, when the stranger came walking towards me with hasty paces; nobody could be more rejoiced than I was, and, forgetting entirely that I had waited so long, I ran towards him. He shook me heartily by the hand, and said, "I am sorry that I have kept you waiting so long."

"I would readily have waited still longer," replied I, "if I had been sure of seeing you at last, for I was anxious to obey your commands, and to get rid of my doubts."

"That you shall," said he; "follow me."

He began to walk so fast that I hardly could keep up with him; he uttered not a word; we arrived at the gate and it was opened at his command; our way led straight through the suburbs, at the bottom of which a solitary house was standing; my conductor knocked at the door; we were let in: the house appeared to be empty and deserted, and we saw no living soul except an old decrepid man, who had opened the door. The stranger ordered a light; a lamp was brought, and he walked without stopping through a dark passage till we came to a door, leading into a garden, in the back of which was a small pleasure-house; my conductor opened the door, and we entered a small damp room.

"Now we are on the spot," said he, after having carefully secured the door, "tell me what you want to know."

First of all, I wanted to give him a brief account of the recovery of my effects, and then began to ask him, if he had been my benefactor. However, he prevented me from doing it, exclaiming, "I know it all, I beg you will concentrate all you want to know into one question."

I mused awhile, but I was not able to bring all my wishes to one point, and it is very likely that the presence of that extraordinary man, had greatly contributed to my perplexity. I found it impossible to make the question he had ordered me to do.

Seeing my distress, he said, "Well, then, inquire after the name of the friend who has taken so much care of you."

That was the very question which I was most eager to ask. I had wished to propose, but I would not venture to do it for fear of offending the stranger; with great joy I replied that is what I wish to know.

"Well then," replied he, "you shall get personally acquainted with that friend of yours."—"Then I do not know him yet personally?" resumed I, "I thought it was you, sir." The stranger shook his head. "I am only his deputy," was his answer, "and," added he, after a short pause, "only through the third hand."

I gazed at him with amazement, but he seemed to take no notice of it, and began to make preparations for introducing my friend in a most mysterious manner. He strewed sand on the floor, and drew two circles with an ebony wand, placing me in one and himself in the other.

"How will this end?" thought I.

The stranger was now standing opposite to me, in a solemn posture; he folded his hand upon his breast, his looks being lifted up to heaven. Silent and motionless like a statue was he standing there. A chilly sensation of horror penetrated me. I did not dare fetch breath.

The stranger remained in that posture for a quarter of an hour; my fear was swallowed up in dumb amazement, and my heart began soon to fail me from fear and awful expectations. At length my conductor broke his mysterious silence; I heard his voice, but I could not understand what he said; the words he pronounced seemed to belong to a foreign language. The lamp afforded but a faint light, and I could not well distinguish the objects around me. All was silent as the grave. My conductor whispered only now and then some mysterious words, drawing figures in the sand with his ebony wand.

Now I heard the clock strike twelve, with the last stroke the stranger began to turn himself round about, within the circle, with an astonishing velocity, pronouncing the christian and surname of my deceased mother. I staggered back thrilled with chilly horror. On a sudden I heard a noise underground, like the distant rolling of thunder. The stranger pronounced the name of my mother a second time, and in a more solemn and tremendous voice than at first. A flash of lightning hissed through the room, and the voice of thunder grew louder and louder beneath my feet. Now he pronounced the name of my mother a third time, still louder and more tremendous. At once the whole pleasure-house appeared to be surrounded with fire. The ground began to shake under me, and I sank suddenly down. The ghost of my mother hovered before my eyes, with a grim, ghastly look; a chilly sweat bedewed my face and my senses forsook me.

A violent shaking roused me at length from my stupefaction.

The shaking did not cease, and I felt as if I was tossed to and fro: at the same time I heard a terrible creaking and whizzing not far off. As soon as I had recovered my recollection, I perceived that I was sitting in a coach, driving onward with an incredible velocity, and found myself closely confined. Something was snoring by my side, but I could not distinguish what it was, being surrounded with impenetrable darkness.

You cannot imagine what I suffered in that terrible situation. I was seized with anxiety and apprehension, creating the most tormenting sensations, which cannot be described.

The road my human or supernatural coachman had taken seemed to be very uneven, or, perhaps, he did not know the road, for I felt every moment the most violent jolts, which increased my anxiety still more, by the additional apprehension of being overturned. My bones, which already had been hurt very much by my falling down in the pleasure-house, seemed to be quite dislocated. I had been in that state of agony about half an hour, when a most violent jolt overturned the coach. A voice roared, "Jesu Maria!" Methought I felt the freezing hand of death upon my heart, and lost the power of recollection.

At length I was roused from that state of insensibility, by the most excruciating pains. I opened my eyes; two men, each of them holding a horse by the bridle, were standing by me; a countryman, with a lanthorn, was in their company, and the broken coach was lying on the ground at a small distance. They wanted to raise me up, but being pierced by terrible pains, I entreated them, for God's sake, not to touch me. My leg was fractured in two places: the horsemen promised to ride to a neighbouring town for assistance, and disappeared; the countryman remained with me and endeavoured to comfort me.

I waited half an hour and nobody appeared; the night was cold: I waited an hour and no assistance came; one fainting fit followed the other. At length I heard the rolling of a coach, the countryman went with his lanthorn into the middle of the road, and saw a coach and four; the honest man begged the driver to stop, and related my misfortune.

An old reverend man got out of the vehicle, lifted me, with the assistance of the good peasant, into the coach, and ordered the coachman to drive slowly onward.

With the dawn of the morning we came to a village. My kind deliverer was the lord of it. Having been carried to the castle, a surgeon was sent for, and meanwhile the old nobleman endeavoured, by his kind conversation, to make me forget part of my pains.

The surgeon arrived a little while after, my wounds were dressed, and I was carried to bed. At first my deliverer would not leave me, and visited me afterwards three times a day. May heaven reward him for his generous and humane behaviour.

As soon as I had related to him all that had happened to me, he sent some of his people to look after the coach; but it could be found nowhere.

After nine weeks' confinement I was recovered so far that I could return to F—. The benevolent nobleman accompanied me thither, and my landlord was rejoiced to see me. Inquiring after the mysterious stranger I was told that he had been seen no more since I had left the inn. My deliverer stayed three days with me, and then we parted in a most affectionate manner. The next day I set out for my own country, where I happily arrived without any further accident.

Here Elfrid concluded his wonderful tale, which he, as he added, never had been able to unfold, though he had taken the greatest pains to come at the bottom of it. He looked at his friend, eager to hear what he would say to those extraordinary adventures; but Herman was lost in profound meditation for many minutes, at length he began: "Brother, thy tale is very wonderful, so wonderful, that I should not have believed it, if I had not met, on my travels, with adventures, which seem to have some connexion with thine."

Elfrid had apprehended that Herman would laugh at his story, as many of his friends had done; he was therefore very much astonished at Herman's words, and besought him to give a short account of the adventures he had hinted at. Herman promised to give a full account of whatever had happened to him, partly by way of narration and partly in writing; however, he begged him to wait till tomorrow, that he might be able to arrange the necessary papers. Elfrid very readily consented to it.

The next morning was uncommonly fine, yet Herman's guest had no inclination for a hunting party. As soon as breakfast was over he reminded his friend of his promise, asking whether he had found the papers he had been mentioning. Herman said he had, telling his friend at the same time that he intended to relate only that part of those adventures in which he had been personally concerned; the remainder he would give him in writing, but not before his departure, lest ghosts and necromancers might deprive him of the pleasure of making his dear visitor as comfortable and happy as possible. Elfrid having consented to it, the two friends took their places by the fireside, lighted their pipes, and Herman began as follows:

Thou knowest, brother, that I, having finished my studies, was appointed governor to the young Baron de R—, to conduct him on his travels. On our return from Italy we took our way through Switzerland and Germany, and met, on this last tour, with the most remarkable adventure of our whole journey.

Being arrived at the skirts of the Black Forest, our postillion missed his way, as it began to grow dark, and at length, did not know what direction he should take. Our fright was not little, when he apprised us of his distress, being desirous to get out of that dreadful forest as soon as possible, on account of the many instances of robberies and murders committed within its precincts, which the postillion had enlarged upon on the road; we therefore exhorted the fellow to go on, whatever might be the consequence. He did so, and after half an hour we came to an open spot.

"Now we are safe!" exclaimed the postillion joyfully, "and, if I am not mistaken, not far from a village."

He was right. We soon heard the welcome barking of dogs not far off, and a little while after we saw lights.

We entered a large village, but the inn was very indifferent, and the landlord was amazed at the uncommon sight of gentlemen. His whole stock of eatables consisted in some smoaked puddings, and a coarse sort of bread; he told us that neither wine nor beer could be got within the distance of many leagues and even our postillion could not drink his brandy. We asked him where the lord of the village resided; he answered that he never lived there, because the castle had not been habitable for many years. I enquired the reason of it.

"At present," replied the host, "I dare not give you an account of it, tomorrow you shall know everything; but, very likely, this night will make you guess the reason."

The Baron and I entreated him to satisfy our curiosity, but he shook his head and left the room.

Pinched by hunger we took up with our scanty supper, and then asked the landlord to show us to our beds, but, alas! there was not one bed unoccupied in the whole house, and we were obliged to rest our weary limbs upon a bed of clean straw in the middle of the room.

The Baron soon began to snore, but I could not get a wink of sleep. Now the watchman announced the hour of midnight with a hoarse voice, and on a sudden I heard the trampling of horses and the sound of horns. The noise came nearer, and methought I heard a number of horsemen rushing by, and sounding their horns as if a large hunting party were passing through the village; the troop darted like lightning through the street close by the windows of the inn. The Baron started up, asking me with a fearful voice, "What is this?"—"don't know," replied I abruptly. I listened attentively, and the troop had not been far from our inn, when on a sudden all was again as silent as the grave; the Baron began to snore as before, and I to muse on that strange incident.

I could not think it possible that anybody would go a hunting in so large a company, at that unseasonable hour, and was much inclined to think all had been a deluding dream, when I suddenly recollected the mysterious words of our landlord, I cannot but confess that I was seized with horror. I was just falling asleep when the voice of the watchman, crying one o'clock, roused me from my slumber. No sooner had he finished his round than the former noise was heard again at a small distance. I started up and ran to the window, but before I could open it the whole troop had rushed by like a hurricane. A little while after all was silent again, yet in vain did I beseech the god of slumber to take me in his arms.

The Baron had heard nothing the second time, snoring quietly by my side whilst I was ardently wishing for the morning, in order to satisfy my curiosity. I was too impatient to await the landlord's account of the castle, and when the watchman was crying two o'clock I hastened to the window, and began to converse with him.

"Watchman," exclaimed I, "what did that noise at twelve and one o'clock mean?" "Your honour," replied he, "is certainly a stranger, for there's not a child in our village that does not know what that noise means; it is sometimes heard every night for several weeks, afterwards everything is quiet again for a considerable time."

"But," said I, "who is that person that goes a hunting at night?"

"That I can't tell you at present," answered the watchman, "ask your landlord, he will tell you all the particulars. I am here on my duty, and under the protection of Providence, but I dare not speak of what I hear and see."

With these words he went away:—I wrapped myself up in my cloak, and sitting down by the window on a chair, expected, with anxious impatience, the rising of the sun. At length the eastern sky began to be embroidered with purple streaks, the crowing of the cocks sounded through the village, and the watchman announced the approach of day. The Baron awoke.

"You are very early," said he, rubbing his eyes, "pray tell me, what noise was it I heard in the night?"

"I myself am impatient to know it," replied I, "I wish the landlord would rise and unfold that mystery; the troop has rushed by again at one o'clock with the same terrible noise."

While I was talking thus, I heard the trampling of horses, and looking out of the window, saw an officer with a servant. They alighted at the inn, knocked at the door, and entered the room. The officer, a lively young man, wore a Danish uniform, and was on the recruiting business; he had missed his way like ourselves, and we soon got acquainted with him. When the Baron related the nightly adventure, the officer at first thought he was joking, but when I most seriously affirmed every circumstance, he showed an ardent desire to get acquainted with those nocturnal sportsmen.

"That honour you can easily have," said the Baron; "if you will stay here the ensuing night, we will give you company."

"Bravo!" exclaimed the officer, "perhaps the gentlemen will be so polite to invite us to their sport, and then we may be so fortunate as to get a haunch of venison."

Now the landlord entered the room. "Well," said he, bidding us a good morning, "have you heard anything tonight, gentlemen?"

"More than I liked," answered I; "who are those sportsmen that go a-hunting at midnight."

"Why," replied he, "we don't talk of it: I would not tell you anything about it last night, for fear your curiosity might expose you to some misfortune; yet, having promised you yesterday to tell you as much of it as I know, I will be as good as my word."

After having paused awhile, he began thus, in a confidential tone: "Close by our village is a very large building, where formerly the Lord of this village used to reside. One of the former masters of the castle was a very wicked and irreligious man, who found great delight in tormenting the poor peasants; everybody trembled when he appeared. He trampled with his feet upon his own children, and confined them in dark dungeons, where they were often kept for many days without a morsel of bread. He used to call his tenants dogs, and to treat them as such—in short, he was cruelty itself.

"Hunting was his only amusement, and he always kept a vast number of deer, which were the ruin of the peasants' little property, and reduced them to the utmost poverty; no one dared to drive them from his fields, and if he did, he was confined in a damp dungeon, underground, for many weeks. When that wicked man wanted to hunt, then the whole village was called together to serve him instead of dogs; if anyone was not alert enough, then he would hunt him instead of the deer, till he fell down expiring under the lashes of his whip.

"One time after he had roved about from morning till night, he fell from his horse and broke his neck. He was buried in his garden. But now he was terribly punished for his wickedness, having had no rest in his grave to the present day. At certain times of the year he is doomed to appear in the village, at twelve o'clock at night, and to make his entry into the castle with his infernal crew, but as soon as the clock strikes one he is plunged back again into the lake of fire burning with brimstone. Nobody can inhabit the castle! Many who have been so foolhardy to attempt it have lost their lives; whoever ventures to look out of the window when the infernal hosts are passing by gets a swollen face as a punishment for his curiosity. We are now used to that nocturnal sport, and do not care for those infernal spirits, but many strangers have fallen ill through fright."

Here the landlord finished his tale, and seemed to be pleased with our astonishment; however, his pleasure was soon damped when the Lieutenant broke out in a roaring laughter.

"Laugh as long as you please," said he; "stay here till night if you have courage, and then we shall see if you will laugh."

"That I will," replied the officer, "I will not only stay in your house, but I will also spend the coming night at that dreadful castle. I dare say, gentlemen," added he, "you will keep me company."

The Baron, being a man of honour, thought it a great disgrace to betray the least want of courage in the presence of the soldier; he therefore promised to accompany him thither: I made several objections, representing to the officer the danger we should run, not knowing who those spirits might be; however, he silenced all my remonstrances: "I am a soldier," said he, "and all ghosts and hobgoblins have ever been kept at a respectful distance by a martial dress."

At length I was obliged to take a part in the expedition, if I would not desert the Baron. The landlord, who had all that time been staring at us in dumb amazement, lifted up his hands when I had consented to go to the castle, and entreated us, for God's sake, to desist from our undertaking: "If you go," added he, "then all of you will be dead before tomorrow morning: for heaven's sake, dear gentlemen, do not run into the very mouth of the devil thus wantonly!"

However, the raillery of the Lieutenant put him soon so much out of temper, that he left us in great wrath, swearing in the height of his anger, that the devil would make us smart for our foolhardiness and unbelief.

"Gentlemen," began now the officer, "pray let us take a walk to that terrible place, where we are going to spend the night, and reconnoitre it before dinner,"—Approving of that proposal, we went all three to that residence of terror.

We approached and beheld the gothic remains of a half-decayed castle; the gate was open and we entered the fabric. The arched walls, overgrown with moss and ivy, echoed to the sound of our footsteps; a long narrow passage led to a spacious court-yard, paved with stones; now we espied a spiral staircase of stone, and ascended it in dumb silence. A second long and narrow passage, which received a faint glimmering of light through several small windows, strongly guarded by iron bars, led us to a back door; the chilly damps of the long confined air rushed from the aperture when the Lieutenant had pushed it open; the apartment to which it led bore the gloomy appearance of a prison— the remains of half-decayed tapestry, covered with cobwebs, gave the room a dark dreary appearance; pieces of broken furniture were scattered about on the floor, a lamp hung in the middle from an iron chain fastened to the arched ceiling.

Just as we were going to leave this abode of gloom and horror, I perceived a little door in the remotest corner of the room; it was likewise unbolted, and we entered a second room, which bore the same gloomy aspect with the former apartment, being covered with half-rotten remains of broken furniture; another door led us at length into a spacious hall, where the cheering light of the day hailed us at last, many of the arched windows being either open or broken to pieces; the fresh air, the beautiful view meeting our eye from every side, chased at once from our countenance the solemn awe.

"Here," exclaimed the Lieutenant, "here we will meet the airy Lords of this Manor; Let us try, gentlemen, whether we cannot fit a table and some seats among the rotten relics of furniture."

We succeeded in our attempt, dragged a round massy table in the middle of the hall, supported it by four worm-eaten poles, then we fetched some pieces of wood from the adjacent apartments, placing them upon large stones round the table, and thus secured a resting place for the night.

Now we rambled through several apartments on the other side of the hall, and meeting with nothing worthy of our notice, except the traces of desolation, we returned by the way we had entered that gloomy mansion.

We descended into the courtyard and made there likewise our observations: spurred on by curiosity, we entered through a ruinous side building, a garden, which still bore some marks of former grandeur; broken statues of marble were here and there lying on the ground. We cleared with our sabres a way through brambles and nettles to a grove of beech trees; it likewise was hardly penetrable.

Having worked our way for more than half an hour, with much toil and difficulty, through a thicket of thistles and brambles, we arrived at length wearied and fatigued at an open spot; in the middle of it we beheld a statue, bearing in one hand an urn of black marble—we approached and read the following inscription on the pedestal:

HIC JACET
GODOFREDUS HAUSSINGERUS,
PECCATOR.
(*Here lieth Godfrey Haussinger, a Sinner.*)

A little lower down we perceived a cross engraved in the stone, and under it

A.D. 1603.

We stared at each other in dumb amazement, and being already too much fatigued, we did not like to work our way farther into the garden, and returned.

"Gentlemen," began the officer, as we were going back, "what do you think of the inscription on that tomb?"

"I think," replied I, "it strongly corroborates what the landlord has told us."

My companions smiled, and we came again into the courtyard, looking around we observed an arched wall opposite the staircase; as we came nearer we saw a flight of steps leading to a cellar, which was shut up by a massy iron door, strongly secured by an enormous padlock.

Having now examined every corner we returned to our inn.

The landlord, who was ignorant of what we had been about, was struck with horror and amazement when we related where we had been, and did his utmost to persuade us to desist from our design; however, when he saw he was spending his breath in vain, he kept his peace, and mentioned not a single word more about it during the whole day—we did the same—for the Lieutenant's conversation amused us so well, that evening stole upon us unawares.

Our dinner was better than our scanty supper on the preceding day, because the Lieutenant had brought with him an ample provision of ham and cold beef; some bottles of excellent wine, which he was also provided with, raised our spirits, and increased his and the Baron's courage, in such a manner, that they expected the approach of night with the greatest impatience—they were constantly looking at their watches, and as soon as the clock had struck nine, thought it high time to go to the castle.

We called the landlord to pay our bill, and the poor fellow tried once more to persuade us not to go to the castle: he entreated us not to expose our lives thus daringly to certain danger, and at last fell on his knees;—but when we left the room, without taking notice of his entreaties and ardent prayers, he lamented beforehand our untimely death, gave us a lamp, and bolted the door, fetching a deep sigh.

The Lieutenant's servant walked before us, carrying the lighted lamp in his hand, and a portmanteau stocked with provisions under his arm, and we kept close to his heels, armed with sabres and pistols.

It was autumn, and of course very dark. We arrived at the castle; the faint glimmering of the lamp spread a kind of awful twilight around us as we were walking through the lofty arches of the vaulted passage leading to the courtyard. Having fired our pistols and loaded them again with bullets, we ascended the staircase; the doors leading to the hall we left open, that we might have a view of the courtyard, and sat cheerfully down to supper; a bottle of wine we had taken with us to keep us alert, was handed round: however, we missed our aim, for every one of us began to grow drowsy soon after we had finished our meal—we rose and walked about in order to avoid falling asleep, but we were soon tired of it, the ground being so very uneven, and returned to our seats. I recollected now, very fortunately, that I had put the fables of Gellert in my pocket. I took the book out, and began to read to the company; then I gave it to the Baron, and he was relieved by the Lieutenant—thus we were enabled to resist the powerful charms of sleep.

Now it struck eleven. All around us was buried in awful silence, which only now and then was interrupted by the creaking of our feeble chairs; the Lieutenant wound up his watch and put it before him on the table.

"One hour more," began now the officer, "and we shall be in another world." Then he awoke his servant, who was fast asleep, and the Baron began again to read to us.—When the Lieutenant's turn came for the second time, he looked at his watch and exclaimed, "three quarters past eleven, we must be on our guard."

He got up and went to the window; I followed him. Impenetrable darkness surrounded us, no star could be seen; awful silence was still all around, interrupted only by the snoring John, and the creaking of the wood; the pale light of our lamp produced a horrid glimmering in the spacious dreary hall; the Baron, leaning his head upon his arm, struggled to forget every object around him, and the officer uttered not a single word.

Now we heard a clock toll twelve at a great distance, and I walked softly back to my seat, the Lieutenant did the same, taking up one of his pistols, and rubbing the lock with his handkerchief. We looked at each other, and every one of us strove in vain to hide the horror he was struggling against. The watchman cried the hour, the crowing of the cocks told us midnight was set in, and still all around us was as silent as the grave. The Baron laid the book upon the table, and the Lieutenant was going to raise a loud laughter, asking us where the spirits might be, when suddenly the trampling of horses and the sound of horns was heard—we all were fixed to our seats, staring at each other with a ghastly look; now the noise seemed to be under our window; the Lieutenant ran towards it, with a cocked pistol in his hand, but he was too late.

All was quiet again, and an awful stillness swayed around the castle: however, a few seconds after we heard suddenly a most tremendous noise in the court-yard, which was followed by a terrible trampling and a jingling of spurs on the staircase, as if a great number of people in boots was coming up. The noise came nearer and nearer, my feet began to fail, my teeth to chatter in my mouth, and my hair to rise like bristles, while every sense was lost in anxious bodings; at length the noise grew fainter and fainter, and soon we could hear it no more, and midnight stillness resumed her awful sway.

A long pause of dumb astonishment ensued, until at last the Lieutenant, who had recovered his spirits first, exclaimed, "Shall we go down?" I shook my head without uttering a word, and the Baron was likewise silent. "Then I will go alone," said the Lieutenant, snatched up a brace of pistols, drew his sabre, and hurried down. He returned a few minutes after, exclaiming, "It is surprising; I cannot see the least traces of either men or horses."

Now he retook his seat, casting down his looks in a pensive manner —his servant was still snoring—the Baron began again to read, and I fell fast asleep. At once I was roused by the report of a pistol. I and honest John started up at the same moment, and we heard once more the trampling of horses and the sound of horns, but it soon died away at a distance, and the Lieutenant entered the hall with the Baron.

They also had not been able to resist the leaden wand of sleep, but the same noise in the courtyard we had heard at twelve o'clock had soon roused them from their slumber. "As soon as we heard the noise," said the Baron, "we hastened to the outer room, our pistols cocked, but before we could reach it the noise was under the window of the castle; the Lieutenant knocked through one of the windows in the room close to the hall, and sent a bullet after the troop, which was rushing by like an hurricane; however, he was prevented by the darkness of the night from distinguishing anything except some white horses."

"The spirits are afraid of us," exclaimed the Lieutenant now, "but come, let us return to our inn, we shall rest more comfortable on a bed of clean straw than on this damp ground." We all consented to it, and left the gloomy abode of those nocturnal sportsmen. We knocked a good while at the door of the inn before it was opened: and at last the landlord appeared, stammering, lost in wonder, "God be praised that you are still alive, how did you escape?"

The Lieutenant silenced him by some hasty lies, and promised to give him a full account of the whole adventure after he should have rested a little.

"Gentlemen," said he, as soon as he got up in the morning, "next night I will go once more to the haunted castle, and spend the night in the courtyard, will you keep me company?"

The Baron looked at me as if he wished me to refuse the proposal; I did so. "We cannot," said I, "stay here a day longer, and such an under-taking would, besides, be too dangerous for only four people."

"O!" exclaimed the Lieutenant, "if that is all you have to say against it, then I will soon make you easy. We will take a dozen stout fellows from the village with us; they will not hesitate to accompany us if we give them a couple of dollars and a good dram; it will be devilish good fun, and tomorrow, with the first dawn of day, I will depart with you."

The Baron consented to the proposal, and I myself did not dislike it; in short, we remained, and sent our postillion through the village to publish, "that all young fellows who would go with us to the castle next night, should have sixpence each, and as much brandy as they could drink."

In less than half an hour the whole village was assembled round the door of the inn. We selected fifteen of the stoutest, ordered them to provide themselves with proper arms, and to appear by ten o'clock at night at the inn. Our landlord, who beheld these preparations in dumb amazement, believed firmly that we must be arch necromancers, and his fancy having been fired by the wonderful account of our nocturnal adventure, which the Lieutenant had given him, he was himself not unwilling to go with us to the castle, and to bid defiance to the infernal hosts. However, as soon as it grew dark, his courage died away, and he wished success to our undertaking, telling us he could not leave his house.

Our little army was assembled before ten o'clock, armed with scythes, poles, hay forks and flails. We ordered the landlord to give a dram to every one; took some tables, benches, lamps, and a small cask of brandy with us, and marched in triumph towards the castle.

We pitched our camp in the courtyard, not far from the entrance; the peasants placed themselves round the brandy cask, lighted their pipes, and expected with pleasure the appearance of the airy gentlemen.

Another advantage we reaped from that honest company was that we had no need to keep sleep at a distance by reading, for the merriment of our little army soon rose to the highest pitch, and these jovial fellows, being heated by the contents of our little cask, challenged his satanic majesty and all his infernal hosts amid peals of roaring laughter.

It was now past eleven o'clock, and the noise began to abate, some of our gentlemen were nodding, and some snoring, we were therefore obliged to beg those who had not yet yielded to the powerful charms of sleep,to give us a song, which they instantly did in so vociferous a manner, that our hearing organs were most painfully affected—the sleepers started up when they heard that terrible noise, and joined the jovial songsters with all their might. Thus we chased away the god of sleep, who seemed not in the least to relish the disharmonious notes of our jolly companions.

Now the Lieutenant beckoned to the blithesome crew, and the clamorous noise was suddenly hushed in awful silence. It struck twelve o'clock, and the sound of horns and the trampling of horses was heard at a distance. The peasants listened, their mouths wide open, and gazed at each other struck with chilly terror. No sound was heard, except the

palpitating of their hearts, and here and there the chattering of teeth—
all of them moved their lips as if praying ardently. The noise came
nearer and nearer, and now it seemed to be in the castle. Again everything was silent, but in an instant the former noise struck once more
our listening ears, and the infernal hosts rushed by like lightning—the
Lieutenant, the Baron, and I darted through the passage leading to the
gate, but the airy gentlemen were already out of sight, and we could see
nothing, save a faint glimmering of some white horses. The mingled
noise of their horns and of the trampling of their horses soon died
away; the stillness of midnight swayed all around, and we returned to
the courtyard.

Our valiant crew was still fixed to the ground, seized with horror
and astonishment. None of them were able to distinguish whether we
were ghosts or their fellow-adventurers; however, they recovered their
spirits by degrees, and prepared to leave the residence of the infernal
sportsmen.

We left the castle, fully convinced that these nocturnal ramblers
must be beings who were afraid of us, discharged our courageous troop
and went to rest.

I awoke with the first ray of the morning sun, and roused the Baron
and the Lieutenant; the latter seemed not to be inclined to fulfil his
promise, being desirous to try his fortune once more, and to hide
himself either in the courtyard or before the gate. When he saw that we
would not stay any longer, he postponed the execution of his design to a
future time, and followed our example.

We left our inn at six o'clock. The morning was gloomy and rainy,
the wind swept furiously over the heath, and drove the black clouds still
closer and closer together; after a few minutes we entered the Black
Forest. Looking out of the coach I saw the Lieutenant and his servant
turn to the left towards a brook, where we beheld an odd incident. A
reverend old man was sitting there, and reading in a large book; bewildered in profound meditation, he seemed to take no notice of the
howling storm; and not to be sensible of the rain rushing down in large
drops upon his uncovered head, the tempest was sporting with his
reverend grey locks, and the rain beating in his face, yet he did not stir.

His long brown robe seemed to denote a traveller from the East—a long staff and a black wallet were lying by his side.

I got out of the coach to view that strange being a little closer, and to speak to him, but before I could accost him, the Lieutenant exclaimed, "Greybeard, what art thou reading?"

The old man appeared to take no notice of his question, and went on reading as if nobody had been there.

"What art thou reading?" exclaimed the Lieutenant once more, alighting and looking over his shoulder at the book.

The old man answered not a word, but still continued to read. I also was now standing behind him, and looking at the book, its leaves were of yellow parchment, the characters large and of different colours.

The Baron was close at my heels, and the Lieutenant being provoked by the man's obstinate silence, shook him now violently by the shoulder, thundering in his ears, "Greybeard, what art thou reading?"

Now the old man lifted his reverend head slowly up, stared at us with angry looks, and then said, with a solemn awful voice, "Wisdom!"

"What language is it?"

OLD MAN.—(Reading again)—"The language of wisdom."

"What dost thou call wisdom?"

OLD MAN.—"All that thou dost not comprehend."

LIEUTENANT.—"If thou knowest what other people cannot comprehend, then I should like to ask thee a question."

OLD MAN.—(Staring again at him)—"What question?"

LIEUTENANT.—"There is a castle not far from the next village, where every night a numerous troop of spirits make their entry; I and these two gentlemen have watched there these two nights."

OLD MAN.—(Interrupting him)—"And art not a bit wiser for't, for thou seemest not to be fit to converse with spirits."

LIEUTENANT.—"But thou—?"

OLD MAN.—"I understand the language of Wisdom."

The Lieutenant bit his lips, shaking his head with a contemptuous smile. Now the Baron accosted the old man, who again was immersed in profound meditation.

BARON.—"Well, then, if thy book contains such a treasure of wisdom, then tell us why that castle is haunted by spirits, and for what reason they go their nightly rounds?"

OLD MAN.—"That the spirits must tell thee themselves."

BARON.—"What does then thy book contain?"

OLD MAN.—"The ways and means of forcing them to a confession."

BARON.—"But why hast thou not forced them long ago to confess everything?"

OLD MAN.—"Because I never cared for it."

BARON.—(Laughing)—"But if we should entreat thee to do it, and pull our purses, would'st thou not do us that favour?"

OLD MAN.—(Frowning)—"Vile mortal, can wisdom be bought with gold and silver?"

BARON.—"How can one then purchase it?"

OLD MAN.—"With nothing—hast thou courage?"

BARON.—"Else we could not have watched in the dreadful castle."

OLD MAN.—"Then spend another night in it. I will be there a quarter before twelve o'clock—now leave me."

We gazed at each other with doubtful looks. The old man resumed his reading, and seemed to take no further notice of us, who were still standing behind him lost in silent wonder. At length the Lieutenant mounted his horse, and we went back to our coach. "Well," said the officer, as we were getting in our carriage, "well, gentlemen, will you return with me?"

In vain did I make objections, the expectation of the two hot-headed young men was strained too much; it was impossible to subdue the eager curiosity of the young Baron, and the presence of the Lieutenant made me apprehend that all reasoning would not only be spent in vain, but at the same time make me contemptible. I therefore was forced to go back with them, and to embark in an enterprise, which, being not only useless, but also very dangerous, would plunge me in great distress.

Our host was highly rejoiced and struck with astonishment when he saw us come back with the intention (as he believed) to engage once more with the nightly sportsmen. Our valiant companions of the preceding night had given a wonderful account of our adventure, relating how horribly the ghosts had looked, how courageously they had encountered the infernal crew, and how the strange conjurors at last had banished the tremendous host from the castle forever.

The whole village assembled, therefore, as soon as our return was known, gazing at us as supernatural beings, and consulting us about several matters. The Lieutenant had his fun with the simplicity of those honest people and the day was spent merrily.

It was already dark, and the villagers had not yet left the inn; they unanimously intreated us to take them along with us to the castle. We were obliged to disavow our design, to feign sleepiness, and to order a bed of straw to be got ready.

At ten o'clock we stole silently to the castle without a light; the Lieutenant's servant lighted our lamp in the courtyard, and we went to the hall, where we had spent the first night, waiting with impatience for the last quarter before midnight. The lieutenant did not believe the old man would be as good as his word; I joyfully seconded his opinion, and should have been glad if we had not waited for him; but the Baron, who, from his juvenile days, had been fond of everything bearing the aspect of mysteriousness, was quite charmed with the reverend appearance of the old man, and maintained, upon his honour, that he certainly would stick to his appointment.

The Lieutenant began to discourse with the Baron on apparitions and necromancers, maintaining by experience and reasoning, that all was either deceit or the effects of a deluded fancy; yet the Baron would not relinquish his opinion, adding that one ought not to speak lightly of those matters, and that the old man certainly would prove the truth of his assertion. We were still conjecturing who that strange wanderer might be, when we saw by our watches that there were but sixteen minutes wanting to twelve; as soon as it was three quarters after eleven we heard the sound of gentle steps in the passage.

"Our Greybeard," said the Lieutenant, "is a man of honour," and took up the lamp to meet the old man.

Now he entered the hall, his black wallet on his back, and beckoned in a solemn manner to follow him. We did so, and he led us through the apartments and the vaulted passage down stairs. We followed him through the courtyard to the iron gate of the cellar without uttering a word; there he stopped, turning towards us, and eyeing us awhile with a ghastly look; after an awful pause of expectation, he said with a low trembling voice, "Don't utter a word as you value your lives." Then he went down the two first steps; taking from his bosom an enormous key which had been suspended round his neck by an iron chain, and opened, without the least difficulty, the monstrous padlock; the door flew open, and the old man took the lamp from the Lieutenant, leading us down a large staircase of stone. We descended into a spacious cellar, vaulted with hewn stone, and beheld all around large iron doors, secured by strong padlocks. Our hoary leader went slowly towards an iron folding door, opposite to the staircase, and opened it likewise with his key; it flew suddenly open, and we beheld with horror a black vault, which received a faint light from a lamp suspended to the ceiling by an iron chain.

The old man entered, uncovering his reverend head, and we did the same, standing by his side in trembling expectation, awed by the solemnity that reigned around us; a dreadful chilliness seized us, we felt the grasp of the icy fangs of horror, being in a burying vault surrounded by rotten coffins. Skulls and mouldered bones rattled beneath our feet, the grisly phantom of death stared in our faces from every side, with a grim, ghastly aspect. In the centre of the vault we beheld a black marble coffin, supported by a pedestal of stone, over it was suspended to the ceiling a lamp spreading a dismal, dying glimmering around. The air was heavy and of a musty smell, we could hardly respire, the objects around seemed to be wrapped in a blueish mist. The hollow sound of our footsteps re-echoed through the dreary abode of horror as we walked nigher.

The old man stopped at a small distance from the marble coffin, beckoning to us to come nigher; we moved slowly on, and he made a sign not to advance farther than he could reach with extended arms. The Lieutenant placed himself at his right, I took my station at his left, and the Baron opposite to him.

He put the lamp on the ground before him, taking his book, an ebony wand, and a box of white plate out of his wallet. Out of the latter he strewed a reddish sand around him, drew a circle with his wand, and folded his hands across the breast, then he pronounced, amid terrible convulsions, some mysterious words, opened the book and began to read, whilst his face was distorted in a ghastly manner; his convulsions grew more horrible as he went on reading; all his limbs seemed to be contracted by a convulsive fit. His eyebrows shrunk up, his forehead was covered with wrinkles, and large drops of sweat were running down his cheeks—at once he threw down his book, gazing with a staring look, and his hands lifted up at the marble coffin.

We soon perceived that midnight had set in; the trampling of horses and the sound of horns was heard, the Necromancer did not move a limb, still staring at the coffin with a haggard look. Now the noise was on the staircase of the cellar and still he was motionless, his eyes being immoveably directed towards the coffin. But now the noise was in the cellar, he brandished his wand and all around was buried in awful silence. He pronounced again three times an unintelligible word with a horrible thundering voice. A flash of lightning hissed suddenly through the dreary vault, licking the damp walls, and a hollow clap of thunder roared through the subterraneous abode of chilly horror. The light in the lamp was now extinguished, silence and darkness swayed all around; soon after we heard a gentle rustling just before us, and a faint glimmering was spreading through the gloomy vault. It grew lighter and lighter, and we soon perceived rays of dazzling lights hooting from the marble coffin, the lid of which began to rise higher and higher; at once the whole vault was illuminated, and a grisly human figure rose slow and awful from the coffin. The phantom, which was wrapped up in a shroud, bore a dying aspect, it trembled violently as it rose and emitted a hollow groan, looking around with chilly horror. Now the spectre descended from the pedestal, and moved with trembling steps and haggard looks towards the circle where we were standing.

"Who dares," groaned it, in a faltering hollow accent; "who dares to disturb the rest of the dead?"

"And who art thou?" replied our leader, with a threatening frowning aspect, "who art thou, that thou darest to disturb the stillness of this castle, and the nocturnal slumber of those that inhabit its environs?"

The phantom shuddered back, groaning in a most lamentable accent, "Not I, not I, my cursed husband disturbs the peace around and mine."

OLD MAN.—"For what reason?"

GHOST.—"I was assassinated, and he who judges men has thrown my sins upon the murderer."

OLD MAN.—"I comprehend thee, unhappy spirit, betake thyself again to rest; by my power, which every spirit dreads, he shall disturb thee no more—begone—"

The phantom bowed respectfully, staggered towards the pedestal, climbed up, got into the coffin, and disappeared; the lid sunk slowly down, and the light which had illuminated the dismal mansion of mortality died away by degrees. A flash of lightning hissed again through the vault, licking the damp walls, the hollow sound of thunder roared through the subterraneous abode of horror, the lamp began again to burn, and the awful silence of the grave swayed all around.

The old man took up his wallet and his book, beckoning us to follow him. We returned to the adjoining vault, through which we had entered that abode of awful dread; it was as lonesome as we had left it; our leader locked the iron folding-door carefully; then he took out of his wallet a large piece of parchment on which a number of strange characters were written, a piece of black sealing wax, and a monstrous iron seal. Having made several crosses over those things with his ebony wand, he fixed the parchment above the lock, and sealed it hastily on the four corners.

This done, he went into the middle of the cellar assigning us our places; then he strewed sand on the ground, drew a circle with his wand, and began again to read in his book amid horrible convulsions. He brandished his wand, pronouncing three times with a most tremendous voice the same word he had made use of in the burying vault. A flash of lightning hissed through the cellar, a clap of thunder shook the subterraneous fabric, all the doors save that which had been sealed up were suddenly forced open with a thundering noise, the lamp was extinguished, and a blue light reflected in a grisly manner from the staircase against the damp wall; woeful groans, lamentations, and the dismal clashing of chains resounded through the spacious caverns. The noise seemed to come from the staircase—gentle steps were heard—a numerous troop seemed to be descending into the cellar; the lamentations and the woeful groans advanced nearer, and louder resounded the clashing of chains.

Horrid to behold did now a second phantom appear before our gazing looks, staggering slowly towards us, and leaving a numerous retinue on the staircase; the garment of the spectre was stained with blood, the skull fractured, the eyes like two portentous comets!

"Who art thou?" roared our leader with a thundering voice, and the dreary cavern echoed to the sound.

The phantom answered with a hollow, dismal voice, "A damned soul!"

OLD MAN.—"What business hast thou in this castle?"

GHOST.—"I want to be redeemed from hell."

OLD MAN.—"How canst thou be redeemed?"

GHOST.—"By the forgiveness of my wife."

OLD MAN.—"How darest thou claim it, reprobate villain? Return to thy damned companions in hell. Respect this seal, respect these characters."

Here the old man pointed at the door of the vault which had been sealed up: the phantom staggered towards it, but suddenly shuddered back and sunk groaning on the ground; a flash of lightning illuminated the cellar, and a tremendous peal of thunder resounded through the lofty vault; all the doors were shut again with a terrible noise, a frightful howling filled our ears, and horrid phantoms hovered before our eyes; flashes of lightning hissed through the vault and roaring claps of thunder threatened to overturn the whole fabric.

The lightning ceased by degrees, and the roaring of the thunder died away, a blue flame was still glimmering on the staircase, but it soon died away, and we were surrounded with darkness; groans and dreadful lamentations resounded still through the winding caverns, but soon all around was hushed in profound silence. After a short pause of horrid stillness, the trampling of horses and the sound of horns was heard again; yet that noise died also away before we recovered our recollection.

When our astonishment began to subside, we perceived that we were standing in a dark cellar, without knowing whether any one of us was missing. A disagreeable sulphurous odour affected our smelling organs, and bereft us almost of the power of respiration; not a whisper interrupted the dead midnight silence which surrounded us. At length, somebody took me by the hand, I shuddered back, my imagination being still the wrestling place of horrid wild phantoms, and my soul divining a thousand dreadful thoughts.

"It is I," said the Lieutenant, and I felt at once as if a heavy load had been taken from my breast. Now the Baron began also to speak, "Where are you?" whispered he, "are you still alive?"

We groped about in the dark, and at last found him leaning against the wall.

"How shall we get out of this cursed residence of horror?" exclaimed the Lieutenant. "Come, let us try whether we can find the staircase; It must be just opposite to us, if I am not mistaken." Then he began to walk on, and we groped after him, tumbling now and then over loose stones.

"I have found the staircase," cried our fellow adventurer, "at last, after a long fruitless search, I feel the first step."

A ray of joy beamed through our hearts as we were climbing up, but alas! it was soon most cruelly damped; the cellar door was locked up, and the blood congealed in our veins when the Lieutenant told it us. We exerted all our strength to force it open, but in vain, it was bolted on the outside. The Lieutenant called as loud as he could for his servant, whom he had left snoring in the hall; we joined our voices with his, calling with all our might "John! John!"

The hollow echo repeated in a tremendous accent, John! John! but no human footstep would gladden our desponding hearts. Frantic with black despair did we now begin to knock at the massy door till the blood was running down from our hands, and to cry John, John, till our voices grew hoarse—the hollow echo still repeated in an awful tremendous accent our knocking and crying, but no human footstep was heard. "The fellow sleeps and cannot hear us," said the Lieutenant, at length with a faint voice, "let us sit down and watch him when he shall come down."

We did so, but I had no hope that the servant would come, yet I concealed my apprehension within my breast. The Lieutenant dissembled to be easy, and began to converse on what we had seen and heard; however his broken accent, the faltering of his speech, and his low voice, betrayed the anxiety of his mind. The Baron and I spoke little, and when we had been sitting about an hour not one uttered a word more; all was silent around us. Nothing interrupted the death-like stillness of the night, except the violent beating of our hearts.

At length the Lieutenant asked if we were asleep; however, the anxiety of our minds and the dreadful apprehensions which assailed us, drove far away even the idea of sleep. We sat some hours in the dreadful situation, and it was now about five o'clock in the morning when the Lieutenant exclaimed, "I fear we wait in vain for my servant, he cannot sleep so fast that he should not hear us! But where can he be?" Then he began again to knock violently against the massy iron door, but all was in vain. No human footsteps were heard, we remained some hours on the staircase, but all our waiting and listening was fruitless, no cheering sound of human footsteps would gladden our desponding hearts.

"I will not torment you by vain apprehensions," began the Lieutenant at length, "however, we seem to be doomed to destruction, yet let us try if we cannot escape some way or other, come down with me into the cellar, there we shall have a better chance to espy an outlet than here."

We descended, with trembling knees, without saying a word, and groped along in the dark a good while, knocking our heads against the damp wall, and the iron doors. Alas! our search seemed to be in vain, and the grim spectre of a lingering death stared us grisly in the face, my feet could support me no longer, and I dropt down wearied with anxiety.

Now I began to reproach myself for having plunged into the gulph of destruction not only myself but also him who had been entrusted to my care. The apprehension of being famished in that infernal abode, thrilled my soul with horror and black despair; at first I heard the Baron and the Lieutenant still groping about; neither of them uttered a word;

the hollow sound of their footsteps re-echoed horribly through the vault—at length the sound of the Baron's footsteps died away at a distance, and only one of my companions in destruction remained with me.

"Where are you?" exclaimed the Lieutenant.

"Here I am," replied I, "but where is the Baron?"

The Lieutenant called him, and I did the same, but we received no answer. At once a sudden hollow noise struck our ears, and at the same time a faint glimmering of light darted from a remote corner of our dungeon. I started up, half frantic with joy, and we pursued the gladdening ray of light; it seemed to come from an opening in the wall. No words can express the rapture we felt when we beheld one of the iron doors half open; we went through it with hasty steps, and entered a long vaulted passage. A faint dawn of light hailed our joyful looks at a great distance from below. We descended a declivity, the farther we went the more the light increased, at length we reached the end of the avenue, and perceived some steps leading into a spacious apartment, at the entrance of which some boards on the floor had given way. We descended the steps, and, who can paint the horror which rushed upon us, when we beheld the Baron lying lifeless in the deep vault, upon some mouldering straw? I leaped down without a moment's hesitation, the Lieutenant did the same, and now we began to shake the Baron till we at length perceived signs of returning life. We continued our endeavours to recall his senses, he breathed, gave a hollow groan, and opened his eyes: his fainting fit had been the effect of sudden terror, and he had not received the least hurt.

He now told us that he had met in the dark with a long narrow passage which he had pursued, in a kind of insensibility, till he had staggered down from an elevated spot, when the boards suddenly gave way, dragging him along into the deep vault.

Looking around we perceived that we were in a spacious cavern, which appeared to have been formerly a kind of stable. High over our heads were two large round holes, grated with strong iron bars, through which the daylight was admitted, and after a closer examination we espied a gloomy outlet in a remote corner, shut up by a wooden door, which we forced open without difficulty. We now ascended through a dark passage, higher and higher, till we at length with rapture beheld an outlet which opened into the garden; we were obliged to cut our way with our sabres through the underwood and the entangled weeds, and soon came to the court yard. Tears of joy sparkled in our eyes, rays of unspeakable rapture beamed through our hearts, and we praised God for our unexpected deliverance from the grisly jaws of a lingering death.

The dreary desolated courtyard appeared to us a paradise; the dazzling splendour of the bright morning sun, and the pure air which we now inhaled, filled our hearts with the strongest sensations of bliss. We congratulated each other on our resurrection from the dreary abode of mortality, where we were doomed to be entombed alive, and shook each other by the hand half frantic with joy.

We went now to the hall in search of the Lieutenant's servant; the table and everything was in the same condition we had left them, but John was not there. We went through the whole gloomy fabric shouting and hallooing, discharging our pistols, but no sound was heard except the hollow echo repeating our shouts and the reports of our pistols all over the dreary building.

"Very likely he is returned to the inn," said the Lieutenant, "and we shall find him there."

We left that dangerous abode of black horror, praising God again and again for our deliverance.

As we entered the inn we beheld the landlord surrounded by a number of villagers, who were come to inquire whether we were returned from the castle. They were very much surprised when we entered the room, and, respectfully taking off their hats, told us, that the uproar at the village last night had been more tremendous than ever. Everyone was impatient to know the particulars of our adventure, but the Lieutenant having then no inclination of amusing himself with their simplicity, gave them a short answer, and asked the landlord where his servant was.

"I have not seen him since yesterday," replied he.

"It is impossible," resumed the Lieutenant; "where are the horses?"

"They are in the stable," replied the landlord, "I have just been looking after them."

The Lieutenant gave us an apprehensive look, and begged the gaping peasants to look after him, all over the village and the adjacent places: they all were very willing to do it, and left the inn.

It was nine o'clock when we entered the inn, and it struck twelve when our honest villagers returned, with the disagreeable news that they could find poor John nowhere.

The Lieutenant thought it not prudent to remain any longer at that fatal place; the Baron likewise wished to depart and I too was impatient to be gone. As soon as we had finished our scanty dinner, we departed a second time; the tears started from our landlord's eyes, and from those of the good villagers, when we bade them farewell, after having made them a small present, and they saw us depart with regret.

The Lieutenant knew the ways through the Black Forest pretty well, he rode by our chaise leading his servant's horse with one hand, and we reached without any farther accident the limits of that dreadful forest. We parted company at the close of the second day, bidding each other a tender adieu.

"I thank you, gentlemen," said the Lieutenant, as we were getting into our chaise at the door of the inn. "I thank you for your kind and faithful assistance in the most dreadful adventure of my life; if I should be so fortunate to get at the bottom of the mystery which hangs over that castle, as I shall endeavour to do, I will take the first opportunity to apprise you of my success. Farewell, remember now and then the 20th of September, 1750, and do not forget your friend."

The postillion smacked his whip, and we went different roads. On the fifth day we arrived, without any further accident, at the castle of Baron R—, the father of my pupil.

"And here," added Herman, "my narration is finished. A letter which the Baron wrote me, and a manuscript sent me by the Lieutenant, contains everything that has happened afterwards. But these papers you shall not get before your departure."

Though Elfrid's curiosity had been spurred very much, yet he could not but consent to his friend's proposal, and spent a fortnight more with him in uninterrupted pleasure.

The days rolled swiftly on, shortened by the conversation of his friend, by hunting and other diversions, and he at length was obliged to bid his host adieu.

Before he parted with his Elfrid, he gave him the above-mentioned manuscript, assuring him that he would have given it him sooner, if he had been able to find it amongst a great many papers. He added, that he had searched for it in vain several days, and would have given him the continuation and conclusion of those mysterious adventures, by way of narration, if he could not have found the manuscript, but he had fortunately traced it out the day before his departure amongst a number of old musty papers. Herman cleaned it from the dust and gave it to his friend, saying to him, "Take, brother, take here the continuation of my tale, and if thou thinkest the publication of it will amuse and benefit the world thou art welcome to publish it."

Then they parted, alas! for ever. Herman's wish was accomplished, he had seen once more the faithful friend of his younger days, and soon after went to that better world where good men will meet again the friends of their bosom, never to part again. Elfrid, too, is awaiting the solemn morn of resurrection in his grave, and he, before he died, set down in writing the foregoing narration.

Now let us see what the writings which his friend had given him contain.

PART TWO

I

BARON R—TO MR. HERMAN B—, NOV. 11, 1772.

Dear Friend,—It is with the greatest pleasure I am going to communi-
cate to you a remarkable incident I met with this summer, when at
Pyrmont. I would have given you the following account some time ago,
if it had not been for some papers which I was obliged to wait for; they
are arrived at last, and here I send them, beseeching you to remit them
to me as soon as you shall have perused them.

I had been three weeks at Pyrmont, when I one time went to the
promenade on a very beautiful evening; there I happened to meet a
gentleman whose features interested me very much though they were
unknown to me. Walking slowly on I soon saw him come after me; he
passed me with hasty steps, and turning suddenly stared me in the face;
I did the same, being surprised that I also had attracted the notice of the
stranger. He went on, but soon after turned round once more, directing
his steps towards me and staring again at me. I stopped and did the
same. He moved his lips as if he wanted to speak to me, just when I was
going to ask him whether he wanted something; however, we both

remained silent, pursuing our walk. That pantomime we repeated several times, neither of us uttering a word; at length it began to grow dark and I went to my lodgings.

The next morning I awoke with the first ray of the sun, and went again to the promenade, to inhale the salubrious breeze of the morning air, and to hail the rising king of the day under the canopy of heaven. I was no sooner seated on a bench beneath a majestic beech-tree, admiring the greatness of the Creator so striking in the beautiful scenes of a fine summer's morning, when I once more beheld the stranger who had interested me so much the preceding evening. He came nearer, saluted me, and took a seat on the bench where I was sitting. We both admired, in profound silence, the beautiful scene around for a quarter of an hour. Every object which surrounded us pronounced the greatness of God: numbers of feathered songsters hailed the rising sun; diamonds and rubies sparkled on the leaves of the trees, loaded with the pearly drops of dew. Now the sun darted his warming cheerful rays all around, and the stranger looked at me with an inquisitive eye. "Sir," he at length began, "you will excuse me if I should be mistaken. I think I have had, some years past, the pleasure of being in your company somewhere or other."

"It is possible," replied I, "that I have had that honour. Will you favour me with your name?"

"My name is B—, and I am Major in the service of the King of Denmark."

"B—! I think I remember that name, yet I cannot recollect where I have had the honour of seeing you."

"Perhaps I may," replied he, "if you will be so kind to favour me with your name."

"My name is R—."

"Did not you return from your travels to Germany in the year 1750?"

I replied in the affirmative.

"Then I am not mistaken," said he smiling, "don't you remember the adventure at the Haunted Castle on the skirts of the Black Forest, and that villainous Necromancer?"

I was struck with amazement, "How," exclaimed I, "is it you? Do I not dream?"

"Yes, dear friend, it is I," he replied, "you are not mistaken. How strangely and how unexpectedly do friends meet sometimes in this world! I am at present governor to a young prince who is on his travels. We are here incognito, yet I could not resist the ardent desire of making myself known to you. Did you never wish to get some further intelligence of the mystery of that terrible castle and its strange inhabitants? With the greatest pleasure I would have communicated to you what came to my knowledge since we parted, had I but known the place of your residence; I travelled on purpose to your native town as soon as I had finished my recruiting business, but I was told you had been sent by your prince to England on affairs of state."

"Your kindness deserves my warmest acknowledgment, and I am very sorry that I had the misfortune of being absent when you intended to do me the honour of seeing me."

"Your absence vexed me very much,' he replied, "because it not only deprived me of the pleasure of seeing once more an old friend, but also prevented me from performing the promise I had given you when we parted. This happy meeting affords me, therefore, the greatest pleasure, and if you will favour me with your company, at my apartments, I can give you a satisfactory account of several accidents which happened before and after our adventure at the castle, and which are nearly connected with what we have encountered."

I accepted his kind invitation, and went with him to breakfast in his apartments. On the way he inquired after you, and was rejoiced to hear that you are well and happy, blessed with the love of a dear and virtuous wife. He particularly seemed to be pleased with my little narrative of your matrimonial bliss—I forbore to inquire after the reason of it, fearing to renew the pains, which perhaps the recent loss of a dear beloved object might have inflicted upon him, and gave our conversation another turn until we arrived at his apartments.

After we had breakfasted we seated ourselves by the window, and he began a tale which took an unexpected and a most wonderful turn, but the accidents were so various and many, that he only could give me a short sketch, which being interspersed with many episodes, was rather confused. He was himself sensible of the defects of his narrative, and promised to send me a written account of those wonderful accidents as soon as he should have finished his travels.

I spent five happy days in his company, and then we parted reluctantly. Two months after he sent me the enclosed continuation of his adventures, which will strike you with astonishment.

Major B— sends you his best wishes; he longs ardently to see you once more.

Farewell, and remember

Your faithful,
R—.

II

ADVENTURES OF LIEUT. B—

I was lost in profound meditation after I had parted with my compan-
ions; all the horrid scenes of the adventure at the castle hovered before
my imagination;

I fancied myself at the inn, in the ruinous hall, and then in the cellar, still
beholding the Necromancer and the phantoms, seeing the flashes of
lightning, and hearing the roaring of the thunder, and the hollow voices
of the spectres. My fancy renewed all the horrors which had rushed
upon me when shut up in the cellar, as well as the joy I felt when we had
the good fortune to find an outlet from our infernal dungeon; my restless fancy painted all these pictures with the strongest colours, painted
them so grisly, that I sent up to heaven the most fervent thanksgiving
for my delivery from that infernal abode.

These horrid dreams vanished at length, giving room to contemplations of a more serious cast. I was every moment reminded of the
unhappy fate of my faithful John, and felt an ardent desire to get at the
bottom of those mysterious events, that I might be enabled to deliver

my poor servant from the clutches of the spirits, or, at least, revenge his death. I was however sensible, that I alone should not be equal to it; the peasants of the village I did not think fit for assisting me in my enterprise, and the whole undertaking too hazardous without the assistance and the counsel of an experienced and resolute man. I therefore was determined to search for such a man, and, aided by his counsel and assistance, once more to encounter those nocturnal sportsmen.

This resolution was the result of my meditations on the first morning after my separation from my companions, and I burned with impatient desire to rid myself of that load of uncertainty which lay heavy upon my mind. At length I arrived at the place of my destination, and resumed my recruiting business, assisted by two old serjeants.

I hastened to return to the skirts of the Black Forest, and went to F —; while there I met with Prussian, Austrian, Hessian, and Swedish recruiting officers, and now and then with an old acquaintance of mine.

Amongst others I got acquainted with an old Austrian officer, who was highly respected by everyone; when he said anything, which happened not often, then everybody listened with the greatest attention, and when, now and then, a quarrel arose, everything was soon settled by his interference.

A man who thus powerfully could influence a set of people who admit no law but that of superiority soon engaged my admiration in the highest degree, and I concluded he would be the fittest person to assist me in the execution of my design, to unfold the mystery of the Haunted Castle, if I could but gain his confidence; yet I was sensible that it would be no easy task to ingratiate myself so far with him that he should not refuse believing a tale like mine, which bore such glaring marks of fiction. I apprehended a veteran of so much experience, and so serious a turn of mind, would laugh at my narrative, and treat it as a nursery tale.

I was the more inclined to fear this apprehension might prove true, when I learned by experience that his curiosity was always guided by cool and just reasoning. His cheerfulness never exceeded the limits of moderated seriousness, and his smile was nothing more than an almost imperceptible unfolding of the wrinkles, which contracted his reverend brow; his mirth bore the resemblance of his carriage, and whoever knew him, trembled at his anger, though none of his acquaintances had ever experienced the least mark of passion in his countenance, and much less had he ever betrayed a symptom of unbridled wrath.

I let slip no opportunity of doing him some little services, and thus endeavoured to gain his favour; however, he appeared to take no notice of my unremitted zeal to please him; I treated him with marks of the highest veneration, whenever I was in his company, but he seemed not to regard it. All my most anxious endeavours to win that strange man over to my interest proved abortive, and, at last, I gave over every hope of engaging his attention.

Chance befriended me, at length, unexpectedly, and I got by accident what I already had despaired to attain by the most indefatigable endeavours.

The inn where one of the recruiting officers lodged was reported to be haunted; many strange stories circulated on account of that report, which the then owner of the house endeavoured to laugh off, because he had lived a fortnight in it without perceiving anything uncommon.

This subject afforded one evening matter for a serious discourse among the officers. The Austrian veteran maintained, contrary to our expectation, that one ought not to treat with ridicule some events of supernatural appearance, and no argument could make him relinquish his opinion. My heart panted for joy, for now I could hope he would not refuse to credit my wondrous tale.

I was already going to relate the strange events which I had witnessed at the Haunted Castle, when I suddenly was checked by the apprehension of drawing upon me the laugh of the company, or that someone or other would offer to encounter with me the nightly sportsmen, without being equal to that hazardous undertaking.

The Austrian spoke with uncommon warmth, his eyes sparkled, and the wrinkles on his brow were contracting closer and closer, and when the company persisted in contradicting his opinion, he offered to enforce his arguments by undeniable facts, which he himself had experienced, requesting to be heard in profound silence, which could not but be granted to a man like him. We expected to hear something very uncommon, and for some time gazed at him in dumb expectation, till he at length began as follows:—

"If I maintain that apparitions of supernatural beings ought not wholly to be rejected, then I must tell you, gentlemen, that I do not only mean that it is merely possible that departed souls, or supernatural beings of another class, can appear when and wherever they please; but I also promise to convince you by my own experience, that there are people who can affect apparitions of that kind, at certain times and under certain conditions."

We stared at each other in silent wonder: the preamble of the Austrian gave us reason to expect some horrid tale, and the seriousness of his looks and the solemn accent of his words commanded general awe. After a short pause, our solemn narrator related the following tale:

III

THE AUSTRIAN OFFICER'S TALE OF GODFRIED BURGHER'S GHOST:

> In a regiment of the garrison in which I served as Lieutenant, about twenty years ago, was a man who gave the most undeniable proofs of the truth of my assertion; he was a serjeant, about forty years old, and of a morose and gloomy appearance; he was respected by his superiors, prompt and exact in the service, and never would brook an affront.

The unthinking called him a sorcerer, and people of a more serious cast of mind talked of his connexion with superior beings, taking great care not to offend that terrible man, whose name was Volkert. On the whole he was a very good sort of a man, never offended anybody, if not provoked, was averse to company, and fond of solitude.

He was reported to have performed many strange and wonderful exploits; an ensign, who had severely chastised him for a slight neglect in his duty, was said to have been deprived ever since of the proper use of his right arm; and a captain, who had scolded him without reason, to be afflicted with a deficiency in his speaking organs. In short, strange things were everywhere related of Volkert, and in so serious a manner, that no impartial man would laugh at those reports.

I had not, as yet, got an opportunity of getting more nearly acquainted with that wonderful man, and I must confess I was not very desirous of being introduced to him, for I always treated with scorn such supernatural events, yet I never liked to make those matters a subject for ridicule.

Some of my comrades were frequently inclined to have a fun, as they used to call it, and to request the sorcerer, Volkert, to raise up the ghost of one of their companions who had died suddenly in order to ask his departed spirit whether he had found pretty girls and good wine in the other world; but I always dissuaded them from it, endeavouring to direct them to some other amusement. Meanwhile the rumour of Volkert's exploits increased from day to day, and some people would swear solemnly, that they had seen and conversed with their departed relations, through his assistance.

Among those who related such strange things of Volkert was a woman whose husband had died suddenly some months ago, and entreated her, before he expired, not to give her daughter in marriage to a certain tradesman who had courted her. The girl doated on the young man, and he likewise was exceedingly fond of her; the distress this young couple felt at that sad and cruel prohibition cannot be expressed by words; their grief was unspeakable when they were thus unexpectedly removed for ever from the happiness of being united by the bonds of holy wedlock, just when they flattered themselves to have reached the aim of their fondest wishes.

Volkert was quartered in the same street where the unhappy girl's mother lived. She requested him to find out, by means of his supernatural skill, what reason might have induced her departed husband to forbid his daughter, on his death-bed, to marry the man of her choice, though he had not only never the least objection against the union, but also had always looked upon it with the greatest satisfaction. Volkert promised to take the matter into consideration and answered, some days after, that the deceased himself must be applied to.

The poor girl was very much frightened at this declaration; however, the hope of being at last united to the darling of her lovesick heart, revived her spirits, and she consented at length to suffer the rest of her parent to be disturbed. The mother refused for a considerable time to consent to it; however, at last she agreed to Volkert's proposal, and the day, or rather the night, for the execution of the conjuration was fixed. —"The mother," added the Austrian, "has related to me the whole transaction, and I will let her speak herself."

"It was on a Saturday," said the good old woman, "when we were assembled in a back room, the same wherein my late husband had breathed his last, myself, my daughter, her lover, and two of my neighbours being present."

At eleven o'clock we began to sing, as Volkert had ordered us, penitential hymns and psalms till the clock struck twelve, when we left off singing, and Volkert entered the room, clad in a white garment, barefoot, and with a pale and disordered countenance; under his arm he carried a black carpet, a naked sword, and a crucifix, and in each hand a lighted taper. As soon as he entered the room, he beckoned us to rise, and made a sign not to utter a word; then he placed a table in the middle of the room, covered it with the black carpet, and put the crucifix and the tapers upon it, holding the sword in his hand. This done, he took out of his pocket a bottle with consecrated water, and sprinkled us and the floor with it. After we had pulled off our shoes and stockings, he burned perfumes in a chafing-dish, and began the conjuration, mumbling many mysterious words, and brandishing his sword as if fighting with an invisible enemy; at once the combat seemed to cease, he grew quiet, and turning towards us who had been standing around him, exclaimed, "I have succeeded, he is coming!"

A thick smoke overdarkened suddenly the room, the lights were extinguished, and a shiny figure, resembling in a most striking manner my deceased husband appeared.

"Ask him," said the Necromancer, "ask him before he vanishes."

I shuddered, seized with horror, and was unable to utter a single word: my daughter was in the same situation; the phantom gave us a ghastly look, shaking his head, as if denying something. The Necromancer exhorted us once more to ask the spectre, and one of my neighbours took courage to question him. "Who art thou?" asked he with a faltering voice. "Godfried Burgher," answered the phantom, in a hollow woeful accent.

"May thy daughter marry Anthony Smith?"

"No! no!" replied the apparition, gave a deep hollow groan and shook his head in a ghastly manner.

"Why not?" resumed my neighbour.

The phantom shuddered, lifting up his hands in a menacing manner, staggered back, and, when disappearing, added in a most rueful accent,

"'He is her brother!"

Night surrounded us, the Necromancer pushed the window open, and the tapers began again to burn. Now I could breathe again, and looking anxiously around, beheld my poor child stretched on the floor in a fainting fit. The unhappy girl recovered soon, but alas! her reason was gone. We were seized by the chilly hand of horror when we beheld her roving like a frantic person, wringing her hands, in a grisly manner, tearing her dishevelled hair, and beating her breast in an agony of despair. A burning fever had disordered her mind, and, alas! after three days she was no more! Wild despair drove her lover into the wide world, and heaven knows whether he is still alive or has fallen a victim of his wretched fate. I am a poor disconsolate mother, and haunted by the agonizing pangs of a tormenting conscience, can find neither rest nor comfort here below; the spirit of my poor child, murdered, by my consent to that wicked infernal transaction, hovers constantly before my bewildered fancy; my peace is gone forever; I dare not to pray to the supreme ruler of the world, for comfort and mercy, though he who dwelleth in heaven knows that I reluctantly consented to that wicked transaction, for no other reason but to promote the happiness of my murdered child, murdered by her own mother, who ought to have been her guardian angel! Oh! God of mercy, what! what will become of me, when I shall be called to the tribunal of the All-seeing! when I shall behold her standing before the Supreme Judge, and hear her accuse me in the face of heaven as her murderer? How shall I, how can I answer the stern questions of him who has entrusted her to my care, to watch with a mother's tenderness, over her life and happiness?

> I tremble, seized with chilly horror when my frantic mind antici-
> pates that awful moment, when he who sitteth on the throne of
> majesty shall, with the voice of thunder, say unto me, Wretch!
> who hast cruelly murdered thy child, depart from me into ever-
> lasting fire, prepared for the devil and his angels!—Alas! I feel
> already within my breast, the worm that shall never die, and the
> fire that shall not be quenched.

Having thus given vent to her grief, she tore her hair in wild agony, beating her breast, and the tears of sorrow trickled down her cheeks— she appeared a grisly, ghastly figure.

Her narrative, though incredible in the highest degree, made an unspeakable impression on me. I beheld the poor disconsolate mother standing before me in an agony of unutterable grief; saw the briny tears of her who had with her own eyes witnessed the apparition, and heard her bemoan her unhappy child.

Having mused awhile on these dreadful events, I felt an ardent desire to unfold the mystery hanging over that wonderful transaction; or, if I should not succeed, to convince myself by my own experience of Volkert's supernatural skill.

I interrogated the woman about several circumstances, which had appeared to me rather suspicious; and asking her, at last, whether she had any reason to think that the lover of her daughter had really been a son of her deceased husband, she was prevented, by her tears and sobs, from answering that question, I therefore dismissed her, with the firm resolution to make the strictest inquiries at her neighbours, which I did the same day, but all my endeavours to unfold that mysterious transaction proved abortive; they could tell me no more than what I had known already, repeating the unhappy widow's tale without any material alterations; I was left in the dark and found myself necessitated to check my ardent curiosity.

I now waited with impatience for an opportunity of witnessing Volkert's skill, being determined to be present if he should perform another transaction of that kind.

I went to him, requesting him to give me notice if he should happen to make a new experiment, and to admit me as a spectator. He hesitated not to give me his word, but seemed very little inclined to perform his promise, being terrified by the last transaction and its fatal consequences; the whole town talked of it, and the widow was sued at law on account of the death of her daughter. Volkert was prohibited by his General from making any further experiment of that kind. He had not mentioned to me that interdiction of his commanding officer, yet I perceived that my request gave him some uneasiness, which I took for mistrust when I afterwards came to know that circumstance.

A few months after my application to him, a new accident happened, which gave him an opportunity to exhibit an astonishing proof of his supernatural skill, and tempted him forcibly to disregard the earnest prohibition of his General.

A friend of mine happened to fall out with a foreign officer, who had been visiting his parents, the foreigner challenged my friend, who most readily consented to decide the quarrel by the sword. Business of the greatest consequence obliged the foreigner to depart in the night preceding the morning on which the duel was to be fought—he wrote a note to my friend, promising upon his honour to appear at the appointed place on the ninth day, and my brother officer consented to the delay.

I and a few more officers of our regiment paid a visit to my friend who had been challenged, two days before the duel was to be fought; we were in high spirits, played, ate and drank amid the cheerful laughter of merriment, not recollecting, that after three days our host, perhaps, might not be more. He himself appeared to have entirely forgotten the quarrel, 'til he at last, at the close of our merriment, recollected the duel he was going to fight, telling me who was to be his second, to remind him the following day of his killing business, lest his valiant adversary, Captain T—, might wait in vain for him.

"Upon my soul," added he, heated with wine, "I wish he was here now, d—n me if I would not send him to Paradise, to rest in Abraham's bosom."

"Why, brother," exclaimed one of the visitors, "could you not have him summoned hither by Volkert?"

"That would indeed be excellent fun!" resumed my friend, "but you know Volkert dare not do it, we must of course let him alone; yet, if the rascal does not come the day after tomorrow, Volkert must be applied to, and, even if I should be obliged to ask the General's permission he shall conjure him hither, that I may pierce his cowardly soul."

A unanimous bravo rewarded this unripe joke of our jovial host; we separated, and I went home, lost in profound meditation. Having some reason to suspect that Baron T— would let us wait in vain, his departure having been so abrupt, I thought this would prove a fair opportunity of putting Volkert's supernatural power to the test. At last I resolved to wait quietly the issue of that affair; and if T— should give us the slip, to try whether I should be able to persuade Volkert to give us a sample of his skill.

Though I had unjustly doubted Baron T—'s courage, as it will appear in the sequel of my narrative, yet what we had suspected happened afterwards.

The day fixed for the duel came, but no Baron T— appeared. We waited for him six hours, and still he did not come. Now I hastened to Volkert without telling a syllable of my design to my friends. The mysterious man smiled as I entered the room, and appeared to have a little more confidence in my honesty than when I paid him my first visit. I broke the business to him without circumlocution, and he seemed not unwilling to chastise the foreign officer for his want of courage, yet he endeavoured to make me sensible of the disagreeable consequences which likely would arise, if the transaction should transpire. I summoned up all my little rhetoric, and refuted his objections, by assuring him, that my friends would give him their word of honour never to betray him, and thus screen him from every disagreeable consequence; and that, if an unforeseen accident should unhappily make the transaction known, our joint interference should save him from punishment.

These arguments, accompanied by golden encouragements, conquered at last all his remaining fear; he promised to serve me at any time; however, he entreated me not to invite too great a number of friends, that the danger of detection might not be increased without need. Having promised to act according to his desire, I left him with the greatest satisfaction, and went directly to my disappointed friend, who was railing with much asperity against the cowardice of his adversary.

"What, brother," exclaimed I, "what will all this anger boot thee? It certainly will not give courage to Baron T—, and thou canst not be blamed on account of his ungentleman-like behaviour, having not challenged him. There are a great many who would be glad to sneak off so cheaply and yet so gloriously; you rather ought to pity the white-livered fellow than to be angry with him, yet, if you like, we may hit him a blow when he least suspects it."

Not knowing whether my friend would approve my plan or not, I pronounced the last words in a jocose tone to secure a fair retreat, in case he should not relish my proposal.

"How else," resumed I, "could one get at him, than by *forcing* him to wait on us? Didst thou not lately swear to have him conjured hither by Volkert, if he should give us the slip?"

My friend seemed at first to be offended, looking upon my proposal as an unseasonable joke; but when I went on talking of Volkert, and his occult arts, he asked me at last, "Seriously, friend, dost thou believe in the secret arts of that fellow?"

"I believe nothing," replied I, "that I have not seen; let us make a trial how far the common talk of his supernatural arts deserves to be credited."

He stared at me with astonishment, asking me, after a short pause, "Dost thou expect to prevail on that necromancer to agree with our wishes?"

"What wouldst thou say," replied I, "if he had already consented to give us his assistance?"

My friend stared again at me, and exclaimed at last with visible satisfaction, "Well then, let us see what honest Volkert can do."

Everything requisite for the accomplishment of our design was now talked over and settled. Two of our brother officers, whose discretion we could rely upon, were chosen to be of the party, and my friend agreed to win them over to our purpose.

I returned to Volkert, and was not a little surprised when I found him less willing than ever to assist us in our undertaking. He pretended to have pondered my proposal, but thought it too dangerous to exert his supernatural knowledge in the present case, because the conjuring of a living person could have the most dreadful consequences, which very likely might happen on the present because the Baron seemed not at all to be over-stocked with courage. Though I could not contradict him, yet I endeavoured once more to dispel his apprehensions, by the repeated assurance to screen him, with the assistance of my friends, against every disagreeable consequence. At length he appeared to be easy in respect to that point; yet he did not think it convenient to execute our design in the apartment of my friend, but when I proposed my room, he consented, after many persuasions, to look at it. Having gained his consent, I left him with rapturous joy.

Volkert came the next day to my lodgings, faithful to his promise, but having looked over my apartments, he raised new objections, telling me that none of my rooms were fit for the undertaking. I could not conceal my displeasure, which he, however, did not seem to notice.

At last he made me another proposal before he left me, offering to speak to an honest tradesman, who had an empty room, which would exactly fit his purpose, and, as he hoped, be at our service, if we would but make a reasonable acknowledgment to its owner. I consented to that proposal, Volkert went away, and returned after half an hour with the joyful tidings that he had prevailed on the man to let us have the room, fixing, at the same time, the ensuing night, for the execution of our design. He requested me to repair to the place of rendezvous after nine o'clock, describing the street so minutely that I could not miss it. Having reminded me once more of my promise, he left my room, and I went out to tell my friend and our two associates to resort in good time, to the place of appointment. At eight o'clock they came to my apartment, burning with impatience to witness the mysterious transaction, and we hastened a quarter before nine o'clock, to the house where our curiosity was to be satisfied.

I knew the owner of the room which Volkert had chosen, as a worthy, honest man. When we entered his house he accosted us with much good nature, requesting leave to be admitted to the experiment, which we the more readily consented to when he cautioned us to be on our guard against the cunning of Volkert, whom he very much suspected to be an artful impostor.

"I, for my part," added he, "have taken all possible care to prevent the Necromancer from imposing upon us, and I would lay anything that we shall catch him in some foul play or other."

When we told him that imposition would be impossible, because the gentleman who was to be summoned was still alive, he burst out into a loud laughter, requesting us to wait in his parlour 'til Volkert should call us upstairs.

"He will not be disturbed in his toilsome labour," added he, smiling, "and has made the whole evening such a tremendous noise, that one should think he had been hunting up and down the whole infernal crew of his satanic Majesty."

Time had passed quickly on in the company of that queer good-natured man, who fetched two bottles of excellent old wine, bidding us to be of good cheer. The clock struck ten before we were aware of it, and as soon as the last stroke was heard, Volkert entered the parlour, holding a lighted taper in his hand, his looks were wild and ghastly, his face pale, and every muscle of his countenance distorted, as if some horrid accident had filled him with terror. Every smile of merriment took its flight as he entered the room, our jovial mood was checked at once, and our faces grew deadly wan, like his, bearing all the marks of secret awe. He beckoned us to follow him, and we obeyed his solemn command like machines, forgetting where we were.

He led the way, with tottering knees, in awful solemn silence, and we followed him with beating hearts, expecting to behold unheard and wondrous things. We stepped into a spacious room, in the back part of which we saw a little door. Volkert opened it, leading us through an empty narrow ante-chamber to a folding door; there he stopped,

302

looking back with a ghastly boding aspect, and put the key in the lock—now he turned it slowly and carefully, the folding doors flew suddenly open, a thick smoke broke from it, as we entered, and darkened at first all the objects around.

Ere long I observed in the back part of the spacious apartment a human figure clad in a white garment. The smoke evaporated by degrees through the open door, and the figure grew brighter and brighter, and, advancing a few steps towards it, I fancied to discern some known lineaments. The smoke was now entirely evaporated, and the vision hovered clear and discernible before our gazing looks; I shuddered back when I beheld the exact image of Baron T— before me. His tall slender figure, clad in a white night-gown, struck our senses with awe, as he stood motionless before us—his looks denoted a man in the agony of death, his long black hair covered partly his pallid woe-worn cheeks, floating in a grisly manner down his shoulders.

The vision stared at me and my companions with a ghastly rueful aspect, it made my blood congeal, thrilling my soul with deadly horror; my hair rose up like bristles, and I staggered back towards my friends, who were standing by the door like lifeless statues, their faces wan, their looks bewildered—they resembled midnight spectres, just risen from the yawning grave. I collected all the small relics of courage, advancing again some paces towards the dreadful phantom, and saw the vision hovering nearer, making some feeble signs with his left hand. I made an attempt to speak, but what I said I do not know. The phantom uttered not a word, but was still making anxious signs with his left arm. Now I understood what he meant—the right arm hung in a sling as if fractured.

As soon as I comprehended this pantomime, the phantom staggered back, a dark mist arose from under his feet and surrounded the vision by degrees until we at last could see him no more. I panted for breath, my senses forsook me, a horrid humming noise filled my ears, my eyes grew dim, I staggered to the wall and was nearly fainting. At once I felt my senses returning, and, opening my eyes, beheld myself in a spacious, empty room, my companions around me, panting for breath like myself—Volkert was nowhere to be seen.

It lasted a good while before we could entirely recover the proper use of our benumbed senses. My comrades were chilled with horror, and everyone seemed to ask his neighbour, by his inquisitive looks, whether what our senses had witnessed had been a deluding dream or reality.

The landlord was standing behind me, trembling like my companions, with crossed arms and downcast looks, buried in profound meditation, and exhibiting a woeful picture of pallid fright; at length he begged us to follow him down stairs, and we went into the parlour with dejected spirits, he offered us a dish of tea, but we refused staying any longer, gave him two louis d'ors, and left his house.

The next morning I awoke, wearied and dispirited, having had only a few moments of restless sleep. I expected Volkert would come to fetch his stipulated reward, but I was disappointed, and esteemed him higher for his seeming disinterestedness. At noon my friend who had been challenged paid me a visit.

"Brother," exclaimed he, as he entered the room, "tell me, what did the vision of last night mean by the anxious motion of his arm?"

"That his right arm was fractured," replied I hastily.

"There, read that letter," resumed he, throwing an open letter on the table; I took it up and read as follows:

Sir,—An unhappy accident prevents me from fulfilling my promise this day, having been thrown from my horse and fractured my right arm. However, as soon as I shall have sufficient strength to make a journey of twenty leagues, I shall insist upon your giving me satisfaction. I am fully persuaded that you would suspect me of foul play, though I should not have sent you the enclosed certificate; yet, not to give you the least room to suspect my honour, and to screen yourself by mean subterfuges, I send you the enclosed certificate of our Surgeon-Major. Within six weeks at farthest I hope to recover the use of my right arm, by the skill of that honest man, until then I remain, without either spite or enmity,

Baron T—.
Signed with my left hand.

I gazed in dumb amazement at my friend, who was walking up and down the room with hasty steps and in a pensive attitude.

"Well," exclaimed he at length, "what dost thou think of that letter? It was, as I suppose, only owing to the carelessness of the postman, that I received it so late. The certificate cannot be suspected, and I would have believed the Baron though he should not have sent it."

I remained silent, reading over again and again the letter of the unfortunate T—. The preceding night and the whole morning I had been wavering between doubt and belief, but now I was convinced of the Necromancer's skill, as I am still, and dreaded to see his face. At length I suffered myself to be persuaded by my friend to pay him a visit; he was not at home, and we went several times to his lodgings without seeing him, until we at last, on the third day, met him on the parade. I approached him, and my three fellow adventurers did the same, Volkert wanted to give us the slip, when he saw us coming towards him; however, we came up with him, and with great difficulty persuaded him to come to my lodgings in the afternoon—having promised to meet us, he went instantly away with hasty steps.

At three o'clock he made his appearance; we showed him the Baron's letter—having read it with apparent unconcern, he said, that he as well as ourselves had known the contents of it three days ago. We persuaded him with great difficulty to accept four louis d'ors for his trouble, and he promised to see us now and then, and to convince us of his warmest gratitude by every service in his power, if we would but promise him, on our word of honour, never to desire him any more to raise up ghosts.

"I have suffered very much," added he, "and I am determined to expose myself no more to like dangers. I am afraid some additional disaster awaits me. Baron T— is no poltroon, which I am glad of, but I fear, I fear lest—"

Here he stopped, taking up his hat; we asked for the reason of his apprehensions, entreating him to speak without reserve; but all was in vain, and he left the room with these words, "I wish all may end well."

We could not comprehend the meaning of these words, and did indeed not much mind them, my friend being quite unconcerned about the duel, which we thought Volkert had been hinting at.

Eight days were now elapsed without any disagreeable accident. None of us had spoken a word, as well of our adventure as of the duel, but on the ninth day we were reminded of it in a most terrible manner. My friend entered my apartment at a very early hour, with a pallid, disordered countenance, flinging a folded letter on the table. I took it up, seized with terrible apprehensions, and saw that it was a second letter from Baron T—. "If you will give me leave, gentlemen, I will read it to you." We all consented to it, and he read as follows:

Sir,—Having recovered my strength a little, I hasten to request you to acquaint me with the particulars of a dreadful accident, which you, without doubt, will be able to unfold.

In the night succeeding the day which was fixed for our meeting, an accident happened to me which I cannot unriddle, and most willingly would suppose to have been nothing but the delusion of a disordered imagination; if not, many of my friends had witnessed the unspeakable sufferings I have endured. I was seized after eight o'clock in the evening with an agony more terrible and excruciating than that of a dying person, expiring amid the most pungent horrors and torments of a violent death. Drops of cold sweat bedewed my face, a chilly trembling shook my limbs violently, and the leaden hue of death rendered my countenance wan. I hoped to find relief if I was to walk up and down the room; however, I was seized by the burning fangs of still greater, still more agonizing pains, and the despondency preying on my bewildered fancy increased every minute. I shivered and trembled in such a manner that the chattering of my teeth could be heard at a great distance; all my muscles were contracted by horrid convulsions; the pangs of excruciating agony increased for two hours of infernal torture, until at last, my friends, despairing of my life, carried me to bed; there I lay for half an hour as if my spirit had been separated from my body, which really has been the case. I can give no better description of the last degree of my agonising pains, than by comparing my feelings with the torments of one whose whole frame suddenly is pierced with a red hot iron.

After that terrible shock I was in a state of lethargy, but I dreamed, a horrid, frightful dream. Methought I was violently dragged away from my weeping friends, and, on a sudden beheld myself in the company of some known persons, who seemed to be highly delighted with my torments, and inflicted still greater pangs on my woe-worn frame.

Suddenly I recovered my recollection, to the utter astonishment of my afflicted friends, but I awoke in such a pitiful state of weakness, that everyone present, and even the physician who attended me, despaired of my recovery. They all are of opinion that my enemies must have effected those infernal torments by supernatural means, and I myself cannot think otherwise.

You certainly must have some knowledge of that shameless, horrid transaction, and it is you to whom I ought to "apply for an explanation. I expect your answer by the returning mail. I repeat it once more, you must know the particulars of that infernal transaction, &c., &c.

"The impression this letter made on us," resumed the Austrian, "cannot be described. I read in the countenance of my friend the bitterest reproaches, for having seduced him to employ the infernal arts of Volkert to so shameless a purport."

The serious turn which this dark transaction began to take made us apprehend that it would end with a most melancholy catastrophe, yet all our apprehensions were trifles light as air in comparison to the dreadful anxiety which poor Volkert was overwhelmed with, when these tidings were reported to him. We now plainly comprehended the tendency of the mysterious words he had uttered, when we had seen him last—I never saw a man in a more distressing situation than he was as he perused the Baron's letter. His agony rendered him almost distracted when he came to the conclusion of that melancholy epistle. He wrung his hands in wild despair, was beating his breast, and tearing his hair, exclaiming in an accent of unspeakable agony, "I am undone!"

Then he fell on his knees, imploring us for God's sake to spare him, and to save him from ignominy and ruin. "I have foreseen it," groaned he, "I have foreseen it; O, had I but that time not suffered myself to be deluded to lend a helping hand to that wicked, infernal transaction!"

We did all that lay in our power to make him easy, and promised him to take all disagreeable consequences upon ourselves; however, he would not listen to the comfort we administered to him.

"I am too much known," exclaimed he, and left us in wild despair.

I now consulted with my friend what was to be done, and we agreed at last that it would be best not to answer the Baron's letter, but quietly to await his arrival.

Volkert, who was now more submissive and humble than ever, came frequently to see us, and approved our resolution; but he was always in the greatest anxiety when the idea of the Baron's arrival crossed his mind. Meanwhile the time when we were to expect the Baron drew nearer and nearer.

Six weeks were now nearly elapsed since we had received his last letter. One morning, as I was reading and smoking my pipe with much tranquillity, my servant entered my room, telling me a foreign officer desired to see me. Not suspecting that I should be the first person to whom the Baron would give notice of his being arrived, I was struck with surprise when I beheld Baron T— before me, and I cannot but confess that I was seized with horror when I saw him. The marks of a recent dangerous illness were still visible on his pale countenance; his gloomy, melancholy aspect strongly denoted the sufferings of a deeply afflicted mind, and his whole carriage horribly reminded me of the detestable, dark transaction of that unhappy, fatal night. He entered my room bowing silently, and began, after a portentous pause, to address me thus:

"Sir, you are the second of Mr. C—, who has injured me in a most glaring and disgraceful manner; first, by having insulted me in public, and then by having employed infernal arts to torment me. I dare say you are no stranger to the horrid means your friend has made use of in order to let me feel his wrath. I will not publicly accuse your friend of that black, shameless transaction, the dreadful effects of which you can still read in my countenance; however, he shall answer me with his heart's blood for that ignominious transaction, and for the sufferings he has made me undergo. I have written to him, but he has not thought it proper to answer my letter, which is a certain proof of his having been concerned in that horrid deed, the reality of which I am now fully convinced of: I know everything, even the wretch who has assisted in the performance of that diabolical business. Do not ask me how I came to know it."

He spoke this with such an emphasis that I was unable to utter a single word in defence of my friend, and he appearing not to expect anything of that kind, added, after a short pause,—

"My arm is not yet fit to manage the sword, for which reason I request he may bring with him two brace of pistols. You may tell this; your friend: I hope he will not oblige me to *force* him to accept my terms. At seven O'clock next morning I shall be at the spot we have appointed long ago; till then farewell, and tell your friend that I have not waited on him, because he prefers to converse with unbodied beings, and that I have written to him no more, because he has not thought proper to answer my last letter."

So saying, the Baron rose and left me in such perplexity that I was not able to utter a word in reply. My friend was not less frightened than myself when I told him his antagonist pretended to know the whole of our secret transaction. The remainder of the day was spent in preparations for the duel, and in settling all the affairs of my friend, in case he should be killed.

Volkert came in the evening as usual, being afraid of being known to have any connexion with us. He trembled violently when we told him that the Baron was arrived, but understanding that he would not make public the dreadful wrongs which he had suffered, the poor fellow recovered from his fright, and offered to assist the Lieutenant's servant, who was scouring his master's pistols. This task was soon finished, the two brace of pistols cleaned and charged with bullets.

We sat down conversing and drinking punch till midnight, when Volkert left us with the promise to see my friend once more next morning. He seemed little inclined to give us his opinion on the means by which the Baron could have got intelligence of the conjuration, and the man who had performed it; yet he promised to tell us next morning all he knew about it. I remained with my friend the whole night, and began to sleep a little towards morning. At six o'clock Volkert interrupted our slumber, telling us that he came to take leave of us.

We gazed at him with astonishment and surprise.

"Yes, gentlemen," exclaimed he, "I am going to leave this town, and I am very fortunate that I can do it in an honourable manner. I promised you last night to tell you how Baron T— has traced out his tormentor; know, then, that he has written to his family the same that he wrote to you in his second letter; his relations soon suspected me, being known here as a Necromancer these many years; they gave notice to the governor of the supposed transaction, and he bearing me a great regard, would not meddle with this affair; he has, however, requested my General to remove me to some other place as soon as possible, which my commanding officer was very willing to grant. He sent for me the day before yesterday, and when I appeared before him accosted me thus:

'Volkert, I have warned thee several times to practise no more thine infernal tricks, I expected thou wouldst show some regard for thy General, but seeing that all my endeavours to recall thee to thy duty are fruitless, I must send thee away, yet do not fear that I shall be unkind to thee. I know thou art a clever fellow, and I will give thee a commission as recruiting officer, which employment, I suppose, will not be disagreeable to thee, because it will afford thee an opportunity to make a proper use of thy talents.'"

"My heart was ready to leap into my mouth for joy," added Volkert, "when I heard these welcome tidings, for this is the very situation I had been hankering after. Yesterday I received my instructions, my commission, and plenty of money, and I shall set off as soon as I shall have seen the decision of Mr. C—'s affair, and begin my new employment with pleasure and vigour."

We were surprised to see the gloomy, melancholic Volkert on a sudden so cheerful and merry, but he did not give us time to disclose our astonishment, taking a hasty leave. Having wished success to my friend, he shook us heartily by the hand, and told us, that if Mr. C— should kill the Baron he expected him to join him on the road, adding,

"Perhaps I may then have a better opportunity to convince you of the love and high esteem I bear you." Having promised to see me once more after the duel, if possible, he left us; however, I saw him no more. The hour fixed for the fight drew nearer and nearer. We now took a hasty breakfast and went to the appointed place, where we found the Baron awaiting our arrival in company with a foreign officer, his second. He was impatient to begin the combat directly, but I begged him to have patience, and to remove a little farther from the town, into the field, lest the report of their pistols might be heard by the sentinels on the ramparts. Though the young spark thought it needless to be over cautious, as he scornfully called it, he consented at last to my proposal, riding a good distance farther. We thanked him for his readiness to oblige us, and alighted.

The combatants were placed opposite each other, within the short distance of four paces. My friend fired first, but missed his antagonist; the Baron doing the same was not more successful; my friend fired a second time, but he missed his aim once more; Baron T—'s second ball grazed his antagonist's cheek; Lieutenant C— was vexed, and seeing him take up the third pistol, with a trembling hand, I asked the foreigner whether he was satisfied; he shook silently his head, and my friend missed him again: the Baron returned the shot, and his ball entered the shoulder of C—. I entreated the foreigner to desist from farther animosities; however, he would not listen to me and turning with a malicious grin towards his second, he took the fourth pistol from his hand; my friend discharged his into the air, but the Baron, less generous, took his aim, and his ball whizzed through his antagonist's hat; then shaking my friend smiling by the hand, he mounted his horse, and rode in full speed to the town, accompanied by his second.

The Lieutenant grew fainter and fainter from the loss of blood, and all my endeavours to stop it were fruitless. At length my servant, whom I had sent to town, arrived with a coach and a surgeon, who declared that the wound was of no consequence, and, having dressed it, we conducted my friend to his apartments.

On our arrival we were told that the Baron with his second had been arrested as they had entered the town gate, but nobody could tell us who had been the informer. The auditor of the regiment made his appearance soon after, and examined me strictly, yet he assured me that we had nothing to fear. "It is known," added he, "that your friend has not been the aggressor."

When I begged him to tell me the name of that informer, he paused awhile and then replied,

"Well! I will tell you to whom you owe that kind service, he is no more here; it was Volkert, the noted Serjeant of Colonel R—'s regiment."

"Volkert!" exclaimed I, the words dying on my lips.

The auditor affirmed it and left me. I followed him to the door, inquiring whether Volkert had said anything else.

"I don't think he has," replied he, "he departed this morning on the recruiting business, and before he left the town has told the governor, that a foreign officer, a notorious wrangler, had challenged Lieutenant C—, and that they were going to fight a duel this morning. The governor ordered a file of soldiers to arrest you, but they were too late. When Baron T— returned to town, he was arrested along with his second. That is all I know of the matter."

I returned to my wounded friend in a pensive mood, not knowing what to think of Volkert's strange proceedings. I was inclined to look upon this step as a proof of his concern for my friend's safety, yet I could not conceive why he had not given earlier notice to the governor, having known the hour when the duel was to be fought.

The wound of my friend was not dangerous, and he was able to go abroad after the tenth day, when he went to the governor to make his submission. Having expected to be condemned at least to four weeks' confinement, he was surprised when that gentleman, who was known to be very rigorous, dismissed him with a slight reprimand. Our General took not least notice of the whole transaction, and Baron T— returned to his garrison after having been arrested four weeks. All our brother officers spoke highly of his noble behaviour, telling us that he had rejected all the proposals of his relations to interfere in his behalf.

"However," added the Austrian, "I will not abuse your patience any longer, and here conclude my wonderful tale, thinking to have fully proved my paradoxical opinions, by the account I have given you of Volkert's experiment, and I thank you cordially for your kind attention to my long mysterious narrative; you will excuse my prolixity, having been desirous to give you a faithful account of that strange man. Although I am not able to clear up his character in a more satisfactory manner, yet I am convinced that you now will believe that spirits can appear to the eye of mortals."

Here he ended, seeming to care little what sensations his odd tale might have produced in the mind of his hearers. The serious tone in which he had been speaking, and the high respect we bore him, prevented us from making our observations on his tale; I, for my part, could not help thinking it very extraordinary and fabulous, yet I could not harbour the least mistrust in the narrator's veracity, in despite of the struggles of reason, being fully convinced of his honesty. My design of relating to him our adventures at the Haunted Castle began now to ripen, and I was determined to catch the first opportunity that should offer to impart to him my secret.

The other officers sat in dumb silence, seeming to ponder how to abide by their first opinion without opposing their reverend antagonist: "It is a pity," one of them exclaimed at last, after a long solemn silence, "it is a pity that Volkert is not present, for I am sure he would convince us also, by ocular proofs, of a matter which bears such evident marks of impossibility, in the eye of the impartial friend of truth. I do not in the least suspect your veracity, being fully persuaded that you are convinced by your own experience of a reality of the strange incident you have related; yet you will not take it unkind if I assure you, that my reason will prevent me from becoming a convert to your opinions, until I shall have been an ocular witness of an experiment of that kind."

The Austrian replied not a word to that speech, but rose and took up his hat in dumb silence.

"But, pray sir," resumed another, "have you had no further account of Volkert? did he never return from his recruiting business?"

"He is dead," replied the Austrian.

"Dead!" we repeated with one voice.

"He is," repeated the veteran, coolly, "he met with a sad misfortune in the second year of his employment; ten of his best recruits gave him the slip, and, being called to an account for his negligence, he fell a victim of wild despair, blowing his own brains out."

"A sad exit for a Necromancer," resumed he who had put the question to the Austrian.

"But a common one with gentlemen of that line," added another, rather forward.

The Austrian gave him a stern, scornful look.

"I wish Volkert was still alive," said he who lodged at the haunted inn, "I wish he was still alive, he soon would restore tranquillity to the house of my landlord, and put a stop to the disagreeable talk that is rumoured about, and so hurtful to the poor man."

The Austrian made a silent bow to the company, and left the room. I followed him with hasty steps, and, coming up with him, accosted him respectfully. "You will excuse the liberty I am going to take to request of you a private hearing, wishing to impart to you something."

"That I will hear tomorrow," interrupted he drily, and went away.

The night being far advanced I went to my lodging. I awoke with the first dawn of day, arose, and, having put on my clothes, waited with impatience till it should strike eight o'clock, at which hour I intended to pay a visit to the Austrian. It was about five o'clock when I got up, and the seeming slow progress of time was very painful to me. At length the wished-for hour arrived, and I went with hasty steps to the veteran's lodging. He received me as he was wont to do, with great kindness, giving me a pipe, and after I had lighted it he asked me what my pleasure was?

After some circumlocution I broke the matter to him, giving him a full account of our adventures at the Haunted Castle. He listened with great attention to my tale, and hinting, at the conclusion of it, that I wished he would assist me in unfolding that mysterious matter, he looked seriously at me without uttering a word. Having waited some time for his answer with anxious impatience, he arose, and walked up and down the room in profound meditation.

"Friend," said he at last, after a long and painful silence, "what reason have you to engage in that dangerous undertaking?"

"I have no other motive," replied I, "than to chastise the impostors, and to deliver my servant from their clutches."

He shook his head: "Are you certain," resumed he at length, after a short pause, "that your servant has not been associated with those nightly sportsmen?"

I stared at him and replied, after having meditated awhile, "No, it is impossible, the fellow was too honest; and what motive—" —"You are right," interrupted he, "it cannot have been a preconcerted plan."

He walked again up and down the room in a pensive mood, and then exclaimed suddenly in a determined tone, "Well, I will be one of the party, and, if you like, we will set off instantly."

I eagerly accepted his proposal, and having put in readiness everything necessary, we agreed to depart in the evening. He proposed to take one of his serjeants with him, and I resolved to do the same. I returned to my lodging against noon, highly pleased with my success, in order to prepare myself for a speedy departure.

We left F— at eight o'clock in the evening; nobody was privy to our design, and our serjeants fancied we were going on business, wondering very much how recruiting officers in the service of two different princes could act thus in concord. But on the road we undeceived them, and were much rejoiced that our hoary veterans did not dislike our enterprise.

Three days after our departure from F— we arrived within a small distance from the place of our destination, without having met with any sinister accident.

We were now on the skirts of the Black Forest, but could see no village; the spot where the houses leading to the castle had began was deeply impressed on my memory. I showed to my fellow traveller the rivulet, on the borders of which the old man had been sitting when we first had met him; we looked about for the houses but we could find none. I did not know what to think of the matter.

Pursuing our route, we ascended a rising ground. Gracious heaven!

how was I shocked when I at once beheld a heap of ruins on the spot where the village had stood! We could still trace the marks of conflagration. In the background we saw only a few miserable huts left, and a little further distant the castle presented itself to our view. We gazed at each other in dumb astonishment, and the Austrian alighted; I and our two hoary veterans did the same, and we climbed, after much difficulty, over the heap of ruins. As we approached the few remaining houses, the inhabitants came running towards us covered with rags, and exhibiting pale, woe-worn countenances. I never beheld such a horrid picture of wretchedness and misery;—they wrung their hands, crying for alms, and wept bitterly.

Having distributed money amongst them, I inquired when that misfortune had happened. "Alas!" groaned they, "who should have thought, when your honour left us, that you ever would see us in such a miserable state? We are all ruined; all our little property has been consumed by the flames. Good heaven! how shall we keep our little helpless babes from starving?"

Repeating my question, when that terrible accident had happened, the poor unfortunate people told me their village had been set on fire the day after we had left them.

Dreadful apprehensions filled my soul, and the Austrian's looks seemed to confirm them.

When I inquired after my former host, I was told that he had lost his life in the flames. "The fire," said the poor people, "broke out suddenly, in different places, in the dead of night; they had not been able to save their property, and a great number of the inhabitants, with their cattle, had perished in the flames." This horrid tale made my blood run chill, being convinced that I had been the primary cause of that dreadful event.

As we entered one of the miserable huts, we were met by the lamentations of people half-naked; they all recollected me, receiving me with hideous groans. All my money was not sufficient to comfort the unhappy sufferers, but I divided it willingly amongst them, feeling an inward pleasure in being able to ease at least their sufferings a little. The Austrian, smiling at me, followed my example as far as the expenses of our journey would admit.

At last I ventured to inquire after the Haunted Castle; the poor sufferers shuddered at the question, telling me, without reserve, that they did not doubt that the last visit we had paid to that abode of horror had drawn upon them the dreadful ire of the revengeful spirits, which I in vain wished to be able to contradict. Unwilling to behold any longer the marks of sorrow and distress so deeply imprinted on the faces around me, and stung to the heart by the tormenting thought to have partly contributed, by my idle curiosity, to provoke the lurking tempest of woe that had thus cruelly crushed the earthly happiness of the wretched villagers, I hastily inquired for the next village, they showed us the way, and we bade them farewell with a bleeding heart, riding away in full speed.

But, alas! I could not escape the hideous spectre of self-reproach, pursuing me with icy fangs. The scene of misery which my eyes had witnessed hovered constantly before my gloomy fancy, the groans of woe which I had heard still vibrated in my ears, the haggard looks of these unhappy people, undone by my heedlessness, stared me in the face ever and anon, and I struggled in vain to shake off the grisly spectre pursuing me with unrelenting resentment. "How comfortless and miserable is the man," said I to myself, "whom conscience accuses of having plunged into the gaping gulph of misery a fellow creature!"

The Austrian saw the painful workings of my soul, kindly striving to dispel the gloomy clouds hovering over my brow. "How can you accuse yourself," spoke the reverend veteran, "of having been, though involuntarily, accessory to the fatal blow that has thus cruelly destroyed the happiness of these people, whose fate you are bemoaning? It was the high decree of a superior power, that rules the fate of man. The ways of the All-wise are ever good and just, though surrounded sometimes with impenetrable darkness. Men are but tools in the hand of Providence, and never ought to murmur against the Father of the universe. It is not you who have destroyed the happiness of these poor sufferers; your heart is good, and you could not foresee the dreadful consequences of your juvenile rashness; cheer up, young man, and trust to the Supreme Ruler of all things, that he knows best what is good and fit; he produces light from the womb of darkness, and leads sometimes his children to greater bliss over the thorny path of misery and woe."

I listened with eager attention to the soothing speech of comfort flowing from the reverend lips of my sage companion, and a heavy load was taken from my heart; when he had finished, the clouds of gloominess dispersed by degrees, and a ray of cheerfulness darted through my mind. After half an hour's ride we beheld a large village before us; we agreed to wait there the setting in of night, and then to visit the Haunted Castle secretly.

Our host could not, or perhaps would not, answer our inquiries concerning the desolated castle, and we endeavoured in vain to know whether the mighty sportsmen were still housing there or not; my serjeant went abroad to get some information, and was so fortunate as to draw from the schoolmaster of the village as much as we wanted to know; returning after an hour with the corroboration of our suspicion, that the spirits residing at the castle had set fire to the desolated village, and that they since that time had forsaken their former abode.

Although the latter part of his intelligence gave us but little hope that we should succeed in our design to unfold the mystery of the ruinous castle, yet we determined to make at least a trial, the Austrian being very desirous to explore the noted building, and we went all four to the Haunted Castle as soon as it was dark.

We arrived at the gloomy fabric after a short walk, lighted some torches we had brought with us from F—, entered the courtyard, and ascended the spiral staircase; the Austrian searched every corner, and I found all the rooms in their former condition, the seats and the table we had constructed were still as we had left them, unmoved, untouched.

When the Austrian had carefully searched everything, we descended the stairs leading to the cellar, but found the iron door strongly fastened as before. We entered the garden, searching and prying round, till we at length espied the aperture of the cavern through which we had effected our escape from the grisly jaws of a lingering death. The hollow sound of our footsteps re-echoed horribly through the dreary subterraneous abode as we entered, and the light of our torches reflected grisly from the damp mossy walls of the deep and narrow passage.

Stepping into the ruinous stable, we espied, with pleasure, the hole in the boards through which the Baron had fallen down, and detected in one of the corners a ladder, and above the place where it was standing a trapdoor. Having ascended the ladder, I opened the half-decayed door, with one violent push, and entered with my fellow-adventurers the well-known spacious apartment, leaping over the gaping opening where the boards had given way. Looking around we beheld several small iron doors, one of which flew open at the first push of the Austrian, and presented to our eyes the avenue of a damp arched vault, from which a stone staircase led to that part of the fabric which faced the cellar door.

Without stopping there, we pursued our way to the large folding door leading to the great hall underground, but found it strongly bolted on the inside, and all our hopes of further discovery were blasted at once. We made the utmost efforts to disengage the massy door from its rusty hinges, but all our labour was lost, its strength proved superior to our united endeavours of forcing it.

While we were standing before that door, consulting whether we should go back or not, we heard suddenly a distant noise, as if a lock was opening, and soon after a folding door seemed to fly open, with a hideous creaking, which instantly was followed by a terrible noise of numerous steps as if people in boots were descending. When the noise drew nearer, we could distinguish the clattering of many spurs, and the harsh voices of men; the whole subterraneous cavern was at length filled with a most tremendous noise, and we gazed at each other rather pleased than frightened, being four vigorous men, used to danger, provided with four sabres and as many brace of double-barrelled pistols. The Austrian, standing nearest to the door, retained his equanimity unimpaired and, ere long, a hollow voice, like the distant rolling of thunder, exclaimed, "Come hither with the booty." A confused bustle ensued, the tinkling of money was heard, some quarrelled and some cursed and scolded, but were soon reconciled. At length the bustle ceased, a door was opened close by us, and money locked up in a chest. Meanwhile the following discourse took place in the unknown assembly.

First Voice. "Tomorrow we will waylay the gentlemen of Norrinberg, and ease them of their golden burthen. I trust you will behave like men, my jolly boys! It would be a pity if they should give us the slip once more."

SECOND VOICE. "By holy Peter! they shall not escape."

MANY VOICES. "They shall not, they shall not."

THIRD VOICE. "I wonder where our grey-beard may stay so long. I have not seen his holy face since our last fun."

FOURTH VOICE. "Take my word, brother, he sits by the fireside and chaunts penitential hymns. The fellow is of no further use to our community, we must send him to the devil."

FIRST VOICE. "Let him alone, my boys, he has rendered us many good services, has saved many of our brave companions from the hangman's ruthless fangs; don't grudge him a little rest, he will soon return and bring us joyful tidings."

SECOND VOICE. "He has procured us many a golden booty; has, by his cunning, extricated us from many neck-breaking difficulties; it would be ungrateful to be angry with him. What would become of our noble band if he did not guide our arm by his sage counsels?"

THIRD VOICE. "Bravely spoken, my lad, he is a good sort of a fellow; it is a thousand pities that he begins to grow old and infirm."

FIRST VOICE. "Let him grow old and infirm, if he but escapes the gallows."

Here somebody was locking the door of an adjoining room, a hollow bustle and humming ensued, and the robbers (for such they must have been) were going to withdraw.

"Shall we break in upon the scoundrels?" whispered the Austrian to me.

"By what means?" replied I, shrugging up my shoulders.

"Through the garden, or the adjoining wing of the castle," resumed he.

"But the danger," said I,—"Is not so great as you fancy," interrupted the Austrian; "yet it will be better to force the gentlemen to open the door; if they should refuse to do it, then it will be time enough to surprise them in the court-yard, for I do not think it prudent to venture on the staircase, because they would then have too much advantage over us."

Now all was silent in the cellar, till after a short pause a new conversation began.

First Voice. "I say, brother, what shall we do with the officer's servant we have entrapped? The dog is good for nothing, and we are in danger that he will betray us one time or other."

Second Voice. "Let us knock his brains out."

Third Voice. "Let us give him his liberty."

Fourth Voice. "Or sell him to a recruiting officer."

First Voice. "We will take thy advice, brother Rasch, and set him at liberty. If his master has saved his life, the servant may share the same fortune with him; but first the blockhead shall swear a terrible oath never to betray us, else I will break his rascally neck."

Many Voices. "Well spoken, Captain, let us break the scoundrel's neck if he refuses to swear."

Now we heard them ascend the staircase with a terrible noise, and instantly the Austrian knocked with his hands and feet against the door; a momentary silence ensued.

"Open the door, ye miscreants!" roared my friend with a thundering voice. "Open the door, ye rascals," exclaimed I and my fellow adventurers, but before the hollow sound of our voices had ceased re-echoing through the vaulted passage where we were standing, the whole crew was running upstairs with a tremendous noise, and we hurried with all possible speed through the long winding passage, with pistols cocked, but before we could reach the end of the subterraneous avenue, we heard the trampling of horses, which soon was dying away at a distance. A gust of wind had extinguished our torches, but the light of the moon was shining so clear that we soon beheld an opening in the garden wall leading to the field, where we could see at a small distance, a numerous troop of horsemen galloping away at a furious rate. On our return we observed that the horsemen had taken their flight through the garden, which appeared to have been their common in and outlet since the burning down of the village.

I left the residence of these robbers very much dissatisfied; the

Austrian, on the contrary, was highly pleased, representing to me that we should not know much more of the matter than we had heard, even if we had surprised them; that I did wrong if I complained of having been disappointed, being now informed of my servant's fate, and the mystery of the castle; and that every wish of taking personal vengeance on these miscreants was not becoming men like ourselves, because the hangman would have been defrauded of his perquisites if we had killed some of them.

"All we could do," added he, "would be to give notice of what we have seen and heard to the magistrates of the next town; but I fear the gang is too numerous than that they could be taken prisoners; besides, they will take care not to suffer themselves to be entrapped; and if the magistrates were to take cognizance of our denunciation, and should fail in their attempt to destroy the whole crew, they perhaps would be made a second example of the revengeful daring spirit of these lawless wretches, and pay dearly for having enacted the laws against them. Remember the agony of grief you felt when you beheld the horrid consequences of opposition against these outlaws, in viewing the ruins of the village which but lately has fallen a victim to their cruel resentment, and then tell me whether it is advisable to inform against them? We had better leave their punishment to that supreme Judge who certainly will overtake them with his vengeance when their measure shall be full."

I returned to our inn at the next village, comforted by the seasonable reasoning of my worthy friend, and I never shall forget the wise instructions he gave me on the way; I never shall forget his tender exhortations to take care not to follow the first impulse of the moment, but always to listen attentively to the voice of reason before I should engage in any undertaking, and to bridle the youthful ardour of heedlessness by prudence and cool reflection.

We entered our inn at two o'clock in the morning, and we were met by the landlord, who had been very uneasy at our staying away so long, because many murders had been committed lately within the environs of the village. We told him we had taken a walk, but having missed our way, had strayed about until the dawn of day had assisted us in finding our way back. He appeared to believe our words and we went to rest.

We awoke at eight o'clock, and departed at nine for F—, where our absence had not been much taken notice of, those secret journeys being very common among recruiting officers; yet some of my friends puzzled themselves very much by various conjectures about the reasons of my connexion with the Austrian; but neither we nor our trusty serjeants communicated our adventure to anyone of our acquaintance.

During our absence a strange accident had happened to one of our comrades, which had made every one wish for the return of the Austrian, and no sooner were we arrived before all the officers repaired to my room to inform us of it.

The officer who lodged at the haunted inn, coming home against midnight three days ago, sat down to finish a letter to his Colonel. As soon as it had struck twelve O'clock, he heard a tremendous rap at the door, which he did not mind at first, but continued writing. A second rap, more violent than the first, disturbed him soon after, but he still took little notice of it. A third, not unlike a clap of thunder, ensued after a short pause, the door of his apartment flew open, and a white figure was going to enter the room.

"Fearless," these are his own words, "did I start up, unsheath my sword and run towards the phantom; it retreated, but I pursued, and pierced it with my sword, it gave a hollow scream, but what further happened I cannot tell; I awoke as if from a deluding dream, and was lying stretched on the floor at the bottom of the stairs, surrounded by a great number of people with lighted candles; terrible pains had seized me, and my sword was still in my hand."

When the narrator had finished his wonderful tale, I perceived visible marks of its authenticity on his face, and inquired whether he had been hurt by the fall. He told me he had suffered no material injury except a few bruises.

The Austrian began now to question him.

"Have you perceived anything uncommon before that strange accident happened?"

OFFICER.—"Nothing at all except an insignificant noise, after twelve o'clock."

AUSTRIAN.—"Have you, perhaps, before you met with that misfortune, been thinking on my tale of Volkert's exploits?"

OFFICER.—(Vexed) "I was writing to my Colonel; how could I therefore think on that fellow? Or do you think it impossible that any one besides you can experience things the possibility of which you have proved by facts?"

The Austrian, apparently lost in profound meditation, gave him no answer, but was walking up and down in solemn silence.

Our companions acquainted us now with the purport of their visit, signifying a desire to encounter the kingdom of spirits and hobgoblins *in pleno corpore*, under the command of my serious friend. Thinking the veteran would relish their proposal as little as myself, I thought it would be agreeable to him, if I could prevail on the spirited sons of Mars not to urge the matter further, addressing them in a jocose manner:

"Gentlemen, it seems you do not consider that these airy disturbers of nocturnal rest are not fond of large companies; or do you suppose the apparition, which I suspect to be a female one, a second Semiramis?"

However, it was in vain to attempt persuading them to drop the adventure, their imagination having been heated too much by the Austrian's tale, as that they would give up their design. Turning their backs against me, highly displeased with my harangue, they solicited my friend with the greatest impetuosity to comply with their request. He inquired whether Lieutenant N— was still an inhabitant of the haunted inn, and being told that the valiant son of Mars had removed to another lodging the next morning after the nocturnal encounter, he refused flatly to yield to their entreaties, telling them he was sure the apparition would give them the slip.

"Well, well," exclaimed the undaunted warriors, "we will run the risk and watch the ghost, though we should sit up ten nights for it; we are determined to unfold that mystery."

So saying they left the room in great hurry.

"What do you think of the matter?" said I, when the visitors had left us.

"Nothing," replied he, with much *sang froid*, shrugging up his shoulders.

"But the ghost," said I—

"Is an offspring of their childish fancy," replied the Austrian.

"The fall of Lieutenant N—?" asked I.

"Is very natural," replied the Austrian; "I could cite you more than one hundred incidents corroborating the truth, that people have a very confused idea when their senses are tied up by fear and anxiety. As soon as cool reflection gives way to the horrors of a disordered fancy, we are but too apt to create phantoms and spectres around us, we do not see what really exists, but what we fear to behold."

I could oppose nothing to this reasoning of his, founded so strongly on experience, and suspected the courage of our valiant Lieutenant very much, having no doubt but his fear had made him miss the stair-case; I therefore took no farther notice of our bravado and his companions, not caring what would be the finale of their trifling adventure. My friend was likewise quite unconcerned about the matter, and, without mentioning it any farther, we went about our business.

When night invited us to rest from the toils of the day, we dedicated the remaining hours to the mutual enjoyment of hallowed friendship's cheerful bliss.

Eight days of peaceful happiness were now elapsed, when Lieutenant N— entered my apartment one morning, with a countenance exhibiting the strongest marks of horror.

"I come to you," said he, "because I apprehend a second refusal from your friend, if you do not support my request."

Asking him whether he intended to apply once more to my friend to encounter the ghost, he replied, it was his intention to try his fortune once more with my obstinate friend.

"Then you must excuse me," exclaimed I, peevishly.

Having stared at me awhile in profound silence, he began walking up and down the room, and at last seated himself by my side, resuming, in a cool and tranquil tone, "Hear what I am going to say before you refuse to intercede with your friend, and I will acknowledge myself to be unworthy of your confidence if you persist any longer in your resolution, not to speak in my behalf to your worthy friend."

The solemn manner in which he pronounced the last words engaged my attention, and made me apprehend to hear a tale of horror. Having moved my chair closer to his he went on.

"You know what I and my friends intended to do; we have executed our design. All our efforts to make the ghost appear proved abortive at first; in vain did we watch, make a noise, search every corner of the house, and try to provoke the spirit for three nights; we could neither hear nor see anything uncommon."

I was going to interrupt him, and to argue the imprudence of their proceedings, but he squeezed my hand gently, and begged me not to interrupt his narrative.

"The fourth night appeared," thus he continued after an awful pause, "it still makes my blood freeze when I recollect the horrible scene of terror my eye beheld in that night of dreadful note."

We all repaired to the abode of that airy disturber of the stillness of night, taking our residence in a lonely hall, in the apartment. We sat down to the inviting punch bowl after eleven o'clock, as we had done the preceding nights, filling our pipes and cursing the cowardice of the spectre, seemingly afraid of meeting an assembly of hardy soldiers; but it took ample vengeance on our forwardness, in so horrid a manner, that one must have been an eye-witness of its ire, if one will form a just idea of our situation.

Our impatience increased as the punch began to heat our blood, we took the candles from the table, unsheathed our swords, and began to search every corner of the house and the cellar without success. My friends looked gloomy, the clouds of dissatisfaction were hovering over their brows, and a storm was gathering, which perhaps would have ended in a serious quarrel, if it had not been for the Austrian's tale, which, as yet, had sheltered me against their boiling anger, and from the suspicion of being an impostor or a coward. They began ridiculing the landlord and myself on account of our self-created fright, as they called it, declaring all we had heard and seen to be a mere phantom, the offspring of a deluded fancy; however, they were soon convinced of the truth of our narration, in a most shocking manner.

We were ascending the staircase, and the foremost had not yet reached the last step, when a sudden hollow noise arose. It was not unlike the howling of the tempest rushing through the chinks of an old ruinous building. The noise carried something frightful with it, which cannot be expressed by words. My hair rose up like bristles, an irresistible horror made my blood run chill, and my ridiculing friends became as serious as if a magic wand had touched them, gazing at each other in dumb astonishment. The dismal noise continued a few seconds, and then everything was as silent as the grave.

We pursued our way to the hall, and retook our seats, wondering what could have caused that dreadful howling, and one of the company opened the window to see whether a tempest had gathered in the air, but the sky was clear, and not the least wind blowing. Sensations of unspeakable awe thrilled our souls, the fumes of punch evaporated, and solemn stillness swayed all around; nothing was heard save the violent palpitations of the heart, the chattering of our poor landlord's teeth, and the knocking together of his trembling knees.

A few moments more of profound silence, and then the dismal howling arose again with redoubled force; a sudden violent gust of wind threw the windows open, and the door from its hinges, extinguishing all the candles; a tremendous clap of thunder shook the house, a terrible flash of lightning hissed through the room, and prostrated us to the ground; a hideous lamenting noise assailed our ears, and lifting up my head I beheld the phantom that once had frightened me, advancing with a threatening grin; grisly was its shape, and its eyes rolling like two flaming comets.

I was the first who recovered the use of his senses, and, calling in vain for the landlord, my companions started up, and we found the poor fellow prostrate on the floor, half frantic with terror. At length he also recovered a little from his fright, and after many persuasions ventured down stairs, accompanied by me, to strike a light. Everybody in the house was snoring, except our crest-fallen fellow adventurers, who exhibited a rueful ghastly group, being all as pale as ashes. Looking at our watches we saw it was past two o'clock, sat an hour longer without perceiving anything farther, and returned against morning to our respective lodgings.

I would not have troubled you with an account of this strange incident if an accident was not connected with it, which has happened last night.

My recruiting business having called me abroad yesterday, I returned in the afternoon; in the dusk of evening I entered a thicket in a gloomy pensive mood, all around was lonely and buried in profound silence; no sound was heard except the dismal dirge of the screech-owl, and the shrill chirping of the amorous cricket. At length I heard a whispering within a small distance, and cocking one of my pistols, I rode on with the greatest circumspection. At once I saw a manly figure coming out of the thicket, but could not distinguish his dress; advancing a little farther, I beheld somebody in a peasant's garb, walking on briskly and talking to himself. As I came up with him I observed a black wallet on his back, and a thick branch of a tree in his hand, serving him instead of a walking cane. He seemed to take no notice of me, pursuing his way with hasty steps, and still muttering between his teeth. I saluted him but he gave me no answer.

"Whither art thou going, good friend?" exclaimed I.

"To men!" replied he, to my utter astonishment.

"Very likely to F—," resumed I.

"Yes," said he, "there are men."

Supposing him to be a lunatic, I passed him, pursuing my way in a brisk trot; when I came out of the thicket I saw that I was nearer the town than I thought, and made my horse quicken his pace; but how was I astonished when I beheld again the same figure walking before me.

"Old gentleman," exclaimed I, "it seems thou knowest the road better than I do."

"I think so myself," added he drily; "and I believe I know many things better than you do."

"Strange being," resumed I, "who art thou?"

"A friend of wisdom!" was his answer.

"Thy wisdom," replied I, "must be as odd as thyself! But pray what dost thou call wisdom?"

"What you do not understand," was his reply.

Hearing the words friend of wisdom, I was suddenly struck with a suspicion which my readers will easily guess, and that suspicion was strengthened when the narrator informed me of his definition of wisdom. I strongly suspected that he was the same person I had met in the Black Forest, under the garb of a pilgrim, and I hardly could refrain from exclaiming, "Art thou here, impostor?"

Every one may guess the conclusion of the Lieutenant's wonderful tale. I scarcely had patience to await it. The narrator being highly charmed with the hoary juggler, could not find words to express the sensations his reverend aspect had raised within his breast. He had fancied to be in a company with a robust countryman, but when he entered his house in the suburbs, to which he kindly had invited him, he beheld the countenance of an old man with silver hair, and a mien exciting awful respect. He offered him a glass of excellent wine, and began by degrees to become more cheerful and communicative.

The old man's conversation on the road having betrayed a high degree of occult knowledge, had very nearly tempted the Lieutenant to communicate to him his adventure at the haunted inn; that temptation returning with redoubled force he could no longer resist, and told him everything that had happened. The result of the ensuing conversation was that he entreated the old man to come and conjure up the apparition, to which he, after many seeming struggles, at last consented, under the condition that no more than six persons should be present, and the landlord's leave could be obtained. The Lieutenant left him in high spirits, after having promised to fulfil strictly these two conditions.

I could not bridle any longer my ardent desire to hasten to the Austrian and to get rid of my visitor, who now became exceeding troublesome to me, being tired of his overstrained encomiums on the old deceiver. I therefore, anticipating the renewal of his request to speak to my friend, promised that I not only would engage to persuade him to assist at the conjuration, which was to be performed the ensuing night, but I also assured him that I myself would be present.

The Lieutenant's raptures exceeded all bounds, he almost stifled me by his embraces, and called me more than a hundred times his kind benefactor, and his dear obliging friend. I was, however, entirely indifferent to his raptures and endearments, pondering how I might best confound the vile dissembler, and put a final stop to his enormous cheats. I begged the poor hoodwinked Lieutenant to give me leave to go directly to my friend, and to win him over to the party, which he instantly did, after having fixed an hour in the afternoon when he would wait on me to hear how far I should have succeeded with the Austrian.

"Meanwhile," added he, "I will go to the owner of the haunted inn, in order to talk the business over with him, and to engage three able assistants more from among our friends."

Not finding the veteran at home I was vexed very much, but when dinner-time came I had the pleasure of meeting him. The recapitulation of Lieutenant N—'s account of his late adventure at the inn, and his conversation with the hoary juggler, produced the desired effect. Though a man like him, who was of a cool temper, and never suffered his passion to get the better of his reason, could not be seized with a fit of amazement, yet I never saw him so violently agitated.

Having with apparent emotion awaited the conclusion of my tale, he exclaimed at last, after a short pause, during which his desire for vengeance and punishment seemed to struggle with his reflection and prudence—

"Friend, what do you intend to do?"

"To seize the Necromancer."

"Before or after the conjuration?" asked the Austrian.

"After it," replied I.

Now the dinner bell rang, and he left me with the promise to repair at night to the place of action.

Having accustomed myself by degrees to examine minutely what likeliest might be the result of my noble friend's almost unfathomable considerations, before I determined on anything he was concerned in, I succeeded sometimes in my anxious endeavours to act in unison with his principles, and to coincide with his ideas, but in the present case I was quite at a loss how to proceed conformably to his wish, having not the least clue by which I could expect to extricate myself out of the labyrinths into which he had led me, leaving everything to myself.

However, after much reflection, I was at last so fortunate to hit upon a plan which he fully approved, proposing to conceal myself until the whole transaction should be finished, and then to rush like lightning upon the hoary deceiver, to upbraid him with his glaring cheats, to force him to a confession of the dark, fraudulent means he had employed to play that infernal trick upon us, when he left us in the lurch in the cellar of the Haunted Castle, and then to make him a prisoner without farther ceremony.

We both agreed to deliver him up to the civil power, after having convicted him of his roguery, and to order four stout corporals to rush into the room at the first signal, in order to arrest the shameless, cunning deceiver. Flattering ourselves with hopes of good success, we parted, after a mutual promise to repair to the place of action at eleven o'clock.

Lieutenant N— came to my lodging at three o'clock in the afternoon, to inform me that everything was ready for the performance of our nocturnal adventure. The landlord had made no difficulty to give his consent to the conjuration, and was desirous to be admitted one of the spectators, being elated with the hope that his house soon would be cleared of that troublesome being which had until now banished all his customers, and very much impaired his circumstances. He knew the reverend Necromancer, as the lieutenant was pleased to call him, and was in raptures that the honest old man was returned to F—, and had consented to restore the tranquillity of his house, exclaiming,

"Now I am easy; Father Francis is the very man. It is a thousand pities that he visits these parts so seldom, and that he, if present, buries himself in solitude."

"He could not tell me precisely," added the lieutenant, "how the old man employs his time, because nobody was on an intimate footing with him, nor could anyone tell where he came from, or whither he was travelling so often, but that it was universally known that he possessed houses in most of the adjacent towns, where he was living in the same retired and harmless manner as here."

The lieutenant, highly pleased when I told him that the Austrian had consented to be present at our nocturnal meeting, went now to the other associates, in order to settle everything, and invited myself and my friend to supper, which I readily consented to.

Having shifted my clothes, that the old deceiver might not know me so easily, I went to the Austrian, whom I, without difficulty, persuaded to sup with me and Lieutenant N—. We repeated our orders to our trusty corporals and left the house.

Strange sensations occupied my mind, spreading a gloom over my countenance. The expectation of seeing something extraordinary and wonderful thrilled my soul with awe, and an unaccountable chill trembled through my limbs; perhaps it was the effect of a foreboding of my approaching separation from my ever-beloved friend, who appeared as cool and unconcerned as ever. When he saw me so silent and gloomy, he said, "So solemn, my friend, it seems you wish very little for your old acquaintance."

"It is no pleasant task to unmask an impostor," said I.

"But a useful one," answered he, taking me under the arm.

I endeavoured to appear cheerful, in which painful task I succeeded at length; however, there was still lurking in my soul an awful, strange sensation, quite foreign to my character, though the latter had been tinged with a sombre hue since I had frequented the company of my new friend.

When we came to Lieutenant N—'s apartment, we met two of his most intimate friends, who had been present at the late alarming apparition of the ghost, and were determined to engage the spectre once more.

They all were rejoiced at the Austrian's coming, and soon began to recount the terrible visitation of the ghost, and the anxiety they had suffered, which they did in a most prolix and tedious manner. The Austrian begged them to talk of something else and not to deprive themselves of the necessary firmness of mind by the recollection of what was past; he at the same time endeavoured to give the conversation a more cheerful turn, and I cannot but confess that he never had been so amusing and pleasing since I had known him.

The cloth being laid we sat down to supper, but none of us did honour to the meal except the Austrian; the wine promised to dispel the clouds of gloominess from our circle; however, our host plied us in vain with bumpers, the heart-elevating juice of the grape could not raise our crestfallen spirits, and the Austrian was the only one who relished it, and experienced "its powers divine."

The farther the night advanced the lower our spirits sunk, in despite of my friend's endeavours to spread the glow of merriment around, and to encourage us to join him heartily in his libations. Though he sounded the praise of the wine's excellence, by words and deeds, yet he kept within the bounds of soberness, and when it struck eleven o'clock, bade us drink a final bumper to good success, and then took up his hat and sword.

I did the same, and our companions followed our example with fear and trembling. We went down stairs in solemn taciturnity, and groped our way through midnight darkness to the Haunted Inn.

The master of the house welcomed us most cordially, thanking us beforehand for the expected tranquillity of his house and the return of his prosperity; he led us to the hall where the above-mentioned dreadful apparition had appeared, enlarging with indefatigable garrulity on many horrible incidents which had taken place, within the space of a twelve-month, in that disastrous apartment.

The Austrian uttered not a word, but searched closely every corner of the spacious lonely room, and then took a candle and went out. Having been absent a good while, he returned at length, pulled his greatcoat off, and entered into a long conversation with the master of the house, asking him many questions, which betrayed his diffidence in the poor fellow's honesty. I was not much pleased with his unequivocal marks of suspicion, knowing the innkeeper as an upright, honest man, void of disguise and art, and that he himself had suffered the utmost damage by those nocturnal apparitions. His inn had been unfrequented by travellers these many months, on account of that sleep-disturbing phantom which haunted the weary wanderer in the dead of night, and he swore by everything holy and sacred that he had never seen Father Francis (so he called the hoary deceiver) though he had heard of many deeds perpetrated by that wonderful man.

"It is now," added he, "a good while since I have heard of that sagacious old man; they say he is gone to a distant place, offended at the ingratitude of the people of our country. Formerly he has told the people's fortunes, but without fee. My father, the late possessor of this house, has told me many marvellous instances of his astonishing skill in detecting thefts, and recovering stolen goods; as how he has been possessed of a wonderful sagacity to read in people's looks, at first sight, whatever they had done all their life long; discovered and solved the spell of witchcraft, and horribly punished the old hags that dared to bewitch the countrymen's cattle. In short, said my father, God rest his honest soul, Father Francis has indeed been a father and a friend to everyone in distress, and a baneful foe to the Black Spirit and his infernal hosts."

The Austrian appearing still to harbour thoughts of suspicion against the simple innkeeper, watched closely all his motions, was always at his heels when he left the room, and ever busy to ply him with various questions. I and my companions kept close together, myself burning with desire for the beginning of the drama, and my fellow adventurers awaiting it with fear and trembling.

It struck twelve when the innkeeper was still in close conversation with the circumspect Austrian. The door opened, and Father Francis entered the room; the sight of the hoary deceiver made my blood boil in my veins, and I clapped my hand involuntarily to my sword; the Austrian, who was standing at a small distance from me, hiding a part of his face under his hat, and holding a brace of pistols in his hands, seemed to ask me, by a side glance, whether Father Francis and my old acquaintance in the Black Forest were one and the same person. I affirmed it by a quick motion of my eyelids, and the Austrian turned his back to the Necromancer; I removed behind Lieutenant N—, and peeping over his shoulders, watched the proceedings of the juggler, who advanced with solemn steps into the middle of the apartment, where he stopped, resting his inquisitive looks on the countenances of the company.

Profound silence swayed all around, and we were fixed to the ground like so many statues, thrilled with anxious expectation, and scarce ventured to breathe.

The old man was clad in a long robe of black silk, his snow-white head uncovered, a white silken sash, marked with strange characters, was tied round his waist, and the well-known black wallet hung on his back; having taken it down he untied it, and exhibited the mysterious instruments of conjuration: at his mute command the host carried a table to the centre of the room, put two lighted torches upon it and bolted the door.

Now he gave us a signal to form a circle round him; the Austrian placed himself to his left side, turning his face towards the door, Lieutenant N—, by the conjurer's own desire, to his right; the innkeeper stood close by the Austrian, one of Lieutenant N—'s friends took his station by the landlord, and I placed myself close to the latter. The Necromancer appeared to care little for the right wing, and I could clearly observe that his left neighbour raised his suspicion.

However, he began his conjuration with apparent firmness, after he had strewed a reddish sand on the floor, and delineated a treble circle with his ebony wand. The particulars of the act of conjuring were nearly the same as in the cellar of the Haunted Castle, except his reading aloud the greatest part of the form of the conjuration, and his face being not so horribly distorted by convulsions as in the subterraneous rooms of that terrible haunt of robbers.

Now the ceremony was finished, he cast his book on the table, and pronounced thrice the well-known mysterious word. Suddenly a howling blast of wind rushed against our faces, a thick column of smoke ascended from the floor, overcasting the whole apartment, and extinguishing the torches. Darkness and horror surrounded us.

Ere long a faint gleam was breaking from the floor, sparingly illuminating the objects around, and rising higher and higher on the opposite wall till it reached the ceiling. At once the floor seemed to shake beneath our feet, and we beheld with chilly horror a human figure hovering on the wall; its garments and face, bearing the grisly marks of corruption, appeared to have suffered by the flames. It shook its head and fiery sparks flew around. A sudden smell of brimstone almost suffocated us.

After we had gazed at the phantom some time, with secret horror, the Necromancer exclaimed with a thundering voice, "Who art thou?"

PHANTOM (staggering back).—"A soul from purgatory."

OLD MAN.—"What is thy desire?"

PHANTOM.—"To be redeemed from the flames."

OLD MAN.—"By what means?"

PHANTOM.—"By the sale of this house."

OLD MAN.—"For what reason?"

PHANTOM.—"Because I have got it by fraudulent means."

OLD MAN.—"How can the sale of this house expiate thy crime?"

PHANTOM.—"It can, because my children will be saved."

The Necromancer was silent and the phantom disappeared.

A violent gust of wind rushed again in our faces, the smoke evaporated, and the torches began to burn. Lieutenant N—, with his friends and the landlord, were struck with amazement, and unable to stir; the Austrian lifted his hat, which had hidden part of his face, staring wildly at the hoary cheat, and I expected with impatience the signal for seizing the rascal, who, with great tranquillity and unconcern, was busied with putting his gewgaws again into his wallet.

Now the Austrian came forth, and I clapped my hand to my sword; awful silence reigned around, and our companions were still fixed to their places, whilst the Austrian's sparkling looks rested on the Necromancer, who now had packed up the instruments of fraud, and thrown the wallet over his shoulders. Just when he was going to leave the room his eye caught the glowing face of my friend, and he seemed thunderstruck. Their looks evinced a mutual emotion of an uncommon nature: my friend's stern looks grew more and more terrible, and the old man was apparently grasped by horror's icy fangs: our expectation rose to the highest pitch, and we were standing around them in a grisly attitude, most of us thrilled with secret awe, and I not without chill.

"Yes," began now the Austrian with a trembling voice, "yes, it is thou, Volkert! it is thou!"

The old deceiver shivered violently, his face was distorted by terrible convulsions, he gave a hollow groan, and fell lifeless on the floor.

We all seemed touched by a magic wand, and the Austrian was standing a good while in our middle, in a state of stupefaction; at length he recovered his recollection, drew with his wonted firmness nearer to the lifeless Necromancer, raised him up, shook him with all his might and exclaimed:

"Volkert, Volkert, return to life once more."

But all was in vain, the old man gave no sign of life.

"Volkert, Volkert," exclaimed my friend once more, but he did not hear him.

The innkeeper ran down stairs, fetching a glass of water and some drops, but our endeavours to restore the hoary villain to the use of his senses proved abortive, and he remained senseless in our arms.

"Well then," resumed the Austrian, his eyes flashing with anger, "if amicable means will not do, then I must have recourse to violence." So saying, he discharged a pistol, the door flew open, and four corporals rushed in with their swords unsheathed.

"Tie the rascal's arms and legs," roared the Austrian, "away with the villain, he is our prisoner."

"Your prisoner!" replied the grey deceiver, who had recovered at last, "your prisoner!" roared he with a ghastly grin, disengaging himself from our grasp.

The corporals rushed upon him.

"I am a citizen of F—, of a free imperial town, who dares to touch me?"

The corporals retired hastily, and the Austrian's brow was covered with terrible wrinkles, his eyes flashed anger, his mouth foamed, and his whole frame trembled in an agony of furious rage. I never beheld a more terrible aspect.

"Infernal spirit! hell-born villain!" roared he, gnashing his teeth, "I am deceived!—deceived by thee, Volkert!—Volkert!"

At once the thunder of his voice lowered to an entreating accent.

"Volkert, Volkert, for God's sake have mercy on me; save me from an ocean of doubts; spare me, O spare me; save me from the disgrace of appearing to myself and my friends a fool and a superstitious fanatic! Tell me, O tell me, am I indeed deceived? O, I will forgive thee, I will pronounce thee my benefactor, my saviour, only speak—tell me I am not deceived!"

The tears ran down his cheeks as he pronounced these words, spoken in a most violent passion.

It is a terrible, awful sight to see a man weep. I turned my eye away from the affecting scene, not being able to behold it any longer. The rest of my companions were seized anew with dumb stupefaction when they saw the violent emotions of my venerable friend, and a pause of unutterable horror ensued after the Austrian's speech. The old man either would or could not speak, and the Austrian began once more to address the hoary deceiver in an accent of utter insensibility, and with a sternness of look not to be described.

"Volkert, thou wilt not know me. I will spare thee the disgrace of confessing thine own guilt, but if thou wert in my power—"

His eyes darted flashes of lightning, and his voice was like the roaring of thunder.

"If thou wert in my power, I would make thee confess thy cheats, and if I should be forced to beat thy old rascally limbs to atoms, and to draw thy black blood from thy diabolical heart by single drops, I would make thee confess; but," added he in a more gentle accent, "thou art not within the reach of my power, and it is well that it is so. Volkert, here is my hand, I forgive thee. Thou not only deservest my forgiveness, but also my sincere gratitude, because thou hast given me a wholesome lesson, hast taught me, that everybody, though ever so wise, may be deceived; and I think I have not paid too dear for it."

Volkert wanted to speak, but he could not, being overcome by a sudden emotion, and hid his face with his hands.

"Well, Volkert," resumed the Austrian, "I see thou art not quite so bad as I thought. I will not compel thee to a confession, though I am wishing most ardently to have my doubts cleared up, and trust that thou wouldst tell me more than I want to know. I will not distress thee any longer by my presence; I am going to leave this house and this town for ever."

"'Gentlemen,' added he, addressing us, "I have deceived you, by supporting the reality of things which have been nothing but illusion; from this moment I have forfeited your good opinion, and the honour of being admitted any longer to a circle where I have been respected. You may call my resolution pride, caprice, or whatever you please, I cannot remain here any longer, and I am determined to depart this instant; farewell, live happy."

Having addressed us in so unexpected a manner, he hurried out of the room, taking no particular leave of me. Sympathising with his feelings, I thought it proper not to pay him a parting visit, because I knew it would recall disagreeable recollections, and give him pain.

A parting look which he gave me, when he was leaving the room, told me more than words could have done. Mine eyes were bathed with tears. I have seen him no more, and shall never forget that unhappy night which has robbed me of such a valuable friend, and deprived me of the darling of my soul.

When the Austrian and the corporals had left us, the Necromancer was likewise going to leave the room. His appearance was sullen and gloomy, his looks cast down. My friends were also stirring and stopped him, forming a circle round him.

The landlord was still in a maze of silent wonder, not knowing what to think of what had happened. I was dejected and melancholy, and had banished from my soul every idea of vengeance; my companions, however, seemed not inclined to let him get off so cheaply, and insisted on his explaining how he had contrived to cheat us; but the innkeeper interfered, imploring them not to ruin him entirely, by quarrelling in his house.

Lieutenant N— threatened at last to give him up to the civil power, if he would not confess, which I at first likewise had determined to do, how he had deceived us; however, his stubbornness could not be shaken, and he remained as silent as the grave.

Seeing that every further means to break his obstinacy would prove fruitless, I interfered, advising my fellow adventurers to let him depart in peace.

"Upon the whole," added I, "it matters not how we have been deceived; our friend the Austrian has set us an example how one ought to behave on such an occasion. Let us, like him, forgive the wretch, he is below our resentment."

These words produced the desired effect on the minds of my fellow adventurers, who were stung with shame and remorse, but none of them more than Lieutenant N—. He blushed at his idle fears and his credulity, leaving the room abruptly, accompanied by his friends and the landlord.

Being now left alone with the Necromancer, I flattered myself to succeed better than my companions, and to get informed of what I so eagerly wanted to know; but I was mistaken, his stubborn reserve baffled all my solicitations.

"Farewell, Lieutenant," said he, as he was going to leave the room, "I did not know you at first, and I am rejoiced that you have escaped your doom. I do not deserve your noble, generous treatment: Farewell, and remember sometimes Volkert the Necromancer. If you could see my heart, you rather would pity than despise me; I may perhaps one time find an opportunity of being serviceable to you, and of proving my gratitude by deeds."

I went down stairs with him, and having seen him to the door he squeezed my hand and hurried away. I left the fatal house in a strange situation of mind, and it struck one o'clock when I came home. I went to bed, but not to rest, my fancy being haunted by gloomy ideas, which kept sleep and repose at a distance. Early in the morning my fellow adventurers came to see me, requesting me to unfold the mysteries of the preceding night.

"We know," began Lieutenant N—, their spokesman, "we know that you are, or at least have been, very intimate with the Austrian, and you will, of course, be able to inform us, how your friend came to be acquainted with the cheats of the Necromancer. We have reason to think that he would have acted with more circumspection, if he had known that the Necromancer was no other person than Volkert, his former intimate favourite. We hope you will be so kind to clear up the matter. The Austrian's firmness of mind, his solid character, and his unshaken belief in the possibility of apparitions, give us strong reasons to think that he cannot have acted thus without mature deliberation."

Being but ill-disposed to enter into a circumstantial narrative, and not at all inclined to inform the intruding gentlemen of our adventures at the Haunted Castle, I called one of my corporals, who had been on the watch in the fatal inn the preceding night. "This man," said I, "will tell you more of the matter than I know, having watched every motion of the Necromancer, and discovered all his secret machination."

The old veteran was very willing to satisfy their curiosity, and began a prolix narration of every proceeding in the lower apartment of the inn. The innkeeper was, he related, deceived like ourselves, but his servants had acted in concert with Volkert, and enabled by their assistance to impose upon us.

Not being disposed to listen to his tale, I did not mind what he related, but my visitors, more attentive than myself, appeared at least to be fully satisfied and left me, after a profusion of thanks for having freed them of the doubts and errors.

The separation from my venerable friend had spread a melancholy gloom over my mind, which nothing could dispel.

The third day after his departure, I could no longer stay in a place where every object reminded me of so many hours of bliss, and of the man, whose friendship had made me so truly happy; I bade my servant pack my trunks, ordered my corporals to keep themselves ready, and left F— after a few days.

My journey afforded me but little amusement, being not able to wean my gloomy mind from the painful recollection of the time past, the image of my friend rushing ever and anon on my soul, and I could not resist the ardent desire of being re-united to him.

I sat in the stage musing on what was past, revolving in my mind the strange events of the Haunted Castle, and the inn, and examining minutely all the particulars, but I grew not a bit wiser: that Volkert was an impostor could not be doubted, but how he had managed his artful cheats and what his views had been in deceiving us, I could not unravel in a satisfactory manner; I examined singly all his transactions I knew, pondered with the greatest accuracy what the Austrian had related of his earlier exploits, but I was not able to dispel the impenetrable darkness which I was bewildered in.

The final result of my meditations was, that anybody, though ever so circumspect and wise, would, like my worthy friend, have been deceived by his intricate machinations, and tempted to adopt the opinion that enlightened officer had once defended so stoutly.

I was almost angry with myself for having let slip the opportunity of forcing that dangerous man to a confession of his dark and diabolical transgressions. It is true, I myself knew him as a hardened impostor, but could he not drag into the gulf of perdition many of my fellow creatures, who, like myself, would fall an easy victim to his deceitful hypocrisy?

This thought overwhelmed me with a load of uneasiness, and I reproached myself severely for having imitated the over-generous example of the Austrian, and suffered the accomplished villain to decamp without punishment. I had, indeed, reason to apprehend that the magistrate of F— would not have regarded much the information of a recruiting officer against a citizen, and that the innkeeper would have been induced, by fear or bribe, to contradict our denunciation; nevertheless, I should have had the satisfaction of having performed my duty, and cautioned the inhabitants of F— against that dangerous villain.

Tormented with this and similar thoughts did I finish my first day's journey, struggling in vain to recover my wonted cheerfulness, my mind being then too much occupied by gloominess, and an entire stranger to joyful feelings.

Not being able to get a wink of sleep all night long, I was haunted without rest, by the gloomy offsprings of my fancy, distressed by the appearing slowness of time, and entirely cut off from every comfort by the snoring disposition of my fellow travellers, which made me resolve to leave the stage next morning, and to continue my journey on horseback. I left, therefore, my cheerless and sullen companions, with the first dawn of day, bought a horse in the first village where we stopped, and trotted briskly onward.

I was not in the least acquainted with the roads in those parts, a circumstance which ought to have come sooner in my mind; I was obliged to ride back several times, and when it began to grow dark, found myself bewildered in a dreary forest, without knowledge which way to turn. My jaded horse being hardly able to stir; I alighted, leading the poor beast by the bridle, in order to advance with more expedition.

It was now so dark that I could hardly distinguish the objects before my eyes, when a sudden rustling in the thicket made me start; I listened, but all was silent again and I pursued my way without apprehension, thinking it might have been a deer; but I was not gone far when I heard the rustling again much louder than at first, and close by me: I now beheld, on a sudden, a man with a sack on his back, and a staff in his hand, coming out of the thicket, within the short distance of two or three paces. This unexpected sight gladdened my heart, flattering me with the sweet hope of getting a friendly conductor out of that dreary wilderness, who would direct my weary steps to a place of rest.

"Whither art thou going, good friend?" exclaimed I.

"To the mill," answered he, groaning under his burden.

"Is the mill far from hence?" said I.

"No farther than half a league," he replied.

"May I find shelter there for myself and horse?"

"No," replied he.

"Why not?" asked I.

"Because," replied he, "the miller does not admit strangers."

"I am sorry for it; but is there no house hereabouts where one could get a night's lodging?"

"O yes," answered he, "not far from hence, if you turn to the right lives a woodcutter who lodges travellers."

"But do you think I shall be safe there?" asked I.

"What do you mean by that?" said he.

"Don't you know, good friend," replied I, "that this part of the country is the constant haunt for robbers?"

"Would to God I could stay this night with good Master Max, I would not be uneasy on that score; but I must go on, and alas my burden is heavy."

"If my poor beast was not so jaded, and so much tired, I would be glad to lend it you," said I.

"Thank you, Master," returned he; "I am used to hardships, and have laid in a good stock of patience."

Discoursing thus we went slowly on together, till we came to a foot-path, where the wanderer stopped to direct me to the woodcutter's cottage: "You cannot miss your way," said he; "if you pursue this path you will soon see light."

I hesitated a little while, whether I should follow the advice of the honest man, or not, but the increasing darkness, and a rising tempest, which shook the oaks around, fixed soon my wavering resolution, and I pursued the path, bidding the honest wanderer good night.

I soon found myself on an unbeaten footway, obstructed by bram-bles and underwood; my poor horse threatened every moment to sink down, and I could not resist the apprehension of having been sent on a fool's errand by the unknown man, and misled into an unfrequented lonesome part of the forest. This made me look about with more circumspection, till I had ascended a rising ground with great difficulty, my horse fell frequently on his knees, and it would have been impos-sible to proceed a mile farther; you may therefore easily think how rejoiced I was when the glimmering of a light, apparently at a small distance, bade me hope a speedy end of my distress.

Quickening my steps, I soon perceived a small cottage, the owner of which made his appearance as soon as I had knocked at his humble door, hailed me with a hearty welcome, and bade me, with much good nature, enter his hospitable abode.

Not expecting much convenience, I was struck with wonder when he showed me into a neat little room, not in the least corresponding with the poor appearance of his hut; I had expected to be introduced to the residence of poverty, and found a habitation that bore evident marks of prosperity, and seemed rather to be the abode of a gentleman than that of a poor woodcutter.

Mr. Max—this he told me was his name—Mr. Max took no notice of my astonishment, but prepared, with much alacrity, to provide me and my weary horse with food and drink.

While he was busy to prove his hospitality, I had full leisure to satisfy my curiosity, and to take a view of the objects around me, assisted by the faint glimmering of a lamp.

The first object that struck my fancy was an enormous sword, hanging by his bed-side, which, as I thought at first, was rather an improper furniture for a woodcutter's dwelling; but I soon made myself easy when I recollected, that he, living in an unfrequented part of the forest, might want sometimes an instrument of that kind to defend himself against unwelcome visitors, but my apprehension returned when I beheld a brace of pistols hanging on the wall, which I found were charged with ball.

I went farther in my search, and saw a great number of guns, pistols, and swords in a recess close by the fireside; I was chilled with terror, and just as I had taken the lamp in my hand to have a closer view at this alarming furniture, Mr. Max entered the room, with a large plate of greens, a piece of ham, and a bottle of wine.

"Well," exclaimed he merrily, as he entered the room, "there, I have brought you something to silence your grumbling stomach with; sit down, good sir, and take up with my frugal fare."

Alas! my appetite was gone, but he fetched knives and forks and a large loaf of bread, and began to eat with great avidity, taking at first no notice of my backwardness to follow his example; perceiving at length that I did not eat, he exclaimed, "Well, sir, why don't you eat? I think one must be hungry, if one has travelled far and missed one's way."

His joviality revived a little my spirits, but his country-like simplicity, and his seeming honesty, appeared to me very little corresponding with the great number of fire-arms and swords which I had seen, yet I joined him at last in eating and drinking.

When supper was over I could no longer suppress my curiosity, and asked him why he kept so many guns and swords in his house.

"What," replied he rather angry, "what is this to you? I get sometimes visitors for whom I must keep them."

"But why," resumed I, "so great a number as I have seen in the recess by the fireside?"

"These are fine doings," said he angrily, "who bade you to search my room? Is this becoming a guest?"

I arose, and asked him how much I had to pay for my supper? He fell a laughing, and exclaimed, with marks of astonishment—

"You don't intend to depart in this dark and tempestuous night!

Don't you hear how the tempest roars, and how the rain beats against the windows? I hope you don't think you will be shot or stabbed because there are so many fire-arms and swords in that recess? No no, good friend, you need not be afraid, all these things are not mine, they belong to sportsmen who have laid them up here, that they may have them when they are a hunting in this part of the forest; perhaps you may see them yourself tomorrow morning; and the sword by my bedside I bought some years ago from an Austrian deserter."

Though I was not inclined to stay for the sportsmen, I did not know whither I should go with my jaded horse in that dark tempestuous night, and dreaded to run the risk of escaping from an imaginary danger, only to fly in the face of a real one, which, at last, determined me to stay. I begged Mr. Max to show me the place where I was to sleep, intending to charge my pistols with balls before I should go to bed in case of accident.

My host opened a side door leading to a small chamber, where a bed was.

"Here," said he, "you may sleep till it is broad day, and rest your weary limbs at your ease. I keep this chamber on purpose for travellers; take this lamp, I will fetch it when you shall be asleep."

So saying, he left me, shutting the door after him.

Taking a nearer view of my bed chamber, I observed that it had no windows, and, in order to be prepared for the worst, I charged my pistols, which I had put in my pockets before I had entered the cottage. This done, I considered whether I should go to bed, and thus deceive my host, which, on mature deliberation, I thought would be best.

With that intention I took my lamp to see whether the bed was fastened, lest I might sink down with it into the cellar. Though this apprehension was groundless, I made another discovery which filled my soul with horror. Perceiving traces of blood on the pillow, I was seized with a sudden terror, my hands trembled violently, the lamp fell on the floor, and I was in the dark.

As soon as I had recovered a little from my fright, I searched for my pistols, groping about a good while before I could find them in the dark. My fear abated a little when I found them at last, after a long and fruitless search, and I sat myself down on a little stool by the bedside, listening whether anybody was coming. All was quiet at first, but after a quarter of an hour I heard somebody entering the adjacent room, and approaching the door of my chamber, which was gently opened, and the voice of my host called, "Are you asleep?" I uttered not a word, and after a short pause the same voice resounded once more, "Have you extinguished the lamp?" I still gave no answer, and the host retired.

All was hushed again in profound silence, but it lasted not long, my ears being suddenly assailed by the sound of many voices, the tinkling of spurs, and humming noise, as if a number of people were discoursing; I could understand nothing, the discourse being held in so low an accent, that I was unable to distinguish the sound of their words. At once I saw, through the crevices in the door, somebody striking a light, which gave me some comfort. The discourse was still carried on in that secret mysterious manner. At last, it seemed as if the company were sitting down, and I could now better distinguish the different sounds. The voices of those that spoke were rough, and the words seemed to belong to a foreign language.

I sat near an hour on my stool, like a poor culprit who awaits his doom, but was determined to defend myself to the last drop of blood. I intended several times to rush into the room, and to force my escape through the company with cocked pistols, but something within my breast admonished me to stay where I was, and patiently to wait till they should think it proper to pay *me* a visit.

My situation was exceedingly painful, and at the least noise which seemed to approach my chamber I started up, putting myself in a posture of defence. My fears not having been realized as yet, my apprehensions began to vanish a little, and I thought Mr. Max might be an honest man, and his company the sportsmen he had been speaking of, although their language seemed to contradict that opinion. Hope soothed my terrors for some time, till at length I recollected the traces of blood I had seen on the pillow, which recalled all my apprehensions with redoubled anxiety.

Sleep, whom till now I had carefully kept at a distance, began, by degrees, to steal upon me, and shut at last, with his leaden wand, my heavy eyes. But I was scarce fallen asleep, when one of my pistols dropt on the floor, and went off. I started up, seized by the chilly fangs of terror, and in the same moment the other pistol slipped out of my hand. I had scarcely picked it up when the door suddenly flew open, and three fellows, of a gigantic size, entered my room with naked swords. Sleep, the report of my pistol, and the sudden appearance of those terrible men, had stunned me so much, that I, without knowing what I was doing, discharged my pistol, at which one of the villains dropt on the floor with a roaring yelp. A numerous crew, armed with guns, cutlasses, and daggers, rushed like lightning into my chamber, and before I could unsheath my sword, I felt myself in their clutches, bereft of all power of self-defence.

A tremendous voice roared like thunder from the adjoining room, "Hither with the rascal."

Before I could recover my recollection, I felt myself dragged out of my chamber, and beheld in an instant a man of the most terrible forbidding aspect, who, with a rough thundering voice, menacing looks, and sparkling eyes, asked me "If I could not have patiently waited my doom."

"Tie the daring wretch," added he in a rage, "and throw him into the cellar, until sentence shall be pronounced against him." His commands were obeyed, and Mr. Max himself assisted; I was seized with a despairing stupor, and uttered not a word. I was shut up in a damp cellar; how long I remained in my dungeon I cannot tell, having been in a situation which suspended all my powers of reflection.

After a long interval of the most desponding agony, I was at length dragged forth, and brought before the tribunal of the terrible looking man. The villain whom I had wounded was stretched on the bed, his head tied up, and his associates standing round him, bemoaning his hapless fate, and amongst them a venerable old man, whom I at first had not observed.

Now the grim judge began to speak, and the whole assembly to dart furious and bloodthirsty looks at me. The old man likewise turned his face towards me, and it cannot be expressed by words what my sensations were when I discerned the features of Volkert. A poor culprit cannot feel greater joy when, under the hangman's merciless fangs, his guardian angel appears to save him from his impending doom. I did indeed not know whether he could save me or not, however, the sweet soothing voice of hope silenced all my apprehensions; I had saved him once from ignominy, and, perhaps, from death itself; he had promised me to prove his gratitude, how could I therefore doubt that he would save me from destruction. "Volkert!" exclaimed I, in a supplicating accent, "Volkert!" The terrible man staggered back, staring by turns at me and him.

"Volkert!" exclaimed I, again lifting up my fettered hands; he knew me, and without the least delay took a knife out of his pocket, and cut asunder the cords my hands had been tied with. The whole frightful assembly was fixed to the ground, seized with wonder and aston-ishment.

"Thou hast saved me," began my guardian angel now, in a solemn awful accent, "thou hast given me liberty, take back thy gift, and life into the bargain."

"Friends," said he, addressing the gaping crew, "friends, he is the preserver of my honour and my liberty, what may he expect?"

"Pardon, pardon," was the unanimous cry, "pardon, pardon, he shall live."

"Bravo, my boys," said now their formidable Captain, who was sitting in judgment upon me, "bravo, my honest lads, you are noble fellows: farewell Andrew," added he, addressing his dying companion, "farewell, Andrew, thou art avenged, art doubly avenged by the generosity of thy companions!"

At the same instant the whole crew hurried out of the room, leaving me alone with Volkert. "Farewell, Lieutenant," said he, shaking me by the hand, "you have wisely acted, in leaving F—, like the Austrian; I shall never return to that town. If any similar sinister accident should happen to you, need but to pronounce my name and you will be safe."

I was going to embrace, and to assure him of my warmest gratitude, but he tore himself from my arms, and hastened to join his associates. Soon after I heard a confused noise before the door of the cottage, and, ere long, the whole band rode away in full speed. Now I was surrounded by midnight stillness, interrupted only by the groans of the dying robber. Max did not dare to enter the room while I was there.

I was no longer able to remain in the house, the roaring of the tempest was hushed in silence, and the dawn of morn peeping through the windows; I found my horse sleeping in a corner behind the cottage, got on his back, and rode away in a slow pace.

The morning sun rose in all his dazzling splendour, and still I was bewildered between trees and bushes, straying about two tedious hours without being able to find an outlet, until at length I was so fortunate to meet a countryman, who, for a small reward, directed me to the road leading to N—.

Warned by my dangerous adventure, I now inquired at every village for the route I was to take, and thus reached at last the place of my destination without having met with any farther misfortune. Before I arrived at N—, an incident happened, which being connected with my adventure at the Haunted Castle, I cannot omit mentioning.

Coming to a village about three miles distant from N—, a great noise struck my ears, proceeding, as I soon could distinguish, from a great number of recruits, carousing and singing at the inn. I alighted and entered the residence of merriment and intoxication, in order to inform myself who the commanding officer was, in hopes to meet with an old acquaintance, but I was disappointed. Two serjeants, entirely unknown to me, conducted the transport, and, inquiring after their officer's name, I found that he was an utter stranger to me.

Having surveyed the recruits, I was going to leave the room, when my eyes by accident fell on a man standing in a musing attitude by the fireside, his looks fixed on the floor. Thinking to recollect his features I advanced nearer to him; he started up from his reverie, and, seeing me standing before him, staggered back with evident marks of astonishment; however, his terror soon gave way to rapturous joy; he ran towards me, caught me by the hand, and exclaimed, flushed with pleasure,—

"Dear, dear Lieutenant, is it you? God be praised that you are still alive! God be praised that I have once more the happiness of seeing my kind old master!"

His voice, his accent, and his transport, gave me no room to doubt that he was my late servant, whom I had lost in the castle.

The honest fellow could find no words to express his joy, at my not having been famished with my companions in the cellar, as it had been the intention of the robbers. He expressed his joy in so noisy a manner, that we were soon surrounded by the recruits. I begged the serjeants to indulge with me with a private conversation with my honest servant, which they granted me with great politeness. I called for the host, requesting him to let us have a room to ourselves, that we might converse without being interrupted by the curiosity of his noisy guests.

As soon as we were in private, I requested John to give me a brief account of what had happened to him after we had left him snoring in the great hall of the Castle; he was very willing to satisfy my curiosity, and related as follows:

I was aroused from my sleep by a violent shaking, and, recovering from my drowsiness, saw myself seized by two ill-looking fellows, who were employed to drag me forcibly away.

Fear and terror bereft me at first of all power of utterance and resistance. I attempted several times to cry, but I could not pronounce a single word, and, as much as I could observe through the midnight darkness, saw myself carried down the spiral staircase, over the courtyard. When we were arrived at the gate, I was tied upon a horse, and surrounded by a numerous crew, who took me between them and rode away in full speed. My feet being tied together under the horse's belly, it was out of my power to stir, which rendered my situation exceedingly painful.

The dawn of morn appeared, but not a single ray of hope cheered my desponding soul, being in the power of those merciless ruffians, who were still sweeping the field with all possible expedition, not caring for the excruciating pains I suffered, and forcing my horse to leap over hedges and ditches.

The swiftness of the race and my uncomfortable situation deprived me, at length, of all power of recollection, and threw me into a kind of stupefaction which prevented me from observing how long our journey had lasted. I was seized with a fainting fit, and when my recollection returned, observed that I was shut up in a subterraneous dungeon, an old hag was rubbing me with onions, and, when I recovered from the state of stupefaction, occasioned by the cruelty of my leaders, she fetched a bottle of brandy, admonishing me, in a rough uncouth dialect, to drink plenty of it, which I declined, requesting her to rub my lacerated limbs with it.

Having performed my request with great alacrity she left me, and I had full leisure to contemplate the horrors of my dreary abode, the walls of which were blackened by the hand of time, and overgrown with moss; muddy straw spread on the damp ground served me for a couch, and the faint glimmering of a lamp heightened the horrors of my dungeon; the thick corrupted air made it difficult to fetch breath, to which were added most excruciating pains, not in the least alleviated by the use of brandy, but rather increased on account of the sores my poor frame was covered with; only the agony of my tortured mind surpassed the sufferings of my body; futurity stared me grisly in the face, and the consciousness being in the power of a set of villains, who would either sacrifice my life, to their thirst of blood, or force me, by threats and exquisite torments, to commit deeds of the most atrocious nature, filled my mind with dreadful apprehensions.

I remained two days in a state of unspeakable despondency; although my bodily pains had abated, and I could move my limbs with more ease, yet the fear of futurity had weakened me so much that I could not stir from my miserable couch; my misery was augmented by the troublesome officiousness of the old hag, who every instant came to torment me. One time she wanted to apply to my sores poultices of roasted flour, and at another she would make me swallow a spoonful of disgusting nauseous drops; now she would force down my throat a soup of a most uninviting appearance, and a few minutes after she brought straw, which was half rotten, to place it under my head; in short, she tormented me so much by plying me with her unwelcome officiousness and kindness, that the gloominess of my mind hourly increased, and my little remaining strength was entirely spent by my efforts to resist her torturing care for my health and ease.

On the fourth day of my confinement I was taken out of my dungeon, and my apprehensions were realised. The infernal villains intending to make me one of their associates in wickedness, ordered me to mount a horse, and forced me to follow them in full speed through fields and forests, notwithstanding the weak state of my body. My conductors, at first only three in number, and clad in linen frocks, blackened with coal dust, rode ahead, looking back now and then; their black faces and sooty hands evidently foreboded their dark design.

After half an hour's ride my infernal guides stopped at a lonely public house, alighted, and bade me take care of the horses until they should return.

I obeyed their stern command with gloomy silence, tied the horses to a tree, and sat myself down upon a bench before the house. The haunts of my disordered fancy made the time pass quickly on; I revolved in my afflicted mind my former occupation, the happy hours I had spent in the service of a kind, indulgent master, and the horrors of my present situation, the briny drops of sorrow and affliction moistened my pallid cheeks. "What will become of thee?" said I to myself; "a robber, and perhaps a murderer, too." A chilly trembling glided through my veins, I started up, and was resolved to mount one of the horses, and make my escape, but the want of strength reminded me soon of the utter impossibility of the execution of my rash design. I sunk down upon the bench, imploring heaven rather to put an end to my miserable life than to suffer me to become an associate of these hell-born fiends. After I had ejaculated this fervent prayer I felt my despondency abate a little, awaiting with impatience the re-appearance of my fell conductors.

A short time after they came, accompanied by three more ruffians of a most frightful aspect, who, with the greatest expedition, fetched their horses from an adjacent stable, mounted them without delay, and rode away like lightning; my conductors did the same, ordered me to follow their example, and galloped over fields as fast as their coursers could run; coming up with our ill-looking companions we pursued our journey with all possible swiftness.

Having, by accident, mounted the wrong horse, which was the fleetest of all, I kept always ahead, and could distinctly hear every word they spoke, though I could not understand a syllable of their conversation. After it had grown dark, we alighted again at a solitary public house, the horses being once more committed to my care, and I awaited with patience the end of an adventure that boded no good.

I had been standing in the chilly air of night above an hour, musing on my deplorable fate, when the innkeeper brought me a piece of bread and butter and a mug of beer, but I could neither eat nor drink, shaking with cold.

The night was dark and the sky overcast, a thick dampish fog had wetted my clothes, and not one friendly star was to be seen in the firmament, which was as gloomy as my mind. After I had been exposed for half an hour longer to the inclemency of the chilly air, my conductors reappeared, their number being increased to twelve, and their sooty dress exchanged for green hunting coats; every one of them was armed with a gun, a brace of pistols, and a cutlass.

The feelings which were rushing on my mind at that sight admit of no description; the blood froze in my veins, my soul was harrowed up in dreadful suspense, and I mounted my horse more dead than alive, galloping over the heath with my conductors in senseless stupefaction, like a poor culprit who is dragged along to be delivered to the merciless fangs of the grim fiendly-looking executioner, till I at length was roused from my stupor by the sounds of horns assailing my ears from afar, and the loud clamorous shouts of our troop.

The sound of horns drew nearer, and my conductors answered by blowing theirs. Now I perceived a powerful troop of horsemen, sweeping the heath like a hurricane. In an instant I was surrounded by a numerous crew on horseback, and rough dismal voices vibrated in my ear in a confused manner. One of them struck fire, a number of torches were lighted, and I beheld with amazement and dismay, a large troop of terrible beings around me.

Whithersoever I turned my eyes, I was frightened almost out of my wits by stern, threatening looks. They soon perceived the workings of my desponding mind, laughed at my fear, and uttered terrible execrations. One of them, who bore a more tremendous aspect than the rest, came forth, the noisy crew was awed in solemn silence, and the terrible man began to address them thus:

"You know, my brave companions, that this rascal here," pointing at me, "is the servant of the wretch who has dared to watch in our Castle, with armed numbers. The daring scoundrel and his two associates are punished; famine and thirst have seized their victims with merciless fangs, tormenting them with excruciating pains, with agony and black despair; on our next visit nocturnal to the castle we shall see them lifeless on the ground. You know how the daring fools have been vexed, teased, and tormented by Father Francis. It was glorious fun, we have been amused with their foolish credulity, and are now amply avenged on these bold disturbers of our nocturnal assembly."

"The villagers are not yet punished," continued he, "for having assisted them, but they shall not escape their doom. Our future safety demands the destruction of the village, and its environs, but, tell me, what shall we do with that fellow there? He is well fed, and seems not to be without strength, my advice is to make him our companion."

"We will, we will," roared the whole troop.

Then their terrible leader resumed, "he must give us tonight a specimen of his dexterity."

"He shall, he shall," was the universal cry. I trembled like a wretched culprit who hears his sentence pronounced, when the speaker addressed me thus:—"Fellow! thou hast heard what an honour we have conferred on thee, we expect that thou wilt be faithful to us, oaths are as little valued among robbers as they are in hell, and a hand-stroke will satisfy us, give me thy right hand as a token of unshaken fidelity."

Trembling did I obey his stern command, and he bade me to take courage, to abandon all fear, and to follow him. The torches were extinguished, the robbers began to converse in an unintelligible accent, the horns were sounded, the whole troop set spurs to their horses, rushing over the fields like a midnight tempest; I felt myself seized by the arm, and my horse pulled by the bridle after them. After a short ride the voice of the terrible leader ordered us to halt.

"Here," said he to me, "is a gun and a whistle! The former thou art to use in case of necessity, and the latter as soon as a waggon or a coach passes the road."

This said, he rode away, but methought I heard another horseman not far from me.

Now I began to consult with myself what I should do, whether I should betray the innocent traveller, or suffer him to escape. My mind shrank back from the horrid idea of becoming accessory to the destruction of a fellow-creature, but how could I avoid it if I would not myself fall a victim to the cruelty of my infernal companions? Life is the sweetest gift of heaven, and not easy to be parted with.

While I was in deliberation with myself what course to take, I heard the rattling of a coach within a little distance from me, and a violent trembling seized my limbs: the coach came nearer and my trembling increased. Without knowing what I was about, I was going to apply the whistle to my lips, my hand trembled, a sudden stupor seized me, the whistle dropt to the ground, and the coach passed by in full speed; at the same time I heard somebody whistle behind me, soon after the report of three guns, accompanied with cries and lamentations, struck my ear; a female voice was praying for mercy, loud acclamations filled the air, and soon after all was hushed in profound silence.

I was sitting on my horse in dumb stupefaction, when on a sudden I perceived somebody laying hold of the bridle of my steed, and pulling her forcibly after him. After a few minutes I saw at a distance a glimmering light shining through the bushes; as we came near to the spot I beheld in my conductor the terrible leader of the band, and we at length arrived at a place surrounded with bushes, where the robbers were seated round a fire, dividing the spoil; they all gave a loud shriek, as if they already knew how badly I had acquitted myself of my first task.

"Let us pronounce sentence against the rascal!" exclaimed my conductor, with a thundering voice.

"Let us knock his brains out," roared one of the robbers.

"Send him to the dungeon," exclaimed a second.

"The latter we will do," resumed the Captain, "punishment may, perhaps, recall him to reason."

Having said this, he ordered two of the gang to carry me to the place of confinement; they mounted their horses, took me between them, and hurried away with me at a furious rate. We arrived with the first dawn of day at the bottom of a hill, where I forcibly was dragged through the bushes and thorns fettered with heavy chains, and carried through a narrow passage into a dark dungeon; groping about I found myself surrounded with straw, the muddy smell of which left me no doubt that it was half rotten.

Having lingered many hours in that terrible abode of misery, without either hearing or seeing anybody, I at last was hailed by the distant, hollow sound of approaching footsteps, dying away sometimes, and then vibrating again faintly on my ear; at once they grew more and more audible, and the glimmering of a light began to illuminate the subterraneous cave.

Turning round with much difficulty, I perceived that it emerged from a deep grotto behind me. The glimmering grew lighter, and the sound of footsteps drew nearer; at length I beheld a figure more frightful than the robbers themselves; the old hideous hag, adorned with all the graces of hell, ascended with alacrity from the gloomy abyss, panting for breath; and now I had a full view of the horrors of my den: the faint rays of my lamp were reflected in a grisly manner from the lofty walls, hewn into the solid rock, and mixed with the midnight darkness, which was hovering beneath the high-vaulted ceiling. My dungeon was of a small circumference, but appeared to be far removed from the surface of the earth; the dreadful abode of horror was infected by a damp, pestilential air, through which the light was glimmering as if through a bluish fog.

The antiquated scarecrow began to pity and to bemoan my miserable doom, exhorting me to obey more strictly the commands of my masters, and, having put a pitcher with water, and a piece of bread before me, unfettered my hands, admonishing me to submit patiently to my fate, and never to attempt an escape, which not only would prove abortive, but at the same time prolong and increase my punishment. I uttered not a syllable, and she left me to muse in solitude on my forlorn and unhappy situation.

Three gloomy days of misery and dismay were now elapsed since I had been thrown into that terrible abode of silence and melancholy, before I saw anybody except the old witch, by whose visits alone I could guess the progress of time. No year of my whole life has ever appeared to me so long as those three days of woe; I strove in vain to loosen the fetters which chained my feet, the lock that confined them together baffled all my endeavours, and, after many fruitless efforts, I was obliged to bid a mournful adieu to every ray of hope of making my escape from the fangs of my cruel tyrants: black despair hovered over me with sooty wings, the greedy tooth of grief was gnawing on my vitals, and the recollection of former times of ease and tranquillity served only to heighten my misery.

The fourth day brought me the visit of the Captain, who entered my dungeon with a lighted torch.

"Well, rascal!" exclaimed he, "how dost thou like this beautiful apartment? art thou tired of thy sepulchre, or dost thou prefer to be entombed alive for ever, to the honour of being one of our brave party? art thou sensible of the foolishness of thy stubborn disobedience, and may I expect that thou wilt be more obsequious in future?"

I groaned a lamentable *yes*, the result of my resolution, which I had been driven to by despair and my forlorn situation.

"Well," resumed my tyrant, unfastening my chains, "I hope thou art sensible that it is more eligible to be a gentleman of the high road than to be buried alive amid spiders and toads; I will try once more whether I can make thee a worthy member of our society, rise and follow me!"

I attempted to get on my legs, but I sunk down again upon my damp couch; my legs, which were become quite useless by the pressure of the chains, were now pierced with most excruciating pains, and unable to support my miserable carcass. The robber seeing me struggle in vain to obey his command, seized me with a powerful arm, and dragged me forcibly over the rocky ground. I was trailed along the winding passage of the subterraneous fabric, like a victim to the altar, where it is to receive the finishing stroke. I was every now and then forced to crawl on my knees through narrow holes, and to climb with much difficulty over gaping chasms in the rock, till at length an iron door obstructed our passage; my conductor opened it, and I beheld a spacious lofty hall, illuminated with a great number of torches, where some of the robbers were seated at table, eating, drinking, and conversing merrily with each other, and some cleaning guns and pistols, and charging them.

They all spoke kindly to me, inviting me to partake of their blithesome meal, and congratulating me on the wise resolution I had taken to become a sharer of their fortune. I relished the roasted meat, the turkeys, and hams exceeding well, and swallowed plentiful draughts of most delicious wine. Though I was not remiss to ply briskly the knife and fork and the cheerful goblet, and strove to do honour to the table, yet the robbers chided me every now and then, finding fault with my tardiness.

The exhilarating juice of the grape spread mirth and cheerfulness around; the spacious cavern re-echoed their jocund songs, the tales of their exploits gave variety to the entertainment, and it seemed as if the sting of conscience had entirely lost, with them, its pungent point. The cloth was at length removed, the beldam who had been waiting at table began now likewise to eat, and the robbers made themselves ready to leave their subterraneous haunt.

"Today," said the captain to me, before they departed, "thou shalt stay at home, but tomorrow thou art to be of our party, and thy deportment must decide whether we can enlist thee in our noble company, or shall knock thy brains out."

Then the whole crew sallied forth through the iron door, without giving me time to answer, and left me alone with the old woman, who was very assiduous to amuse me, relating with much garrulity, many stories of the dear gentlemen, as she called the robbers, and extolling their generosity to the skies.

Perceiving that I did not relish her tiresome tales, she fetched books, cards, and dice, leaving it to my choice what sort of amusement I should fix upon. I preferred reading to a tête-à-tête with the old witch, and endeavoured to dispel the gloom of my mind by perusing an old book of chivalry.

At night my rusty companion wanted me to sit down to supper with her, which I refused, requesting her to show me to my bedroom. Vexed by my refusal, she mumbled something between her few remaining teeth, and opened the door of a small side-room where I found a couch, made of clean straw, and covered with a blanket; throwing myself upon it, I slept for the first time sweet and soundly after eight painful nights of horror.

> The next morning the old woman thundered at my door, telling me it was broad day, and past nine o'clock, and that our gentlemen would soon return to dinner. I got up much refreshed, and assisted her in the kitchen, which pleased her so well that she promised to recommend me to the good graces of the Captain.

Thus far had my servant proceeded in his narration, without having been interrupted by me, though he had been very circumlocutious, and spoken above an hour. It gave me great pleasure to hear a circumstantial description of the robbers and their cave, and honest John's simplicity afforded me great amusement, which proved a very seasonable relief in my then gloomy state of mind; I therefore was very much vexed when one of the serjeants entered to tell him that they were waiting for him to proceed on their march, and bade him make haste, just as he was going to give me a full account of the robbers' deportment towards him after their return, of the splendid dinner which the old woman had prepared, assisted by him, and of their discourses at table.

I entreated the rough son of Mars to resign this recruit to me, and to accept from me double the binding money he had given him, but he did not relish my proposal, and John himself was little inclined to enter again into my service; at last I prevailed, by fair words and a small present, on the serjeant to wait a quarter of an hour longer, and he left the room after we had promised to be as expeditious as possible.

When he was gone I asked John why he would rather be a soldier than enter again into my service.

"What else would you advise me to do?" replied he, with weeping eyes, "my life is exposed to the greatest danger in these parts, and would you like to have a servant who has been a robber?"

"You have not been a robber," interrupted I the poor fellow, but recollected soon that he had not finished his narration, and perhaps might have been compelled at last, by menaces, to become a member of the gang, I therefore requested him to continue his tale, and to be as brief as possible, which he in vain strove to do, going every now and then astray. The substance of his confused continuation was as follows:

The robbers returned, treated John again with kindness, ate, drank, and left him once more, without mentioning a word about his going with them, which did not in the least displease him; he amused himself with reading, and when night invited him to sleep, he went to his couch with a much lighter heart than when he had left it in the morning.

That manner of life he led eight days, during which time the robbers always returned to dinner, in greater or lesser number; the whole gang consisted of twenty-four stout men besides the Captain.

On the ninth, tenth, eleventh, and the three succeeding days, the robbers did not return, but on the fifteenth they all appeared in high spirits, though with empty hands; John concluded, from this circumstance, and what he could gather from their mysterious discourses, that they must have had several other haunts, where they hoarded up their spoils; the old castle on the skirts of the Black Forest seemed, however, to be their usual residence.

After dinner was over, and the goblet had freely circulated, the captain recollected that John was to give them a second sample of his capacity, ordered him to mount a horse, and conducted him, accompanied by two of his associates, to the high road leading through the forest, where he commanded him to lay in ambush, and to rob the first traveller he should see coming along the road.

Poor John was thunderstruck at the stern command of the Captain, fell at his feet, and entreated him to have mercy on him; but the ruffians laughed at him, and their leader repeated his order, swearing he would kill him on the spot, if he did not instantly comply with his desire. The hapless fellow seeing there was no alternative, but to be killed, or to prey on his fellow creatures, concealed himself in a thicket, and the robbers posted themselves opposite to him, behind some bushes, taking the three horses along with them.

The first travellers that passed by were two monks, and John thanked God in his heart that they were two. A little while after a ruddy countryman appeared, he was on horseback, as it seemed returning from the market, carrying two empty sacks behind him, and counting money. That will be an easy task, thought John, but when he was going to leave his hiding-place, his knees trembled he was unable to stir, and the clown pursued his way without being disturbed.

The robbers began to hem, and poor John seized with terror, was going to run after the swain, but, thinking him too far advanced, resolved to wait for the next traveller, and to attack him vigorously.

He had waited a good while for another opportunity to acquit himself of his task, till at length a travelling journeyman appeared. John rushed out of his hiding place before his prey was near enough and as soon as the frightened traveller saw a man running towards him with a pistol, he took to his heels and luckily got out of his reach.

The Captain and his companions seized with a fit of roaring laughter, exhorted their awkward pupil, in a low accent, to have a little more patience in future.

Before John could reach his lurking place, a Jew made his appearance; the sight of the poor Israelite fired the novice in robbery with an unusual courage; he rushed upon the terrified Hebrew like lightning, and, having seized him by the collar, demanded his money with a thundering voice. The petrified Israelite feeling himself thus roughly handled, shrieked and lamented most ruefully, and stoutly refused at first to deliver up his mammon, but when he saw his life at stake, and John put his pistol to his breast, yielded at last, with a woeful visage, to the uncouth demands of his aggressor, "I will give—I will give—all the money I have about me." So saying, he untied a leathern bag with money, fastened round his waist, and offered it to the greedy robber, who, transported with joy at his success, was thrown off his guard, and the cunning Jew taking hold of an opportunity to recover his treasure, seized, with much adroitness, the pistol, wrested it from poor John's trembling hand, and ordered the affrighted fellow, who was almost petrified, to return him his money instantly, if he would not have his brains blown out; John hesitated not a moment to submit to the Jew's demand, restored him his bag, and took to his heels, but the two robbers sallying forth from their hiding-place, retook him soon, while the cunning Israelite got clear off with his money and John's pistol.

The unfortunate fellow was instantly carried back to the robbers' den, and shut up again in the subterraneous dungeon which he had but lately left. Having been confined there some weeks the robbers took him one day out of his hole, and gave him his liberty, and a small sum of money, after he had sworn a dreadful oath never to reveal the least thing of what he had heard and seen in the cavern during his stay with them, and to leave the country as soon as possible.

This is the substance of my late servant's narrative; he had entirely forgotten his oath until he mentioned it, yet he silenced soon his murmuring conscience, persuading himself not to have committed perjury, because he had been intimidated by dreadful menaces to make it, and an oath of that nature could never be binding; he at the same time alleged, that the Captain himself had declared that among robbers swearing was of no importance, and thus soothed his conscience.

I did not think it necessary to undeceive, but gave him a handsome sum of money as a token of my gratitude for his faithful services, and bade him an affectionate farewell. He thanked me with weeping eyes and left the room. When he was gone I mounted my horse, and arrived after a few hours at N—.

Now I come to the last and most important incident I ever met with during the whole time of my recruiting business, which will clear up all the above-related events, and dispel the clouds which are still hanging over some parts of my wonderful tale.

Two years were now elapsed since my last adventure, and I had heard nothing farther either of the Necromancer or his associates. The frequent unwelcome visits at the Castle and their alarming consequences, very likely had made both parties more circumspect, which appeared to me to have been the principal motive of those ruffians to release my servant, lest I might be induced to make a strict search after him; whatever may have been their motive for doing so, I had no farther trace either of the robbers or Volkert, and even at F—, the Necromancer's principal place of action, whither I went shortly after, even there, everything relating to our former adventures was entirely forgotten—the haunted inn had been sold to a new master, the apparition was frightened away, and the house was a respectable auberge.

I also began, by degrees, to forget the adventures which I partly had heard related, and partly experienced myself, being only now and then reminded of those incidents, when, in the lonely hour of solitude the recollection of the Austrian stole on my mind.

My long overclouded serenity had resumed its wonted brightness, and the remembrance of my ever-regretted friend was no longer accompanied by gloominess and melancholy sensations; I could again partake of the pleasures which smile at us wherever we are, and could relish again the innocent sports of merriment.

In that state of mind I arrived towards the end of summer at A—, when the expectation of every inhabitant was engaged by the approaching scene of a bloody execution, which was to take place within a few days.

A church having been robbed about six months ago, several suspected persons had been imprisoned and put to the rack, but could not be brought to confession, upon which the magistrates had been obliged to set them at liberty for want of such witnesses as the law requires, and to give up the inquisition until further proofs should be found. Many months elapsed before the enraged priests, aided by the eagle-eyed assistance of the magistrates, could trace out the sacrilegious robbers of their hallowed treasures, and feast their vengeance on the throes of the victims of their foaming ire, expiring on the flaming pile, until at length an accident delivered into their holy fangs the perpetrators of that daring deed, whom they in vain had endeavoured to discover by advertisements, tortures of the rack, and the promise of reward.

There lived in a suburb of A—, an old unsuspected man, named Peter, loved by the children of the place, whom he oftentimes amused with little tales, and bribed with sweetmeats, but dreaded by the aged, who firmly believed him to be on an intimate footing with his satanic majesty, because he now and then displayed, when in good humour, proofs of his juggling skill, which they beheld with gaping terror. This hoary man, who lived in a mean cottage, in apparent indigence, and could not be suspected of possessing ill-gotten goods, went oftentimes abroad, but whither he journeyed, or what called him so frequently from his abode, nobody could tell with certainty; some said he went a begging, others, more superstitious, pretended to have seen him, through the chinks of the half decayed window shutters, stretched lifeless on the floor; and some insisted upon having seen him riding through the air on a broomstick, to pay, as it was supposed, his court to his infernal master, to whom his soul and body was said to be mortgaged.

Very fortunately this man was not at A— when the church robbery was committed, to the greatest satisfaction of some who thought him to be an harmless man, and to the greater mortification of others, who pretended to have suffered many a malicious trick by his sorcery: for if he had not been absent at that time, his ill wishers would certainly have forged a pretext to deliver him up to the civil power, as a suspicious, because he never went to church, although he was supposed to be a Roman Catholic.

Some days after the above-mentioned prisoners had been set at liberty, he returned to A—, on a holiday after sun set. The children playing in the streets no sooner espied him, than they ran towards him, hailing their hoary benefactor with loud shouts, searching his pockets for sweetmeats, and teasing the poor old man so unmercifully, that he at last grew angry, and threatened to chastise the troublesome crowd with his staff; however, their demands grew still more clamorous, and some of them began to prick him with pins, which at length obliged him to put his threats in execution.

When the mothers of those ill-mannered boys saw the old man plying the backs of their darlings with his staff, they attacked him like furies, to revenge their children's wrongs and the profanation of the holiday, and by their vociferations alarmed the whole neighbourhood. The husbands of the enraged dames came soon to their assistance; the children began terribly to roar when they saw their old friend in danger of being torn to pieces by their parents, and poor Peter was glad when he got off the clutches of the merciless multitude, after having sustained many a hard blow, and hastened with all possible speed to shelter himself from farther insult in his humble cottage.

But who can describe the terror he was seized with, when he perceived that he had lost his wallet in the scuffle! Raving like a madman did he rush out of his hut, to recover his property, which was carried away in triumph by the victorious party. He exhausted all the rhetoric he was master of, entreated them, whined, and swore, but alas! his adversaries had hearts of flint, and stoutly refused to give up their booty, and when he at last, half frantic with despair, endeavoured to regain it by force, a violent shower of stones drove him back to his humble abode, leaving his dear wallet in the ruthless hands of the furious and inexorable mob.

The principal motive that had induced the assailants to retain the wallet, was an impulse of curiosity, to see what the old sorcerer, so they called him, had got by his journey; and the attack of the children was, very likely, a preconcerted matter, in order to provoke his anger, thus to give them an opportunity of satisfying their curiosity.

The wallet having been opened the first object meeting their prying looks was an old pair of breeches, a tattered shirt, and some pairs of stockings, then followed a large book and some unknown instruments, and at last they found at the bottom a heavy leathern bag, the knot by which it was fastened, baffling all their endeavours to untie it, was at length cut asunder, and the amazement of the gaping multitude rose to the highest pitch, when their eyes beheld a great number of gold pieces.

At first the whole crew was struck dumb with astonishment, but their silence was soon interrupted by a voice, exclaiming, "We have entrapped the sacrilegious robber of our church!" which was the signal for the enraged multitude to break out in curses and terrible execrations against the old man; the air resounded with the universal cry, "Church robber! church robber!" and some of them, hastening to the justice of peace, roared with a bellowing voice, "We have found him out! we have detected the sacrilegious robber of our church!"

The justice was astonished at the unexpected tidings, but his amazement increased still more, when he saw the large heaps of gold coin which had been found in the wallet of the old beggar, and instantly sent the beadle to seize poor Peter; meanwhile the rest of the furious mob had stormed the defenceless hut of the old man, dragged him forth, and conducted him towards the judge's house amid numberless blows and curses. He was now delivered up to the grim catchpole, who instantly carried him to the town prison.

His trial began the following day, and he was ordered to give an account of himself, and how he had got such a large sum of money. Refusing to answer that question, and pretending to have earned the money by honest means, he was put to the rack; yet he stoutly maintained his first declaration, and the justice, being unable to convict him of the charge he stood accused of, was obliged to set him at liberty, retaining, however, his money, until he should have proved that he had got by lawful means.

Peter promised to prove his deposition within a short time, and returned to his hut, which, during his confinement, had been closely searched by his busy neighbours, who, however, had found nothing in it but some tattered coats, and broken pieces of furniture.

The justice, being a prudent man, dissembled to have dropt all further inquiry, but secretly appointed some trusty people to watch all his motions. Their vigilance was fruitless a great while, until at length one of Peter's neighbours observed him, one morning, leaving his house, with a wallet on his back and a staff in his hand, setting off in full speed.

The people of the justice, whom he informed of what he had seen, followed Father Peter in different directions, in disguise, and saw him at noontide enter a lonely public house. Having waited in vain for his reappearance, they began to conceive suspicion, and concealed themselves behind some bushes within a small distance from the house, until it grew dark.

As soon as night had spread her dun mantle over the face of the earth, they heard a distant trampling of horses, bending their course towards the spot where they were hidden, and, ere long, a numerous troop of horsemen alighted at the public house and entered it, upon which the spies crept forth from their lurking place, and stole softly to the windows of the house; there they had not listened six minutes, when

367

they heard a jingling of money, and, peeping through the chinks of one of the shutters, beheld a table covered with dollars, and surrounded by a number of armed men, among whom was Father Peter, feasting his looks on the money which was spread before him.

Having now got every information necessary, they mounted each of them one of the horses which the robbers had fastened to some trees, and hurried back to the town with all possible expedition. The public house being distant from A— only two leagues, they arrived there after an hour's ride, and having informed the justice of everything they had heard and seen, were instantly sent back with a great part of the town guard, well-armed, and mounted on the fleetest coursers that could be got.

The whole troop arrived a little before midnight at the public house, where the robbers were seated round a table, eating and drinking in great security, and almost bereft of the use of their senses by frequent libations. They all started up as if roused by a sudden clap of thunder, when the town guard rushed into the room, seizing their arms, and threatening to blow their brains out if they should attempt the least resistance.

Their hands having been tied, Father Peter, the landlord, who had concealed himself under the bed, and all his servants were seized, and, having been properly secured, carried off in triumph.

The robbers, amounting to ten, were clad in hunting coats, and their purses well stored with gold and silver coin; the whole train marching slowly on, with lighted torches, arrived at A— before it was light, and the prisoners were safely lodged in the strongest dungeon.

Their trial commenced early in the morning, and the youngest of the robbers, who was questioned first, refusing to confess, was put to the rack; his stubbornness being soon subdued, by the torments of the rack, he made evidence that their gang was very numerous, and scattered all over the country, where they had a great many hiding places under-ground; their chief residence, he said, was the old Castle, on the skirts of the Black Forest, where a great part of their spoils was concealed. He further confessed that Father Peter was in close connexion with all the different gangs: he had no fixed abode, but resided sometimes in this, and at other times in that town, and enjoyed the burghership in several cities, where he possessed houses and estates. He firmly denied to have had any share in the church robbery, but pointed out three of his fellow prisoners who had been concerned in it: whether Peter had been accessory in it or not he could not tell.

The day following the three robbers charged with the sacrilege were brought to the bar, but none of them would plead guilty. Being put to the rack, the first of them, an aged man, bore the three degrees without uttering a word, and died a few hours after he had been reconducted to the prison. The second confessed at the third degree, that he had been accessory in the church robbery; but declared that the third was innocent, and that he himself had been persuaded by Father Peter to commit the sacrilege.

Now the hoary dissembler was ordered to the bar. Having heard the charges of the justice with a firm countenance, he replied, with great equanimity.

"Yes, I am guilty, and wish to God I had no other crimes on my conscience than that which I stand accused of. The sluggish, gluttonous monks, who, in honour of an image of stone, have ruined and expelled from their own country a whole innocent family to beg their bread in the streets; these vile villains are far greater felons than myself, and I rejoice at having been an instrument in the hand of providence to avenge the wrongs of the hapless objects of their rapacity, and to restore to those innocent sufferers their property. If this action deserves punishment, you may tear my old limbs asunder, break these withering bones, and reduce to dust and ashes my poor worn-out frame; I will not complain nor utter a groan.

"The grim avenger draws near—I feel the hand of the Supreme Judge; he, and not you, poor mortals, forces me to confess my transgressions. I can brave the ire of men, and deride all bodily sufferings; but I must bend my aged knees to him who dwelleth in heaven, and the pangs of conscience are not to be trifled with."

The Judge and the Sheriffs gazed at each other in dumb silence at these words, and none of them were inclined to question him any farther. Seeing this, he informed them voluntarily of every particular of the sacrilege, and of the family which had been plunged into want and misery by the rapacious monks whose church and convent had been robbed, by means of a forged will. He at the same time confessed where and in what manner the jewels, and the gold and silver furniture had been turned into money, and by what means the sums those articles had fetched had been conveyed to the family, without acquainting the innocent sufferers with the names of their secret benefactors.

The astonishment of the whole court increased with every word the old man uttered, and as soon as he had finished his confession, he requested the jailor to reconduct him to the prison. It lasted a good while before the dread arbiters of life and death could recover from their astonishment, and debate on Peter's doom, which they unanimously agreed to mitigate as much as possible.

According to the rigour of the law he should have been burnt alive, but he and the robber who had been convicted of sacrilege, were sentenced to be beheaded first, and then burnt. The rest of the gang were ordered to close confinement for further examination.

When Father Peter with his fellow-sufferer was called to the bar, in order to hear his sentence pronounced, he behaved with the same firmness of mind as on his trial, and comforted him who had betrayed him.

Having heard his sentence pronounced with the greatest equanimity, he thanked his judges for their clemency, and left the court, supporting with his arm his companion, who exhibited a ghastly picture of dismay and despondency. Father Peter did not lose his courage during his confinement, and took all possible pains to soothe the grief of his fellow sufferer, and to inspire him with sentiments superior to black despair.

He was to be executed two days after my arrival at A—, and I hesitated long whether I should go and see this extraordinary man or not, although I was much solicited by my friends to do it; having a secret boding that this reverend old man, who faced the grim spectre of death so cool and undaunted, could be no other person than Father Francis, alias Volkert, and thinking it disingenuous to distress, by my presence, a man who had saved my life two years ago.

Curiosity and sensibility struggled a great while within my breast, until the last day before the execution, when an ardent desire of having cleared up the mysteries of former events got the better of my generous sentiments, and prompted me to see him early in the morning.

Having mustered up all my fortitude, I went to the prison at six o'clock. Perhaps, thought I, the old man may now be more willing to dispel my doubts than formerly, being on the awful brink of eternity, and disclose the mystery of his former impenetrable transactions, and my presence may not distress the unhappy man so much as thou thinkest! Yet I could not get entirely rid of my apprehensions of increasing the sufferings of my benefactor, or being, perhaps, disappointed in my expectation.

In this state of mind I arrived at the prison, which was opened by the gaoler after a violent knocking. I requested him to favour me with a short interview with the prisoner, but was denied access, because it was against the common rule to introduce company to the convicts the day before execution. I offered him a dollar, entreating him to make an exception with me, being a stranger, and having reasons of moment to wish for an interview with the old man. The sight of the money seemed to have more weight with him than my words; he mused awhile, and then said, "Since you are a stranger, I will make an exception from the common rule, but I must insist upon your telling nobody of this indulgence."

So saying, he conducted me without farther ado to a narrow staircase, leading to a long and narrow passage; at length we came to a small black door, marked with three red crosses, through which I followed him into a dark gloomy room; the entrance was guarded by two men half asleep, and in the background close to the wall I beheld two human figures, of a ghastly woe-worn aspect, and drawing near with a beating heart, saw that one of them was Volkert: his countenance was pale and emaciated, but still stamped with his usual dignity of mien; his head reclining against the wall, and his hands resting on his knees.

He seemed not to perceive that a stranger was in the room until the gaoler said to him, "Well, Father Peter, there is a gentleman who will be glad to speak to you and your comrade."

Hearing this, he slowly lifted up his head, staring at me.

"Volkert!" exclaimed I, "Volkert!"

His looks grew wild, his head sunk back, and he heaved a deep groan; whilst I was standing before him like a statue, thrilled with horror and pity.

As soon as the gaoler had left us, Volkert began with a trembling voice, "Lieutenant, are you come to embitter my last hours, or to speak comfort to my afflicted mind?"

"The latter, good Volkert," replied I.

"Then," said he, "you are welcome, sit down, if you please, perhaps I may be able to be useful to you somehow or other, before I fall a victim to my crimes. I can caution you at least against cheats like myself."

"No idle curiosity has prompted me." said I, "to see you, nor am I come to distress you by illiberal reproaches, for having once endangered my life, that would be ungenerous. You have saved me once from imminent destruction, and that atones fully for all former injuries; yet you will not be offended if I earnestly request you to clear up some late events, which have happened to myself and the Austrian, who—"

"Has been imposed upon by me," replied Volkert, "like yourself, whom I had given the lie at F—, in your and your friend's presence. I will give you all the information you desire, and at the same time a short sketch of my life, as well as it is in my power in my present deplorable situation. I wish most ardently I had done what I always intended to do, and set down in writing those events, and the memoirs of my life; they undoubtedly would be very instructive, and greatly lessen the number of impostors, and those that are imposed upon."

Here he stopped, and, having mused awhile, began his narrative, which, indeed, was very defective, but satisfactory enough for me.

I am, thus Volkert began, a native of England, my father died when I was not quite ten years old, and left me an helpless orphan, without either fortune or near relations. A rich Dutchman being moved by my helpless situation, took me in his house, and, leaving England the year following, carried me over with him to the Hague.

This worthy man gave me a very liberal education, and when I was thirteen years old took me in his counting-house; but alas! he died before he could establish my fortune as he intended to do.

His son, who carried on his father's business, had never been partial to me, and found a pretext to quarrel with me, and to send me away. A rich nobleman, just going to set out for Germany, wanted a servant, who occasionally would act as secretary, and I was glad to accept his offer to take me in his service. He directed his way to K—, where his father was one of the ministers of state.

My young master appeared to be little inclined to qualify himself for state business, being possessed of a very small stock of ambition, and entirely addicted to the study of the occult sciences, which had engaged his attention so much that he was unfit for anything else. I soon was infected with an ardent desire to become his pupil, and, after a few months' instruction, was as great a fool as himself.

It would be too tedious if I was to relate all our fruitless endeavours to effect the apparition of a spirit, and I was soon convinced that it lay not in the power of man to lord over these bodiless beings. My master, however, continued his mysterious operations day and night with an indefatigable ardour.

It is very natural, that it at length came into my head to profit by his superstitious enthusiasm, and that I eagerly seized every opportunity to impose upon a man, who promised to fall an easy sacrifice to art and cunning, having great reason to expect that such an attempt would ensure me his affection, and promote my fortune rapidly.

One night as he was conjuring up his guardian angel with much impatience, I entered his room, telling him that all his efforts would be in vain, because he was not acquainted with the proper means of forcing the inhabitants of the other world to make their appearance.

Gazing at me with wonder and surprise, he inquired whether I had improved so much in the occult sciences that I could effect what he so eagerly desired. I neither denied nor confirmed his question, but told him that I would give him the next day a specimen of my skill in Necromancy.

It was an easy task to impose on my credulous enthusiastic Count, having secured the assistance of a fellow-servant. We resided at a country seat his mother had left him, which was the fittest place in the world for the execution of our design. Having succeeded better than I at first expected, I made him my dupe above a twelve-month, and grew at last so bold and impudent that the Count could not but perceive my juggling tricks, and instantly sent me away.

The good credulous man has certainly been convinced afterwards, that the lesson I gave him by my cheats deserved the warmest gratitude.

I had saved a pretty sum of money during my stay with the Count, and being used to an idle life, had not the least thought of looking about for another master. I went back to H—, where I abandoned myself to gambling, drinking, and all sorts of dissipation, until all my money was spent, and no other means of getting an honest livelihood left, than to try my fortune in the army.

A recruiting officer paid me a hundred dollars for my liberty, and I cheerfully enlisted under the banner of Mars.

I had received the promise to be made a serjeant, but saw myself at first very much disappointed, being forced to serve as a common soldier. Being, however, a good penman, well skilled in casting accounts, and leading a sober and regular life, I soon rose so high in the good opinion of my superiors, that I was appointed serjeant after nine months' service. I certainly should have been promoted higher if I had continued to be zealous in the service, sober and attentive to my superiors, but my patience was exhausted, and I relapsed again into my former dissipations.

A dissolute life requires money, and the desire of getting it plunges him who has once been led astray from the path of virtue soon into his former errors. I had once more recourse to my juggling tricks, pretending to possess a supernatural skill in detecting thefts, in tossing up the cup, and in telling people's fortunes; I conjured up spirits, dispelled the power of witchcraft, and raised up the dead. In short, I did everything in my power to drain the purses of the weak and credulous.

This trade was profitable, and very advantageous in many respects; but it lost me the esteem of my superiors, stained my character, poisoned my heart, and reduced me at last to that despicable sort of people whose heedlessness bids defiance to every obstacle, and who have nothing more at heart than how they may enrich themselves to the detriment of their fellow creatures. In short, I became a rogue of the blackest die.

It was natural that my cheats now and again miscarried before I arrived at that degree of skill, which, in later years, has crowned with success most of my roguish tricks. My superiors, who had warned me many a time against committing such villainous actions, became at last tired of admonishing and correcting me by words, and a spirit which I had conjured up played his part so bad, that they found themselves obliged to make an example of me, and to banish me the country.

A healthy well-made man of my age had no need to be uneasy about getting into the service of any foreign power. I had taken a liking to the life of a soldier, and found soon an opportunity of enlisting under the banners of Austria.

A few days after I had began my peregrination, I met with a recruiting officer of that country, who proposed me to enter the Austrian service, but, being grown wiser by experience, I at first feigned to dislike the military profession, and succeeded so well that the officer at last threw a hundred ducats upon the table, assuring me, upon his salvation, that he never had paid such a price to a recruit.

Now I thought it high time to strain the strings a little lower, agreed to his terms, and told him that I had been serjeant in the Hanoverian service. Having given him a specimen of my skill in penmanship, I requested him to recommend me to his commanding officer; he promised it and was as good as his word. The general received me exceeding well, and I occupied my former post, as serjeant, before a year was elapsed.

Having been sent away with disgrace from H—, I had taken a firm resolution to abstain in future from all fraudulent, juggling tricks, and kept my resolution firmly a long while, behaving eight years as it meets a good soldier.

I abstained entirely from art and fraud, minded my duty, and thus ingratiated myself with my superiors to such a degree that I kept firmly my ground, in spite of many complaints which afterwards were made against me. An unhappy accident induced me to have recourse again to my former juggling tricks, and thus to acquire once more the title of a Necromancer.

I will tell you all the particulars of that adventure, in order to enliven a little my tedious narrative, and to convince you that nothing but necessity could tempt me to engage once more in rogueries which already had destroyed my fortune once, and deprived me of my good character and a honourable employment.

I was quartered in a house that was said to be haunted. It was rumoured about, that time out of mind it had been haunted by a spirit who disturbed the tranquillity of the inhabitants, though he never had injured anybody; he had now, for about six months, alarmed very much the people that lived in the house, and the report of that extraordinary perturbance had caused such a general fear that most of the rooms were unoccupied.

Tempted by the cheapness of the lodgings, and desirous to get at the bottom of the alarming apparitions which had given so much uneasiness to the inhabitants of that house, I went to the owner, and agreed with him to pay five dollars a year for the best room; I instantly took possession of my apartment, and, to my greatest surprise, perceived a long while not the least trace of any supernatural inhabitant.

My landlord always disappointed my inquiries by vague ambiguous answers; and his daughter, who, as it was rumoured, had suffered most from the dreadful apparition, replied with nothing but a deep sigh, when I interrogated her about the nocturnal phantom.

That girl had attracted my attention in a high degree, as soon as I had seen her, being adorned with charms which conquered every heart, almost irresistibly, because she seemed to be entirely unconscious of their winning powers. Her face was rather pale, her constitution weak and sickly, and although she could not be called a beauty, yet I thought her very amiable, and more bewitching than any woman my eyes had ever beheld. I never had tasted the heavenly bliss of innocent virtuous love before my thirty-ninth year, but I must confess this girl had infused into my heart, at first sight, sensations I had always been an utter stranger to.

Helen, this was her name, her father, and myself, occupied the first floor of the haunted house, and the second floor was inhabited by a young secretary; all the other rooms, a back parlour on the ground floor where the servants lived excepted, were unoccupied.

The secretary seemed to have no concern for what was passing around him, his whole attention being engaged by his writings, and I happened only now and then to see him in the company of my landlord and his fair daughter, whom he treated as utter strangers. However, I watched my opportunity better than him, and was never so happy as when I could spend a few hours in conversation with the charming maid. I always pretended to have something to say to the father, taking care never to come to his apartment but when he was abroad.

However, all my anxious endeavours to make a tender impression on my charmer's heart proved abortive; Helen neither seemed to take the least notice of the attention I paid her, nor to be pleased with my eager zeal to engage her favour. The discourses I addressed to her consisted mostly in monologues, interrupted by frequent pauses; and her replies in a pantomime, composed of a silent shaking or nodding of the head, accompanied every now and then by a gentle sigh, which of course made me, by degrees, tired of conversing with her, though my heart at first shrunk back at the thought of giving up such a lovely object.

I had now been many weeks in the house without either hearing or seeing the least thing of the phantom, the tranquillity of the mansion not having been interrupted for a single moment. The domestics of my landlord were highly surprised, ascribing the peace which they enjoyed to me; even my landlord thought that I had chased away the dread phantom, and oftentimes thanked me warmly for having restored the tranquillity of his house.

"Dear friend," said he one evening to me, shaking me by the hand with evident marks of satisfaction, "to you I owe the peace and tranquillity I now enjoy; if the nightly phantom shall continue to stay away, my house will not longer remain unoccupied, and you shall live in it without paying rent as long as it shall be in my possession."

These words he spoke in the presence of his daughter, who fetched a deep melancholy sigh.

A few days after that trifling accident, as it appeared to me, I came home late in the night, and was going to lay myself down to rest without calling for a candle, everybody being gone to bed, when I heard gentle footsteps before my door; I started up, and the steps advanced nearer and nearer. Now they seemed to retreat, and silence reigned around a while.

I listened with eager expectation, and at once heard again the sound of fearful steps and somebody moving the latch of my door, which now was opened slowly and shut again. I was just going to see what these strange proceedings meant, when a white figure entered my apartment.

"Who art thou?" exclaimed I, with a furious voice, seizing the phantom with a powerful hand.

"Jesu Maria!" groaned the apparition, "for God's sake be quiet."

Methought I knew the voice, and, asking again who it was that dared to disturb my rest, the ghost whispered, in a faltering accent, "Be quiet, dear Sir, I am Helen!"

Half frantic with rapture, I pressed the trembling girl to my panting bosom, printed a glowing kiss on her sweet lips, and asked her what fortunate accident had procured me the happiness of seeing her so late in the night.

"Oh!" sighed the lovely girl, "you shall save me from destruction."

"With all my heart," answered I, "if it is in my power."

"It is in your power," resumed my sweet visitor, "my father confides in you; O, save me! save me!"

I entreated her to tell me the source of her affliction, and how I could be serviceable to her, upon which she sat herself down and began as follows:

"The apparition which has lately disturbed the tranquillity of our house is my lover, Henry—the secretary in the second floor. Last autumn he asked me in marriage from my father, who refused to comply with his suit, and the unhappy man has been hurried by despair into a resolution which has destroyed the peace of my mind, and has made him likewise miserable.

"Our house has been reported to be haunted by a ghost these many years, because it was formerly a cloister. My Henry took hold of that superstitious rumour, turning it to his advantage, and, alas! accomplished his design without difficulty. My heart was thrilled with terror at first, and several nights elapsed in unspeakable horror, before I knew that my Henry was the spectre that visited me every night, and made my blood run chill with awful dread. At length he undeceived me, but, alas! it was then too late; my virgin honour was gone forever. I feel the dreadful consequences of my guilty connexion with the unhappy man, and disgrace and ruin will seize me with merciless fangs, if you do not save me. O, Mr. Volkert! do not refuse your assistance to a poor helpless girl."

Moved by this woeful speech I promised to procure the consent of her father to her marriage with the secretary, might it cost whatever it would. Her gratitude knew no bounds, she almost suffocated me by her endearments, and left me with these words:—"My happiness, my life, and my honour, are in your power; without your assistance destruction will seize me, and eternal misery will be my dreadful lot."

After a cool deliberation, I grew sensible that I had engaged in a very difficult undertaking. By what natural means could the father of the seduced girl be persuaded to sanction her love? How was it possible to shake the firm resolution of a rigorous headstrong man, if a medium congenial to his manner of thinking was not to be employed which might surprise and prompt him to come to our terms for the sake of his own interest. This medium was no other than what he himself had suggested to me—his belief in the supernaturalness of the apparition, and the power he supposed me to have over it.

I could not get a wink of sleep during the remainder of the night, racking my brain and tormenting my imagination in vain. Whenever I fancied to have hit on a feasible expedient, it soon vanished like a deluding dream, as soon as I applied the undeceiving torch of reason, and I saw but too clearly that nothing would extricate me from the maze I was bewildered in but the magic wand.

I was engaged for three days in a most distressing conflict with my rebelling conscience, and several times on the brink of shifting quarters, and taking a house far enough removed from my then abode, but my resolution was always shaken as soon as it was formed, when the doleful situation of the poor distressed girl recurred to my mind, imploring my assistance with a pallid, ghastly look.

It is true the lover of the afflicted, disconsolate girl did not deserve my assistance; however, poor Helen would certainly have been lost without my assistance. These considerations conquered at last every hesitation which reason and honesty had suggested to my troubled mind, and on the fourth morning I went to work.

I entered at nine o'clock the apartment of my landlord, and could not but observe that Helen's cheeks were tinged with a crimson hue of inward satisfaction; her aspect and her looks supported my resolution.

"Sir," said I, "the tranquillity of your house is dear to me, and I have had the good fortune, last night, to hit upon means, the application of which will certainly secure it forever."

The simple, superstitious man embraced me with visible marks of gratitude, exclaiming in an ecstasy of joy, "O, tell me, tell me, what must I do?"

Then he ordered his daughter to fetch a bottle of Hungarian wine, pressing me to drink; but I declined it, resuming—

"Sir, the ghost that disturbs the peace of your house—"

"Have you seen him?" he interrupted me, with a ghastly look.

"I will see him," replied I; "he is a malicious being, and has given me much trouble; yet I trust I shall be able to get the better of him by the assistance of the occult knowledge which I possess."

"How, how!" stammered the simpleton; "then you are indeed the man I always took you for: then you are really one of those great mortals who understand the wonderful art of necromancy. How happy I am to meet at last, so unexpectedly, with the man I have always most ardently wished to find out. Tell me, dear friend, what must we do?"

"Nothing in the world," answered I, "but conjure up in due form that turbulent spirit."

"And will you undertake to perform that difficult, dangerous task?"

"Why not?"

"And when, dear sir, do you intend to do me that inestimable favour?"

"The ensuing night, if you will consent to it, for without your leave I can do nothing."

"O, that you have! that you have! You may do whatever you please; I will consent to anything, if I can get rid of that infernal disturber of my nocturnal rest!"

I left the credulous man with sensations which sprung from pity rather than exultation at my easy-gotten victory. I instantly made every preparation for executing my roguish plan, being assisted by the secretary, and having won over to my purpose the servants of the house, everything succeeded to admiration.

A little before twelve o'clock all the inhabitants of the house resorted to my room, and an intimate friend of mine acted the ghost admirably well: benumbing perfumes deprived the spectators of the proper use of their senses, and the landlord had previously been made unfit for investigation by a powder mixed with his wine.

The ghost appeared, or rather stepped forth, from behind a partition of paper, which I had contrived to make.

When I asked why he had dared to disturb the tranquillity and peace of the house, he answered, in a tremulous, hollow accent, "Out of resentment to the female sex."

On my further inquiries, he related in short answers, that, a century ago, the cruelty of a lady he had been in love with had driven him to despair, and hurried him into the rash resolution to shut himself up within a cloister's hallowed walls; but having profaned his holy order by entering into it with a worldly heart, polluted by the loose desires of sensual love, he had been condemned to purgatory until a certain condition should be fulfilled.

All these queries and answers, previously set down in writing and got by heart, produced the desired effect on the blinded mind of the credulous father, who at length stammered out the question, by what means could he be relieved from his torments? The ghost replied, that he was doomed to suffer the agonies of purgatory, and to haunt his former abode in the midnight hour until an unhappy couple, separated by a parent's cruel tyranny, should be united in holy wedlock.

Having related his fictitious tale, he disappeared behind the partition of paper, under the cover of a thick smoke, leaving my landlord in a state of mind which seconded our design to the utmost of our wishes.

When the credulous man had recovered a little from his astonishment, I asked him if he could explain the meaning of the ghost's answer, and whether it was in his power to perform the condition he had hinted at; upon which he silently nodded to me, and promised to pay me a visit early in the morning, which he did at six o'clock, confessing his cruelty towards his daughter, which he believed had provoked the resentment of the monk, and pleaded the poverty of the young man, and the cool indifference he had treated his daughter with ever since his offers had been rejected.

"Now," added he, "I see everything in its proper light; the ghost has entirely opened my eyes, blinded by avarice. God be praised that the young man has not yet left my house, as he intended to do, for it would give then much room for scandal, if he should marry my daughter, which I am very well convinced cannot be avoided, if the tranquillity of my house shall be restored."

In short, the secretary was married to the girl, and the ghost appeared no more.

This beneficial fraud—for so I may justly call it, the honour, and perhaps the life of the father and daughter, having been saved by it, and the young man, who was sober and industrious, proving a tender and affectionate husband—this beneficial fraud was the first step, which afterwards led me to ruin and disgrace.

Possessed of a large stock of knowledge of the human heart, of experience, and art, I was no longer satisfied with confining myself to trifling juggling tricks, but I soon began to act after a more extensive plan. In spite of all the precautions I had taken to keep the abovementioned transaction from the knowledge of the public, it soon transpired, with the usual additions, and everybody thought me to be a sort of supernatural being, and so many opportunities of preying on the credulity of mankind were thrown in my way, that I could not stand the temptations which frequently occurred to profit by the superstitions of my fellow creatures.

I hope you will spare me the distressing task to relate all the transgressions I committed afterwards; suffice it to say, that a complete account of my frauds would swell many volumes. The few remaining hours of life allotted me prevent me from relating all the subsequent tricks which I committed, I therefore shall confine myself to the two criminal transactions by which your friend, the brave Austrian has been imposed upon; they will afford you ample means of forming a proper idea of those I am obliged to bury in silence.

I had, for the space of six years, carried on my juggling tricks with so much secrecy, that few of my criminal deeds were known. Although I had been betrayed several times by my associates, and reprimanded by my superiors, yet I always suffered myself to be blinded by the too powerful charms of gold and false ambition, and was ever ready to lend my assistance to deeds of the blackest hue.

One day the widow of an honest citizen sent for me and, having bribed me by some pieces of gold, requested me to assist her in the execution of a most criminal design.

Her husband, lately deceased, so she told me, had promised her daughter in marriage to a man whom she could not suffer to become her son-in-law, because he had behaved very disrespectfully towards her while her husband had been living, and scorned to apply for her consent; moreover, she told me, he was a lazy drunkard and a gambler; in one word, a good-for-nothing fellow.

"I know, Mr. Volkert," added she, "that you are in high favour with the Devil, and entreat you to raise up one of the angels of darkness, commanding him to appear to my daughter, and to threaten her to carry her to hell if she will not desist from her intended marriage."

Shocked at that infernal proposal I was going to throw the money at her feet; would to God I had done it! but three ducats more soothed my indignation, and allured me to promise that I would take the matter into consideration, and inform her of the result of it the following day.

I kept my promise, enjoining the woman to tell her daughter, as a secret, that her deceased father had, on his death-bed, compelled her to make a solemn promise never to consent to that marriage. She readily executed my order, and the poor girl was overwhelmed with grief.

Then I bade the inhuman mother assume a melancholy aspect, to treat her daughter with more kindness than ever, to mingle her tears with those of her child, to inveigh now and then against the caprice of the deceased, to inflame the girl, by degrees, with a desire of knowing the reason her father might have had to forbid, on his death-bed, her union with a man he had always seemed to be fond of; and, after these preparations, to mention, as if by accident, my name, and my skill in necromancy, yet to take care, not to betray her design of having conjured up her deceased husband.

The cruel, unnatural mother executed my orders with all possible dexterity and art, wept with her afflicted, disconsolate child, and, by these means, beguiled the unsuspecting heart of her unhappy daughter. The poor victim of a mother's infernal cruelty listened eagerly to the deceitful speeches of her artful parent, and her curiosity was soon raised to so high a pitch, that she one evening came to my lodgings trembling and shivering to acquaint me with her woe, and to implore my assistance, which I instantly promised to grant her.

The rest you very likely know from the relation of your friend. One of my comrades, who was always ready to execute my commands, acted the ghost, and everything succeeded, alas! too well.

But suffer me to drop the dreadful, horrid tale; this black, infernal deed lies heavy on my conscience, for it has rendered me guilty of the murder of two innocent persons.

Your friend requested me, soon after, to give him a specimen of my talents, which I readily promised to do as soon as an opportunity should offer; but, God knows, I did not mean to perform my promise.

However, the quarrel between the two officers afforded me very soon such an alluring opportunity to display my skill, that I could not stand the temptation to perform the most cunning and subtle trick. The whole transaction bears such strong marks of the marvellous, that you will expect a long explanation, but the contrivance was so simple that a few words will suffice to unfold to you that strange affair.

One morning a foreign officer sent for and requested me, to compose an ointment which would make him invulnerable. I stared at him with wonder and astonishment; however, when he covered the whole table with gold, I was tempted to profit by his folly, and asked him who his antagonist was. Being told it was Lieutenant C—, I would not run the risk of exposing myself to his resentment, and left the valiant son of Mars without listening to his proposal.

The succeeding day your friend visited me; "Volkert," said he, as he entered the room, "I have a job for you: I can give you an excellent opportunity to favour me with a proof of your skill, and to get a handsome sum of money into the bargain."

I pricked up my ears, made a few faint objections, and at length suffered myself to be persuaded.

As soon as your friend had left me I went to Baron T—, who was still in bed, without having the least inclination of fighting a duel.

"Baron," exclaimed I, as I entered his room, "give me the money, I am ready to execute your orders; you shall not only be invulnerable, but also leave the field of battle and this town as a man of honour, provided nobody knows that you are returned from your journey."

"That is charming!" exclaimed the undaunted Baron, "nobody besides you and my landlord know that I am returned, and him we can easily silence if secrecy is necessary."

Then he jumped nimbly out of his bed, and gave me the money. I laid my plan before him, and he joyfully submitted to everything proposed. His landlord and the owner of the house where the conjuration was performed, were bribed. The Baron, who acted the ghost, was concealed in a small closet, to which he, when the whole transaction was finished, retired, under the cover of a thick benumbing smoke, which concealed his retreat, and left the town that very night. The postman had likewise been bribed to deliver the letter, composed by me and copied by the Baron. The certificate of the surgeon-major was forged, and everything succeeded to our satisfaction.

As to the duel, everything was effected by natural means. I cleaned and charged the pistols of Lieutenant C—, and took care to spoil the locks of one brace, and to charge the other with wrong bullets. I informed the governor of the duel, that Baron T—'s courage might be known, and he returned, for the same reason, to town, as soon as the duel was fought, delivering himself into the hands of the soldiers who had been ordered to arrest the combatants.

That he might be thought generous, he supplicated for the enlargement of his antagonist, and procured him the governor's pardon.

The heinousness of this deed of mine will be lessened in your eyes, if I tell you, that the bullets in the Baron's pistols were likewise too small, so that Lieutenant C— could not be wounded dangerously, and the baron took care not to hurt him materially.

Volkert had as yet spoken with great hilarity, and it almost appeared as if he had entirely forgotten his impending doom; but suddenly he grew more serious and solemn. Gloomy clouds of sorrow were gathering on his brow, the paleness of his countenance increased, his lips were contorted, he gave a deep groan of anguish, and after an awful pause of inward agony, he went on in a faltering accent—

Oh that I here could conclude the dreadful tale of my transgressions! Oh, that I had not to relate deeds more glaring and abominable! Deeds which thrill my soul with anguish, and pierce my guilty heart with a thousand daggers, pointed by unutterable pangs of a polluted conscience. However, I promised you a sketch of my whole life, and will be as good as my word. Although I shall not be able to give you a full narrative of deeds which fill my soul with horror, yet I will go on as well as I can.

The intercession of Baron T— in my behalf had so much weight with the governor, that he suffered me to escape without punishment, and sent me on the recruiting business, in order to get rid of me without provoking my anger. O that he had rather loaded me with his resentment than with his bounty, and punished me as I deserved; perhaps it would have opened my eyes and brought me back to the path of honesty.

My ruin was now completed. I began my recruiting business with great alacrity and cheerfulness, and found but too many opportunities of exerting my plotting skill, which I did with so much success, that my comrades were astonished, and my superiors so highly pleased with my zeal, that they put the greatest confidence in me, and entrusted me with sums which enabled me to abandon myself to all manner of dissipation; the few remaining sparks of honesty and virtue were extinguished by degrees, and I was hurrying with rapid steps into the abyss of destruction.

My dissipations tempted me to defraud my superiors, and soon intricated me in a maze of embarrassment, where I found myself entirely bewildered. I got acquainted and intimately connected with the most dangerous sort of people, with robbers and their infernal associates. Allured by my cunning and artful tricks, they did everything in their power to gain my confidence, and to win me over to their party, which, alas! laid the foundation to my ruin. I became a spy, a traitor, and, at last, their accomplice in the perpetration of the most shocking crimes.

My recruiting business was neglected, and my superiors were going to call me back. Being not able to give an account of large sums that had been entrusted to me, I could not appear before my commanding officer, and no other means were left me to escape the impending storm, but to disappear entirely, which I effected in such a manner that everyone firmly believed I was no more.

I conducted ten robbers, disguised as recruits, through a large town, where many of my profession resided, and, as soon as we had reached the adjacent wood, they took to their heels. I ran to the next village, raving like a madman, related my misfortune, wept, cried, and then returned to the wood, dissembling to be in the greatest despair.

The robbers, who were waiting for me, made me pull off my uniform, dressed a dead man in it, who, perhaps, had been murdered for that purpose, put a pistol in his hand, and disfigured him by blowing his brains out.

Now I was no longer Volkert the serjeant; I was Volkert the robber and murderer. I painted my face, feigned to be twenty years older than I really was, and thus escaped being known by my former acquaintances. I soon became famous under the name of Father Francis, bought houses in several towns, and everybody took me for what I appeared to be, an old, harmless man. Yet I was known at length by one of my former messmates, when in the H— service, who was recruiting in the empire, and forced me to assist him in his business.

The cunning rogue had not forgotten my skill in executing deceitful plots, and his expectation that I should be of great service to him by my artifices did not deceive him. I never spread my nets in vain when I wanted to catch a well-made young fellow, and we had enlisted within a short time a great number of recruits. How easily I could remove every obstacle I will prove by a single instance, which will give you a true notion of my intricate artifices.

A well-made, young, and amiable Livonian, lodged with me at the same inn, at T—, and my associate took such a liking to him, that he offered to acquit me of all farther services, if I could ensnare this young man.

I promised to do my utmost, and went instantly to work, ordering some of the gang I was connected with, and who then resided at T— on account of the great fair, to purloin his ring, snuff-box, purse, and watch, returning him the latter in a public place, telling him that I had detected the thief admirably well.

This done, I left him suddenly, without giving him time to make farther inquiries, my sole view being to excite his curiosity, and to gain his confidence, in which I succeeded admirably well.

The Livonian became very anxious to get acquainted with me, watched my return to the inn several nights, and attempted to converse with me; in short, he was very impatient to draw from me an information of the means by which I had detected the thief, but I always shunned him, and baffled his endeavours a great while, until, at last, I found it necessary to pay him a visit, in order to console him about the loss of a bill of exchange which my myrmidons had got in their power, along with his pocket-book.

This bill having contained all the little wealth he had got about him, he was under the necessity of either remaining some time longer at T—, or of selling his linen and everything of value, and thus return to his own country, in a most distressing condition. I gave him two notes, each of a hundred dollars, the binding money from the recruiting officer.

My unexpected visit and my seeming generosity put him into the greatest astonishment, and I left him again abruptly, without entering into conversation with him.

He was now enlisted without suspecting it, but I did not, as yet, know how I could put him into the power of my employer; however, my inventive genius soon suggested to me the proper means of effecting my purpose. By some letters from his mother, which I had found in his pocket-book, I had learned that she had died a little time before, very ill satisfied with his conduct, on account of his dissipations when at the university.

The characters engraved on the inside of the ring which I had taken from him, being the same with those the letters of his mother were signed with, put it out of doubt that the miniature picture of an old lady it was adorned with, must be the likeness of his mother.

One of my associates, whose features had by accident some resemblance with those of the picture, concealed himself at the inn, painted his face with chalk, wrapped himself in a sheet, and went at night into the room of the young Livonian, who seemed to wait for my return, to inquire, as I suppose, some particulars about the two notes I had given him the preceding day, and was not a little frightened when he saw the ghost of his deceased mother entering his room. The phantom walked through his apartment, looked at the watch which was on the table to signify that it wanted rest, sighed, gave him a menacing look, and left him thrilled with horror and amazement.

The day following I ordered my myrmidons to watch every step of the Livonian and was informed that he was gone into a tea garden, after he had changed the two notes.

I hastened after him without delay, and found him sitting in a lonely bower; he did not see me, though I was standing close by him, being bewildered in gloomy meditations, and talking to himself. Suddenly he exclaimed, 'No, it was a dream!' 'It was no dream,' replied I instantly. He looked up, seized with terror and surprise. I promised to unfold, at ten o'clock at night, all the mysterious accidents which had happened to him at T—, and, having appointed to meet me at the city gate, which was within a small distance from our inn, disappeared suddenly.

My spies continued to watch his motions during the remainder of the day, and one of them carried everything that he had lost to the land-lord of the inn where we lodged, that he might be the more eager to meet me and to satisfy his curiosity, which had the desired effect.

He kept the appointment very punctually, but I made him wait above an hour. Just when he was on the point of going home I came walking towards him with hasty steps, and conducted him to a lonely public house within a small distance from the town, which was the usual haunt of the recruiting officers and their associates.

Having conducted him into a pleasure-house in the garden, built over a cellar, to which a trapdoor led from the room where we then were, I asked him what he desired to know, and seeing him hesitate to fix on a question, I inquired if he should not like to know his benefactor, who had interested himself so much for him? he consented to it, and, having drawn a circle round the trapdoor, which could be let down from below, I placed him in the centre of it. Some of my associates, who were concealed in the cellar, imitated the roaring of thunder, during my conjurations, opened the trapdoor, and caused him to sink down into the cellar: he, who already had acted the ghost of his mother, appeared again in his former disguise; some blew powder of calophony through the windows of the pleasure-house, and everything succeeded as well as I could wish.

The poor young man was stunned with wonder and surprise and seeing the ghost of his mother as he was sinking down into the cellar, lost all power of recollection. He was instantly carried in a coach, one serjeant of the recruiting officer seated himself by his side, and another mounted the box, driving on with all possible speed, but being a very indifferent coachman, the vehicle was suddenly overturned and one of the unhappy young man's legs was broken.

When the serjeants saw it they disengaged the horses from the coach and rode away. This was indeed a great disaster, but still it turned out very fortunate for the young man, for a neighbouring nobleman, who saw him in his deplorable situation as he passed the road, took him to his castle, sent for proper assistance, and took so much care of the young man, that he, after a few months, was able to return to his native

THE NECROMANCER

country, where he safely arrived without having met with any farther sinister accident.

The recruiting officer, vexed at the miscarrying of our design, now dropt all connexion with me, and I abandoned myself entirely to a life of rapine and plunder.

You will now expect me to unfold your adventure at the ruinous Castle, on the skirts of the Black Forest, but I hope you will spare me the disagreeable task of enlarging on the particulars, since you have a clue, by the assistance of which you will easily extricate yourself from the maze of mystery and wonder in which you have been bewildered.

As to the strange apparitions in the subterraneous vaults, they have likewise been effected by the assistance of the robbers. Some of them were concealed in the vaults joining to the principal cellar, and the burying vault, blowing the artificial flashes of lightning through the chinks in the wall, and others being concealed in the hidden recesses of the subterraneous fabric, produced the thunder by means of large kettle drums. The lid of the coffin was opened by a cord, which the darkness concealed from your sight; the female figure was the son of a neighbouring publican, closely connected with our gang, who already had acted the ghost several times, when curious travellers had visited the castle: the light shooting from the coffin was effected by a dark lanthorn, which previously had been placed to it: the bluish glimmering you saw in the other vault, came from a lanthorn composed of blue glass, and placed on the staircase of the cellar.

The second ghost was one of the robbers; his fractured, disfigured head was made of a hollowed pumpkin. Our sudden retreat we effected through the iron doors, and the ruinous side building opposite the cellar door.

The stench you smelt was effected by some brimstone we had left burning on the staircase; the extinguishing of the light in the lamp, hanging over the cenotaph, and of that which you had taken with you was caused by a certain spirit I had poured in it as we descended the staircase; perhaps you will recollect that I took it from you before I began my juggling tricks, as I was leading the way into the cellar. The spirit in the lamp over the cenotaph had previously been poured into it by one of my associates; and the smoke caused by the artificial lightning smothered the light until it evaporated in the arched vault. After the second apparition had disappeared I overturned the lamp; and the rest you will be able to unravel without my assistance.

Now I come to the incident which gave you and your friend an opportunity of seeing me in my real character, and of detecting my juggling, cheating tricks. Everything has been carried on and executed under my direction; here is the key to it.

Ever since the H— recruiting officer had known me at T— I visited that town very seldom, though I possessed a house there, and was esteemed by my neighbours and fellow citizens.

An acquaintance of mine who kept a public house within a small distance from T—, took a large inn at that town, and expected to do very well, but an adjacent inn which was in great renown, disappointed all his hopes, and reduced him soon to very distressing circumstances. He disclosed his distresses to me as I once happened to come to T—, and I advised him to ruin the neighbouring inn by the introduction of a ghost.

The owner of the house had died a little time ago, and his son, a young inexperienced and simple lad, carried on the business. We bribed some of his servants to make a noise in the night, and to spread the rumour about, that the house was haunted, and that the late possessor of it appeared at midnight, frightening the guests in a terrible manner.

This artifice succeeded to the utmost of our wishes, and when I left T—, a few months after, the inn of my friend, which always had been empty, was crowded with travellers, while that of his neighbour was the lonely haunt of the disguised spectres.

Having great reason to apprehend that out machination would be detected sooner or later, I promised my friend, who dreaded the same, to return within a twelve-month, and to procure him an opportunity of purchasing the haunted inn on reasonable terms. I was as good as my word, returned to T—, and what farther happened you know.

At first I was rather uneasy that the foreign officer had taken lodgings at the haunted inn, and prohibited every nocturnal disturbance, apprehending the whole artifice would be detected; but just as I was going to leave T—, without having attempted anything, the cowardice of that officer gave me an opportunity of executing my design.

His comrades, chicken-hearted like himself, proposed to watch with him in the haunted house, and their imagination played them a trick which most unexpectedly favoured the execution of my plan.

They had watched three successive nights without either hearing or seeing anything uncommon; the fourth night a tempest was raging, without their perceiving it, being prevented from doing it by the great quantity of punch they had swallowed, and the roaring noise which was the natural consequence of their inebriation.

When they entered the room, after having been frightened by the howling of the storm, on their return from the search they had been making, the tempest ceased for a few seconds, and it was natural that one of them, who very wisely looked out of the window, could perceive nothing. Being chilled with dread and apprehension, he forgot to bolt the window, his companions had, from like reasons, neglected to shut the door, and the first gust of wind finding no resistance threw the window and the door suddenly open, the lights were extinguished, and their disordered fancy effected now, what I, perhaps, would have attempted in vain, with all my juggling skill. Flashes of lightning illuminated the room, the tremendous roaring of thunder shook the house, one of the company overturned the table in his fright, and they really fancied to see a phantom, which only existed in their disordered imagination, harrowed up by fearful apprehensions and superstitious terror. What further happened I need not tell you.

My spies informed me of the departure of the officer who had resided at the haunted inn, and of the route he had taken; they likewise apprised me of his return. I hastened to meet him on the road, and the conjuration of the ghost was agreed on.

Being no stranger to the cowardly disposition of his friends, I apprehended not the least danger from their being present at the experiment, and willingly consented that he should bring with him some of them. However, I was very much mistaken, because two of them were gentlemen for whom I was not prepared, and who had been already once deceived by Volkert; yet I did not entirely miss my aim, and the haunted inn was sold soon after to my friend on very low terms; the simpleton who had been the owner of it, and who believed still in the reality of the apparition in spite of what he had seen and heard when I conjured up the spirit, and in spite of reason and good sense, having no peace nor rest until he had disencumbered himself of the possession of ill-gotten wealth. The apparition itself was effected by means of a camera obscura in an apartment beneath that where I performed the cheat, some boards in the floor having, the night before, been sawed through, after we had made a hole in the ceiling of the lower chamber. The boards which covered the opening close to the wall were replaced in such a manner that they could be removed from below, by means of which the smoke could ascend from the lower apartment, and represent the picture in the machine—smoke and darkness put the finishing stroke to the deception.

I left, like your friend, T— the next morning, with the firm resolution to return no more, apprehending to be delivered up to the vengeance of the civil power, in spite of your generosity, and having lost my good character forever. On my journey I happened to come to the house where you was confined, and felt the highest satisfaction when I had it in my power to make you some atonement for the many wrongs you had suffered by me. My intention was to live here in A— in solitude and retirement, and to dedicate the rest of my miserable life to repentance, and thus to make my peace with God. But my former lawless companions soon found out my retreat and forced me to renew my crimes, and to assist them in their infernal deeds.

> The crime for which I am confined here you very likely know. All I can say in order to palliate this last transgression is, that it is one of the noblest deeds I ever performed, and it would not give me the least uneasiness if the execution of it had not brought destruction on other people beside myself.

Here Volkert stopped fatigued and exhausted by the long narrative. I conversed a good while longer with him on his conjurations, and could not help mentioning, that I was very much surprised that his deceptions could have been kept so concealed, though he had always been obliged to rely on the assistance of other people, to which he replied—

"Your observation is very just, but your surprise will vanish, if you consider that my assistants in cheating people bore their share in the frauds I committed, and, of course, would not have escaped punishment if they had not kept secret all transactions of that nature."

"It is more surprising," added he, "that one is always certain to find people who will lend their assistance in cheating their fellow citizens, and it is almost incredible how willing everyone is to assist any impostor in deceiving others; yet I do not think that the source of that intriguing disposition, so common among all classes of men, springs from the depravity of human nature; I rather would attribute it to the pleasure everyone feels when he can prove the superior powers of his genius, which is the head spring which animates us as well to good as to bad actions, and, if guided by a benevolent heart and good principles, raises us above the common herd, and leads us to honour and glory."

As I rose and was going to leave the prison, Volkert squeezed my hand, and said, with a faltering voice—

"Tomorrow, at this hour, I shall be no more,—tomorrow, at this hour, I shall have seen the Supreme Judge of human kind. I shudder when I think that I must appear before His awful throne. Yet, there is one consolation supporting me,—one consolation, that, as yet, has warded off the deadly arrows of despair, and, I trust, will comfort me in my trying hour, and when He who dwelleth in heaven shall speak to me. This consolation, friend—give me leave to call you by that sacred name —this consolation is not the vain, groundless expectation that I shall atone for my sins by suffering the punishment that awaits me. No; if I had a hundred lives to lose, I could not atone for my manifold crimes. This consolation consists in the persuasion that I shall be made a warning example of the dread consequences attending the criminal abuse of the intellectual powers the great Ruler of the universe has given us, and that the world will be warned against impostors like myself."

When he had finished, I bade him a last farewell, in a faltering accent, and left the unhappy man, who said to me, as I opened the door—

"Come tomorrow to the place of execution, your presence will give me comfort!"

I left the prison lost in gloomy thought, and with a bleeding heart. The dismal idea of the awful scene which was to be exhibited the next day haunted me wherever I went, and I struggled in vain to chase it from my mind. The solemn stillness of the night rather increased than diminished my uneasiness, and sleep entirely fled from my weary eyes. The dawn of the rosy morn cheered the whole creation, but my soul was pierced with horror when the first ray of the rising sun hailed me on my couch.

At length the solemn sound of bells announced the approaching hour of execution. I wrapped myself in my cloak, and repaired with trembling steps to the place where Volkert was to atone for his crimes. The streets were crowded with a noisy multitude. Haunted by secret awe did I arrive at the place of execution, and horror made my blood run chill as I beheld the dreadful pile which soon was to reduce to ashes the preserver of my life.

A gaping multitude was standing around, awaiting with cruel insensibility, and with more than beastly satisfaction, the dreadful catastrophe which was to terminate the life of their fellow creatures.

Without recollection was I standing amid the crowd, when suddenly a confused noise was heard, and every eye directed to one spot. Lifting my downcast looks, I beheld the funeral procession drawing near with slow solemnity. Volkert was walking in the front with firm and manly steps, followed by his ghastly-looking fellow sufferer. The procession stopped at the enclosure encircling the scaffold, and Volkert's eyes were anxiously looking around; at length he saw me, nodded to me with a grateful smile, and entered the enclosure.

His trembling fellow sufferer was first sacrificed by the avenging hand of justice. I cast my eyes to the ground until I perceived by the murmuring noise around that his sufferings were over. Now I directed again my melancholy looks towards the dread place of execution, and beheld Volkert undressing himself, and approaching with firmness the stool stained with the smoking blood of his friend. Now he was seated, the sword of the executioner lifted up—now it glittered in the morning sun ready to strike the fatal blow. I shut my eyes involuntarily—a sudden hollow humming told me that Volkert had conquered. Awful sensations thrilled my palpitating heart, and I forced my way through the gaping multitude without looking once more towards the horrid place where Volkert had expired.

At the city gate I looked back and beheld with horror a thick column of smoke ascending aloft and darkening the pure, serene air; I could not stand the horrible sight, and hastened to my apartments, determining to leave a place immediately in which my peace of mind had been so much disturbed.

But being informed that the Captain of the gang would be examined the following day, curiosity got so far the better of my impatience to leave as soon as possible a town where every object recalled to my mind the hapless state of my preserver, that I resolved to stay one day longer, and very glad I am that I took that resolution. The account this man gave of himself being so singular and remarkable, that I was amply repaid for the melancholy and grief which haunted me with unabating fury, whilst I tarried within the walls of the town where my benefactor had been executed.

The trial began at six o'clock in the morning, and I took care to be in the town house before the terrible leader of the robbers had made his appearance at the bar. Every one present seemed struck with terror when he entered the hall.

He was of a gigantic make, near seven feet high, his robust limbs corresponding with his extraordinary size; his black and bushy hair covered part of his sun-burnt face, which was disfigured by two gaping scars across his left cheek. His eye, for he had but one left, flashed like lightning when he beheld the dread arbiters of life and death eager to pronounce his doom. The judge exhorted him to speak the truth, and not to aggravate his guilt by stubbornness. However, nobody expected that a wretch of his appearance would pay the least regard to gentle admonitions, and perhaps remain silent even under the tortures of the rack. His savage look and lofty mien seemed to betoken a haughty spirit, not easy to be subdued. I at least had entertained not the most distant hope of having my curiosity gratified in so satisfactory a manner as he really did. Imagine therefore my astonishment when, contrary to all expectation, he began:

"My Lord and Gentlemen,—I am in your power, and well aware that nothing can avert my impending doom; I scorn the tortures of the rack and bid defiance to every human effort, to force me to a confession of my crimes. You might tear my limbs asunder, and kill me by inches, and yet would never extort a single word from my lips if I had no other reasons to deal candidly with you. However, I will spare you that trouble, and honestly confess my crimes, their origin, and their progress; being strongly persuaded that the history of my life will afford a useful lesson to judges, and teach the guardians of the people to be careful how they inflict punishments if they will not make a complete rogue of many a hapless wretch, who would have been recalled to his duty, and preserved to human society, by gentle treatment. I never should have become a robber, had not the too great severity of laws made me an enemy to the human race, and hurried me to the brink of black despair. I know my doom is fixed; however, if your heart is no stranger to pity you will at least not refuse a tear of humanity to a poor unhappy man, who has been dragged by dire fatality into the path of vice, and forced to commit deeds his soul abhors."

Here he stopped. Awful silence swayed around, and my curiosity was harrowed up to the highest degree, when he began nearly in the following strain:

I am the son of an innkeeper at A—, whose name was Wolfe, and who died when I had reached my twenty-fourth year. I succeeded him in his business, which being indifferent, many of my hours were unemployed.

Being the only son, I had been spoiled by my parents, who were delighted with my wanton pranks and indulged me in everything. Grown-up girls complained of my impudence when I was but twelve years old; and the boys of the village paid homage to my inventive genius. Nature had not dealt niggardly with me in respect of bodily endowments; however, an unfortunate kick from a horse disfigured my face in such a manner, that the girls of the village shunned me, and my play-fellows took frequent opportunities to make me an object of their merriment. The more my female acquaintances avoided me, the more the desire of pleasing took root in my heart. As I grew up, I was given to sensuality and persuaded myself to be in love. The object of my flame treated me with scorn, and I had reason to apprehend that my rivals were more successful than I; however, the girl was poor, and I had reason to hope that her heart, which was inaccessible to my vows and prayers, would yield to presents, which I knew not how to procure, the small income my business afforded me being entirely swallowed up by the vain efforts I made to render my person less disgusting. Being too much addicted to idleness to exert myself in amending my circumstances, and too ambitious to change my expensive mode of life, I had only one means left to improve my fortune, which thousands before me had tried with more success.

The village in which I lived gave me an opportunity of committing depredations on the game, and the money I raised in that way wandered regularly into the hands of my mistress. Robert, a gamekeeper to the Lord of the Manor, was one of the admirers of Jenny, which was the name of my paramour; he soon observed the advantage which my presents procured me over him, and being spurred by envy and jealousy he watched me closely. By degrees he began to resort to the "Sun," which was the sign of my inn, more frequently than ever, and his prying eye soon detected the source of my liberal gifts.

A very rigorous law against game-stealing had been renewed not long before, and Robert was indefatigable to find an opportunity of getting rid of his rival. He succeeded but too soon; I was caught in the very act of shooting a deer, and condemned to be sent to the house of correction. It cost me all my little remaining fortune to buy off that punishment. Robert had gained his aim, and Jenny"s heart was lost to me.

Glowing resentment rankled in my breast, and I was determined to be revenged as soon as a proper opportunity should offer. Poverty and want, hunger and despair, tempted me once more to have recourse to game stealing, and Robert's watchfulness surprised me a second time. Being reduced to the lowest degree of poverty, it was not in my power to gild the hands of justice a second time, and I was committed for a whole year to the house of correction in the residence. Every lash of the gaoler's whip gave new strength to my resentment, the separation from my mistress increased my passion, and I hastened on the wings of love and revenge to my native place as soon as I had been set at liberty. I flew to Jenny, but was denied admittance and treated with scorn. The pinching want having subdued my pride and laziness, I offered my services to the rich, in the village, but nobody would employ a fellow who had been imprisoned in the house of correction.

Pressed by hunger and dire necessity, and foiled in all my attempts at getting an honest livelihood, I renewed my depredations on the game, and was entrapped a third time through Robert's watchfulness. The repeated infringements on the game laws had aggravated my guilt. The judges looked into the records of the law, but not into the heart of the transgressor, paid no regard to the plea of want and dire necessity, and sentenced me to have the mark of a gibbet burnt on my back, and to work three years in the fortifications.

At the close of that term I recovered my liberty a second time, and here begins a new period of my life.

I was entirely changed, having entered the fortress as a common transgressor, and left it as a consummate villain. I was not entirely divested of all sentiments of honour when I was confined; however, the few remaining sparks of ambition were soon extinguished by ignominy, being confined in one room with twenty-three malefactors, two of whom were murderers, and all the rest famous thieves and vagabonds. I was laughed at when mentioning the name of God, and urged every day to utter blasphemies against our Holy Redeemer! My fellow prisoners sung obscene songs to me, which I could not hear without disgust and horror, and committed actions which I could not behold without blushing. Every day new rogueries were related, or wicked designs fabricated.

At first I avoided the company of that abominable set of wretches as much as possible, hiding myself in the remotest corners of the prison; however, I wanted a companion in my solitude, and the cruelty of my gaoler had refused me even the poor consolation of taking my dog with me. My labour was hard and my health declining: I wanted assistance, and, to be sincere with you, I was in need of comfort, which, scanty as it was, I could not obtain without sacrificing the last remains of my conscience.

Thus I used myself by degrees to hear without disgust the most horrid language, and to behold without aversion, and at length with secret pleasure, the most shocking actions; before the termination of my confinement I was superior in wickedness to my instructors in villainy, and began to thirst with increasing impatience for liberty and revenge. I hated the whole human race because every one of my fellow creatures was either happier or less wicked than myself; I fancied to be a martyr to the natural rights of man, and a victim of glaring injustice. I rubbed my chains against the wall in a fit of frenzy, grinding my teeth when the sun was rising behind the rock on which the fortress stood, and experienced with unutterable agony, what a hell an extensive view creates in the bosom of a prisoner.

The free air whistling through the iron gates of my window, and the swallow perching on the massy bars, seemed to mock me with their liberty, and rendered my imprisonment more hateful and horrid to me. Seized with the burning fangs of despair, I vowed unrelenting and burning revenge to the whole human race, and have been as good as my word.

The first idea which rushed upon my mind as soon as I saw myself at liberty, was that of my native village. I had indeed not the least glimmering of hope to meet there with the smallest assistance in my distress; however, I entertained sanguine hopes to glut my revenge, which gave wings to my steps. My heart beat violently when my impatient eye beheld the steeple of the village; however, it was not that sweet satisfaction which I had felt on my first pilgrimage, which was now heaving in my bosom. The recollection of all the misfortunes and cruel persecutions I once had suffered there awakened me suddenly from a kind of stupefaction; all my wounds began to bleed anew. I quickened my steps, anticipating the pleasure it would afford me to strike my enemies with terror by my sudden appearance, and to feast my eyes on the pangs of the devoted victims of my vengeance.

The bells were ringing to summon the inhabitants to the church when I went to the market-place. I was soon known by the inhabitants, who were going to church, and everyone who met me started back at the sight of me.—Having always been very fond of children, I could not resist the involuntary impulse of giving a penny to a boy who was skipping by; he stared at me for a moment and then threw the money in my face. If my blood had not been heated so much, I should have recollected that my long and bushy beard had frightened the poor boy; however, my polluted heart had infected my reason, and tears, which I never had shed in my life, were trickling down my cheeks.

The boy does not know who I am, nor whence I came, said I, half aloud to myself, and yet he avoids me like a wild ferocious beast. Is my black heart marked on my brow, or have I ceased resembling a human being, because I am sensible that I hate all human kind? The contempt of that boy grieved me more than my long imprisonment, because I had treated him kindly, and could not accuse him of personal hatred.

I seated myself on a large stone opposite the church. What intention I had I do not know; however, I remember very well that I rose up in a fit of burning rage when I saw that all my former acquaintances passed by with visible contempt, and scarcely deigned to look at me.

I left my station in an agony of vexation, to find out a lodging, and as I was turning round the corner of a street I met my Jenny. "My dear Wolfe," she exclaimed, and offered to embrace me, "God be praised that you are returned at last; I have shed many a bitter tear during your absence!" Hunger and misery were marked in her face, and I beheld with horror that she was infected with an ignominious illness. Her tattered raiment and her whole appearance told me plainly what a miserable wretch she was. I soon guessed the origin of her abject situation, concluding by the sight of some dragoons that soldiers had been quartered in the village. "Soldier's strumpet!" I exclaimed, and turned my back to her with an exulting laughter. It gave me some satisfaction to see her infidelity rewarded in so shocking a manner. I never had loved her sincerely.

My mother was dead, and my house had been sold for the benefit of the creditors. I had no friend, no money, except a few groats; everybody fled me like a mad dog; however, I was dead to shame and disgrace. After my first imprisonment I had shunned all human society, because I could not stand the contempt I met with everywhere. Now I intruded upon them, and it afforded me a malicious satisfaction to drive them away by my appearance; it gave me a pleasure, because I had nothing farther to lose, and nobody to care for; I had no further occasion for the least good quality, because nobody believed I had one left; the whole world was open to me, and perhaps I should have been able to recover the character of an honest man in a distant province. However, I had no courage to assume even the mask of honesty; despair and disgrace had forced these sentiments upon me, and I persuaded myself that every sense of honour was useless to me, since I had no claim to the smallest share of it. If my vanity and pride had maintained their dominion over me, I certainly should have put an end to my existence. I did not know myself what my intentions were; I wanted to do mischief—so much I knew; I wished to deserve my fate. "The laws," said I to myself, "are the guardians of human happiness, and therefore I will do whatever is in my power to subvert them. Necessity and thoughtlessness had once compelled me to sin, but now I did it voluntarily, because it gave me pleasure."

I had again recourse to game-stealing, for hunting had always been my chief passion, and life called for support; but this was not the sole motive which prompted me to reassume my former favourite occupation; the desire of bidding defiance to the laws, and to infringe the prerogatives of the prince, was an additional impulse. I had no apprehension of being taken up once more, for now I had a ball in readiness to stop the mouth of my informer, and was sure I could not miss my aim.

I killed all the deer which came in my way, selling only a few pieces on the frontiers, the remainder I left behind to rot. I lived very sparing, in order to be able to afford the expenses for powder and shot. My depredations, and the havoc I made in the forest, caused a great alarm, but nobody suspected me; my miserable appearance screened me from suspicion, and my name was forgotten.

This mode of life I continued for several months without being detected. One morning I was rambling through the forest, pursuing the traces of a deer; having hunted without success two tedious hours, I began to give up every hope of coming at my prey, when I saw it at once within the reach of my gun. I took my aim, and was going to fire, but started suddenly back, when I saw a hat upon the ground not far from me. I looked around with great circumspection and beheld Robert, the gamekeeper, standing behind the trunk of an oak, and aiming at the same deer which I intended to kill. My blood froze in my veins as I beheld the author of all my misfortunes; and this very man, whom I hated most among the whole human race, was within reach of my fusee. Infernal joy thrilled my whole frame, I would not have exchanged my gun for the universe; the burning revenge which till then had been rankling in my bosom rose up to my finger's end, which was going to put an end to my adversary's life; however, an invisible hand seemed to retain my arm to prevent the horrid deed. I trembled violently as I directed my gun against my foe—a chilly sweat bedewed my face—my teeth began to chatter, as if a fever frost had seized my frame; methought I felt the icy fang of death upon my heart, and every nerve was quivering.

I hesitated a minute—one more elapsed—and now a third. Revenge and conscience were struggling violently for victory,—the former gained, and Robert lay weltering in his blood!—

My gun dropt on the ground when Robert fell. "Murderer," stammered I, with quivering lips. The forest was as silent as a church-yard, and I heard distinctly the word murderer. Creeping nearer to the spot where my enemy was swimming in his blood, I saw him just expire. I stood a dreadful minute of grisly horror before my murdered foe, as if petrified; a yelling laughter restored me to the use of my senses. "Wilt thou any more tell tales, good friend?" said I, stepping boldly nearer, and turning him upon his back. His eyes were wide open. I grew serious, and every power of utterance fled; strange and horrid sensations chilled my heart.

Till then I had been a transgressor of the laws on the score of the disgrace I had suffered, but now I had perpetrated a deed for which I had not yet atoned. An hour before that horrid action, no man living would have been able to persuade me that there was a more abject being upon the earth than myself, but now I began to fancy that I had been enviable an hour ago.

Not the most distant idea of God's judgments came in my mind; however, I had a confused notion of halter and gibbet, and of the execution of a murderer which I had witnessed when a boy. The idea of having forfeited my life froze my very soul with dreadful fear. I wished ardently that it might be in my power to restore to life my slain enemy, and racked my brain to recall to my recollection all the injuries he had made me suffer, but, strange to tell, my memory seemed to be entirely extinguished, I could not recall a shadow of all the ideas which, but a quarter of an hour ago, had filled my soul with glowing revenge, I could not conceive how I could commit such a horrid deed.

I was still standing by the corpse in a kind of stupefaction, when I was roused from my desponding reverie by the cracking of whips and the creaking of waggons on the high road, which was about a mile distant from the spot where I then was.

I went mechanically deeper into the forest, and recollecting on the way that Robert had been used to wear a watch, I wished to get it in my possession. I wanted money to reach the frontier, and yet I had no courage to return to the place where the corpse lay; the idea of the devil and the omnipresence of God rushing suddenly on my mind, I struggled a few moments, and having summoned all my boldness determined to go back and fetch the watch in defiance of God and the devil.

I found what I had expected, and in a green purse a little more than a dollar, silver coin. As I was going to put both in my pocket, I started suddenly back and considered whether I should take it or not. It was no fit of shame, nor was it fear to aggravate my crime through robbery; it was rather scorn which prompted me to fling the watch upon the ground, and to take only one half the money. I wanted to be thought an enemy of the gamekeeper but not his robber.

Now I fled deeper into the forest. I knew that it extended itself four German miles towards the north, where the frontiers of the country began. I fled on the wings of fear till noon; the swiftness of my flight had dispelled the agony of my conscience; however, it returned with redoubled violence as my strength began to be exhausted: a thousand grisly phantoms tortured my fancy and filled my soul with dreadful bodings. I had no other choice but either to put an end to my wretched existence, or to drag on a life embittered by a continual fear of dying under the hand of the executioner. I had not the courage to rid myself of a painful existence, and shuddered at the idea of leading a life of never-ceasing torments.

Hemmed in between the certain tortures of life and the uncertain horrors of eternity, equally averse to life and to death, I finished the sixth hour of my flight, an hour abounding with agonies which no living man can form an idea of.

Gloomy and slow I had pursued a narrow footpath which led through the darkest thicket, when suddenly a rough commanding voice ordered me to stop. The voice was not far off. Agony and the horrors of despair, which had assumed their dreadful sway over me, had made me entirely regardless to the objects around me; my eyes were cast to the ground, and I had covered part of my face with my hat, as if that could have hidden me from the eye of the lifeless creation. Starting and lifting up my eyes I saw a savage looking man coming towards me; he was armed with an enormous club, his figure was of a monstrous size, my first surprise at least had made me think so, and the colour of his face was of the mulatto hue, which gave to the white of a squinting eye additional terrors. Instead of a girdle he had his green buttonless great coat tied with a thick cord, to which an enormous knife and a brace of pistols were fastened. I had quickened my steps when his terrible voice assailed my ears, but he soon came up with me and stopped me with a powerful arm. The sound of a human voice had filled my soul with terror, however, the sight of a ruffian raised my spirits. In my miserable situation I had full reason to tremble at the sight of an honest man, but none at all at that of a robber.

"Who art thou?" thundered the frightful apparition in my ear.

"Thy equal," was my reply, "if thou really art what thy appearance bespeaks."

"This is not the right way. What business hast thou here?"

"And what right hast thou to question me?" I replied in a determined accent.

The terrible man measured me with his looks from top to toe. He seemed to compare my haughty answer with my defenceless situation— "Thou art impudent like a beggar," he resumed at length.

"Very possible, I have been one but yesterday."

He laughed, exclaiming with a horrid grin, "My honest friend, I hope thou dost not presume to be thought something better."

"That is nothing to thee;" so saying, I wanted to pursue my way.

"Fairly and softly, my dear boy, why in such a hurry; what weighty business is it which makes thee run so fast?"

I mused a moment, and cannot conceive what prompted me to reply in a slow accent, "Life is short and hell everlasting."

He stared at me with a ghastly look, "I'll be d—d," he resumed at length, "if thou hast not stumbled against a gallows on thy way."

"I may come to that one time; farewell, comrade."

"Stay a moment longer," he exclaimed, taking a tin bottle from his hunting pouch and offering it to me after he had swallowed a large draught. The hurry of my fright and the dreadful agonies of mind I had undergone had reduced my strength very low, and my parched lips had not been moistened with one refreshing draught that whole unfortunate day. Famine had already stared me horribly in the face, in that extensive forest, where three miles around no refreshment could be procured; you may therefore easily think how joyfully I accepted his offer. I swallowed greedily the contents of the bottle, and new strength animated my whole frame, my heart was expanded with new courage, and hope and love for life returned in my desponding heart; I began to fancy that I was not wholly miserable, so much relief afforded me that welcome draught; and I must confess that my situation began to appear less dreadful to me, since, I after a thousand miscarried hopes, had found at last a being that bore some resemblance with me. In the desponding situation in which I was, I would not have hesitated to pledge the health of an infernal spirit, in order to have a confidant.

Meanwhile my new companion had stretched himself upon the grass, and I followed his example.

"Thy brandy has given me new life," said I, "we must be better acquainted with each other."

He struck fire and lighted his pipe.

"Is it long since thou hast carried on this trade?"

He stared at me—"What means that question?"

I took the knife from his girdle, resuming, "Has this instrument done much execution?"

"Who art thou?" he roared in a terrible accent, flinging his pipe on the grass and starting up.

"A murderer like thyself—but only a beginner."

He gazed at me and took up his pipe.

"Thou art no inhabitant of these districts," he resumed at length.

"I am; hast thou heard of Wolfe the innkeeper, at A—?"

He started up as if frantic, exclaiming in a rapturous accent, "Wolfe the innkeeper, who has been punished so severely for game-stealing?"

"That very man I am."

"Welcome, comrade, a thousand times welcome!" he exclaimed, shaking me joyfully by the hand, "how glad am I that I have found thee at last, I have been many, many months in search of thee; I know thee very well, know all that thou hast suffered, and have been longing for thy assistance this great while."

"For *my* assistance? To what purpose?"

"Everybody speaks of thee. Thou hast many enemies, hast suffered glaring injuries, hast been entirely ruined, and persecuted with unheard-of severity."—He grew warm.—"They have immured thee in the house of correction, have treated thee like a galley slave at the fortress, have stripped thee of thy fortune, and reduced thee to beggary, because thou hast killed a few paltry deer, which the Prince suffers to prey on our corn, and to rob us of the fruit of our diligence. Is it come to that, brother, that a human being is valued less than a hare or a boar? Are we not better than the wild beasts of the field? And a fellow like thyself could brook not such injury."

"What could I do?"

"That we shall see. But, pray tell me, whence dost thou come, and on what errand?"

I related my whole history to him, and, without awaiting the end of it, he jumped up with joyful impatience, pulling me after him with all his might.

"Come along, brother," he said, "now art thou ripe, art the very man I wanted for my purpose. I shall reap great honour by introducing thee to our commonwealth. Make haste and follow me."

"Whither art thou going to conduct me?"

"Don't ask questions, but come and see;" so saying, he dragged me forcibly after him.

As we proceeded, the forest grew more and more intricate, impenetrable and gloomy. None of us spoke a word until I was suddenly roused from my apathy by the whistle of my leader. I looked around and beheld myself at the declivity of a steep rock, projecting over a deep cavern. A second whistle answered from the womb of the rock, and a ladder rose slowly from the abyss; a thundering voice hallooed from the deep, and the winding cavern echoed to the sound. My leader descended, first bidding me to wait till he should return. "I first must secure the mastiff which guards the entrance to our abode," he said, "thou art a stranger, and the ferocious beast would tear thee to pieces." So saying, he disappeared.

Now I was standing alone before the precipice, and was well aware of it. The imprudence of my leader did not escape my notice. It would have cost me no more but a resolute effort to pull up the ladder, and I would have been restored to liberty, and effected my escape without the least danger of being overtaken by the inhabitants of the cavern; I cannot but confess that I had some temptation to do it. Looking down into the abyss I was struck with an obscure idea of the bottomless gulf of hell, from whence there is no redemption to be expected. I began to shudder at the new course of life which I was going to commence. A sudden flight only could have saved me. I was half determined to effect my escape, and already stretching out my hand to pull up the ladder, when suddenly I fancied to hear a thundering voice as if from the womb of hell, "What has a murderer to risk?" and my arm lost its hold and every power of motion. My doom was fixed, the time of repentance past, and the murder I had committed was towering behind me like a mountain shutting up for ever my return to the path of virtue.

My leader reappeared the same moment, bidding me descend into the cavern. I had now no other choice left but to submit to necessity, and climbed down. Having advanced a few steps under the excavated rock, our passage grew larger, and I beheld some huts at a distance, and as I approached nearer, a round spot covered with grass appeared to my view. About twenty people were sitting round a blazing fire. "Here," my leader exclaimed, "here I bring you a new member of our society, whose name is not unknown to you; rise and welcome the celebrated Wolfe of A—."

"Wolfe!" they all exclaimed with one voice, starting up and forming a circle around me, men, women, and children. Their joy was unfeigned and cordial; confidence and even respect was marked in their looks; one squeezed my hand, the other clapped me on the shoulder in a confidential manner; all seemed sincerely rejoiced at seeing me, and the scene was not unlike the meeting again of an old beloved acquaintance.

My arrival had interrupted their dinner, they retook their seats and pressed me to partake of their inviting meal, which consisted of venison of all kind and stewed fruits. The goblet filled with delicious wine wandered from hand to hand, and spread merriment and joviality around; plenty and concord seemed to reign in that little society, and every one strove to manifest his joy at my presence.

I was seated between two females, which was the place of honour at table, and having expected to meet with the refuse of their sex, how great was my astonishment when I found amid this gang of robbers the most beautiful female figures my eyes ever beheld. Margaret the eldest and handsomest of the two, was called Miss, and could not be much above eighteen; her language was very licentious, and her looks still more so. Maria, the youngest, was married, but had run away from a husband who had treated her ill; her form was superior to that of my other neighbour, however, she was pale and of delicate constitution, and on the whole less striking at first sight than the lively Margaret. They seemed to rival who first should kindle my desires; the beautiful Margaret strove to dispel my timidity by wanton jokes: however, I soon conceived an invincible dislike to that woman, and the modest Maria fettered my heart forever.

"You see, brother," said the man who had been my conductor to that place, "you see how we live here, and every day passes like the present. Is it not true, comrades?"

"Yes, every day passes like the present," the whole gang exclaimed.

"If therefore you think you can accustom yourself to our manner of life, then stay with us and be our captain. Do you consent to it, comrades?"

An unanimous "Yes," rent the air.

My imagination was fired with wine and loose desires, my reason fettered, and my blood heated. Human society had banished me—and there I found brotherly affection, good living and honour. Whatever might have been my choice, I could not escape the hand of punishing justice; however, in a situation like that which was offered me, I could at least sell my life dear. Voluptuousness was my ruling passion, and I had till then always been treated with scorn and contempt by the other sex, but here I could expect to satisfy my desires, and to be received with pleasure. My resolution cost me but very little, and I exclaimed, after a moment's consideration, I will stay with you, comrades, if you will cede to me my beautiful neighbour.

All of them agreed to consent to my request, and I then became unexpectedly the avowed possessor of a whore, and the chief of a gang of robbers!

To be revenged on the prince in whose dominions I had suffered so much disgrace was the chief desire of my heart, and to effect that purpose was the first use I made of my new acquired authority. Our gang consisted in eight stout fellows besides myself, the rest was composed of women and children. My new associates had contented themselves, till I was joined to their society, with clandestine depredations in the pantries and cellars of the rich peasants, and game-stealing, and never had recourse to violent means. My views went farther. I proposed to declare open war against the game, which had brought on my disgrace and ruin, and to rob the houses of the judges who had punished me so severely.

To effect our purpose we wanted horses, the frontiers where the dominions of my former sovereign terminated being three miles distant. By means of house-breaking and some highway robberies we soon got possession of a sufficient sum of money, with which we dispatched one of our associates to a distant town to buy four horses, fire-arms, powder and ball. The houses of the hated judges were pillaged in a tempestuous night, and whenever the face of the earth was covered with midnight darkness, we sallied forth from our den to destroy the game in those parts where my misfortunes had commenced, and I took care to let my persecutors know that it was Wolfe who committed these depredations.

Meeting with success in our nocturnal rambles, our temerity increased, and we waylaid the traveller on the high road; however, I took great care not to perpetrate a second murder. The terror of my name soon spread itself all over the country, and the neighbouring magistrates tried every means to get me in their power; a great reward was promised to him who should take me, dead or alive, and if one of my associates, a full pardon; however, I was so fortunate as to elude the watchfulness of my pursuers for a considerable time, and to frustrate every attempt on my liberty.

I had carried on this infernal trade a whole year, when I began to be tired of it. The gang whose leader I was having disappointed my sanguine hopes, I soon perceived, with terror, how much my fancy, heated by wine and loose desires, had been imposed upon when I consented to become the captain of my associates. Hunger and want frequently supplied the place of superfluity and ease, which I had expected, and I was necessitated many a time to risk my life in order to procure a scanty meal, which hardly sufficed to appease the violent cravings of my empty stomach. The visionary image of brotherly concord disappeared, and envy, suspicion, and jealousy stepped in its place, loosening the ties of our society; the solemn promise of a full pardon to him who should deliver me into the hands of justice was a powerful temptation to lawless robbers, and I was well aware of the dangers which surrounded me. I became a stranger to sleep, a victim to never-ceasing apprehensions; the phantom of suspicion pursued me everywhere, tormented me when awake, laid down with me upon my couch, and created frightful dreams, when my weary eyes were now and then closed by the hand of slumber. My conscience, which had been lulled asleep, recovered its power by degrees, and the sleeping viper of remorse was roused by the general tempest which was raging within my breast; the hatred I bore the human race turned its dagger against myself—I was reconciled to human kind, and cursed nobody but myself. The dreadful consequences of vice stared me grisly in the face, and my natural good sense dispelled at length the delusions which had led me astray from the blessed path of virtue. I felt how deep I had fallen, and gloomy melancholy stepped in the place of gnashing despair. I wished, with weeping eyes, to have it in my power to recall the times past, and was convinced that I would make a better use of the hours I had dedicated to the vile service of guilt. I began to hope that I yet would reform, being sensible that I should be able to effect a reformation. On the highest summit of depravity I was more inclined to tread in the steps of virtue than before I had committed the first lawless deed.

A war had broken out in Germany at that time, and recruits were raising everywhere, which gave me some hopes to retreat in an honourable manner from my associates, and turn a useful member of human society. I wrote a letter to my prince, the copy of which you will find in my pocket-book.

The letter was produced and read by the clerk; the purport of it ran, as much as I can remember, as follows:

If your Highness does not think it beneath your dignity to condescend to a villain like myself—if a criminal of my atrocity is not entirely excluded from your mercy, O then do not reject the humble petition of a repenting sinner.

I am a murderer and robber, have forfeited my life, and am pursued by the avenging hand of justice. I will deliver myself into the hand of the executive power; but I, at the same time, am going to lay a very strange prayer at the feet of your throne. I detest life, and do not fear to die; it would, however, be dreadful to me to die without having lived. I wish to live, in order to repair my crimes past, and to make my peace with human society, which I have offended. My execution will be a warning example to the world, but will not atone for my wicked deeds. I hate vice, and have a strong desire to try the path of honesty and virtue. I have shown great capacities to become a terror to the state, and I flatter myself that I yet have some abilities to render services to the country which I have injured.

I am well aware that I supplicate for something quite uncommon. My life being forfeited, it does not become me to propose conditions to punishing justice; however, I am not yet chained in fetters, am yet at liberty and fear has the least share in my prayer.

It is mercy that I crave, and if I had some claim to justice I would not attempt now to enforce it; yet there is one circumstance which I have reason to recall to the recollection of my judges. The period of my crimes commences with that rigorous sentence which has deprived me of my honour. If my judges had not been too severe, if they had listened to the voice of equity and humanity, I should perhaps not have been reduced to the necessity of craving the mercy of your highness—their want of feeling has plunged me in the fatal gulf of guilt.

Let mercy supply the place of justice and spare my life; if it is in your power to intercede with the law in my behalf, the remainder of my life shall be entirely devoted to your service.

If you can grant my humble prayer, let me know it by way of the public prints, and I will throw myself at your feet, confiding in your princely word; if not, then justice may proceed as it shall be deemed proper, and I must act as necessity shall require.

This petition, 'thus resumed the delinquent,' was not taken notice of, as well as a second and third, and having not the least glimmering of

414

hope left to be pardoned, I took the resolution to leave the country, and to die in the service of the King of Prussia as a brave soldier.

I gave my gang the slip, and began my journey. My road led me through a small country town, where I intended to stay the night. A few weeks previously a proclamation had been published through the whole country, commanding a strict examination of every traveller, because the Prince had taken a part in the war as a member of the German Empire. The gate-keeper of the town which I was going to enter was sitting upon a bench before his house as I rode by; my forbidding countenance and motley dress raised his suspicion, and as soon as I had entered the gate he shut it and demanded my passport, after he had first secured the bridle of my horse. I was prepared for accidents of that sort, having provided myself with a passport, which I had taken from a merchant whom I had robbed. However, this testimony would not satisfy the eagle-eyed gate-keeper, my physiognomy being in contradiction with it, and I was obliged to follow him to the bailiff's house. He ordered me to await his return at the door.

The passport was examined, and meanwhile a rabble began to assemble around me, attracted by my strange figure; a whispering arose among the multitude, and some of the crowd were pointing alternately at me and my horse; the latter having been stolen by one of my former associates, my conscience gave the alarm. The gate-keeper returned with the passport, and told me that the bailiff, understanding that I came from the seat of the war, would be glad to have half an hour's conversation with me, and to get some information of the situation of our army. This message increased my apprehension of being known, and fearing the invitation of bailiff to be a snare to get me in his power without resistance, I clapt spurs to my horse without returning an answer.

My sudden flight gave the signal to an universal hue and cry: "A thief! a thief!" exclaimed the whole multitude, pursuing me with all possible speed. The iron hand of punishing vengeance seemed ready to grasp me; my life was at stake, and I redoubled the swiftness of my flight, goading the sides of my horse without mercy.

My pursuers were soon far behind me, panting for breath, and liberty promised to gladden my heart again, when the fleetness of my flight was suddenly stopped by a dead wall. My pursuers gave a loud shout when they saw me entrapped, and I had given over every hope of effecting my escape, when a sudden thought struck me that the wall might be the city wall, and that perhaps I would regain my liberty through a window of one of the houses on the bottom of the street. The door of that on the left side was open; I jumped from my horse, and entered it with a pistol in each hand, bolting the door after me, and hastening upstairs without being seen by any one of the inhabitants. My pursuers were close at my heels, and thundered at the door when I was rushing into a room where nobody was but an old woman. Seeing a man with a brace of pistols, terror fettered her tongue, and she fell into a swoon. I opened the window, and imagine my joy when the open field hailed my anxious looks; I bolted the door, placed chairs and tables against it, threw the bed out of the window, and concealed myself in the chimney to await there the setting in of night.

This was the work of a few moments, and I was safely housed in my hiding place when the door was forced open with a thundering noise. My calculations had not deceived me, and my plan succeeded as well as I could expect it. My pursuers, seeing the window open and the feather-bed lying in the field, believed firmly I had effected my escape: some young men jumped boldly down, and others went to pursue me on horseback; the old woman who could tell no tales, was carried to another part of the house, and I was left alone to muse on my awkward situation.

Soon after, the owner of the house came into the room with some of his neighbours, and confirmed by his discourses my hope that nobody suspected my hiding place. One of the company thought I might be concealed under the bed, but his idea of my still being in the house was, to my inexpressible satisfaction, treated with ridicule. At length my situation became extremely painful to me, and I wished fervently my unwelcome visitors might be gone.

After two tedious hours I was at length released of my fear to be detected by some unforeseen accident, when the landlord and his friends left also the room where I was hidden. As soon as the coast was clear, and the tranquillity of the house restored, I climbed higher up into the chimney, with the intention to get upon the roof; however, on maturer consideration, I thought it safer to remain where I was, hearing many voices in the field, which made me afraid of being detected.

The time crept slowly on, and I thought the wished-for hour of midnight would never set in; hunger and thirst increased the horrors of my situation, and that ever-watchful remembrancer of the mortal race, conscience, began to remind me of my wickedness, and the punishments of never-sleeping justice, which sooner or later would overtake me. My resolution of leaving the path of vice acquired new strength, and I vowed fervently never to sin again if I should escape once more.

Amidst these salutary meditations and resolutions night began to set in, and I breathed freer. At length the feather-bed was brought back, but nobody came to sleep in it that night, and the room remained unoccupied.

As soon as midnight silence announced to me that everybody was gone to rest, I slided softly down the chimney, tore one of the bed sheets and twisted it in a line to make use of it in getting into the field. No sooner had I touched the ground than I took to my heels to reach, before daybreak, the Black Forest, which I knew was only two miles distant, being well aware that the whole country would be in a hue and cry after me, as soon as my nocturnal escape should be known. Fear gave me strength and winged my feet; fatigued and entirely spent I reached the skirts of the Black Forest, and threw myself into the first thicket to rest my weary limbs.

Fatigued by the long journey I had made and the anxiety and fear which continually had harassed my mind, I fell asleep. I had not slept two hours, as I could guess by the sun, when I was suddenly roused by the distant barking of dogs: I started up and listened, when the hallooing of two huntsmen vibrated in my ear. They seemed to direct their course towards the spot where I was concealed, and no other means of escape were left me but to climb up an adjoining oak tree, and to hide myself amid its thickest branches, where I fancied to find security.

However, all my fears and apprehensions returned with redoubled force, when the dogs came to the tree which sheltered me, and began to bark in a terrible manner. The hunters were close at their heels, but seeing no game, they recalled my new persecutors and pursued their way. Fear of falling into the hands of my enemies obliged me to remain where I was until the dark mantle of night should cover once more my flight.

Hunger and thirst had hardly left me sufficient strength to keep my situation any longer, when I, to my inexpressible joy, espied the nest of a raven in the top of a tree, and six eggs in it. This unexpected relief gave me new strength, new life, new hope, and I awaited with patience the setting in of night, when I got down, pursuing my way through the forest.

The night was dark, and a rising tempest shook the tops of the lofty oaks; the distant lightning and the hollow voice of the thunder announced a dreadful night. The thunder soon began to shake the firmament, flashes of lightning illuminated, by intervals, the dark and dreary forest, and to increase the miseries of my situation, a storm of rain rushed down with such violence as if all the flood-gates of heaven had been opened at once. I sought shelter beneath an ancient oak, but, alas! a flash of lightning which shivered to atoms a lofty beech tree, not above fifty paces from the spot where I was standing, made me soon quit my dangerous asylum, and drove me to an open spot, where I was exposed to all the violence of the storm. I was soon wet to the skin, my teeth began to chatter, and all my little courage fled on the wings of despondency.

I had stood the fury of the elements two horrid, dreadful hours; no sound was heard but the screech of the owl, the croaking of the raven, the roaring of thunder, and the howling of furious winds: midnight was past, and the hurricane still raged with unabated fury. My wounded conscience brought all my crimes to my recollection: I fancied the day of judgment was near, and was seized with a violent trembling. My tortured soul, divined a thousand horrid thoughts, and I vowed fervently to pursue the steps of virtue.

My whole frame shaking with cold I began to run without knowing whither I was directing my course, in order to warm my blood, which was almost chilled, when suddenly the ground gave way beneath my feet, and I fell into a deep pit. My fall was violent; however, I received no other hurt except a few bruises, my coat being entangled in the root of a tree about four yards from the bottom of my subterraneous dungeon. I strove to climb up the wall, which appeared to be horizontal, but all my endeavours were fruitless, and the dreadful spectre of famine stared me grisly in the face. I sat down upon the damp ground and began to muse on my forlorn situation, when a sudden flash of vivid lightning illuminated my prison, and disclosed to my eyes a narrow passage; I groped along the winding passage with fearful steps, not knowing whether it would lead me upwards or downwards.

I had walked above half an hour and not yet found an outlet, the little hope I had to extricate myself from my subterraneous dungeon began to die away by degrees, and seemed to be entirely frustrated, when a massy iron door suddenly obstructed my way. I exerted all my little remaining strength to force it open; however, the impenetrable darkness which surrounded me rendered all my labours abortive. The punishment of my crimes seemed to be arrived, and I sunk down upon the damp ground in a fit of despair, entirely spent, and incapable to attempt any farther efforts to open the fatal door; cold drops of sweat bedewed my wearied limbs, and I began, the first time in my life, fervently to pray.

At length a thought struck me, that perhaps the flash of the powder would disclose to me an outlet, if I was to fire a pistol. I hastily took one out of my pocket and discharged it; my hope had not deceived me entirely, and I beheld another passage to the left, which I instantly pursued with alacrity. Ere long I came to a second iron door, which, however, soon yielded to my efforts to open it, and let me into a spacious vault.

Having groped about half an hour longer I was thrilled with unutterable joy when I discovered, after many fruitless researches, a narrow staircase, which led me into a roomy hall, faintly illuminated by the rays of the moon, who was peeping through the lofty windows, composed of stained glass.

419

Here the robber gave a full description of the Haunted Castle, on the skirts of the Black Forest, which you, my dear friend, know too well to require a repetition of the faithful picture he drew.

> Having explored every corner of the ancient fabric, thus he continued, without meeting a living soul, I descended into a spacious courtyard, from whence a lofty gateway led me into the open field.

The dawn of morn began to break in the east from the purple clouds, and I heard the crowing of cocks within a small distance. He only who has been in a situation like mine can form an idea of the rapture which rushed on my soul when I perceived myself to be so near an inhabited spot.

Quickening my tottering steps I saw two country wenches with baskets on their heads coming from the adjacent village, which seemed to be not above a quarter of a mile distant. I was just going to inquire of them the name of the village, when both of them raised a dreadful scream, running back as fast as possible. Being desirous to know, previous to my entrance into the village, where I was, lest I might unknowingly run into the hands of my pursuers; I summoned up all the few remains of strength, which hunger and fatigue had left me, in order to come up with them, but when the frightened girls perceived me close at their heels, they threw down their baskets, and fled with the swiftness of an arrow.

Fearing to be known, and apprehending the wenches would alarm the village, I was obliged to desist from my pursuit, and to seek a hiding-place until I should be able to advance a mile farther. No place promising a safer asylum than the desolated castle, I resolved to return, but previously to examine the baskets the girls had dropt, whether they might not contain some victuals to appease the pinching hunger which tormented me.

It seemed they had been on their way to the market, their baskets containing some lumps of butter, two earthen jars with milk, some small cheeses, and two large pieces of coarse bread. The milk, which was not all run out of the earthen vessels, quenched my thirst, and the bread and cheese I took with me to the castle to satisfy the pressing demands of my stomach.

On my arrival in the great hall of the castle I struck fire with the help of a steel I had in my pocket, and the flint of one of my pistols, and soon was seated by the blazing flame drying my wet garments and appeasing my hunger. Casting my looks accidentally on my hands, I saw that they were as black as those of a coal-heaver, from the soot of the chimney where I had sheltered myself against the first onset of my pursuers, and having every reason to believe that my face must be of the same hue, I easily could account for the sudden flight of the two girls, who very likely took me for the devil.

This idea silenced my fears of a visit from the alarmed villagers tolerably, and the soothing hand of sleep began to close my eyes.

Thus far the captain of the robbers had related his extraordinary tale, when the chief Justice commending the apparent sincerity of his voluntary confession, broke up the court, ordering the prisoner to be reconducted to his dungeon until the following day, when he would hear the continuation of his adventures.

My business not allowing me to stay a day longer, I departed reluctantly at four o'clock in the afternoon. However, before I left N— I obtained the promise of a friend of mine whom I accidentally had met, that he would send me the continuation of the robber's further confession, and four weeks after I received the following letter, which contains everything you may wish to know.

PART THREE

I

CONTINUATION OF WOLFE'S CONFESSION,
AND THE FINAL ISSUE OF HIS TRIAL

My worthy friend,

It is with the sincerest satisfaction I am going to give you a faithful account of the remainder of Wolfe's confession, and the final issue of his trial, according to my promise.

You will remember that he closed the narration of his singular adventures which he gave on the first day of his trial, with his reluctant return to the castle, where he intended to stay till the darkness of night should shelter him against the pursuit of his persecutors. The great fatigue he had sustained on his flight soon closed his weary eyes, and he slept till after sunset, when he left the castle to pursue his way to F—, where he intended to enlist in the Prussian service.

Directed by the silver rays of the rising moon he soon found his way to the high road. At the first well he fell in with he cleaned his sooty face and hands and then went briskly on. Being well stocked with provisions, he determined not to enter any inhabited place before he should be obliged by necessity to do it, lest some new misfortunes might cross his military scheme. With that view he left the high road whenever it led through a village, walked all night long and slept in the day time. Thus he travelled onwards two nights without having met with any accident, when he, at the close of the third day, was obliged to direct his course to a small hamlet, in order to provide himself with provisions. As soon as it was dark he went with fearful steps to a baker's shop to purchase some bread, but great was his terror when he wanted to pay for the small loaf of coarse bread he had bought, and could not find his purse, which must have dropt out of his pocket when he dried his garments in the hall of the castle.

Being entirely destitute of money he offered one of his pistols, which he took out of his pocket, in lieu of payment. The baker viewed him from top to toe, and after some hesitation agreed to the bargain. Unfortunately the house of this man had been robbed some weeks before by a gang of thieves, and Wolfe's savage look, joined with his singular appearance, rendered him suspicious to the baker, who, ever since the robbery had been committed in his house, took every ill-looking stranger for a thief.

Prompted by that notion he ordered one of his people to follow Wolfe at some distance as soon as he had left the house, and went instantly to the bailiff to inform him of his suspicions, and the strange bargain he had just concluded.

The magistrate who had been indefatigable in his researches after the daring robbers, without succeeding in his endeavours to find them out, soon fell in with his opinion, and ordered some stout fellows to follow the suspected robber, and to secure him by surprise.

Wolfe, who had meanwhile struck again into the forest, seated himself behind some bushes by the banks of a rivulet, and began to appease the demands of his grumbling stomach, not observing that he was followed, when suddenly four sinewy arms seized him from behind.

The unexpected surprise, the continual fatigues he had undergone, and the strength of his adversaries rendered it impossible to disengage himself from their powerful grasps, and he was dragged before the magistrate of the hamlet, who demanded his passport. Having been obliged to leave it behind when his alarmed conscience had drawn upon him his late disaster, he had no other choice left but to pretend being an Austrian deserter, who wanted to go into the Prussian service. The bailiff, mistrusting his veracity, ordered him to be searched, when a loaded pistol and a large knife were found upon him, which increased the suspicion of the zealous magistrate, who, without farther ado, sent him to the prison.

New apprehensions of a dreadful nature assailed now the unhappy man. The fear that all his former crimes would be detected filled his desponding soul with black despair; however, his lamentable situation took soon a turn more favourable than he could have expected. A transport of Prussian recruits passing through the village in the afternoon, the bailiff ordered him to be delivered to the commanding officer, thinking this to be the most commodious way to rid the country of a fellow whose whole appearance bore evident marks of his thievish profession, and to spare himself the trouble of a tedious examination. His size and the robust make of his limbs rendered him a very acceptable acquisition to the recruiting officer, and he was enrolled as a Prussian soldier, to his unutterable joy.

Wolfe, the robber, was now at once appointed to fight the battles of Frederic the Great, and make a solemn vow to fulfil cheerfully the duties of his honourable calling.

The transport arrived safe at Magdeburg, and the new soldier was with his companions instructed in the art of killing lawfully his fellow creatures. The Corporal who was appointed to instruct him in the manual exercise was famous for his severity, conforming strictly to the military principles of his royal master, who, as it is universally known, had it laid down as a rule to inspire his martial bands with heroism by the frequent application of wooden arguments. Wolfe, who was not in the least partial to that sort of reasoning, found it very difficult to brook the brutality of his drilling master, who seemed to have a particular predilection for him, plying his back so frequently and so severely that the new soldier was soon rendered too sensible of his instructor's partiality for him.

Wolfe exerted himself to the utmost of his ability to please the rigorous Corporal and to shelter himself against the frequent heavy showers of blows and cuffs, but not being able to attain his end, resentment and hatred began at length to rankle in his heart, his whole stock of patience was exhausted, and he began to have frequent recourse to drinking in order to dispel the gloominess of mind which haunted him incessantly, and to drown the recollection of his forlorn situation.

One day as he came half-intoxicated to the parade, he acquitted himself so badly of his task that his military mentor plied his back most unmercifully. Wolfe's anger was roused, his blood was boiling, and he called his chastiser a savage beast, a bloodhound, and many other names of the same stamp. The fury of his tyrant being raised to the highest degree by that language, he inflicted his blows with so much violence that Wolfe, in a fit of despair, struck him to the ground with the butt end of his gun. He was instantly seized, carried to the prison, and sentenced by a court martial to run the gauntlet.

The day of execution appeared, the soldiers were drawn up, and his back was bared, when lo! the mark of his ignominy was seen between his shoulders. It being evident, by the sign of a gallows which was seen between his shoulders, that he had been under the hands of the common hangman, he was declared unworthy to undergo military punishment, and sentenced to work in the fortification.

Confined with the dregs of human kind, and ever in company with the basest of villains, his weak virtuous resolutions died away by degrees. He once more began to consider himself as the sport of injustice and barbarous cruelty; his belief in the Providence of the benevolent Ruler of the world soon gave way to atheistical principles, and his former desire for doing mischief returned with redoubled force, when he saw his sincere endeavours to become a useful member of human society were thwarted again in a most cruel manner. He began to think that he was doomed to be a villain, and being driven to despair by hard labour and frequent blows, he concerted plans of effecting his escape.

One of his fellow-prisoners, a most consummate ruffian, joined with him in devising means of regaining their liberty; and after many fruitless efforts they at length effected their escape, assisted by an impenetrable fog which covered their flight. As soon as their escape was known in the fortress, the cannons were fired and the country roused. However, they happily eluded their pursuers, and reached, at the close of day, a wood, where they resolved to conceal themselves in the tops of the trees till the heat of the pursuit should have abated.

In this uncomfortable situation they remained as long as their small stock of provisions lasted, consulting with each other by what means they could best procure an independent livelihood, and at last agreed to resort to the Haunted Castle in the Black Forest, and there to commence robbery. After many fatiguing rambles and alarming fears, they arrived at length at the wished-for asylum.

Wolfe's inventive genius begot the scheme to render that desolate fabric more secure against the intrusion of unwelcome visitors, by raising an idea in the fancy of the neighbouring villagers of its being haunted by evil spirits. In order to accomplish their design, they set up a dreadful howling and doleful lamentations whenever they perceived some of the villagers near the environs of the castle. The gloomy appearance of that half-decayed fabric, aided by the superstition of the credulous peasantry, rendered their artful schemes successful, and in a short time none of the villagers dared to approach their lurking-place, from which they sallied out every night, disguised in the skin of goats, which they had stolen and fleeced, and committed numberless robberies in the village.

Having procured a sufficient stock of money, Wolfe's associate was dispatched to a neighbouring town to procure fire-arms, powder, and ball, and then they began to prey on the unwary wanderer. To relate the numberless robberies they committed before they were joined by new associates would swell volumes. As their numbers augmented they became more daring, and extended their depredations many miles over the country, till after a series of thirty successful years their infernal society sustained a deadly blow by the nocturnal surprise which delivered them into the power of punishing justice. Wolfe has since confessed that they have a great number of hiding places besides the solitary castle, and that their gang consists of fifty-three ruffians, who are dispersed all over the country.

The useful information he has given to his Judges has enabled them to secure a great number of innkeepers and publicans, who were leagued with that infernal set of ruffians, of whom six more have been taken up since you left me; however, their money, and the great booty they have hoarded up, has not been detected as yet, and is supposed to have been removed on the first alarm by the rest of the gang. Wolfe's life will be spared on account of his faithful confession, and the great assistance he has afforded his Judges in putting a final stop to the depredations which have been committed for a series of years in the environs of the Black Forest; he is to be committed for life to the house of correction, where he will have ample scope to reflect on his life past, and to prepare to meet that eternal Judge who sooner or later overtakes the wicked in his vile pursuits.

Thus I have executed my task as well as it was in my power, and trust you will kindly overlook the defects of my narrative, and always believe me to be, with the greatest sincerity,

Your affectionate friend,
P—.
FINIS

ABOUT THE AUTHORS

Eliza Parsons was an English author best known for having penned two of the seven Northanger Horrid Novels. Parsons is presumed, based on a baptismal certificate, to have been born in 1739. Her father, John Phelp, was a successful wine merchant and used his wealth to provide his only daughter with a better education than many of her contemporaries. She married James Parsons at age 21 and had eight children. The decline in James Parsons's health and subsequent death, as well as the death of all three of her sons, led Eliza Parsons to seek means to support her remaining children and herself. She began writing, and over the course of the next seventeen years wrote nineteen novels and one play. Though prodigious, Parsons often struggled with money until her death in 1811. *The Castle of Wolfenbach* is her most famous work.

Lawrence Flammenberg was born Karl Friedrich Kahlert in 1765 and died in 1813. He also wrote under the pseudonym Ludwig Flammenberg. His work, *Das Geisterbanner* was translated into English by Peter Will (writing as Peter Tuethold) into The Necromancer; or, The Tale of the Black Forest. Kahlert is credited as a major influence for Matthew Lewis's *The Monk*.

ABOUT THE TRANSLATOR

Peter Teuthold was the pseudonym for Peter Will. Teuthold is best known for his translation of Lawrence Flammenberg's *Der Geisterbanner: Eine Wundergeschichte aus mündlichen und schriftlichen Traditionen* into *The Necromancer; or, The Tale of the Black Forest* and Carl Grosse's *Der Genius, Horrid Mysteries*, which is also included in the Northanger Horrid Novels list. Little is known beyond his work on these projects.

ABOUT THE EDITOR

Ann Marie Hormeku is a writer obsessed with the intersection of place and identity. She is currently attending Western Colorado University's Master's program in Publishing where she is collaborating with her cohort on an anthology highlighting new mythology, fairy tales, and folklore. She previously interned at the University of Georgia Press and *The Chattahoochee Review*. In the future she hopes to establish a press that will print evocative and experimental poetry, nonfiction, and fiction from diverse voices as well as share her own work with the world. She lives on a small acreage outside of Athens, Georgia, with her husband and children and enjoys wasting summer days swimming in the backyard pond with her daughters and their pup, Cocoa.

WORDFIRE CLASSICS

The Lost World
The Poison Belt
by A. Conan Doyle

The Wolf Leader
by Alexandre Dumas

The Cthulhu Stories of Robert E. Howard
by Robert E. Howard

The Detective Stories of Edgar Allan Poe
by Edgar Allan Poe

The Jewel of Seven Stars (Annotated)
by Bram Stoker

From the Earth to the Moon and Around the Moon
by Jules Verne

The Complete War of the Worlds
The War in the Air
Kipps: The Story of a Simple Man
The Sleeper Awakes and Men Like Gods
by H.G. Wells

Mother of Frankenstein: Maria: or, The Wrongs of Woman & Memoirs of the Author of A Vindication of the Rights of Woman
by Mary Wollstonecraft

We: The 100th Anniversary Edition
by Yevgeny Zamyatin

One Stormy Night : A Story Challenge That Created the Gothic Horror Genre
by Lord Byron, Dr. John William Polidori, and Mary Shelley

HOLIDAY CLASSICS
The Ghost of Christmas Always
by Charles Dickens & Kevin J. Anderson

The Santa Claus Stories
by L. Frank Baum

Our list of other WordFire Press authors and titles is always growing.
To find out more and to shop our selection of titles, visit us at:
wordfirepress.com

 facebook.com/WordfireIncWordfirePress
twitter.com/WordFirePress
instagram.com/WordFirePress
bookbub.com/profile/4109784512